This
special
signed
edition is
limited to
750
numbered
copies.

This is copy _176_.

DAVID J. SCHOW

DJSturbia

DJSTURBIA

David J. Schow

Subterranean Press 2016

By David J. Schow

Novels

The Kill Riff
The Shaft
Rock Breaks Scissors Cut (novella)
Bullets of Rain
Gun Work
Hunt Among the Killers of Men
Internecine
Upgunned

Short Story Collections

Seeing Red
Lost Angels
Black Leather Required
Crypt Orchids
Eye
Havoc Swims Jaded
A Little Aqua Book of Creature Tails

Nonfiction

The Outer Limits Companion
Wild Hairs (essay collection)
The Art of Drew Struzan
The Outer Limits at 50

As Editor

Silver Scream
The Lost Bloch Volume One: The Devil with You!
The Lost Bloch Volume Two: Hell on Earth
The Lost Bloch Volume Three: Crimes and Punishments
Elvisland (John Farris story collection)

First Edition

ISBN
978-1-59606-772-1

Subterranean Press
PO Box 190106
Burton, MI 48519

subterraneanpress.com
Black Leather Required: **davidjschow.com**

Contents

NOW HOLD STILL

Sorry I woke you up again.

You always ask the same dumb questions. *Why me* (meaning you)? Or *who are you* (meaning me)? Which paves the way for *what do you want* (meaning what do I want from you and how can you talk your way out of it)? That's okay because I expect you to say that—you always do. Last time this happened it occurred to me that you want a story, a justification that might reduce your fear or make sense of your apparently random victimization.

I used to have this girlfriend who once said I had to learn to look at a situation from the other person's point of view, and I first thought what the hell for? This is fairly cut and dried. So I thought about it some more.

Here's the story I came up with. We've got time.

You know what a soul-mate is? I don't mean the mainstay of cheap romance—that flowery, idealistic bullshit people use to excuse the ruination of their lives. Seriously, now. Don't most people assess what they have by smacking it against the wall of True Luv? And it never sticks. Hence many otherwise normal folks squander their well-being on an altar of whom-meets-whom and happy endings all designed to rub your nose in what a crap life you have anyway.

The pisser about such clichés is that sometimes they're real—a random synergy, that ole thunderbolt that must exist if for no other reason than to cause us to writhe and pillory ourselves because it never exists for you and me. That's just infuriating, like not getting picked in the natural selection choose-up. It forces you to watch people effortlessly achieve a precise chemistry while you sit, a failure in a puddle of missed ingredients.

Buck and Nikki had a chemistry like that, the kind that could leave you pissed, envious, covetous, sourpussed.

But you probably wouldn't want to pay the price such a rarity costs, because you've always wanted things easy and convenient. A couple like Buck and Nikki, they could be your shining beacon of hope or your best reason to kill yourself. Especially if you're the kind of person who thinks finding a soul-mate is oh-so-special, and not merely a lie unforgiving mothers use to reassure loser children.

Buck and Nikki met by accident. Catalyst, reaction. Saw the essence of their beings in each other. Got married. Got divorced, because even ideal relationships need maintenance. Eventually they hooked back up. Buck needed larger goals. Nikki needed the illusion of freedom. They hit upon a course that was brutally honest, yet directly required them to be creative.

They sat down and made lists of every person with whom they'd gotten sexually involved since their breakup. No omissions, no cheats, no tricks and no also-rans. Basically, anybody who could be considered an assault on their unity. Then they added the people with whom they'd each had relationships prior to hooking up. (Buck had another marriage back in the weeds, somewhere.)

When they were finished they had to give full disclosure on each name. Buck's list had 72 and Nikki's 153, because getting laid for her was always a matter of simple consent (except for the rapes), whereas for Buck it was more a male pursuit thing.

They laughed over their sub-lists of "almosts."

Then they added their lists together—and this is the creative part—and Buck said *we should just kill every single one of them,* and Nikki's eyes lit up.

Think about that for a moment. Think about the commitment, the conviction it would take as an expression of an ultimate kind of love, a sealant bond of genuine weight and consequence, a process and an involute puzzle demanding bottomlessly creative solutions. A self-renewing, auto-refreshing task.

Now think about your own personal list. The people you've fucked. Who've fucked you over. The ones you loved who didn't love you. The liars and con artists, the opportunists and abusers, the rotten choices, the impulse-buys and the gauntlet of faces you've had to survive in order to develop what you call a persona and some sort of half-assed working philosophy.

I use the comparison of good memories versus bad. Good ones tend to shrink on the shelf while bad ones swell up to absorb more space, and that's a problem. The good boils down to fleeting impressions, fast moments, partial incidents—that long and unexpected kiss in a taxi; those fiery wrestling matches where you got what you wanted for once; a sudden spark of passion out of nowhere; the rare instance of transcendence or actual comfort. Now stack that one good feeling against the two weeks of misgivings it probably cost and you'll see the disparity—the year wasted versus the perfect moment; the downside of feeling good; the bitter, endless hours that taught you to be better or different with your next partner.

Obviously we're not just talking about sex here, although that's all that matters to the drones out there in yahoo-land. Who's fucking whom really does make the world go 'round. It's often the *only* piece of intel that matters.

Buck and Nikki, see, had found a way to cut right to the steak, stay happy, and build their love.

Let's go back to those lists: First thing you do is check off anybody who might have died without your help. Okay, that left 210 people.

Next thing you'd normally do is omit special circumstances or those candidates who were inapplicable or immune. Buck and Nikki looked at each other. Soul-mates, right? No fucking exceptions; still 210.

Then Nikki remembered this one guy who wound up (deservedly) as a paraplegic in an iron lung. She wanted him to spend every waking moment of his life suffering, and Buck agreed—209.

Three people in prison. Tougher to reach, so—206.

Four impossible to trace, gone to ground (perhaps literally), out of the world without a shove. It happens. Fair enough—202.

Or: a hundred and one times two. The symmetry was irresistible.

Hell, bullets come fifty rounds to a box; shotgun shells are five-per, and if you looked at it that way, the whole massacre barely added up to a full grocery bag.

The strategy was this: Any hesitancy, inability, or misgivings by one would be compensated by the other. If Buck couldn't bring himself to lay a sledgehammer upside the skull of his #8 from high school, then Nikki would batter-up. If Nikki felt a ping of remorse about stabbing her #43 (her longest liaison before Buck), Buck would move in smartly with the appropriate gutting tool. (Besides, ole #43 turned out to be a gosh-danged drug dealer.)

It was like collecting, in a way. Or catching the bug for library skills—research, data, deduction, checklists. The first items in your collection come fast and hard, in a flurry. The final ones are the most difficult to collect because the grails are the most subterranean, difficult, or costly.

As to bank, well, their parents had died in such a timely fashion that providence, not coincidence, was credited. Instead of a portfolio, golf, condos or early retirement they chose their special mission, which also fulfilled the old itch for a bit of world travel. Buck and Nikki were, after all, responsible adults who had to make their own way. All they really had was each other (and they had each other *a lot*).

Still, you're asking why, meaning you want all kinds of explanations you hope will prolong your clock. An "arc," as they say in the movie business, a through-line.

When stories explain everything to you, that's called "exposition."

Ever notice how most stories try that old "calm before the storm" routine? They try to set up something "normal" and then mess with it; make it abnormal to provide a fulcrum to restore the status quo. Except in them stories they usually get "normal" all wrong. It rings false. Or it ain't normal for half the people who read it. I mean, what is "normal," anyway? The Fifties nuclear family? The Nineties drag of soccer moms, SUVs and cellphones? Gold watches, gardening and grandkids? That stuff was never normal for me, and hearing about it all the time sounded like fairytales of zombie life from another planet, like Mars.

"Normal" is relative.

Think about the bad things. The secret things you've done in your life. The stuff so bad you've never shared it. Never even made teasing hints.

The maybes are endless. So are the excuses. Some of that crap might break your heart. But you love patterns and order, so you break your own heart over and over.

Ever mourn the dead? You think dead people give a sour rat fart about your self-humiliations and your displays designed to be noticed and overheard?

Ever hurt somebody on purpose? Perhaps relieve them of the burden of their lives? Is that too extreme for you?

How about all the people you've killed without murdering them? The lies you've spun, the dreams you've crushed, the trodden victims of your own screwed-up personality?

There are no karmic checks and balances, and the universe doesn't give a good goddamn about you.

Yet you think you have some jumped-up moral superiority to Buck and Nikki, don't you? You think you're "normal."

I could say, well, it was because of the baby. Nikki pushed really hard and Buck watched the spawn of their union dribble out in pieces. An arm with an elbow joint, a foot, half a head. And then you'd say, *oh, now I get it,* because you got your exposition. You think you know the mission, the plot.

But I wouldn't want you to *analyze* this to death and miss its value.

I would say Buck and Nikki found other ways to sanctify the covenant of their love, and then I would ask: Have you ever really been in love like that?

Now define "normal." I dare you.

At this stage I probably don't need to tell you that Buck and Nikki aren't their real names. You know that, right? If you didn't know that, you would still be sleeping. No duct tape, no gag. Enjoying a dream of love, perhaps, absent the real thing.

What you and I have right now is intimate, but it sure ain't love.

As might be normally expected, Buck and Nikki's verve began to flag about the time they hit the century mark, one hundred down. Leaving a hundred to go, plus stragglers. It might have been boredom or weariness or satiation. Whatever. So they started farming out a few jobs. Which is why I woke you up this way tonight, when you thought you were sleeping safely alone. Like I woke you up two nights ago, in another town. When you were wearing a different face, asking all the same dumb questions.

You're all the same to me.

And as intriguing as you may have found my tale of Buck and Nikki, I have no interest in what your own story might be. What your real name is. Who you might or might not have slept with in the past.

Story or no story, you'll ask the same dumb questions every time. Giving you all the exposition changes nothing.

You'll come awake in the dark, thinking yourself innocent and normal, and there I'll be, standing over you. You'll open your eyes and get it. No story; just is.

....

After 9/11

(Interview conducted by Drew McWeeny for Ain't It Cool News in late September, 2001)

Drew: First off, in light of the events that took place in New York, what do you feel your primary duty is as a writer serving an audience in a Post-WTC America?

DJS: Primary duty = Not to write in fear. Not to coddle or massage the hypocritical concept of a bogus "sensitivity" in media that time-out from the horrific WTC news images to sell easy armchair patriotism and SUVs called the "Liberty." Less than a week after the terrorist attack, news coverage focused primarily on how brave TV anchorpeople were "suffering;" these glory hogs being spelled only by an endless parade of religious nitwits braying on about their god's plan. From my non-partisan religious viewpoint, it looks to me like Allah kicked "God"'s ass, this time out. Gunshy sheep are always quick to make the entertainment industry take it on the chin any time extremists do public damage. Americans have for decades denied the reality of terrorist acts on US soil, always qualifying each new outrage with a convenient disclaimer: "It was a lone nut." Or "It wasn't *really* terrorism." But Hollywood has been warning audiences about terrorism in our own backyard for just as many decades. It's time people stopped averting their eyes; maybe they'll learn something, or at least put their anger and fear in a more deserving receptacle than movies or books or TV—like, for instance, culling all their do-nothing politicians.

As a writer, you've dealt in stark, even brutal imagery in your work. Is there anything that you now feel awkward about in light of recent events?

I'm sure The Coup were embarrassed by the bad timing of their album cover. But where do you draw the line? At *Black Sunday*? At *Die Hard*? At *Independence Day*? At *Godzilla*? At anything featuring a building collapsing, or jet hijacking, or a big cloud of smoke? Do we prohibit *Air Force One* or blacklist Tom Clancy? "Potentially upsetting" imagery is fundamental to most kinds of drama, period. If the WTC doesn't definitively demonstrate the difference between movies—that is, fiction—and reality, let me spell it out for you: In the movies, we're usually victorious over the hijackers, the bombers, the terrorists, as in *Executive Decision*. In real life, Americans don't always "win" just because we're the coolest.

If you were asked to alter past material to somehow reflect the current tragedy, would you feel that was appropriate?

It's cowardly and dishonest to alter original material according to what the news tells us to shun this week. It works no perceivable good. But you have to acknowledge that many such decisions are made anyway, by higher-ups in the corporate food chain—witness the rush to judgement on the *Spiderman* poster, cable networks dropping or shuffling action series or movies as "inappropriate," and Clear Channel's totally ridiculous hit list of songs prohibited from airplay—everything from "Hey Joe" to "Stairway to Heaven"...just because they're terrified that their fourth-quarter earnings will dip half a percentage point if they don't pretend to be "sensitive."

Or do you stand behind the work you've created, even if someone finds unfortunate echoes in it?

If we dope out this theory to its logical conclusion, we'd better start burning Bibles by the truckload, because of all the grief *that* book has fomented throughout history; it's the all-time record holder for unfortunate echoes. Nobody curtailed the Catholic High Mass just because it supposedly influenced Peter Kurten to murder people, and I expect the same courtesy in regard to my writing. No one is forcing people to read or look at so-called "inappropriate" material, and again, who gets to decide what is or isn't appropriate? The worst possible scenario is panic, and the imposition of self-censorship motivated by guilt or a desire to seem "correct." Panic gives you the Us-Vs.-Them brand of all-purpose "enemy," dating all the way back to the World War Two scenarios the Reagan administration was so fond of evoking.

There are currently censorship groups forming around the country to try and get rid of "inappropriate films" with "insensitive content" from not only video stores, but cable and network outlets as well. As a filmmaker and performer, how do you feel films with similar content to tragic circumstances should be viewed...and how do you think they benefit or harm society?

I'd like to maintain the gentle fantasy that most people are not sponges—passive absorbers of whatever is broadcast or published. I'd like to believe that people can exercise choice according to their own tastes, and have the common respect not to foist their choices on others, particularly in a militant way. Zealots are fanatics, whether they're crazed enough to destroy buildings or crazed enough to mandate what everyone else should be looking at or reading. Thomas Jefferson was outraged by this very idea. He said, "Are we to have a censor whose imprimatur shall say what books shall be sold and what we may buy?" If we do, this isn't America anymore. The censorship groups you cite have always been lying in wait, and should be ashamed of using the WTC tragedy to grandstand their narrow and picayune agendas.

What's even more ominous is that CNN is currently running a poll on their website, which asks, "Would you accept more government involvement in your life if it meant more security against terrorism?" That's really an are-you-still-beating-your-wife kind of pseudo-question, since whether you answer YES or NO doesn't matter—it stinks either way. It is, in its own way, a kind of terrorist question. (Everybody stop now and go look up "terrorism" in the dictionary. Don't accept what media tools say; just go look it up for yourself. We'll wait.) What it doesn't address is the bald reality that "security from terrorism" is impossible, due to the nature of terrorist acts. "Security from terrorism" is practically an oxymoron. Security is a comforting illusion, not an absolute. But if you answer NO to the CNN question, the perception is that one "supports terrorism." The Spanish Inquisition couldn't have twisted language any better.

Is there catharsis in images of Americans triumphing over crisis right now, or are these images too much in light of recent reality?

If you're asking "is it possibly beneficial for Americans to watch *Commando* or *True Lies* right now?" I'd say it probably couldn't hurt. It's certainly more cathartic than waiting around for some phantom enemy to declare itself, or persecuting a whole group of people based on the thin ice of a likely suspect. Right now the country is a lynch mob with no one to hang, so the people are looking around for some substitute in which to invest their outrage, and as Jack Valenti says, the movies have always provided a juicy target, particularly for politicians...and most politicians are far more corrupt than most movies. Maybe that's why they go after the movie industry with such fervor—to detour responsibility away from their own fat little taxpayer-supported sinecures.

Drama—fiction—is necessarily exaggerated for point-making purposes. Sometimes these exaggerations, in the name of realism, cause people to confuse realism with actual reality, and the buck-passing of blame begins. If hot-button images upset you, don't look at them—but don't restrict anyone else's right to look at them, because every single person has a completely different ceiling and floor for what's terrible, or what's funny, or what's uplifting.

Americans seem all too willing, right now, to give up their freedoms in the name of flag-waving and ass-kicking. Mob thinking won't work. Hindbrain responses won't work. This isn't a football game. The only freedom worth losing, as Klaatu says in *The Day the Earth Stood Still*, is "the freedom to act irresponsibly."

Where do you draw the line with this sort of thing? Should absolute freedom be protected? Should there be times of temporary censorship, or do people need access to all types of art at all times?

There is no such thing as "temporary censorship." That's a schmooze way of seducing people out of their rights. Any such "temporary," oh-so-sensitive censorship always turns out to be a foothold for more censorship, until artists become so restricted that there's a backlash, at least as long as there are people who enjoy or consume art who don't want to eat pabulum all the time. Do we shut down rollercoasters because some nebulous rider might have a heart attack? Do we herd clowns into detention camps for the duration, since laughter has become deemed "inappropriate" by some? Again, where do you draw the line?

Of course, I wrote a *Chainsaw Massacre* movie, so everything I say is automatically suspect. But I also screenwrote *The Crow*, a very violent movie which nonetheless has a moral center, a heart, if you will. Some of the best and most lasting entertainments

deftly balance both. Art has to be no less than honest, and sometimes that's uplifting, sometimes it's sobering, and sometimes it's
horrifying. Checklists of do's and don't's only force artistic expression into a narrower box, and pretty soon we're *all* buried alive.

I am not trying to sound harsh or unfeeling. I was as stunned
as most others seemed to be by the magnitude of this tragedy, and
I know a *lot* of people in New York City. Fortunately, the internet
was solid gold when it came to making fast contact, especially
when every phone in the state seemed to crap out, even cellu-
lars. The social impact of WTC will be reflected in many movies,
books, and TV shows to come. Right now, *Holy War Inc.: Inside
the Secret World of Osama bin Laden* is being rushed into print in
a mass-market edition. The book was written by CNN producer
Peter Bergen. HarperCollins has fast-tracked a book of essays on
the WTC attack. Is this social conscience, or just another company sniffing a ready market? At the same time, agents are shying
away from marketing books not only invoking terrorist elements,
but (per *Variety*, 19 September 2001) "all violent books." Art of any
sort—even lowbrow art—is a response to our culture, and one
can't just globally delete art's inevitably darker side, be it crass
exploitation or junkfood pop. To creatively hobble artists is to
bury one's head in the sand, and haven't we all had enough of
that by now?

**No one seems ready to stand up as a media voice to advocate
for the curative powers of art.**

I don't know about "curative;" I don't feel the need for a cure;
perhaps I'm not infected with anything. What I do need is creative freedom and access to all varieties of art, unlumbered by
the self-serving agendas of politicians or the stormtrooper tac-
tics of those who would police morals. Movies and books are
my religion, and we all know what happens when you mess with
people's religion...

THE LAST SONG
YOU HEAR

"I can remember the first time I ever saw you."

The woman sitting in the plastic hospital chair nodded back at the man in the bed, lips pursed, daring him to be accurate. *Pray, continue.*

"You were wearing a white dress. You were sitting in my landlady's foyer, in her cane rocker, laughing at something she'd said. Your legs were crossed and she had her tile fireplace going and the light was hitting you from the side. I remember your legs, the firelight on your stockings. The expression on your face. And I thought, whoa, who is *this*? I had just come home from classes and gotten off the bus from the college and I spotted you through the window, and it was getting dark and, I'll admit it, I lingered at that window, watching you. It sped up my heartbeat."

"Great," she said. "A *stalker*."

"I'll admit it."

"And how long were you outside the window, spying on us?" The gleams in their eyes matched.

"A couple of minutes. An hour, tops. Okay, maybe two. Until you got up to leave, anyway. I had to change position. I ducked around the elm tree at the side of the building, and watched you walk to your car. It was a lot of input, I mean, now you were actually *moving around* and stuff."

"I'm amazed your head didn't explode."

"I'm amazed that I had spent a significant time writing about the ridiculousness of clichés—love at first sight, getting struck by the thunderbolt, all that—and there I stood with my brain fried to toast. If I had met you then, I would've gasped like a fish. You had to have been what, all of twenty-one?"

She recollected it as twenty-three and they compared timelines for a while. Did math.

During the ensuing week she had made two more appearances he had been fortunate enough to catch. She knew his landlady, Mrs. Engle, as a co-worker in some department store. This was a boon, an excuse for future collisions. By the time he introduced himself, he was sufficiently immunized so as not to seem a jittery wreck.

"I remember talking in Mrs. Engle's driveway one time," she said. It was a wistful memory for her. "I have no idea what we talked about. I just remember that we talked for a couple of hours, kind of standing there in a trembling-on-the-threshold kind of way. One of those talks that spins off on a hundred tangents and nobody is really in a hurry to leave."

That was how he remembered it, too.

He saw her as popular and social, versus his own introversion. Doubtlessly, other denizens of the popular/social leisure class would vampirize her availability. She had her degree from some Eastern university and had transplanted herself far away from her family, to enjoy kicking it and earning her minimal expenses by working at the shopping center. She danced and drank and played grownup quite well, flirtatious enough to smash more than a few shallow hearts while never jeopardizing her own emotional equilibrium.

So he began calling her on the phone. Plying her with his words. Strictly nonphysical. He told her of his aspirations to write and somehow avoided stunning her into boredom.

He strengthened his resolve by quitting school, hitting the road, following jobs, scraping by, always checking in when his travels brought him within range of Mrs. Engle's.

"That's when you took up with whatsisname," he said. "The executive-cut cannon fodder. The tennis player. The white picket fence guy."

"Oh, he was around before that," she said.

"I remember his car. A Pinto, red lacquer, jacked up like a muscle car."

She was flatly astonished that he remembered her boyfriend's old ride. "You were off in Berkeley, or Alaska. I can never remember which. Banging that stripper."

"Adele wasn't a stripper," he said. "She was an assistant to a stripper. More properly, a retro-burlesque performer who toured. An 'exotic dancer,' she'd say, then later, 'performance artist.' The description changes as the orbit decays. She ended badly. Cancer. I don't know what ever became of Adele."

"I remember those long, dead-of-night calls," she said. "We would just talk and talk, and we weren't scoping each other out or groping toward some hasty, preliminary feel-up. What we said had value, tainted as it was by all that—" she hunted down the correct word "—*exuberance*. The part you missed was how quickly and how completely I was smitten. I tormented myself about it. I tried two thousand logical and practical ways to deny it. I fought not to invest tears in frustration. And every time I thought you were history, well that's that, and you had receded…up you popped again."

"You wrote me a poem," he said.

She rolled her eyes and mock-strangulated. "Oh, not that god-damned poem."

"I remember the part about you pressing your nose up against the glass and seeing me and my life on the other side, louder and in color."

"It was punishable, girly tripe. It didn't even deserve to be scribbled on the back of a spiral notebook, surrounded by hearts and stars and shit."

"It worked at the time. Here I was, trying to seduce you with words because I felt I didn't *have* anything else to deploy, and there you were, coming back at me with words. It took thought. It took time and effort. It took courage to expose it and share it. That's why I made you the cake."

Their birthdays, as it happened, were only a few weeks apart. Re-ensconsed in town, he had whomped up a Stir 'N Serve cake in a foil pan and divided it on the diagonal with two colors of frosting to commemorate their birthdates. He invited her over and she showed up with a half-gallon jug of cheap Carlo Rossi Rhine. He was living in one half of a ramshackle duplex and did not even have a bed, merely a foam pad and a scatter of sleeping bags. They had gleefully dug into that little cake over fifty years ago, clinking mismatched glasses he had swiped from some pizza parlor.

On that night, they did not despoil the bedding, or the second-hand sofa, or the dicey carpet. They had made out a bit, lots of embraces, and stopped short. They were friends who could tease each other goodnaturedly about their dalliances—his dimwits and lunatics, her clubsters and Yuppies, those heat-of-the-moment tactical errors that always ended by waking up naked, craving escape.

He did not see her for a month after the cake. When she returned, it was with resolve and they were naked before half the jug of Carlo was spent. They consumed each other because they were starving. They got dressed, grabbed food, and repaired to her place, a sterile-neat and anonymous unit in some complex. Assigned parking, amenities; actual bed. They did not emerge back into the world for a day and a half.

In the normal world, that commingling would have doomed their relationship to the usual erosion and mandated formalities that murder love.

"You dumped me," she said.

"You always say that," he said, sniffy about terminology. "I got a gig and when I turned around you had already married Mr. Average. Mr. Suitable. Mr. White Picket Fence."

"It seemed like a good idea at the time," she said, despising the cliché. "At least my father saw me get married before he died. My father would have really liked you."

"How did he feel about your marriageable man-thing?"

"He was…polite. You know, I got drunk one night and uprooted that white picket fence outside our house with a shovel."

"Wow."

"Thinking about you drove me crazy sometimes. You were so good for me and so bad for me."

The white picket fence was a metaphor for what the world offered. They had joked about it.

"I wanted it, I got it *literally*…and I hated it. While I was at work the next day, my husband rebuilt it. Left me a bouquet on the dining room table. Wrote *I love you* on the card. While he was porking his secretary. And later, hookers in Tokyo on a business trip. You could say we had a nice, stable dynamic. A normal American marriage."

"What about all your boyfriends after that?"

"I'll admit it—we competed, without really ever saying so."

"I thought it was sweet you put all those eligible men on hold just to see me again."

Glutted with disposable income and money market accounts, she had secured a fancy-ass hotel suite for their reunion. A security floor, fresh cookies at night for guests. Privacy and room service. Whenever the husband went out of town. It went that way for the next decade or two, subject to their schedules.

She finally got divorced about the time he got married. Move a grain of sand on the beach and it changes things on the other side of the planet. He got divorced. She remarried. They vectored on each other like orbitless moons, unpredictable, their collaboration resuming wherever it had been interrupted weeks or years before, always potent enough to render them giddy, spiked with just enough risk, fraught with impossibility, sufficiently potent to be infuriating, later. It was the most honest relationship either of them had ever experienced. At least, that's how they reassured themselves.

"I hated that hotel in Atlanta," he said.

They had not seen each other for about five years. They converged in Atlanta, only for him to discover he had to stand by, on hold, while she ran damage control on her afternoon affair, another jock who ran a sports franchise. The jock's own wife red-lined certain times of day, and evenings were reserved for the hubby.

"Actually, I hated *waiting* in that hotel in Atlanta. Ticking the clock through bad movies. *Doc Hollywood. Father of the Bride.* Sugary happy-ending shit. Endlessly."

"I didn't want to sleep with someone in the afternoon, then sleep with you," she said. "I wanted there to be a gap. Distance. Insulation. I loaded my plate too much and was afraid you'd be poisoned."

"Listen, back in my nastier days, I once slept with three different women I knew in a twenty-four-hour period, just to prove to myself I could do it. I used them. I was not a nice person. One time an old girlfriend called me in tears, obsessing. I was with a new girlfriend and I let her listen in. Watch, I said. I will make this despondent woman laugh, long-distance. Then I made her cry again, all on cue, all by design, all my fault."

"That was cruel."

"Sure was," he said. "It taught me a hard lesson. Apart from that it stood as an example for me not to judge you, or who you chose, or why."

"No it didn't," she said, smiling. "It just hit you upside the head: Pot, kettle, black. What we had always ran outside those parameters. Our history predated whatever else we did on our own. We existed inside a hermetically sealed bubble only we knew about. We were answerable to no one. Still are. That's why when I say I love you, I mean I love you uniquely. This is my private place. Nobody takes away what I have in this bubble. It is outside of time and obligation. It's something you and I have—we own a piece of each other that no one else gets, ever."

"You're forgetting Mrs. Engle," he said.

She laughed out loud. "Oh, god, that time we visited her *together.* What the hell were we thinking?"

He was back in his old haunts and she had arranged to slice away a free weekend to visit friends in 'another town,' specifically, his old landlady. They shacked up in a resort hotel. It was the closest thing they had ever had to a vacation together. They ducked out, had remarkably feverish sex, and returned in time for coffee at Mrs. Engle's. Laughter, anecdotes, catch-up, nostalgia, with him knowing all the while that his ladylove was sitting there, all proper and charming, with no panties beneath her skirt because he had ripped them off. *Going commando*, she had called it.

"I think she knew, on some level, what was really going on," he said, of Mrs. Engle, one of many surrogate Moms throughout his life.

"More than that," she said, "I think she approved. And that means she understood. Maybe this—you and me—was something that Mrs. Engle could understand in her calm way, and maybe that makes it okay."

"Like the seal of approval from the one person in the universe whose opinion we'd give a damn about?"

She nodded and they were both silent for a moment. Mrs. Engle had died a long time ago.

"Do you ever think about what it would have been like if—?"

"I hadn't *dumped* you?" he said. "We had, how you say, hooked up? Bonded? Partnered?"

"We have done all that."

"Just not cohabitated."

"Because we probably would have torn each other to shreds in a week, and I wouldn't be sitting here now, old man."

"You're probably right, old lady. Tell me something: Did you ever sit down with a calendar and add it all up? Us, you and me?"

"No, I never thought of that. But you tried, I'll bet."

He winked. "A futile effort, once, in the midst of some gloom, probably around my fortieth birthday. I tried to cumulate the flybys, the phone calls, the dates and place and times. As far as I got, I figured about forty-five days, total, before I gave it up as stupid."

"About a month and change."

"Yeah, spread out over half a century or more."

"But I came when you called."

"I know. Because you're my family, in here." He thumped his chest and extended his hand to her. She rose, clasped it, and kissed him with considerable passion.

"I won't let you go through this alone," she said. "You'd do the same for me."

He said nothing because he already knew how right she was, had always been.

In the corridor of Ward C she was caught leaving his room by a young woman. Bright eyes hollowed out with fatigue assessed her and did not know her.

"Are you a friend of Dad's?" said the younger woman.

The older woman said, "He was a friend of my late husband's. They went to school together." She was privately pleased at how smoothly this lie slipped out. It would need minimal embellishment.

"That hick college in Dos Piedras?" said the younger woman. "He only went there three semesters."

"I know," the older woman said with a measure of pride. "He quit school to write. And he made the right choice, didn't he? My husband taught him how to play billiards. Not pool—billiards. He always said that was the most useful thing he learned in that academic cemetery."

"Yeah, I remember him saying that once. A long time ago. Before." The younger woman's eyes had blurred with bright tears she could not dam back.

"What's the matter?"

The younger woman pawed out a tissue and spot-checked the corridor for witnesses to her distress. Eyes dutifully averted. Her voice hitched. "He remembers *that*. But he can't place me or my brother. He's totally forgotten Mom. She died two years ago. No, three, I mean. That's when he started to slip. He can vaguely remember the titles of some of his books. But he can't remember his family. His editors or agents for the last thirty years. He doesn't recognize his friends. Anything. It all just fell out of his head." She turned away, wrestling inner demons. "No, *no*, goddammit, I will *not* dissolve into a blubberfest in the middle of this fucking *hospital*!"

She let the older woman embrace her.

"God, I am so sorry," she said, forcing calm. "I'm Pam. Pamela. Did Dad say anything else? Did you—I mean, do you know him well?"

"I only knew your father for about a month and a half," said the older woman. "I never really counted the days, you know."

....

Bloodstock:
Four Days of Stress, Chaos and Wonderment

(2005-2009)

Conventions. Love 'em or hate 'em, they're everywhere.

Regional science fiction conventions used to be simple: You rang up some paperback authors and spent a weekend drinking with them. A film program consisted of two or three 16mm wonders rented from Universal 16 or Films Incorporated (or Swank, Budget, Kit Parker, or Westcoast—if you're old enough, you remember the drill). Catalogue rentals were frequently the only chance you would get to see, say, *Twins of Evil*, nudity and all, after its theatrical run. The themes of science fiction, horror and fantasy were always a reliable envelope for university-sponsored festivals, which tended to favor movies over books, and used cult credibility as a programming scheme to attract audiences larger and less minutely focused than genre fans. But even these had the air of a weekend party—that is, if you can imagine a party with *no alcohol*—instead of a militantly-micromanaged cash cow event.

As film-on-film became too dated and cumbersome, conventions big and small began to succumb to the dreaded "video room syndrome." From the larger and more prestigious literary cons to the smallest regional "fan gathering," the organizational idiom remained hobbled by an unspoken Golden Rule that seemed to mandate every con committee start from scratch every single time, with no learning curve from event to event.

Then *Star Trek* cons redefined the whole playing field in the 1970s, catalyzing the out-of-control growth cycle that spawned many of the present-day Zilla-sized media mashups that look like conventions, call themselves likewise, but operate under the moniker of "shows" or "festivals," and segregate audience from performers behind a nightmarish wall of commerce—autographs for pay, extra fees for preferential seating and a complete absence of return considerations. No freebies. No exceptions. No socializing. No programming after dark. The operative rule seems to be pay up, run the gauntlet, then get out and stay out...unless you have more cash.

Sometimes these assemblies are christened "conferences" to lend them a bogus veneer of respectability. Whatever the social function, and wherever more than five fans gather together in one place with money in their pockets, whether to wear rubber foreheads, wallow in trivia or purchase tchotchkes, such events are generally still called "conventions."

Which is better than calling them "big-ticket media orgies," the better to distract the attendee from the reality that his or her role has been reduced to that of generic consumer. The convention, as once idealized by Trekkie-eyed EquiCon veterans, is no more. There really should be a new word for the sort of event that characterizes such gatherings, now—perhaps one that explains why the San Diego Comic Con has so little to do with actual comic books.

Things were different in 1946, when author Robert Bloch experienced his first convention, a PacifiCon in Los Angeles, which featured a tiny attendance, most of whom already knew each other—A.E. Van Vogt, Leigh Brackett, Ray Bradbury, and many other future genre giants. As Bob said, "That was back in the day when Arthur C. Clarke would drive 500 miles just to pay to be an attendee." The very first World Science Fiction Convention, according to Forry Ackerman, drew 185 people, many of whom could not afford the one-dollar banquet fee.

Imagine, then, the fantasy construct of a damned-near ideal convention, featuring dozens of celebrity guests to whom you could have damned-near unrestricted access, and costing mere mortals a pittance. No way it could break even. The costs would be crippling. It could only truly happen once, like Woodstock, and you just had to be there.

It happened, and I helped run it. It wasn't perfect, but it damned-sure was memorable. And it's probably still my favorite.

It was called the Science Fiction, Horror and Fantasy World Exposition. It was held in Tucson, Arizona in the middle of 1977 (June 2-5). It featured over fifty "official" guests and three tracks of film programming—over 100 features, half in 35mm, not counting numerous shorts, cartoons, and TV episodes—as well as such then-milestones as the first mass public convention showing of original Frank Frazetta paintings (they arrived in a U-Haul truck), overseen by Ellie Frazetta personally, and four tons of Kenneth Strickfaden's Frankensteinian Van de Graaf generators, Jacob's ladders, Tesla coils and "lightning screens" all fired up and discharging electricity, live, under the supervision of Strickfaden himself, shouting "Throw the third switch!" The host hotel featured a life-sized wedge of *Star Trek* bridge. Besides displays from attending artists, exhibit rooms boasted an original Martian dreadnought from *War of the Worlds*, armatures from *Mighty Joe Young* and *When Dinosaurs Ruled the Earth*, and the submarine from *Atlantis, The Lost Continent*. World-famous organist Lee Erwin flew in from New York to play live accompaniment to such silent classics as *The Hunchback of Notre Dame* (for which Erwin composed an original score in 1923) and the Chaney *Phantom of the Opera*—the only 35mm print known to exist at that time.

Guests? They literally ran the gamut from A to Z, including (effects maestro) L.B. Abbott, John Agar, Poul Anderson, Jack Arnold, Ian Ballantine, Whit Bissell (and his ultra-charming wife,

Jennifer Raine), Lin Carter, astronaut Charles "Pete" Conrad Jr., Buster Crabbe, Jim Danforth, Lester del Rey, Gordon Dickson, James Doohan, Harlan Ellison, Philip Jose Farmer, Ellie Frazetta, June Foray (voice of Rocket J. Squirrel and other Jay Ward immortals), Frank Kelly Freas, Friz Freleng, Clyde Geronimi, Jack Haley, Ray Harryhausen (with producer Charles Schneer in tow; *Sinbad and the Eye of the Tiger* was their latest film), Robert and Virginia Heinlein, George Clayton Johnson, Jack Kinney, Richard Matheson, Robert McCall, Clarence Nash (the original voice of Donald Duck), Dennis (Denny) O'Neill, Maureen O'Sullivan, George Pal, Frederik Pohl, Mae Questal, Carl Sagan, Robert Short, Joseph Stefano, Jim Steranko, Kenneth Strickfaden, Douglas Trumbull, William Tuttle, Boris Vallejo, A. E. Van Vogt, Johnny Weissmuller, Jack Williamson, Robert Wise, Roger Zelazny, and, needless to say, Forrest J Ackerman.

(How odd this list strikes me now. Film fans wouldn't have known the writers. Literature fans may not have recognized the names of such cinema immortals as the fellow who played the Tin Woodsman in *The Wizard of Oz*, or the woman who will forever be the voice of Betty Boop. Devotees of Frazetta and Freas might have scratched their heads at names such as Short and Abbott, let alone the Disney animation directors of *Sleeping Beauty* (Geronimi) or the Oscar-winning *Der Fuehrer's Face* (Kinney). You couldn't tell the players without a scorecard...or unless you were a complete geek. Which means opportunities to learn something new abounded, even for the most jaded.)

Convention security was handled by the Dorsai Irregulars, veterans battled-hardened by combat experience won in more *Star Trek* wingdings than I could ever tolerate. This group was captained by soon-to-be-famous writer Robert Asprin, who later brought forth his popular series of punnish-ingly titled fantasy books, starting with *Another Fine Myth* in 1978. The Dorsai were fallout from the Society for Creative Anachronism (by way of Gordon Dickson's *Dorsai* fiction), and Bob's handle was "Yang the

Nauseating." Bob immediately formed a liaison with the Tucson Police Department and obtained 30 walkie-talkies from a golf and tennis resort, the Tucson El Conquistador. Those walkies— powerful FM jobs that could transmit through concrete—really saved our bacon, in the days before cellular anything.

One hundred and fifty pieces of cake were consumed on behalf of Johnny Weissmuller's birthday (there were satellite cakes to the normal-sized one with the inscription). Robert Heinlein, mantled "the Dean of Science Fiction Writers," was spotted hanging out on the patio with Bob and the Dorsai, singing at four o'clock in the morning. It was that sort of gig, primarily because apart from the exhibits, films, and a smatter of hastily-organized panels, there was virtually no programming—at least as that event map is understood in the current context. Over fifty pros with very little to do, except attend a banquet, talk for an hour, and basically hang out with the fans who showed up...which is how I wound up spending a very pleasant break with Carl Sagan, talking about nothing in particular (but all of it fascinating) in the hotel coffee shop one afternoon. As an attendance event, it soared far beneath the expected numbers; out of a projected 5000, fewer than a thousand people showed up.

Price? Ten bucks a head for the weekend if you paid in advance, a staggering $12.50 if you waited until after January 1, 1977 to register.

Organizationally, the Expo was a catastrophe of Woodstockian proportions, underplanned and manic, a crash course in speed spin as it threatened to hurtle beyond control several times during every minute of every day. Insurance concerns nearly killed it in utero since no coverage was in place until the day before opening. Shippers and truckers ransomed waiting exhibits for ready cash. Limousines were procured to ferry guests to a banquet at the Skyline Country Club...which got cancelled, not that anybody was *told* this. Undaunted, the dessert chef from the Skyline showed up in person with Weissmuller's cake, demanding payment on the spot. The program book, for which Boris Vallejo donated an original oil painting as the cover, never made it to the print shop. (The painting, incidentally, was "The Amazon's Pet." I held it in my hands the day it arrived; the convention mastermind hauled it out of the trunk of his beat-up, poop-brown AMC Javelin, where it was propped against a grease-clotted jack, and into my grasp.)

The guy who thought up this extravaganza was Robert Nudelman, a theatre arts student with whom I had helped run several DesertCons at the University of Arizona in the mid-1970s. It was at DesertCon that we hooked up with the likes of Robert Wise, Jim Danforth, Poul Anderson, Doug Trumbull and even Vincent Price, and Bob was itching to ringmaster a larger event outside the confines and technical restrictions imposed by a campus-only function. We brainstormed much of the Expo in my one-room garage apartment.

A very talented artist named Harry S. Robins whomped up flyer illustrations. (Harry was also a fixture at the New Loft Cinema, Tucson's interpretation of an art house, where one memorable evening I saw him participate in a primordial version of *Mystery Science Theatre 3000*-style riffing on a live mike during a screening of *When Dinosaurs Ruled the Earth*.)

Harry's painstakingly hand-lettered come-on, rendered in mid-1976, was festooned with invitee names by me using PressType—some of whom, I note now, had to decline or could not attend due to the usual exigencies. (Tex Avery? Mel Blanc? Robert Bloch? Jeff Jones? Holy crap...Roger *Corman*?!)[1] Producer Saul Zaentz *was* there, presiding over a sneak preview of his *Lord of the Rings* film due the following year.

---

[1] To this day, I have no idea whether the following people were there: Ralph Bakshi, Arnold Gillespie, and weirdest of all, Frank Capra Jr. Many people misremember Robert Bloch as being there but he wasn't; Margaret Hamilton had to bow out due to illness. Saul Zaentz's presence supports the idea Bakshi (director of *Lord of the Rings*) *might* have been there, but I cannot confirm.

The whole shebang took about a year to organize, then the sheer stress plunged Bob into a near-nervous breakdown the day before we opened. At the eleventh hour—more like 11:59:45 and counting—the newly-minted public relations firm of Foudy, Zimmerman & Associates was brought in to arrange events on the fly, cut expenses, and manage run-and-gun damage control. Complete charge of the dealer's room fell to me. I wandered down to a vast basement exhibit space featuring 80-plus empty tables, each with a hotel-issue tablecloth in a wad on top. I stared at them for a couple of quiet moments—the last such of the next five days—and realized that in about ten hours, I would own every logistical problem trucked in by every single dealer, some of whom were bound to arrive late, with a built-in hatred for the leftover spaces they would have no choice but to occupy (thanks again, Steranko!). No sweat. Blood, tears, cerebro-spinal fluid, sure, but no sweat. It had all been scared right out of me. More than once I fell into yelling matches with Bob Asprin, after which we always brooked manly truce. Stupid, to holler at the guy fighting right next to you in the trench.

Miraculously, and with the supremely professional help of the PR firm, we made the boat float. We held war council at 7:00 PM sharp each day in a classic smoke-filled room. Minor guest glitches transformed into solvable bitches; most often, the guests themselves pitched in to organize and concoct impromptu, one-of-a-kind diversions. Then-local writer and KHYT DJ Michael Cassutt coordinated with the Red Cross to bring in Heinlein's newly-inaugurated blood drive (begun at MidAmeriCon the previous year).[2] (Mike also says author G. Harry Stine was in attendance, as well as Fredric Brown's widow, Elizabeth.) A crew for *60 Minutes* showed up to shoot a piece on the L-5 Society; Foudy-Zimmerman shut everything else down and herded all

---

[2] What is now called the Heinlein *Memorial* Blood Drive was begun as a way of "paying it forward," since Heinlein himself had a rare blood type (AB+). The drive is still going strong to this day.

warm bodies into the exhibition hall so the video crew could reap crowd shots with Heinlein as the focus. George Clayton Johnson threw open the doors of a sixth-floor suite to all comers, on a 24-hour basis, providing crash space—for free—passing around a gigantic bong, and videotaping some sort of pagan ceremony in which Forry Ackerman was crowned with a ceramic monstrosity fabricated by a local potter, a sort of Viking helmet commemorating god-knows-what exalted status, which must have weighed 25 pounds. A makeup artist friend of mine stationed himself in the dealer's room and began to mutate anybody who walked up and asked to be...different. For free. Writers staked out the smaller conference rooms and commenced an endless, unscheduled round-robin of readings. Nobody charged dime one for an autograph.

Does this sound like any convention you've ever been to?

As attendee Wolf Forrest noted, "The lack of a formal schedule (just hurriedly typed pages with listed events) left guests 'vulnerable' to attendees for long stretches; folks witnessed the inchoate, the obvious, the sublime, the ridiculous, the terrifying, and the dizzying coalescence of fun from chaos."

Note that "hurriedly." Damned right. Out of some 36 events considered to be "panels" or "talks," the typed sheets misspelled nearly everyone's name, and merely listed a person, a time, and a place, recombining the guests like Bingo balls and leaving theme or topic, if there was actually one, to the deductive prowess of the fan: *Let's see: Crabbe, Weissmuller, O'Sullivan, Farmer—I get it—Tarzan!*

Then there was that *Star Trek* bridge. It was supposed to be a full-sized, 360-degree recreation; by Michael Foudy's recollect, "it turned out to be about thirty degrees." The prior Saturday, the bridge's fabricators announced that there was no way they could make the deadline, and Foudy found himself recruiting carpenters from a Fourth Avenue bar for a bit of flat-wage-plus-all-you-can-drink independent contracting. The construction itself was crawling together miles away, at the JC Penney in the El Con shopping mall (and Penney wanted that thing *outta* there). When the half-intoxicated builders arrived, they found themselves at odds with an army of Trekkies who had come to nitpick and "supervise." Guess who got jettisoned.

Then the whole magilla had to be broken down and trucked to the hotel.

I arranged with room service to break and enter my room each morning and just pour coffee directly into my skull. I think I saw exterior daylight one time in 96 hours. During a brief caesura I sat Jack Arnold down and taped an interview with him. Later that Friday I found out I was in charge of some panel provisionally titled "Fifties Science Fiction Films." Picture, if you can, the panel: George Pal, Jack Arnold, Richard Matheson, Whit Bissell, John Agar.

In an audience of several hundred—easily the largest single panel of the event, scheduled to run 90 minutes—dozens of people were snapping photographs, yet I never saw or possessed a single piece of evidence I had been there...until over thirty years later, when Roger Koch provided one to prove that *yes, that muddy phantom down-stage was me with a mike in my hand.*

For a festival with little planning, there was an enormous amount of sheer *movement,* of people bustling to and fro, hooking up with each other, making dates, having parties. It was like a sudden microcosm, a freefire zone for the fantastic.

Johnny Weissmuller could frequently be heard emitting the Tarzan yell from the bar, where I saw him with a drink in each hand. The bar stools were of such a design that when one leaned back far enough, one fell over, and Johnny *always* leaned back for the signature yodel, providing many people with the opportunity to help him off the floor. (Roger Koch remembers shepherding an inebriate Johnny through a fruitless search for his own hotel room; Johnny vanished somewhere on the fifth floor in search of a corner to pee.) John Agar showed up for the panel a bit, um, *marinated* as well, leading the audience into many spontaneous outbursts of applause for the rest of the panel while Whit Bissell tried to hold him in check. (Poor John, then in the clutches of his drinking problem, nonetheless got off the most-quoted line of the weekend: *"Hey, you wanna know what it was like to fuck America's Sweetheart?"*) The Heinleins hosted a large party in their suite on Saturday night, after doing local radio and TV interviews on behalf of the blood drive and making a sortie to tour the facilities the University of Arizona Medical Center. Thanks to George Clayton Johnson's open-door policy, the entire sixth floor became a London fogbank of pot smoke that wobbled more than a few people waiting on the desperately slow elevators. My friend Susan Thing was waylaid by Mr. and Mrs. George Pal for a local shopping trip in search of Indian jewelry: "The next thing I know," she said, "(George) is making a beeline for me, gesticulating wildly at his wife, telling her, 'Ask her! Ask her! She *lives* here!'" Ken Strickfaden—"Mr. Electricity"—performed several shows per day (his tour support being his "circle of wizards" John Foster, Dick Aurandt, Ed Angell and probably Jim Shaffer). You just had to be there for the tirade of expletives unleashed by the petite and funny June Foray, waiting to speak in a room where the audience was being held in an overtime thrall by the petite and funny Harlan Ellison. Everyone laughed during the Q&A with Charles Schneer and Ray Harryhausen when somebody asked for Taryn Power's phone number. Jack Haley was astonished by the size of the queue waiting for his autograph. To the consternation of hotel management, two women who had been cosmetically enhanced with pointed ears and skyrocket eyebrows jerry-rigged their own "costumes" from hotel sheets and *nothing* else (except for their spike heels). "Ducky" Nash performed *that* voice to the delight of children at Sunday brunch. Buster Crabbe, buff, tanned and fresh from completing his *Energistics* fitness book, spoke of how easily at age 69 he could reprise his Flash Gordon role in the upcoming remake—and then, he averred, "maybe" as Flash's dad. This was Boris Vallejo's first convention appearance ever, and he was quite frankly stunned by the size and diversity, asking, "Are they *all* like this?"

And *everybody* was looking for Bob Nudelman. Doohan and Harryhausen demanded their fees, pronto. One of the projectionists flat-out quit. Travel agents were virtually plucking cash out of the registration box. Our PR paladins sequestered Bob in a top-floor suite at the hotel with a Dorsai guard outside and a strict nobody-in-or-out policy. Result: Bob Nudelman barely got to see what he had wrought. Mike Foudy remembers Bob sneaking out very late one evening, surrounded by a Dorsai escort, like a Mafiosi in witness protection before a trial.

Ultimately, the hours elapsed. Guests needed to catch flights starting Sunday afternoon. The previous Wednesday—the final setup day, when guests began to arrive—seemed decades past. Out of the goodness of their hearts, the folks engineering the portion of the 35mm film program at a Tucson venue then called the Temple of Music and Art continued to run movies all night Sunday and into Monday morning, for the benefit of the staff. I retreated to the theatre and fell asleep in the dark, courted by *A Boy and His Dog, A Clockwork Orange*, and *Psycho*. When I came out, it was still night—or rather, it was night *again*.

Aftermath: Beyond the lack of practical advance publicity, attendance was further hobbled because the U of A's 30,000 student body had ended their term three weeks earlier. Early June is the absolute *worst* time, weather-wise, for the high desert, and we were slotted for the weekend *after* the Memorial Day holiday. The Expo closed over $75,000 in debt, most of which was shouldered by Bob's father, a local doctor who was forced to take out a second mortgage on his house. As Peter Zimmerman said, "There was front money but no *back* money." The convention hotel ate half its own bill for defaulting on various agreements—not maliciously, since they were victimized by having three different booking agents deal with convention management during the year this blowout took to set up. I collapsed an extra day at home and, the following day, was promptly fired from the only "legitimate" wage job I've ever held. It was definitely a watershed period.

In the wake of the Expo, Robert Nudelman fled Tucson for Los Angeles in 1978, where he became a pit-bull activist on behalf of the Hollywood Heritage Foundation, with an eye toward the preservation and/or restoration of Hollywood landmarks against the floodtide of modern development. He helped save the Cinerama Dome and the ABC/Merv Griffin Studios buildings and was fundamental in the massive restorations undergone by the Pantages, Chinese and Egyptian Theatres. (I remember one of the first times I encountered him after I moved to Los Angeles, he was overjoyed at discovering the remains of the Seaview from *Voyage to the Bottom of the Sea* in a junkpile at 20th Century-Fox [for you miniature obsessives, it was the "floater" model with no bottom, for surface water shots]).

Those of us who go back further always recalled the Expo as "Nudelcon" (pronounced *noodle-con*). Bob always recalled it as an ambitious failure, and no mention was made of it when he died of a coronary at age 52 (on 3 May, 2008, in Tucson). For nearly three decades he was a fixture on Hollywood Boulevard, consorting with developers, testifying at hearings and fighting City Hall; as his colleague Fran Offenhauser said, "There probably isn't a single historic building or development project in Hollywood that Mr. Nudelman didn't have a part in."

At the time of his death Bob was the Director of Preservation Issues for Hollywood Heritage, and curator of its museum in the iconographic Lasky-DeMille Barn as well as vice president of the Society for Cinephiles and the Cinecon Classic Film Festival. He was working with Todd Fisher and Debbie Reynolds to realize the long-planned Hollywood Motion Picture Museum in Tennessee, and when he died he had no fewer than 58 separate Hollywood area restoration projects on the boil. He also co-authored two books with Hollywood Heritage's Marc Wanamaker: *Historic Hollywood: A Centennial History* (2005) and *Images of America, Early Hollywood* (2007).

And *that* all started with Nudelcon...I mean, the Expo. Which none of his Hollywood boosters had ever heard of.

Less than three weeks after Bob's demise, the other Bob— Robert Lynn Asprin, our indispensable security chief—died at his home in New Orleans at age 61 (22 May, 2008). When we did the Expo, Bob had just published his first book (*The Cold Cash War*, 1977) and would go on to write or co-write 50 more. I had yet to publish any fiction professionally, although I had just earned a whopping fifty bucks for my first newspaper article.

While checking up on Asprin I discovered that *another* of our DesertCon familiars, Les Reese, had died the year before (29 September, 2007) in New Mexico from injuries sustained in an ATV accident.

At which point I was dismayed to realize that most of our guests have passed on, too.[3]

Like I said, this sort of happenstance cannot be totally planned. Chaos theory will always demand its due, but some-times, in exchange, you get glimpses of something unique and magical. And not replicable.

By the mid-90s, conventions were a tough gig, even if you were a guest—which status is defined as a person for whom the convention picks up travel and expenses, at the very least, in return for using up a weekend of their time. Much preferable is

---

[3] For the morbidly curious: Haley (1979); Pal (1980); Crabbe (1983); Weissmuller & Strickfaden (1984); Abbott & Nash (1985); Heinlein & Carter (1988); Geronimi (1989); Aurandt (1991); Arnold & Kinney (1992); del Rey, Foster & Raine (Mrs. Bissell) (1993); Ballantine, Freleng & Zelazny (1995); Bissell & Sagan (1996); Stine (1997); O'Sullivan & Questal (1998); Conrad (1999); Van Vogt & Erwin (2000); Anderson & Dickson (2001); Agar (2002); Ginny Heinlein (2003); Doohan, Freas & Wise (2005); Stefano & Williamson (2006); Tuttle (2007); Ackerman (2008); Schneer, Farmer & Ellie Frazetta (2009).

the college lecture circuit: Universities not only waste less time and make fewer outrageous last-minute demands (comparatively speaking), but cut actual *contracts* for your performance, like professionals. In addition to travel and expenses, they pay honoraria and per diem. Generally the audiences are not composed of jaded know-it-alls, and the curiosity factor is higher, which helps knock down the performance wall.

Today, the meaning of "guest" has been perverted to label virtually anyone with a professional credit who wanders through the door. Frequently such accredited attendees will find their names all over the convention advertising, without a suggestion of compensation in any form. In return for sitting on a panel, they get to… sit on a panel. The World Fantasy Convention used to kick back the membership fee to any guest who participated in a panel; when this proved cost-prohibitive, the perk was reduced to a free drink at the bar. That one dried up years back, as well. And today it usually costs about a hundred bucks just to enter whatever substandard hotel has been inflicted on the membership this year.

Which may be another reason they're called "cons."

(The Expo's guests were comped travel and lodging, and in many cases, speaking fees. I'm willing to bet a few participants got short-sheeted, merely by the chameleonic minute-to-minute cash flow, because I had to perform paper acrobatics just to lock down a hundred bucks to keep from starving.)

In most present-day convention environments, it is more fun and less waste just to hang at the hotel bar without inflicting the actual convention on yourself. If you have any professional standing at all, you can usually get into the dealer's room, or the art show, or the panels, for nothing. If you're a fan, stake out the bar anyway—and you'll find that the world will walk past your position, as opposed to the frantic seek-and-find missions abortively attempted in the midst of a mob.

While the old warhorses of convention-dom became completely inbred (just traipse to the current nominations for the

World Fantasy Award or the Hugos, and ask yourself if you've even read a tenth of those titles, or care), those amoebically-promulgating autograph and TV-reunion get-togethers were evolving, too.

Whatever is not assimilated is destroyed, and just as the convention as a form of recreation was losing its allure, along came the Mad Model Parties, the Chiller Theatres, the Wonderfests, each seeking a comfort zone for fans who still wanted to mingle for all sorts of reasons (like the resin kit boom of the late 80s, for example)—and most importantly, re-injecting the nostalgia and clubby tree-house camaraderie important to fans who were now courting middle age and beyond.

And there's still a smidge of lingering magic, no matter how naked the grab for your bankroll. Just like in the olden days, most of the downside is obliterated by meeting that one erudite fan who "gets it," or the one pro who will happily give you some face time.

Conventions, conferences, convergences, convocations, festivals and shows are prolific enough today to be a fact of life for any fan in almost any sub-genre. This is a good thing, quite contrary to the attitude that might be gleaned here, i.e., *better then; worse now.* Simply put, getting what you need from any such gathering has merely become more competitive, as such things always do when they evolve. The comparison between Woodstock 1969 and its 1999 corporately-sponsored zombie resurrection remains apt, though, because "then" is a matter of history, and "now" an attempt to recreate history that is venerated. Bottom line: Either you were there, or weren't.

I was there. And boy howdy, was it glorious. But only in hindsight. As Joe Lansdale once said of having kids: "I love my children. I wouldn't take a million dollars for them…and I wouldn't give you two cents for two more just like 'em."

This little reminiscence owes its existence to Roger Koch and Jennifer Fox for the photos as well as Robert Taylor, Wolf Forrest, Chris Wheeler, Trini Ruiz, Mike Cassutt, Sue Thing, Michael Foudy, Peter Zimmerman and Frank Dietz. Thanks, team!—DJS

———————

(This article was finally published—with the photos—in Jim & Marian Clatterburgh's magazine Monsters from the Vault *#27 [Spring 2010].)*

To see a complete film list for the Expo, see pages 298-99.

GRAVESIDE

This is what I remember, years and years later:

After the usual dull speculations about insanity or astral projection or spiritual possession or interloping consciousness or dream planes or an odd, random tilt of chance or dimension at fault, I was able to unfold myself into the idea that I could see through other people's eyes while I was sleeping.

Except it was no longer like sleep to me. It was staying awake, all night, all day, every day, if not in my head then someone else's.

Never the same person twice.

No build. No bullet points for plot. No ascending ladder of incident. No connection or crosstalk among points-of-view. And no sleep. "Rest" for my body but not my brain. My girlfriend claimed I snored. I never knew; how could I?

My surrender came too quickly (four days, give or take) and with rueful glee. People spend their lives trying to know others. To see their thoughts. Get into their heads. Know the worst wormdirt they lust to believe is truth. Dirty little secrets and lies. Hidden agendae unveiled. Deadly baggage and psychiatric footnotes for firebombed relationships. If only they had known. Things were just as so-and-so predicted, suspected, fabricated.

Discovering Stacia has a clit ring carries a tiny voyeuristic thrill. Glimpsing her in a vanity mirror is a minute-movie wet dream. Finding out she had dumped her boyfriend in order to rejigger her persona as a mercenary dyke is disappointingly foreseeable. For her it is a fashion statement. No consequence. I have barely figured out her name—she glanced at a copy of *Vanity Fair* with a subscription label—before I blink and lose her. Unrecoverably. Ships in the night.

Seeing is believing, said a guy I'd experience later via the blink.

I called it a "blink" because I could not confer more sophistication to the transition. Maybe it was a stutter of sleep or a near-wakeup. A cough or a rollover. With every blink, my internal channels changed. The sights I saw and the sensations I experienced through total strangers were maddeningly brief, one-way, and inconclusive. I saw nothing from the provocative vantage of serial killers, murder victims, celebrity fucks or dead relatives.

All people, even on the other side of the planet, spend inordinate overtime staring at themselves in reflective surfaces, so I saw a lot of faces, many more than names culled.

Half the time I wanted to move into a stranger's existence and occupy their life. Perhaps they got to sleep. Half the time I wanted to amputate the freeflow and just collapse comfortably back into my own corpus, thank you. Except my own sleep, as noted, was problematic.

Calvin Federline is a business manager who is very huggy. He embraces his intimates, his friends, clients, especially the chosen few he is embezzling into Chapter 11. I am with him long enough to see him check his hair plugs in a men's room mirror before wire-transferring pilfered funds offshore. Calvin manages a lot of television actors, always repeating his full name with each handshake and hug because no one can recall it. Just by name, you'd recognize the actor he was invisibly robbing this afternoon.

Blink.

Karla thunders through an incredible midafternoon orgasm, which she is faking. All I see are the guy's feet. She is on top of him, turned around so he can watch her ass piston up and down. Also, I realize, so he could not see her actual expression. She does not have to fake her deep excitement—not at the sex, but at the tasty naughtiness of each of them cheating on their respective spouses. I only find out her name because the unseen guy keeps gasping it, like a fish trying to respirate methane. Then, blink.

One of the dopier ideas to lumber the massmind of ordinary citizens is the rote preconception that "normal" people all do the same things at the same time, which perhaps explains why nobody can ever pick up their dry cleaning punctually. Nine to five workers, weekend warriors, gridlock traffic-jammers, the herd faithful of consumer gospel. Those goodfolk who are asleep when "all decent people" are likewise. Having become the opposite of decent, I was thus seeing Calvin and Karla in the middle of the day because nighttime slumber had already become, for me, a purgatorial marathon of exhaustion wrought by lying still, eyes closed, teeth grinding, relentlessly *seeing*.

My girlfriend's name was Constance, and I never got to see anything through her eyes. She suggested I was "dreaming" and I resented her for hooking such a thickly obvious symptomology. After that she proposed doctors, then more doctors, in a simplistic and dismissive way, so I left. No use prolonging an unwinnable argument.

I try drinking myself into a coma but when my eyelids droop, I see.

See Frankie, who lives in kennel filth exercising his protozoan right to deplete resources and distribute waste products, because he believes in free will.

See Norma, who read a magazine article about self-inflicted wounds and has begun cutting herself open so the world would know her pain.

See a guy who spots his best friend's wallet, and hating himself, swipes cash from it.

See a woman who lives every day plotting to kill her husband, who had made the mistake of striking her some ten years previously. Her joy in her routine is perverse.

Ordinary citizens, normal people. I didn't know a single one.

You'd think by sheer averages I might see something remotely encouraging about the human condition. But even a sweet-faced mother turns her nose away from her little girl, thinking: *fat.*

And another daughter, another place, a child who really truly believes her mother is a monster who connives to suck out her soul while she is asleep. That her stuffed animals have hidden teeth.

Some of the usual suspects blinked past with lavalike predictability: The priest and his humid fantasies of sweetly lubricious grade-school cornhole. The junkie's utter devotion to the fix. The failed poet's escalating delusions of worth. The career gal drowning in her own self-loathing. Sad clichés, living, breathing, staring at themselves in mirrors and finding themselves wanting, every waking moment. They found solace in sleep and I came to despise them. Every morning they awoke and experienced that brief caesura before reality rushed in to remind them of all the ways their lives were a boring abyss of dashed hope and sundered aspirations, that solitary moment of calm in a day thence squandered in ennui, pointless oscillating anger and fruitless theoretical vendetta unadmitting of action. They seethed, or rather, steeped. *Someday I'll get even. I'll show you all. I told you so. No one appreciates my suffering.* To glimpse swatches of commonweal life was to gorge on ever-deepening (hence bottomless) despair.

Blink.

In recounting their trivial agonies as my own special complaint, I realized I was no better. I had become them, bleating about all the things I didn't have.

Do you still harbor romantic notions about human self-sacrifice or love as higher virtues? I watched them dash against the reefs of anthropological hardwiring. We are a disease threatening to overrun our petri dish. Blink, I'm a microscope, watching toxins stomp the heads of fellow toxins for a shot at a higher rung on the food chain. Self-sacrifice? Animals do it. Love at first sight? Animals do it. Art? When we managed such sad gestures we treated them no better than would beasts, discarding worth for commodity and consuming our frustrated imperfections along with everything else in a world we doggedly entombed in the excrement of our own feeding frenzy.

Blink. Mrs. DuVal wants to buy a painting to match her sofa group. The limit of her aspiration is to have a living room that looks like the lobby of a Holiday Inn. She only watches Academy Award-winning (or nominated) films. She does not have taste so much as artificial flavor.

Hundreds of such nickelodeon excerpts from other lives cleansed me of all delusion about human nature at its parasitic finest, so you'll forgive me if my tone seems a tot grim.

You know how you save something your entire life—a keep-sake, an heirloom, a tchotchke—only to see it broken or lost at last, and you feel the death of a tiny component of your essential being, then rationalize it as just a thing, an object, a symbol? You try to dismiss it, strip it, belittle its value in terms of who you think you have become.

That's what this felt like, in reverse. Blink: suddenly something is there, of such import that your preceding life is revealed as a futile reflex, a mere chemical reaction. Blink to already-open eyes reviling all they perceive, a vision that beguiles me into phony superiority. Love is a lie next to that caliber of revelation.

Constance didn't even bother searching for me. She was summoned later.

Blink. I see myself. That's different, at least. One time only.

The woman staring at me is named Lorraine (from her Medic Alert bracelet) and her evaluation is that I am an urban derelict adrift on a footpath bench, a blemish on her stroll, staring to infinity, see-ing nothing. She rehearses how she'll refuse to give me spare change. I see her from inside her own head, clearly enough to know that her Medic Alert bracelet will not save her when the time comes, soon.

We mock each other silently. She and I, all of us, we hate every other one of us, and we keep reproducing because our DNA man-dates it.

Why me? What was the distinction that transmogrified me into a receiver? I never blinked to see anyone else lumbered with my new affliction. Perhaps it was a cosmic shell-game, like one of those puzzles composed of sliding tiles. If so, a terminus might be expected. I would learn some sound moral lessons and the curse would shift to the next hapless recipient.

Never happened.

I could recount no cause for the effect. No turning point. I was secure in my own misanthropic cocoon, then blink and I was afflicted. Stories with tidy resolutions were no help. Then again, as Constance posited, I could have been making up the whole thing, id and ego train-wrecking into an embarrassingly self-absorbed scenario of auto-pity. Just what I needed to put me in my place, right?

Exhaustion became a giddy narcotic as the exterior world evanesced to vague input, except through the eyes of others.

Blink. Mr. Rebusi (like a rebus with an eye, he told people) knee-jerks through social discourse entirely in clichés. Fine just fine as wine, he says. Can't say and wouldn't know. Still waters run deep, pretty much. It takes a heap of living to make a house a home. If I'm lyin' I'm dyin'. Enough about me, let's talk about you. You've got to walk a mile in the other person's shoes.

An admirable sentiment, if choice is involved.

According to Mr. Rebusi, a kiss is just a kiss.

The first time I ever kissed a girl was delirious, like smoking crack. Time and space seemed to plunge and morph. The very air seemed alive. Like everybody else I spent the rest of my life trying to recapture that feeling. It started that way with Constance, less potent, less vital, yet adequate. I guess it depends on how desperate you are.

What you see is what you get, as Mr. Rebusi would say. That's all she wrote.

The blink stopped when I heard Constance telling people that I had died with my eyes open. Authority figures hovered over me. I was back in my own head at last, but the sound of Constance weeping told me I was going to miss the suffocation of fellow humans, even at their worst.

·········

Death to Decaf!

(2009)

Media wizard Peter Levin hit the nail square on the head when he posited, some years ago: "The future of entertainment is the arrested development business; sports, videogames, toys and comicbooks."

When *Fandango* posted its annual Hot List of the "Most Anticipated Tentpoles for 2009," it went like this:

According to Men:
1. *Star Trek* 23%
2. *Transformers: Revenge of the Fallen* 17%
3. *Harry Potter and the Half-Blood Prince* 14%
4. *X-Men Origins: Wolverine* 9%
5. *Terminator Salvation* 7%
6. *Watchmen* 7%
7. *Angels & Demons* 5%
8. *Public Enemies* 3%
9. *G.I. Joe* 3%
10. *New Moon* 3%

According to Women:
1. *Harry Potter and the Half-Blood Prince* 25%
2. *New Moon* 15%
3. *Transformers: Revenge of The Fallen* 11%

4. *Angels & Demons* 9%
5. *X-Men Origins: Wolverine* 7%
6. *Star Trek* 6%
7. *Public Enemies* 5%
8. *Night at the Museum: Battle of the Smithsonian* 4%
9. *The Lovely Bones* 3%
10. *Where the Wild Things Are* 2%

According to me: 90% bottom-line, low-common-denominator, PG-13 franchise shite; megabudget crapshoots whose sole soulless purpose is to maintain corporate revenue streams. In other words, *not* movies for moviegoers so much as pretty junkfood. (Plus a Dillinger movie by Michael Mann, starring Johnny Depp, and an adaptation of a frustratingly unreadable novel—if anybody can energize it, Peter Jackson can.)

The days when you could tell a Paramount movie from a Universal movie just by the look of the production drowned long ago, about the same time those studios incorporated into multi-tasked marketing steamrollers. Every time a top-heavy entertainment robot like *The Dark Knight* grosses a bazillion dollars, it succors the preference of corporations to keep churning out the same product in the same way. In obdurate ignorance of digital millennia, industry strikes, or creative latitude, if companies can keep moviegoers gobbling the same old crapburger, executive sinecures are safe for another fiscal year.

It's business, and isn't America all about business?

This affects the tributary of horror in myriad goofy ways.

For one thing, horror is a niche market—always was, always will be. We've watched it subdivide into multifarious eddies on its own—from monster movies and "chillers" to gore films, slasher films, so-called torture porn, "extreme" churners enabled by DTV, and by now even an entire subgenre of "shakycam" flicks as seen through the lens of some hapless character's camcorder. What remains odd about these ventures into the realm of horror is that so few of them cultivate unease or fear. The by-now quaint gore film aesthetic is still present—meaning that while you definitely would not want to see your own eyeball on the end of a nitrogen cork-popper, witnessing same does not automatically generate any kind of raw fear. A flinch, sure; revulsion, a phobic twitch, or perhaps just a warm fulfillment at seeing a gross-out enacted in latex and CGI...but nothing like genuine unease.

For another thing, there's *retcon*. It's a word now, a conflation of "retroactive continuity," which means, in film terms, somebody callously changed the rules you thought you knew. Which means, in horror film terms, that the legendary slashers of the 1970s and 1980s are now less mythic because they all just really had shitty childhoods: Motivation = simple Freudianisms, generally over-cooked. The iconic monsters and supernaturals of the movies you loved as a callow teenager have been defeated at last, neutralized by forces stronger than they are—namely, rethinks, reimaginings, and reboots that are to real horror as decaf is to espresso.

This is something to ponder as *Fangoria* courts its 30-year anniversary. Age 30—you know, the age past which you aren't supposed to trust anybody. (If you're ancient enough you might recall Charlton Heston saying this in *Planet of the Apes*. If you're interested enough, you might also like to know that the attribution is to Jack Weinberg, leader of the Free Speech Movement at Berkeley, who coined the catchphrase in a 1965 interview with the San Francisco *Chronicle* when he was 24.)

So far the 21st Century is the Age of Decaffeinated Horror.

When the Asian contingent checked in to re-energize the moribund horror genre, they were met with a counterattack of whitebread American remakes for people too lazy to read subtitles (or merely unable to read). It's been a decade now since the surge was perceived, and dead wet ghost children have descended into the familiar, sapping their ability to startle.

Original DVD releases lost their direct-to-video ghetto status as soon as the first animated sequel became a cash cow. This was good for horror. DVDs also permitted extreme/uncensored/ unrated cuts to become commonly available. This was also good. The market responded with a floodtide of cheap, derivative tripe; never have so many tried to regurgitate *Dawn of the Dead* so badly to less purpose. Not so good. Downside: Instead of presenting a broader smorgasbord of choices to a wider audience, it became much harder to pick the infrequent jewels out of an exponentially-growing dungheap. How was one supposed to tell what was hot and what was not?

Film criticism in general is on the ropes as print media yield to digital the way dinosaurs yielded to dominance by mammals. That leaves film reviewing, which is simple consumer advocacy— either see it, buy it, or don't. Any idiot with a keyboard can do that (and many do, from behind such trust-inspiring internet handles as "DarthScrotum" or "ineedagirlfriend"), but the idiom itself was polluted long ago by pointless bean counting (i.e., an obsession with boxoffice take over content) and the court jester-dom of thumbs-up or thumbs-down, five stars or no stars, does it rock or is it "teh suck." Scroll most online boards devoted to movies and you'll see they almost invariably decay with astonishing speed toward the topics that really matter to their members: List-making *(VOTE for your Top Ten Lampshades in Film!)* and haters spewing bitchy and spectacularly illiterate bile at one another.

Horror film criticism doesn't exist in a practical sense, which is a shame because a semblance of artistic/cultural context could go a long way toward lifting horror, as a genre, out of the slimepit of ignominy from which so many fans spend so much effort defending it. What critical thinking does persist is more difficult to find than, say, the latest slasher no-brainer with a number behind its title.

In fact, more and more horror films have become essentially critic-proof: Reboots, remakes and rethinks literally sell nothing beyond their own title. They stroke the tropes, tweak the kills, sling the same hash, and all end in exactly the same place (stop me if you've heard this one: *lone female survivor triumphs!*) where the "horror" part looks finished but probably isn't, not really, especially when some mook character fatuously says, "It's over now." Ninety-five percent of modern horror films might as well end with that classic question mark from the 1950s—*The End...Or Is It?*

Consider this plot frame: Everything's crushingly dull and normal until we meet a character who is the darling of destiny, the Chosen One, who taps hitherto unsuspected reserves of courage to prevail over a monstrous and conventionally unstoppable enemy. Sometimes the Chosen One is a fifth wheel. In animated features, it's the least likely or ugliest misfit critter; in horror films, it's generally the lead hottie. Yes—the films that most resemble modern horror films are feature-length cartoons.

Horror audiences exacerbate the downslide by unilaterally supporting anything and everything that fits the label. Fans hope for the best each time, with an earnestness that borders on an act of faith, but have been burned enough times to develop a healthy cynicism easily mistaken for doom-crying. No argument, though, is sufficient to keep them from lining up and handing over their money to this week's debuting brain-eater or bloated-budget cape-and-tights train wreck.

Which is one reason assorted online entities have summed up the general audience as "the popcorn masses" and "the shitkicker crowd."

Get burned enough times, and one begins to pine for the good old days. Except the current fashionable period for nostalgia is the 1980s, which is now so ancient and lost in the mists of time that people are doing documentaries about the golden age of the slasher film.

Seriously?!

If you have to time-stamp the most recent dovetail period for horror movies, 1992 is a good place to land. It was the point at which the slasher movie aesthetic crossed over in the mainstream and Anthony Hopkins received an Academy Award for playing a sociopathic cannibal, something that had not happened since 1932 when Fredric March got a trophy for playing Jekyll and Hyde. Now suspense movies, thrillers, and "grownup" films could freely poach the gore and psycho factors, yet not risk being labeled downmarket as a "horror" movie.

This was very nearly simultaneous with the first practical, common-citizen-friendly penetration of what is now called the internet.

Exploitable elements not assimilated from horror films were cast back down into the pit—the back alleys, the abandoned haunts, the gutter...and the hobby houses provided by websites. Horror is at its most unsullied and potent when it remains determinedly outlaw. Yesterday it was fleapit grindhouse runs of movies you certainly wouldn't want to see with your mom; today it's uncensored cuts on DVD and missing footage on YouTube. It demonstrates that horror was never meant to have any sort of broad mainstream appeal. It remains a niche market, a secret clubhouse, and a sure bet for low-budget filmmakers, because even now, nothing in the world is cheaper than sending a loony with a power tool after a cheerleader, or locking up idiomatic teen types in a room and rolling in the zombie army.

Further, even now, horror movies are still a good boot camp for earnest people with talent.

Some of them, it is hoped, will not be crushed into single-serve patties by studio behemoths and distribution monarchies—you know, those mega-sized monsters whose endless bloated logos at the beginning of a film now add several minutes to the running time before they're repeated.

And blood effects in CGI? They *still* look stupid.

One of the things *Fangoria* continues to do usefully is present politically neutral background on most if not all candidates for your attention. It's certainly not the mag's fault that most cast and crew interviews often come off like studio-spun puffery—you know, akin to the EPK junk on discs where everybody talks about how great and swell and terrific everybody else was, because they're like *sooo* terrified for their jobs, their image, or their future. It is mildly astonishing to me that so much copy has been logged in the name of horror, lo, unto three decades, not to mention that some of that copy was *my fault entirely.*

No news travels faster in the sub-world of fandom than who died and how fast someone can post about same; it's a feeding-frenzy sort of hobby that is always "nasty, brutish and short" (as good ole Thomas Hobbes said in 1651 of life in general). If I was struck by a lightning bolt and fried to medium-well-dead tomorrow, R&D would stand as one of my quick-capsule quote-byte epitaphs (along with that bird movie and maybe a zombie story and a book or two for which nobody will be able to remember the titles). People still remember R&D *thirteen years* after it folded! I have been stopped on the street, in a bar in Shreveport, in a supermarket in North Carolina, in a drugstore in Vancouver, and even collared in the middle of WETA Workshop in New Zealand, by people who read R&D and apparently never forgot it.

Perhaps this is the reason Tony Timpone still indulges me every 50 issues or so...or maybe he's just waiting for me to accrue enough text to do a sequel to *Wild Hairs* (the collected R&Ds with extras; it won the International Horror Guild's prize for Best Nonfiction Book in 2001), so he can blurb *that,* too.

Or maybe Tony thinks that if he gives me enough rope, I'll admit that my favorite recent horror film was *Rambo.*

Either way, if you want a rallying cry for horror as it approaches 2010 *(The Year We Still Don't Make Contact Again)*, I cast my vote for *"Death to Decaf!"*

————

*(This is a stray "Raving & Drooling" column from **Fangoria** Magazine—one of three such uncollected columns, the rest being found in the comprehensive collection of 'em, **Wild Hairs** (Babbage Press, 2000). This wandering installment was written for **Fango**'s 30th Anniversary issue [#284, June 2009].)*

DENKER'S BOOK

You will forgive me if my recollections of Denker seem fragmented. I do know that his Nobel Prize was rescinded; that seemed unfair to me, but at the same time I understand the thinking behind it, the dull necessity of the counter-arguments, all the disparate points of view that had to swim together into a public accord in an attempt to salve the outrage.

It used to be held as common superstition that if you paint an interior door in your home with a certain kind of paint, the door might open into another time. The paint was lead-based and long-prohibited. In 1934, there were doors like this all over the place. The doors generally had to be facing south. People have forgotten this now.

Chinese horticulturalists discovered that dead pets, buried in a specific pattern around the entryways to houses and gardens, not only seemed to restrict access by spirits, but lengthen daylight by as much as half an hour. Type of animal, number of burials, interment pattern and even the sexual history of the pet owner all seemed to have modulating effects.

I cite these stories as examples among thousands—the kind of revelations that seem to defy not only physical laws thought to be immutable, but logic itself.

Nevertheless, they took Langford Meyer Denker's Nobel Prize away from him. They—the big, faceless "they" responsible for everything—probably should not have. Denker made the discovery and fathered the breakthrough. "They" claimed Denker cheated; that is, he did not play by strict rules of science. But there are no such things as rules in science; merely observations that are regularly displaced by new, more consolidated observations.

Some said that the dimensional warp door Denker created was real, that it worked. Others held that it was a flashy deception; sleight-of-hand rather than science. Still others maintained that Denker's demonstration was inconclusive. By the time the furor settled, all of them said Denker had cheated. Denker had used the book.

Denker's machine was a gigantic, Gothic clockwork; an Expressionist maze of gears, liquid reservoirs, lasers and lenses. Lathed brass bins held clumps of humid earth. Common stones were vised by hydraulics in that peculiar way you can squeeze an egg between your palms with all your might and not break it. Particle-emitters were gloved in ancient lead. Imagine a medieval clepsydra wirelessly married to countless yottabytes of computing power and stage-managed by a designer who had been seduced by every mad scientist movie ever made. The containment chamber was made of pitted bronze shot through with rods of chemically pure glass; it weighed several tons and was completely non-aerodynamic, yet Denker claimed that once the whole package was transposed into a realm where earthly physics were irrelevant its properties recombined according to perverse rules to render the device as safe as a pressurized bathysphere or commercial space capsule.

Of course the earliest naysayers called him mad.

I remind you at this point in the story that without a totally arbitrary baseline of normalcy, "insanity" is not possible. (It has been said that normalcy is the majority's form of lunacy, which I suppose explains Christianity.)

Colors can drive people mad. It follows that there are spectra yet unknown to us, flavors and timbres that might catalyze our air, our light, in new and unpredictable ways. "Sounds that were not wholly sounds;" that sort of thing. The scientific community's rebuke of Denker was a denial of the most commonplace protocols of experimentation, but by that time the point was to demonize the man, not disprove the theory.

A portal to another universe different from our own perceived reality? Something that functioned so far out there that what we thought of as our physical laws seemed irrelevant? Fine.

A glimpse into the unutterable? Also fine.

But Denker had used the book. Not fine.

I ask you to stop right now and consider the purpose of a book that was *never intended to be read*. What is the point?

Consider this: You take an ordinary bible, which credits supernatural forces for all the bloodshed and horror in the world. They still make people swear on this book in courts of law; its symbolism has become part of ritual.

Denker's book was no mere opposite pole or gainsaying counterdogma, although many people tried to discredit it that way. That's an irony: the arrogance to assume you can neutralize something that will not be denied.

Where Denker found the book, if he ever truly possessed it, I do not know.

Scholars claimed the book was a repository of forbidden knowledge, therefore much sought or shunned through millennia. Bait for fanatics. A grail for obsessives; a self-destructive prize for the foolhardy. Unless it was akin to a key or a storage battery—a necessary link in a logic chain—it was still a dead end, because in the end (as one story went) you wound up dead too. Denker's philologists rapidly proved that trickle-down translations of the book (about 400 years-worth) were virtually worthless because there was no way to reconcile different languages to the concept of the unnameable. Latin held many of the book's conceits in polar opposition to the Greek interpretation, and so on. In many ways the book was like a tesseract, partially unfolded into a yet-undiscovered realm.

But Denker did not stop at etymology. His scheme advantaged the top skim of curious geniuses all over the world. He used crypto experts to translate partial photo plates from Arabic—an iteration long thought lost forever. No one ever saw more than an eighth of a full page. Then he used colloquialists to defang the language piecemeal, in order to render down the simple sense of highly convoluted and frequently unpronounceable arcana. The resultant text was presented to a hand-picked and highly elite international group preselected by Denker for the interests he knew he could arouse.

When he had exhausted one scholar, Denker moved to the next, and you have probably already heard the story about how Rademacher Asylum gradually filled up with his depleted former colleagues.

These were not dazzled hayseeds or the easily-swoggled rustics of a fictive Red America, nor were they the deluded zealotry of one improbable religion or other. These were minds capable of the most labyrinthine extrapolations—the first, second and third strings of pawns to fall to Denker's inquiry.

Denker followed his instincts, and in the hope of discovering an anti-linear correlation presented his findings to a physicist who was then in the grip of Alzheimer's. He consulted South Seas tribal elders with no word for "insane" in their lexicon. Then philosophers, wizards, the deranged and the disenfranchised. With a brilliant kind of counter-intuitiveness, he allowed children to interpret some of his findings. Then, autistics. The man with Alzheimer's was said to have "lost his mind completely" prior to his death. But as I've told you, the mad are always safe to expose. The mad enjoy hermetic protections unavailable to the mentalities that judge them unfit for normal human congress. "Normal humans" were the last thing Denker wanted.

Darwin pondered natural selection for twenty years before committing to print; Denker did not have that kind of leisure. Our science these days is competitive; cutthroat; the Sixties-era model of the Space Race has overrun all rational strategy. There are very few scientific rockstars and most of our millionaires are invisible. Resources may be accessed at the fierce cost of corporate sponsorship, which often mandates blood sacrifice or the occasional bitterly humbling obeisance—while the former can be a mental snap point, the latter is often a more serious derailment of any kind of exploratory enthusiasm, crushing instinct and logic into the box of fast, visible progress. Expediency becomes cardinal. This was the bind in which Denker found himself, in both senses—he embraced the delirious possibilities of risk and, using stress as a motivator, discovered his own interior limitations.

Coleridge wrote that "we do not feel horror because we are haunted by a sphinx, we dream a sphinx in order to explain the horror that we feel." Borges, after Coleridge, wrote, "If that is true, how might a mere chronicling of its forms transmit the stupor, the exultation, the alarms, the dread, and the joy that wove together that night's dream?" This was in essence the chicken-and-egg riddle that governed Denker's inquiries. Possessed of a fanciful mind, he did not believe the most transporting inspirations to be reduceable to mere mathematical schemata, yet that was the task set before him. Others had failed. Replacements waited hungrily. More tempting, to Denker, was that capacity which Apollonius Rhodius coigned as "the poetics of uncertainty," itself reducible to the 20th Century argot of doing a wrong thing for the right reason.

All this citation makes Denker sound stuffy or cloistered or pretentiously intellectual, so I need to give you an example of the man's humor. He referred to the book as his "ultra-tome-bo"—at once conflating the Spanish *ultratumba* (literally, "from beyond the grave") with the Latin *ultima Thule* (i.e., "the northernmost part of the habitable ancient world")—thereby hinting with a wink that his quest aimed beyond both death and the world as we know it.

Knew it, rather.

(He further corrupted *ultra* into *el otro*—"the other." The other book, the other tomb. He was very witty as well as smart.)

I hope you can follow this without too much trouble. Sometimes my memory itself is like a book with stuck-together pages; huge chunks of missing narrative followed by short sections of over-detail. If I have learned one thing, it is that harmonics are important. You may sense contradictions in some of what I am telling you, and I would urge you to look past them—try to see them with new eyes.

Denker's so-called scientific fraud was revealed when his device was taken from his stewardship and disassembled. The machinery held a bit of nuclear credibility, but the heart of the drive was an iron particle accelerator that resembled a World War Two-era sea mine, a heart fed by cables and hoses and fluid.

Empty inside.

Because Denker had removed his fundamental component—the book.

Having spent three-quarters of a billion dollars in corporate seed money and suffering the deep stresses of delivery-to-schedule that such funds can mandate, Denker cheated the curve. Science failed him, but when he combined science with sorcery, he was able to give his backers what they thought they wanted. All he had to do then was word his interviews precisely enough to feature that hint of arched-eyebrow evasion as to method. Money was already coming at him from all sides.

Most people don't know exactly how an internal combustion engine functions, but they drive automobiles. In kind, Denker's device could transcend space-time boundaries; the point was that it worked. Never mind that on the other side of the boundary might be a group of surly cosmic Vastators, or the displaced First Gods of our entire existence, itching for a rematch now that we have evolved, devised technology, and gotten ourselves so damned civilized.

A long time ago, I used to have a lit-crit friend who was enchanted by the idea of haunts—in particular, living quarters in which resonant works of literature were conceived, the way that James M. Cain wrote *Double Indemnity* while resident in his "Upside-Down House" in the Hollywood Hills. If it was true that the most dedicated writers "lived, ate, slept, drank and shat" their way through their most lasting works, might not some of that ectoplasmic effluvia generate a mood or lingering charge of unsettled energy, the sort of thing ordinary people might classify as a ghost?

My interest was not in Denker's book. That seemed too risky. So I sought out the place where Denker's book was not so much *written* as assembled, collated.

The locale, you might have guessed. It is dead now. The structures engird no whispers. The "charge" was long gone, if it ever existed. No negative energy. No ghosts.

Because it had *all* gone into the book.

By then, naturally, the world was dealing with other problems. Disequilibration was, in many ways, the most predictable outcome.

Throughout history, certain individuals had sought to destroy the book, not realizing the futility of this. In the state Denker used it, it could not be destroyed. It could only be discomponentialized— taken apart the same way it had been put together. Except now that it was whole, it could only be handled in certain limited ways, and none of those would permit its possible destruction. Again, as I have said—contradictions. Did Denker have the book, whole and entire, in a single place? We may never know. Thus, when I reference "the book," we are speaking of whatever grand assembly Denker managed, which stays in my mind as his true achievement.

One mishandling of the book caused peculiar incipient radiations—or new colors and sounds, if you will. Unfathomable byproducts and side-effects. This was one reason Denker insisted his cumbersome bronze-and-cast-iron device had to be tested in outer space.

This achieved two important goals: It removed the book briefly from the physical surface of the Earth, and it guaranteed Denker's deception would be a long time unraveling.

I saw in Denker's journals that he noted, early in the experiment, that animals were profoundly affected by the proximity of the book. Animals lack the ameliorative intellect by which humans justify insanity.

If one is inflexible and devoted to an illusion of normalcy— stability, permanence, reality—then the break is always harsher. The more rules there are to violate, the more violations there will be, because what we call reality is an interpretive construct of the human mind; a reality we re-make every day to deny the howling nothingness of existence and the meaningless tragedy of life. Bacilli have no such concerns. They just are. They can't be horrified or elated.

Denker's two safety margins were time and space. Many of his translations—the words from the book—were not meant to be in the same place at the same time, not even as ones and zeros in a database. The whole of it, as I have said, was tricky to handle. There was no manual for this sort of thing. This was completely new, untried, unsaid, undone.

In the end, Denker realized that ultimately all his equipment was not needed. The physical hardware briefly won him that fickle Nobel prize, but all he had really needed was the book. He had already achieved what we have agreed to call a break from reality, but in the end, people are more comfortable saying that he just snapped.

I think it is overreachingly grandiloquous and silly to blame Denker for the downslide of the entire planet. Haven't you noticed that long before the incident, we had already become so biosensitive that we could not even travel without getting sick? I think the Earth is simply evolving, and it is not *for* us anymore.

In the midst of all that I have told you, it might be said that Denker himself fragmented. His mind went elsewhere.

And if you could find me, you could probably find Denker too, but it's not really Denker you're interested in, is it? You're after the book, just like the ones before you.

Now, of course, the fashion is to impugn Denker for the way the sky looks at night. For the night itself, since I have heard that the sun no longer rises. I have not been able to bear witness to the other stories I have heard about the freezing cold or the sounds of beasts feeding.

But once I find a way to free myself from this room, I am going to seek out Denker, and ask him to explain it to me.

....

Thirty-Eight Days Later:
The Brief Life and Ignominious Death of
Features from the Black Lagoon

(2010)

Plagiarize, plagiarize,
Let no man's work evade your eyes,
Remember why the good Lord made your eyes,
Don't shade your eyes,
But plagiarize, plagiarize, plagiarize.
(Only be sure to call it research.)

— *Tom Lehrer*

I'm usually happy when someone takes the time to cite me or my work. I was cited a couple of times in the text of *Features from the Black Lagoon* (McFarland & Co., 2010), a book ballyhooed as "the ultimate guide" to the eponymous film trilogy. As it turned out, those attributions were the mere micro-tip of a gigantic iceberg of Creature information almost wholly borrowed, appropriated, paraphrased and—let's call it what it was—stolen from work by others with precious little acknowledgement to the people who executed the actual digging, interviewing, and collation of facts. Verdict: Not so jolly.

"He's also *taken credit* for some important findings!" complains David Reed in the original *Creature from the Black Lagoon*, speaking of his opportunist sponsor, Mark Williams. If that Richard Denning character had not been dragged and drowned by the Gill Man, he might have gone on to take sole credit for a book like this, derived from a handy pile of magazine articles, several specific books and DVDs, and the vast resources of Google, IMDb and Wikipedia.

I probably missed something but in 262 text pages I found not one original idea, observation, or criticism from the author, who was swift enough to use the term "Creature ripoff" early and often for anything involving monsters and a body of water. That might charitably be called irony. Although "D. DeAngelo" seemed to fairly scream "pen-name," according to <u>wingedtiger.com</u> Domenic "Danny" DeAngelo "is a freelance writer/artist and self-publisher, originally from Boston, now living in Florida." As "capaware" on Amazon.com, he excoriated John L. Flynn's *75 Years of Universal Monsters* book as "sloppy and unprofessional."

As canon or catalogue, *Features* suffered from enormous gaps in overall knowledge, something you would not expect from an author who was, at the very least, an avowed fan of the subject matter. Page 201 debuted a section called "The Creature in Literature" that totally overlooked the most famous book on the shelf—the 1954 novelization by "Vargo Statten" (John Russell Fearn)—as well as skipping past the two Crestwood House books (*Creature from the Black Lagoon* [1981] by "Ian Thorne" [Julian May], and *The* [sic] *Revenge of the Creature* [1987] by Carl R. Green & William R. Sanford.

DeAngelo's concluding remarks for his (long) synopsis of the 2006 novelization by Paul DiFilippo read: *"...the idea of turning the Gill Man into a 'devolved mockery' of a once-noble alien race not only belittles the character but divorces it from any relation to mankind, which just doesn't fit with its origins as established in the film."* Really? It's only been a plot point of nearly ever proposed film remake, dating all the way back to Nigel Kneale's 1982 screenplay.

A Creature fan as ringmaster of an all-inclusive compendium should know that John Agar and Lori Nelson reprised their roles from *Revenge of the Creature* for a 2005 bargain-basement opus titled *The Naked Monster.* This is mentioned on page 100 with no further illumination. But a genuine Creature fan would also know that the actors had already re-embodied Drs. Clete Ferguson and Helen Dobson in 1998, for video clips featured as part of Universal Studios' online *Hunt for the Creature from the Black Lagoon* Sweepstakes (along with Rex Reason from *The Creature Walks Among Us*). No mention of that, here. Caveat: A self-appointed expert whose sell copy trumpets his book as an "ultimate guide" will be called upon to demonstrate said implied expertise.

Okay, but that's nitpicking, you might say. And you'd be right.

How about the ephemera on the Amazon, the Devonian epoch, evolution in general, or sea creatures in mythology? The bulk of the details given on page 18 about the Tiktaalik, an extinct not-so-missing link between fish and amphibians, was globally imported from Wikipedia. The passage on evolutionary traits? Answers@Yahoo.com. The description of Silver Springs, Florida (page 93) as "a timeless oasis of unparalleled beauty, offering respite to the early settlers who drew sustenance from its 99.8 percent pure artesian spring waters"? Word for word from the Silver Springs website (www.silversprings.com/heritage.html).

Okay, but that's still splitting hairs, you might say.

How about the opposite pole of the information spectrum: cultural trivia? Sideswiping the topic of collectible die-cast metal cars featuring Gill Man artwork (page 258), DeAngelo misses an easy three out of five, including the officially-licensed "Muscle Machine" monster truck done in 2000 to tie in with the remake of *The Mummy.* In describing Bally's Creature-themed pinball machine (p. 249), DeAngelo said it features "such classic '50s songs as 'Around the Clock,' 'a Job,' and 'Blues.'" *Seriously?* No cognizance whatsoever of "Rock Around the Clock," "Get a Job," or "Summertime Blues?" Anybody home?

Okay, this worried scab was starting to bleed, and obviously this game could be played all day.

So let's dive right into the backbone of the subject matter, the central trilogy of Gill Man movies. The single most-plundered work in this regard was Tom Weaver's Volume 2 of the Universal Filmscripts Series (MagicImage Filmbooks Presents *Creature from the Black Lagoon*, 1992). Even casual scrutiny revealed a wild mix-and-match of material from Weaver's book, his cast-and-crew interviews as published in *Fangoria* and *Starlog* (et al), and his audio commentaries on DVD for all three films—most of it in Weaver's own words, strip-mined and transplanted. Other interviews with *Creature* principals were raided from sources less specifically obvious, yet no less apparent. In every instance, DeAngelo could not add a single new factoid to the heavy lifting already done by others, not to mention Weaver, who noted, "Unfortunately for the author, my book was only about the first Creature movie, so for the two sequels, he came up short."

Jumped to the index. Looked under "W," where I found:

Weaver, Tom: 244.

Properly cited, Weaver's contributions alone would have used up an entire index page at minimum. A bibliography (pp. 263-264) provided DeAngelo's basic shoplifting list.

Does that sound harsh? Isn't research common coin once divulged? Isn't there a line between "context" and "ripoff?" Possibly, but in a book that depended so heavily on external sources (and in fact could not exist without them), a seasoned plagiarist would have deployed a much thicker smokescreen to disguise the work of writers whose prose expressions were

appropriated wholesale with little or no amelioration. A neo-
phyte would not have bothered to alter purloined material at
all. Most of the text resided on the slippery slope between the
two, making its lackadaisical sourcing seem less like ignorance
and more like arrogance. The scattershot and often incom-
plete disclosure provided by this book's 125 endnotes, plus the
bibliography, came nowhere near giving due credit under the
shady circumstances.

To belabor the point, raw data is one thing. Personal
inflection, nuance and prose timbre are elements of a writer's
individual style and voice—a distinctive and unique footprint,
and hence, a writer's own intellectual property, something so
fundamental that it is protected by copyright law (that is, you
don't have to file paperwork to enjoy the protection). Facts and
figures are stray black notes until a composer arranges them
into a piece that can sing; sometimes soar. Professional writers earn a living from their words. Steal those words at your
peril. Or, to quote Guido the Killer Pimp from *Risky Business:* "In
times of economic uncertainty, never fuck with another man's
livelihood."

I thought, let's give this fellow DeAngelo a break; he's just
a Floridian who wants to enthuse about the Creature. Then
I read the chapter titled "Jaws 3, Creature 0" (pp. 211-229), and
aha! There's Tom Weaver getting mugged again—for the William
Alland anecdote about the earliest idea for a remake. It's virtually
a verbatim transcription of Weaver's comments on the DVD.

Then DeAngelo attacked the topic of proposed modern
remakes, which I covered in depth for *Filmfax* #73 in 1999. Sure
enough: My words, his book. My sentences transposed and
adjectives re-grafted. No connection between the bibliography
listing for the article and the relevant text. Why bother finding
those scripts, reading them, and forming one's own conclusions
when it's far simpler to cut-and-paste with only the feeblest stab
at paraphrase? Season lightly with interview quotes hijacked

from others, high-carb it with bloated, overlong synopses (that hallmark of the tyro reviewer), and half-bake it until it's book-sized. Serves one—the person whose name is on the cover.

There was an even more labyrinthine permutation: DeAngelo *mis*-credited a Jack Arnold quotation on page 228 to an interview by Al Taylor and Dave Knowles in *Fantastic Film* #21 (but omitted the issue number and January 1981 publication date). I should know because the quote was from my own interview with Arnold, done June 1977, also used in my own *Filmfax* piece ("The Revenge of the Return of the Remake of Creature from the Black Lagoon," issue #73, June-July 1999—I still have the tape, and will happily credit corrections in this regard).

If this book had come out in 1979, it might have been more forgivable. For one thing, DeAngelo would have had to expend actual effort on research, which was much trickier way back then.

McFarland Publishing's genre rep as a niche sanctuary for quirky books on science fiction, horror and fantasy films was initially founded on what could forgivingly be called glorified term papers (the firm's website calls them "scholarly monographs"), whomped into book form and sold principally to libraries as reference volumes. As the 1980s commenced, writers with genre obsessions discovered that McFarland was a great place to get their otherwise-unchampioned longform work published, albeit under the Spartan conditions of no advance payment (McFarland has always been a royalty-only publisher) and severely limited distribution. McFarland's bona fide classics include Bill Warren's *Keep Watching the Skies!* duology (1982/86), and deep-dish spotlight volumes like *Directed by Jack Arnold* (by Dana M. Reemes, 1988), TV's *This is a Thriller* (by Alan Warren, 1996), and *Paul Blaisdell, Monster Maker* (by Randy Palmer, 1997)...as well as nearly all of Tom Weaver's justly-lauded interview compendia.

But the reference shelf for fantastic cinema is yards longer today. General information that was the province of a scarce few worthwhile books in the pre-internet era is now much more commonly known. So a new book on an old topic has to be really special, or break freshly discovered intel to receive serious attention by knowledgeable fans. (For example, nothing here approached the surreal, skull-smacking deconstructionism found in the Creature writeups for Steve Johnson's quirky magazine *Delirious*.) I would go so far as to posit that *Features from the Black Lagoon* violated McFarland's own boilerplate contract clause insofar as the author warrant that *"the Manuscript is original and does not infringe upon any statutory copyright or upon any common law right, proprietary right, or any other right whatsoever."* Not that McFarland would notice; all the company knew was that it could sell this book based on the cover illustration. Here, the non-attention paid to disclosure would seem not just unprofessional, but dependent on the fact that nobody would cross-check the chain-of-title. On the other hand, it's admittedly impossible for a publisher to micro-vet every book this way—*that's why the author warrants are in the contract.*

Instead of one shining piece of news or noteworthy tangent, what the reader got were synopses—endlessly. It is legitimate to cite *The Seven-Year Itch* in the Creature's timeline, but did that mandate a windy recap of the entire movie? And, mamma mia, don't get the guy started on *Jaws*; like Lloyd Bridges on *Sea Hunt*, you'd find your lungs suddenly aching for air. Excruciatingly protracted summations for aquatically-related films sucked up another 80-plus pages. If you'd like to read what DeAngelo had to say about *Zaat/Blood Waters of Dr. Z* (1975, page 164-5) or *Humanoids from the Deep* (1980, page 168-69) for free, you still can—on Wikipedia, where you'll find the same phrasings, but in more detail.

Among the 113 photos was nothing special, further indication of a net cast shallowly, when you consider all the amazing vintage Creature photos that have surfaced in the past decade alone— from *Life* magazine, for example. And dammit, there should have been one thing, at least *one special thing*, in this book to justify separating you from your fifty bucks.

There wasn't.

When you strip away all the material by others, DeAngelo brought nothing to the table on his own. No perspective, no voice, no insight, and certainly nothing new. Even his Introduction and Afterword contradicted each other. (The former argued that the Creature is completely different from the other monsters of Universal's classic canon; the latter argued that they're all basically the same.)

This makes DeAngelo an entrepreneurial regurgitator, but it doesn't make him a writer so much as a literary cuckoo bird (in ornithology circles this behavior is known as "nest predation" or "nest parasitizing"). Or maybe a vampire finch (look it up).

So, from a critical standpoint, any review of this book was hardly necessary. Creature fans would have bought it anyway, no doubt sparkling over the thought of having all this swell information in one place. If McFarland or the author were taken to task, the most optimistic outcome would have been either an amended text to properly credit sources, or withdrawal of the book entirely, both of which would only have served to make this edition a collector's item for the perverse. (*) I said as much in a strongly-worded cease-and-desist letter I sent to McFarland, pessimistic that there would be any official response. *You too have been victimized*, I wrote.

The whole fiasco does point up the current disdain for intellectual property rights by the internet-besotted, who callowly assume everything they can see on a screen comes "for free." Those familiar with the recent Helene Hegemann publishing scandal in Berlin will recognize that plagiarism isn't even

---

(*) Remember the old gag about the movie that "wasn't released; it escaped" (once attributed to Robert Altman, talking about *M*A*S*H*)? Sure enough, the price of *Features* quickly skyrocketed for the few copies that escaped to outlets like eBay, where it was last seen at $270 and counting.

stealing anymore—it's "mixing," as in "mix tape" or "party mix." Hegemann's 2010 novel *Axolotl Roadkill* became a sensation for the 17-year-old author in Germany until it was revealed that most of the text came from an earlier novel, *Strobo* by "Airen," plus liberal lifts from anywhere-and-everywhere online blogs. Far from the outrage that greeted Kaavya Viswanathan in 2006 when she was similarly exposed for plagiarizing Megan McCafferty (with "over 40 passages containing identical language and/or common scene and dialogue structure" [per Crown Publishing's investigation] as well as borrowings from Salman Rushdie, Meg Cabot and Sophie Kinsella), Hegemann defended herself as "a representative of a new generation...there's no such thing as originality anyway, just authenticity."

Which sounds a lot like the rationalizations used by DeAngelo when he sprang up to defend himself in posts on David Colton's Classic Horror Film Board—"*I fail to see that I've committed a crime here*"—which ignited a microcosmic firestorm of blogging once Weaver himself began to post comparison passages in a thread titled *Features from the Black Lagoon—New McFarland Book on the Way*, begun 14 July 2009.

The McFarland street date for the book was 19 January 2010. By 27 January, Tom Weaver had gotten a look at it, made his first post about plagiarized content, and notified McFarland. On 17 February, DeAngelo appeared on the board. Over the ensuing week he was raked over the coals primarily by 8 to 10 repeat posters, some of whom began to e-mail McFarland directly. Apparently the first was a board member handled as "Starta Bilen," who contacted McFarland on 22 February; Margie Turnmire of McFarland responded the following day: "*We are currently studying the situation.*" The same day, 23 February, in the aftermath of a "very strong" phone call to DeAngelo, Cortlandt Hull publicly withdrew his participation from DeAngelo's proposed *Wolf Man* follow-up book. The 23rd was also the date DeAngelo fled the boards, after his operatic mea culpa had spieled onward for more than 10,000 words (over three times the length of this article) of futile post-facto spin-doctoring that all could have been avoided if he had *just asked permission* in the first place. (**)

It was a classic case of too much, too late. By February 25th, McFarland was sending out e-mails advising that *"Features from the Black Lagoon is no longer available,"* and the book's catalogue listing had been withdrawn from the company website. Thirty-eight days, from birth to stake-through-the-heart. A response letter to me dated 1 March and signed by McFarland head honcho Robert Franklin advised that *"the book went out of print last week and no copies are for sale."*

If you plagiarize, expect your book's life to be this nasty, brutish, and short. (That's my rip on Thomas Hobbes' *Leviathan*, just so you'll know; interested parties should read what Hobbes had to say on "injustice" being the failure to perform in a contract, or covenant.) So short that what began as a book review had now become a case study.

In his posted defense, DeAngelo seemed to vacillate between outraged ignorance (*"If Mr. Weaver does not want other authors to quote his work, then I suggest he stop having it printed"*—2/17/10) and clueless naïveté (*"I saw nothing wrong with taking the information Mr. Weaver has obtained over the years and making it available to other fans. After all, the Universal Filmscripts book is out-of-print and very expensive, and it's not easy to look up a specific fact about one of the films on his DVD audio commentaries"*—2/19/10). Whatever his true demeanor—malign conniver or out-of-his-depth amateur—the ultimate adjudicator of his case is simple traffic cop logic: ignorance of the law is no excuse.

"Crowd sourcing" or "open sharing" of the sort that likewise doomed *The Daily Beast*'s Gerald Posner is usually blamed

(**) DeAngelo briefly resurfaced on the Amazon.com comment board for *Features* before his remarks were deleted on March 11th.

on the high velocity of information on the internet. Sara Libby spoke to this point on her *True/Slant* blog: "I went to a solid journalism school that instilled me with plenty of old-old-school values, many of which I don't think are very flexible when it comes to lifting another person's writing or insights without attribution. The Internet makes things happen much faster, but it also makes it relatively simple to give credit where it's due: Just throw up a link to the original story, or put something in quotes, and you're done."

As my pal and fellow author F. Paul Wilson responded: "Stealing is stealing. Passing another person's words and work off as your own is not just lazy or mendacious, it's theft, pure and simple. Nobody gets a pass on this. Nobody."

———

(It would be churlish of me not to extend my appreciation to the frantic bloggists of the Classic Horror Film Board, the source for some of the data included here.—DJS)

———

(This article appeared in Tim & Donna Lucas' magazine Video Watchdog *#157 [July/August, 2010].)*

BLUE AMBER

When Senior Patrol Agent Rixson first spotted the shed human skin draped over the barbed wire fence, she thought it was an item of discarded clothing. Then she saw it had empty arms, legs, fingers, an empty mouth-hole stretched oval in a silent scream, and vacant Hallowe'en-mask eyesockets. Carrion birds had already picked it over. Presently it was covered with ants. It stank.

If you had asked her, before, what her single worst experience working for the Border Patrol had been, Carrie Rixson might have related the story of how she and her partner Cash Dunhill had happened upon a hijacked U-Haul box trailer full of dead Mexicans eighteen feet shy of the Sonora side of Buster Lippert's pony ranch. Something had gone wrong, and the coyotes—the wetback enablers, not the scavengers—had left their clients locked in the box, abandoned, under 101-degree heat for over three days. The Cochise County Coroner concluded that the occupants had died at least two days prior to that. The smell was enough to make even the vultures doubtful. The victims had deliquesced into a undifferentiated mass of meat that had broiled in convection heat that topped 400 degrees, about the same as you'd use to bake a frozen pizza.

That had been bad, but the flyblown husk on the fence seemed somehow worse.

"Should I call it in?" said Dunhill, sweating in the pilot seat of their Bronco. He was a deputy and answerable to Carrie, but neither of them were high enough in the grade chain to warrant collar insignia.

"As what?" Carrie shouted back, from the fence. She was already snapping digital photographs.

Dunhill unsaddled and ambled over for a look-see. No need to hurry, not in this heat. "I think this falls out of the purview of 'accidental death,'" he said. "Unless this ole boy was running away so fast he jumped the bobwire and it shucked off his hide."

"That happened once," said his partner. "Dude in New Jersey. Hefty guy, running away from the cops, tried to jump an iron railing and got his chin caught on the metal spike up top. Tore his head clean off. It was still stuck on the end of the spike. I saw it on the internet."

Cash and Carrie had been the target of department punsters ever since their first pair-up assignment. She was older, 37 to his 29 years. They had never been romantically inclined, although they teased each other a lot. Cash's high school sweetie had divorced him in a legal battle only slightly less acrimonious than the firebombing of Dresden, and Carrie had been about to marry her 10-year live-in life partner—Thomas "Truck" Fitzgerald, a former Pima County sheriff turned Jeep customizer—when he up and died of cancer that took him away in six weeks flat. Neither Cash nor Carrie was in the market for loving just now, although they both suffered the pangs in their own different ways.

"Oh, don't *touch* it, for christsake," Cash told her.

"I'm thinking cartel guys," she said as her hand stopped short of making actual fleshy contact. "This is the sort of shit they do. Skin your enemies. Cut off their heads, stuff their balls into their mouths, dismember them and leave the pieces in a public place with the name of the *cliqua* written in blood."

"You see that on the internet, too?" Cash dug out a toothpick. He was battling mightily to stop smoking.

"Nahh," she said. "I usually only look at lesbian porn. Girl-on-girl, slurpy-burpy." The way Cash usually rose to the bait when she egged him on was reliably amusing, under normal circumstances.

She used a dried stick of ironwood to lift one of the flaps. "Definitely not a scuba suit or a mannequin. There used to be a person wearing this, and not so long ago." The shadow side of the castoff skin was dotted with oily moisture, as though it was still perspiring.

"Whose property is this?" Cash was looking around for landmarks.

"This is outside Puzzi Ranch. I guess it might be Thayer McMillan's fence."

Cash and Carrie's daily grind was to patrol the strip of International Highway (both a description of the actual road and its real name) between Douglas, Arizona and Naco Highway. Naco—the town—straddled the U.S.-Mexico border and had always been a sizzling hot spot for violations of all sorts. In the dead-ass stretches of high desert separating the two towns, there was just too goddamned much open space for something not to go wrong.

"Secure Fence Act, my ass," said Cash, for about the zillionth time. His views on a wetback-proof fence were abundantly known. "I'll call base; see if we can get a number for McMillan." He popped an energy drink from the Bronco's cooler and blew down half the can in one gulp.

"Gross," said Carrie. "That candy-flavored salt water is bad for you." The logo on the can shrieked *Kamikaze!* "'Divine wind.' 'Empty wind' is more like it."

Then Cash would say...

"May the wind at your back never be your own."

They were okay, as partners. When the meatwagon arrived over an hour later, Billy Szwakop, the coroner's assistant, scowled at them at though he was the butt of yet another in an endless series of corpse gags. It wasn't even really a dead body, he said. It was just the skin part. For all they knew, no murder had been committed.

"Yeah, he's probably still walking around, all wound up in duct tape to keep from leaking," Cash said. Billy's gentle disentanglement of the...item...had revealed it to be male.

It had also revealed a broad split from sternum to crotch, not an incision. After it was bagged, Billy added, "I don't think this was a Mex, either."

Carrie got interested. "What makes you say that?"

"Most Mexicans are Catholic, and most Catholic males are circumcised."

"Ugh," said Carrie. "Too much information."

From the concealment of a broad, shaded thicket of skunk-bush and screwbean mesquite, bulbous indigo eyes watched them, then died.

The zigzag access road to the McMillan compound was dead on the eastern property edge, about half a mile back from where Carrie Rixson had spotted the thing on the fence. It paralleled several secure horse corrals before it widened into a gated arch-way featuring a wrought iron double M (itself a zigzag) up top. The building cluster was organized around a broad donut of paved road—big barn, smaller barn, main house, guest house, and a generator-driven industrial icehouse side-by-side with a smaller smokehouse. Further north, in the rear, would be a long, narrow greenhouse with solar panels. Thayer McMillan had made part of his pile breeding quarter horses and Appaloosas. In residence were several trainers and wranglers, in addition to a cook, a housekeeper, and an on-call executive personal assistant. Two of the eight McMillan children still lived at home—Lester, the heir apparent to King Daddy's throne, and his younger sister Desiree, a recent divorcee with two children of her own, both under 10 years old. Thayer, the patriarch, was on his fourth wife, a brassy Houston fireball named Celandine, 25 years his junior, or about Desiree's age. Call it fortyish.

There was also, it was rumored, security staff.

It was further rumored that McMillan was pouring concrete to the north of the greenhouse for a private helicopter landing pad.

There were many other rumors about the McMillans, mostly of the sort slathered about by jealous inferiors, but the one about the chopper pad piqued Cash Dunhill's interest. That close to the border? Cash had always wanted an excuse to investigate further.

The light green Bronco kicked up a tailwind of grit as it barreled along the access road. Half a mile in, there was a red pickup truck parked on the shoulder. One of those showoffy, urban cowboy rigs with a mega-cab, a Hemi V-8 and double rear tires. Nobody inside or close by. The clearcoat was covered in dust.

Cash checked it out. "The keys are inside," he said. It was as though someone had pulled over for a piss and just sank into the earth before he or she could zip up.

"Nobody on the home line," said Carrie, snapping her cellphone shut. "Just voice mail."

"No horses, either," said Cash. He could see the corrals from where they'd stopped. "Not a single one."

"It's midday; maybe they're cooling off in the barn." No doubt the barn was air conditioned.

"Guess we guessed wrong about the security, too," he said, a bit distantly, the way he did when he was trying to puzzle out evidence. "Nobody on us yet, nobody at the gate."

"Maybe they upgraded," said Carrie. "Cameras and lasers instead of people."

"Maybe." You could score useful points by agreeing with your partner on things that did not matter. They rumbled over the cow-catcher rails at the gate, within sight of the Cliff May architectural masterpiece that was the main house—a classic of the modernist California Ranch style that blended hacienda elements with the Western aesthetic of building "out" instead of "up." There was a lot of woodgrain and natural stone. The bold, elongated A-frame of the roof line allowed sunlight to heat the huge pool.

"How many bedrooms, you figure?" said Cash.

"Five," said Carrie. "No, six, and probably at least one bathroom for each. Japanese soaking tubs, I bet. I love those."

A large blob of brown was piled near the gate to the northern-most corral.

"What the hell is that?"

"Horsehide."

"No, it isn't," said Cash, stopping the vehicle again. "Horse."

Hollow, split and empty, just like the thing they had found on the barbed wire fence.

Carrie already had her weapon out. "There's a dog over there. But a whole dog, not just skin." She moved closer to verify. There were spent shotgun cartridges strewn around a dead Rottweiler near the front walkway. "We'd better—"

"Call this in, now!" Partners often completed each others' sentences.

Cash was advised that available law enforcement, this far out, was on a triage basis and they would be required to wait at the scene.

"Cash, look at this."

Carrie indicated a smear of blackish fragments in the dirt, like ash or charcoal. "I stepped on it. But look, here's another one."

It was a dried-up bug. There were several of them in the yard. "Looks like a cicada," said Cash. "Or one of them cockroaches; you know they get three inches long around here."

"But it isn't. Look."

She stabbed it with a Bic pen and held it aloft for inspection. It sounded crispy, desiccated. What resembled an opaque, thornlike stinger protruded from one end, its razor-sharp edge contoured to flare and avoid contact with the body.

"This isn't right," she said. "It can't be. This is mutated or something. Or a hybrid. No bilateral symmetry."

"I don't understand a thing you just said."

"Bilateral," Carrie said. "Identical on both sides. We're all base two—two eyes, two arms, two legs. Ants have six legs. Spiders have eight, and eight eyes. One side of the body is a mirror of the other. But not this. Nothing I know of is based on three."

Cash, prepared to blow her off, grew more interested. "Maybe it's missing a leg."

"From where?" She turned the thing over in the waning sun-light. "There's no obvious wound."

"Maybe that stinger thing is really a leg? Or a tail?"

"Yeah, and maybe it's a dick," she said, disliking patronization.

"Leave it for the plastic bag boys," said Cash. "Just don't touch the sharp thing, okay?"

"No way."

"You suppose maybe a swarm of these locusty things flew in and ate everybody from the inside out?"

"Then why aren't there dead ones inside the…" Carrie sputtered out, groping for the right word. "Carcasses? That much fine dining, there should be a couple thousand of them around."

Cash knocked loudly and rang the bell while Carrie thumbed the latch on a door handle that probably cost three weeks of her pay. "It's open," she said.

"Probable cause?"

"You've gotta be shitting me, Cash."

Then Cash would say…

"I wouldn't shit you, darlin, you're my favorite turd."

But he, too, had his weapon limbered up, a Ruger GP100 double-action revolver in .357 Mag. Carrie packed a full-sized Smith & Wesson M&P-40 that held sixteen rounds with one in the pipe—cartridges that Cash knew to be semi-wadcutters.

Feeling increasingly absurd, they both called into the acousti-cally vacant recesses of the house. The coolers were on full-blast.

"Jesus," she said. "It must be below fifty degrees in here."

"Like the frozen food aisle at the supermarket." They covered each other excellently. Goosebumps speckled their sun-licked flesh.

Cash shook his head. Think of the utility bill.

"Well, room by room, I guess," he said, uncertainly.

The showplace central room was large and vaulted, with a grape-stake ceiling and a fireplace large enough to roast a Smart Car. Very open. All other rooms were peripheral.

The deeper they ventured, the more tenantless the house seemed. Neither one of them called out any more—that was just instinctive, the old telepathy of partners sharing a silent warning.

Carrie checked the behemoth Sub-Zero Pro fridge for sealed bottled water, just for hydration's sake. Do it when you can. Several more of the bugs, chilled and lifeless, were on the top shelf near an open half gallon of milk.

Keeping her voice low, Carrie said, "I'm thinking disease, Cash; what are you thinking?"

Cash nodded. "Something insect-borne, something special. That means government spooks and security. But not here; the goddamned door was open." He gratefully plugged water down his throat. It was so cold it gave him a migraine spike.

"Either that or a really pissed-off butcher with some kind of vendetta. But I don't see any blood anywhere. How about we just back off?"

"Crime scene," said Cash. "We've got to stay."

"What's the crime?"

"We really oughta leave this for larger minds," he said, full up with doubt.

"Don't you chicken out on me, Cash Dunhill. It's not seemly."

"Something is going on; we're just not smart enough to figure it ou—"

She held up her free hand to cut him off. "Hold."

A noise; they both heard it. A soft noise. A soft, shuffling, sliding noise.

Something was moving toward them in the hallway.

———

"Mommy," said the thing.

It appeared at a fast glance to be a little girl in bluejeans and a bright yellow Taylor Swift T-shirt (logoed *You Are the Best Thing That's Ever Been Mine*), lurching along as though drugged, in a pair of blocky K-Swiss Tubes. Her bronze-colored hair was lank and damp.

"Holy shit," whispered Carrie.

The voice was all wrong. That "Mommy" had come out as a froggy, guttural croak. The front of the T-shirt was soaked, as though she had vomited. She looked past the two officers, not at them. Half her face seemed to be melting off. The whole left side was slack and drooping, elongating her eye and hanging her jaw crookedly down.

"Mommy make samwich peen butter gahh."

Thick yellow mucus was cascading out of her nose.

Carrie moved to kneel, arms out. "Honey…?"

"Don't touch her, for godsake!"

"Found it," the girl said, voice hitching with phlegm.

"Found what, sweetie?" Carrie was keeping her distance.

"Pretty," said the girl. She opened her hand. One of the bugs was there. Crouching at the abrupt light, tripod legs tensing. It was alive.

"Oh my god," Carrie said as the bug sprang across the three feet between them like a grasshopper, hit her in the face, and sank its wicked-looking barb into her cheek. In the light, Cash swore he could see fluid drain from the translucent stinger.

Cash shouted and charged, kicking sidelong to lay out the kid, swatting with his hand to dispose of the attacking bug. It hit the floor with its legs up, dead already, like the ones they'd found in the yard.

"Stupid, *stupid*!" Carrie had landed on her ass.

"Lemme see that. Quick, now."

"Squeeze it. Cut it if you have to!" Her cheek was swelling and darkening already. Her right eye was going crimson.

Cash put his thumbs together to try to evacuate the poison—if that's what it was—from the entry wound, but no dice. A tiny dot of bluish wetness welled up at the puncture, but nothing was coming out. He almost tried to suck it, using snakebite protocol.

"Don't put your *mouth* on it, Cash, for fuck's sake!" Carrie was sweeping her arms around, preparatory to trying to stand again, but her movements went thick and wide.

"Astringent," Cash said. "Disinfectant." There had to be something in the kitchen or a nearby bathroom. In a glass-doored liquor cabinet he found some 120-proof Stolichnaya vodka. Stashed behind it was a crumpled soft pack of Camel Lights with two bent cigarettes inside, which he stashed in his uniform blouse's flap pocket. Two wouldn't kill him.

He dashed vodka over Carrie's wound. "I can't even feel it," she said. "It should burn."

The kid was standing back up.

"Bike," she said. Her eyes were looking two different directions. The skin on one arm seemed skewed, as though her hand was mounted backward on the bone. With the other hand, the girl pawed at her face and caught hold of her slack, hanging lower lip. She pulled it downward and it began to peel away. The buttery flesh on her neck split and began to slough. Her yellow shirt absorbed more discharge, from within.

For that single second, Cash and Carrie were transfixed in mute witness.

The little girl's face flopped around her neck like a rubber cowl. In its place was a knob of pale meat resembling a clenched fist, with two bulging button eyes, shiny, featureless orbs that were not black, but a very deep indigo.

Together, Cash and Carrie opened fire.

Their slugs hoisted and dumped the thing, which had begun to walk toward them again. It fell back into the corridor in a broken jackstraw sprawl.

"It was starting to tear off the skin," Carrie said, distantly. Its raised arm lingered, clenching a handful of wadded-up neck. Then it toppled over and hit the marble floor tiles with a juicy slaughterhouse *smack*.

Whatever was leaking out of the bullet holes looked like plain water. Faintly bluish.

"Come on," urged Cash. "To hell with this. We've got to get you out of here, pronto."

"Good idea," said Carrie. Her voice was going furry and opiate, as from a severe allergic reaction. Congestion, histamine levels redlining.

He lifted her bodily, not thinking of all the times he'd wanted to brush her boobs, her butt, just playfully.

Then Cash would say…

"Hang on, darlin, you and me are traveling." Warily he observed the pewter light in the windows. Twilight had already fallen. Sundown came fast in the desert.

Just get to the vehicle, he thought. *Just burn ass outta here.*

But the Bronco, sitting in the front turnaround, had already been dumped on its side, partially spiderwebbing the windshield.

And two more things of full-grown human size were waiting for them, with their bulging, dark, ratlike eyes.

———

They had shucked their human envelopes and stood on either side of the upended Bronco. Like UFO "grays," but lumpier and mottled. Two arms with pincer hands. Two legs. Bilateral symmetry. No facial features except the convex eyes, deep blue, no pupils or irises. They looked spindly. But they had turned the Bronco over.

Cash had to place Carrie on the ground in order to execute a speed reload. If he shot them center mass, they only flinched. Headshots put them down more definitively.

"Shotgun," said Carrie from the ground. "Truck. Keys. Run."

Then Cash would say…

"I'm not leaving you!"

"Don't be an idiot," she said. She managed to prop herself on one elbow to dump the Smith's clip and refresh. "Get the shotgun. Run as fast as you can to the truck and bring it back. I'm not going anywhagh…"

She coughed viscously.

"You sure?" Weapon up, Cash was scanning the perimeter nervously. *Go. Stay. Go. Stay.*

"Go," Carrie said. "I'm a big girl."

Cash wasted several more seconds trying to upright the Bronco by himself. No go. The adrenalin surge of legendary vehicular rescues had failed him. He retrieved the Mossberg pump from the cabin mount (he never locked it unless he was handing over the vehicle; in his worldview, speedy readiness outranked rules). The veins in his head were livid and throbbing. Thirty yards distant was the structure that shaded the big freezer unit and the smokehouse.

The freezer. The cold house. Sunset. These monsters did not like the light or the heat. They coffined up in the daytime. Now it was nighttime.

The bugs stung you, injected you. These things grew inside you, then peeled you off like a chrysalis. When they did, there wasn't any *you* left. You had become nutrient and a medium for gestation.

Their purpose or motive could be hashed out later by others, people with degrees and ordnance and expensive backup. Right now, Carrie was stung and waning. Who knew what her timetable was, or whether the effect could be neutralized? In the movies, monsters who upset the status quo were always defeated by something ordinary and obvious, usually discovered by accident—seawater, dog whistles, paprika, Slim Whitman music. In movies, the salvational curative was always set up in the first act as a throwaway, sure to encore later with deeper meaning.

In movies, you found a cure, gave the victim a pill or an injection, and they were instantly okay. A miracle, wrap it up, the end, roll credits.

Cash ran faster, his bootheels thudding on the roadway, the sound reminding him of a shopping cart with a bum wheel, the kind he always seemed to draw at the market. How did the wheels get those bumps, anyway?

With proper warmup and training, track sprinters could do eight hundred meters in three minutes. That was without a gunbelt and equipment, without cowboy boots or Cash's lamentable diet. Without panic or terror. What a laugh, if he ran himself right into a heart attack.

Then they'd find his body and use him as an incubator.

Then Carrie would say…

Man up. Don't be afraid. Solve the problem. Work fast and sure.

But he was afraid. Normally fear got shoved behind revulsion or duty. Fear was tamped down and tucked away. Cash did not *want* to go back. He wanted to show this place his ass and taillights, never to return.

Carrie would have come for him, so he forced himself to stay on track. To do the manly thing, the brave-and-true thing. He did not wish to look bad in her eyes.

Gunshots echoed behind him. Five, six, seven rounds.

"Dammit to hell!" He spit the toothpick from his already arid mouth.

The red Ram pickup was twenty yards away, chrome bumpers glinting.

Cash roared the truck through the archway, cutting hard left to skid clear of where he had left Carrie. The dual rear wheels churned a broad curtain of dust.

Carrie was not to be seen in the yard or near the porch. Two more of the bipedal things were spreadeagled in the dirt, missing most of their heads, forming big, wet puddles around themselves. Carrie's .40 was there on the ground, too. The action was not locked back; it still had rounds in it.

Cash was sure that if he wanted trouble, he'd find it in the big freezer. The creatures he had seen were pallid, like cadavers; featurelessly smooth, like a reptile's clammy underbelly; undoubtedly alien or aberrant, which suggested a moist toxicity as incomprehensible as a biowar germ. The smart thing to do was *leave*.

The right thing to do was rescue Carrie, if she could still be saved.

Reverse out the strangeness—that's what Cash's thinking mind told him to do. Put yourself in their place. Somehow, some way, they come to consciousness on McMillan's ranch. Maybe they had no idea where they were. Perhaps they lacked the facility to process sounds or smells. Maybe their vision was into the infrared spectrum, like a rattler's. Anyway, they hit the ground (or came up out of the ground, if they didn't fall from outer space or burst out of radioactive pods) and commence reproducing, to strengthen their numbers or gain some kind of immediate survival foothold. They discover that for the most part, they cannot walk around in the daytime because it's too hot, too bright. They wander around and maybe incur a few casualties in their experiential curve. They're like men on the moon, seeking a shelter with oxygen and environment. Perhaps they were transitional beings in the process of adaptation, evolving to live in new circumstances.

Illegal aliens, Cash thought with a sting of irony.

Edging up to the icehouse door was one of the hardest things Cash had ever done. There might not be any ceiling to this madness, but there might be a floor, and that bedrock had to be composed of Cash's own resolve. This could not be about anything, right now, except retrieving his partner. All the rest, the theories, the what-ifs and mad speculation, had to be left for later. And yes, the fear, too. All Cash needed to know was that bullets seemed to put the creatures down just dandy.

The icehouse door was latched by a large silver handle. It made a complicated clockwork sound when Cash cranked it, as though he was breaching an immense safe. Cold air and condensation ghosted out around the insulating gaskets.

Nobody home.

He could not find a lightswitch and so brought up his baton flashlight. There *was* something in here, but it wasn't a cadre of shufflers waiting to eat his face or a line of frozen beef sides to mock his fear.

The object looked like a big, broken section of latticework, laced with frost, propped against the stainless steel wall. About five-by-five, it was obviously a segment of something larger, something elsewhere, or perhaps the sole piece worth salvage. When Cash tilted his head to one side he saw that it resembled a big honeycomb, with rows of orderly, stop-sign-shaped pockets. Each octagonal chamber held one of the bugs, suspended like prehistoric scorpions in amber, although this medium was a pliable, transparent blue gel the consistency of modeling clay. It gave when Cash pressed it with the tip of his ballpoint pen, then sprang back.

Twenty or thirty of the little compartments were empty.

Peek: There were—head count—sixteen creatures outside now, cutting him off from the truck. They had hidden themselves, and waited for him to enter the freezer. The empty area between Cash and his opponents hinted that they had gotten the idea to keep their distance.

They were learning.

Best tally, he could clear twelve with the shotgun and the Ruger before he had to reload, if he did not miss once. He still had little idea of how fast they could move when motivated. He could hang tight and wait for dawn, a fat ten or eleven hours…but not in the freezer. They might not even disperse at dawn. They might wait until noon, when it got hotter.

Beyond fear was exhaustion. How long could Cash keep his eyes open and guard up?

Longer, he realized, than he could go without taking a dump. His last visit to the throne had been over twenty hours ago, and his bowels were threatening to burst like a sausage casing in a centrifuge. Great.

He could surrender. But not yet.

He could spy on them and pick a moment. They might dither around trying to form a plan of attack, or an ambush, or a diversion. Not yet.

He checked the door again. They hadn't moved. He tried to squeeze his ass cheeks to interrupt the inevitable. *Go or no go?* He did not laugh at his own folly, because if he started, he might not be able to stop, and when authorities locked him in a padded cell, he'd still be laughing.

Utterly humiliated, he moved to the back corner of the freezer, dropped his pants and tried to move his bowels as fast as possible.

The tang of his own refrigerated shit brought him about as low as he'd ever felt, and rendered him infantile.

The pack with the two cigarettes rustled in his pocket, beckoning his attention. He craved a smoke, just to purchase a smoke's worth of time. Brilliantly, he lacked the means to light up.

"Emerge. Cash emerge now."

It was a voice from outside. It sounded like a very bad imitation of Carrie's voice, clotted and syrupy.

Cash hurried his pants on and buckled up so he could refill his hands with guns.

All right, full disclosure: Cash had always wanted to see Carrie's breasts. But not this way.

She was naked, striding through the group, her flesh disorganized and baggy. Her face was melting right off her skull. Cash saw her breasts. They hung offsides due to the V-neck rip in the center of her chest. The skin that had drooped along her arms accordioned at the wrists the same way as a paper wrapper mashed down from a drinking straw. She reached up with elephantine hands to grab at the tear in her chest. The tissue rended apart, gone fishy and rotten, as the mouthless being stepped out of the incubation envelope that used to be Cash's partner. Its knot of throat bulged as it mimicked speech via some unguessable mechanism.

"Cash. Emerge."

It had been less than an hour since Carrie had been stung.

When Cash came out, shotgun-first, the entire group moved forward several emboldened steps. He shot one, then another, and they dropped. In the nightmare slow-motion of a fever dream, he saw the one that had issued from Carrie pick up her Smith from the ground. One tendril of the clawlike pincer wrapped the butt while the other sought the trigger. It leveled the pistol at Cash and fired.

The slug went high and wide.

It's not her, not any more...

That hesitation almost killed him. As he brought the Mossberg to bear, a second shot flew in true and punched him in the upper left chest, spoiling his aim. A hot rivet of pain fried his nerves. He grimaced, corrected his muzzle, and cut loose. The thing that had peeled off Carrie's body lost half of its knoblike head and spun down in a shower of gluey mulch, dropping the pistol, slide open.

While the rest rushed him.

Cash side-stepped to the smokehouse, dealing out the remaining rounds from the shotgun and getting one more hit, one miss, and one wing-strike that blew away a pincer at the elbow.

It was at least ninety degrees inside the smokehouse. The air was ripe with cured pork. There was an interior crank handle that could be barricaded if he could find something to wedge under it.

Carrie had favored light loads for diminished recoil. As a result, the semi-wadcutter had lodged in Cash's breast and failed to exit. Dense blood, not completely oxygenated, was already blotting his shirt. Heart blood.

The creature had picked up Carrie's gun, fired once, corrected, and hit him on the second shot. They were learning. Now they would know the purpose of any other firearms loitering around, say, inside the house, if…

Cash remembered the spent shotgun shells in the yard. Someone else had tried earlier, and failed. Someone had shot their own dog, the Rottie, to keep it from changing, too.

Cash hoped they would not come into the smokehouse due to the heat. They might waste time deciding what to do, but wouldn't breeze on in. Not yet. He should have just bolted. Run for the hills and made it someone else's problem. Now he was cornered, low on ammo, and in need of medical attention. But if he ran, he still had no idea of how fast they could pursue him.

Or maybe Cash could wait until they adapted more, or learned enough to come in after him, at which time he still had the option of putting a slug into his own head.

But not yet.

Thudding and thumping, next door. They were inside the icehouse.

They could imprint off horses, dogs, people, anything. Until Cash was all that was left to use.

Outside there came a sputtering noise, like a motor missing cylinder strokes. The generator for the icehouse had been chugging away for the better part of a day or two without being refueled. It was running out of gas. Cash knew the sound. The icehouse would thaw and the stored bugs would melt free. Would the smokehouse cool off as the freezer warmed up?

Buttoning up for hours was no longer an option. Cash had scant cognizance of the passage of time. He did not wear a wristwatch. Almost nobody did, any more; everybody had mobile devices. Cash's own cell was still in the door pocket of the Bronco.

Not yet.

———————

Cash used his fist to hammer a pork shank under the door handle, because the creatures outside had come to test it. Right outside the smokehouse door, they were less than a foot away from his face.

Shooting through the door would get Cash nothing except ricochets and a less secure door. Maybe, if he could get to the roof...

The smokehouse was a wood frame veneered in sheet metal. There was a white oak curing barrel that could be flipped to provide a step-up. Every time Cash tried to correct his balance to bulldog his way through the ceiling, his wounded shoulder blew new spikes of pain all the way down to his feet and the bullet hole began to pump fresh. His life was dribbling out.

Obscured from view was a tiny skylight, probably for ventilation. It was difficult to see since the ceiling had browned to a uniform pattern. Too small for his body, but there. He had to bang the corroded hasp back with the grip of his Ruger.

Yeah, don't attract any attention to yourself with the noise.

The hinges squeaked as he pushed against the hatch with the heel of his good hand. His entire right side was going numb and his vision was getting spotty. Shock was setting in. He could just get his head through the hole if he was willing to sacrifice an ear. Outstanding; his last tetanus shot had been years ago. Amoebic infections from tainted meat were the worst.

Soon he would not be able to trust the evidence of his own senses. He would hallucinate, grow dopey, pass out.

Cash had to clamber down to find a plastic crate for more elevation, then repeat his unsteady ascent. He could just get his head through the hatch. The ceiling was as solid as a carpenter's warranty, no rusty nails to auger loose, firm framing or your money back.

Cash could see the pickup truck. There were no creatures in sight except the ones he'd terminated. They were knocked down in their own mud, near the hideous skin-pile that used to be Senior Patrol Agent Carrie Rixson.

To the left, clear; to the right, ditto. The view to the rear was harder since Cash had to peer through the interstice between the hatch and the roof, but it looked okay behind him, too.

This calm could not hold. They had retreated to regroup, find weapons, or make more. Cash could belay his fear and move now, or try to clench and await what came next, as he grew more helpless by the second. The tension was far worse than trying not to shit. You couldn't win. Your own biology would doom you.

He nearly fell on his face getting down from the clumsy barrel-and-crate arrangement. He nearly started weeping when the chunk of pork stuck under the door handle refused to wiggle loose. But in three more heartbeats, the door was open and he was moving as fast as he could manage for the truck, hoping his adversaries had not become savvy enough to take the keys.

They were gone from the yard.

"I'm sorry," he said to Carrie's remains. She deserved better. "God, am I sorry."

That did not slow him down, though. The pickup's cab door was still open. The keys were still in the ignition. And Cash was alone in the turnaround.

"You fuckers!" he shouted hoarsely. "I'm coming back! I'm coming back for all of you! I'm gonna kill every single one of you!"

No response. Locked into the cab, windows up, Cash unbuckled his gunbelt to get at his trouser belt, which he unthreaded to bind his own wadded-up T-shirt tight against the oozing bullet ditch in his shoulder. The Ram truck fired up positively on the first try. Not like in the movies, where the vehicle won't start while the monsters close in. The seatbelt alarm pinged annoyingly.

Cash laid the pedal down and thundered over the cow-catcher at the archway, highbeams up to max. The fuel stood at half a tank. He did not allow himself to breathe until he rocketed back onto the International Highway. Now it was safe to crack the windows and blow the AC on high.

He remembered the cigarettes in his pocket, dug one out, and lipped it. A little nicotine would be better than nothing at all. But the truck did not have a dashboard lighter. Few of them did, anymore.

The black tarp in the pickup bed, unsecured, blew free just in time for Cash to glimpse the big section of blue amber honeycomb, his cargo, before his dulled eyesight focused on the bug that had been left for him inside the cab. It tensed to spring, just out of swatting reach. That's what the monsters had been up to in the icehouse—setting a trap and backing off, to let Cash ambush himself.

The big Ram truck swerved off the road and stopped. It would sit for a while, metal pinging as it cooled, the AC still blasting. Then, eventually, it would resume its journey into the city.

......

We Have Always Fought Giant Monsters

(2012)

On March 1st, 1954, the 23-man tuna trawler *Daigo Fukuryu Maru* ("Lucky Dragon Five") was hunting the catch of the day some 90 to 118 miles east-northeast from Bikini Atoll just as the first atmospheric test of a dry-fuel thermonuclear bomb kicked up a fireball four and a half miles across, showering the crew in radioactive ash and turning their faces black. The ship was supposedly outside the hazard zone until the H-bomb, code named Castle Bravo, mustered twice the expected yield—15 megatons, where 4 to 6 were expected (think roughly 15 million tons of TNT).

Memorial ceremonies are held to this day in Japan at the gravesite of Aikichi Kuboyama, who was the first Lucky Dragon crewman to die (at age 40), several months after the H-bomb test. His dying wish was "to be the last victim of an atomic bomb."

Surviving victims of Hiroshima/Nagasaki are called *"hibakusha"* and are qualified for government assistance. Although the crew was ineligible for this help, the Lucky Dragon Five became a new national symbol for Japan's nuclear dread. Castle Bravo produced the worst accidental radiological disaster in US history, jeopardizing US-Japan relations when it was called "a second Hiroshima." The land-based food chain on Bikini remains contaminated to this day.

The Japanese got around to making an eponymous movie about the incident in 1959, which also inspired Neville Shute to write his apocalyptic novel, *On the Beach* (1957). You might have seen the film made from it.

Toho Studios, impressed by the success of *The Beast from 20,000 Fathoms* (1953), assigned producer Tomoyuki Tanaka to blend details from the Lucky Dragon Five tragedy into a story first titled *The Giant Monster from 20,000 Miles Beneath the Sea*. Once director Ishiro Honda and special effects wizard Eiji Tsuburaya were engaged, the title was abbreviated to *Project G* (*G-Sakhuin*, the "G" for "giant"). Since *Beast* had been derived from "The Lighthouse" by Ray Bradbury, Tanaka similarly hired author Shigeru Kayama—one of the most prominent mystery writers in post-war Japan, whose tales frequently involved mutant reptiles, fish, and other monsters—to confect what was then described as "a sea monster that was a cross between a whale and a gorilla," hence, "*Gojira*" (from *gorira* [gorilla] + *kujira* [whale]). Thanks to Tsuburaya's fondness for *King Kong, Gojira* almost wound up being an giant octopus. Kayama set the bones and characters, which were fleshed out by Honda and co-screenwriter Takeo Murata.

In the opening scenes of *Gojira*, the Japanese fishing vessel *Bingo Maru* is subsumed from below by broiling, radioactive light, directly quoting the Lucky Dragon Five's fate.

I knew none of this when I first encountered the Big G on television, specifically during a week-long run of *Gigantis the Fire Monster* on Los Angeles' *Million Dollar Movie*. Big monster, rubber suit, crushes cities, breathes radioactivity, looks kind of like Gorgo. *Gigantis* was the American retitling of *Godzilla Raids Again* (*Gojira no Gyakushu*, or "Gojira's Counterattack," 1955), the rushed-out Japanese sequel to the original *Gojira* (released in the US as *Godzilla, King of the Monsters*). Under this pseudonym, Godzilla engages in his very first mano-a-mano battle with another monster (Anguirus), thus inaugurating the entire sprawling genre of the *daikaiju eiga*. Godzilla movies are the biggest continuous film franchise in motion picture history, encompassing several "eras" (*Showa*, 1954-1980; *Hesei*, 1984-1999; and *Millennium*, 1999-2004) as he evolved from his original status as a nightmare vision of Japan's atomic fear to a self-appointed protector, first of Japan, later of the entire planet Earth. Kim Newman quite rightly charts Godzilla's "rehabilitation" in his essential film books *Millennium Movies* (1999) and *Nightmare Movies* (revised third edition, 2011).

Culturally, Godzilla rules. His trademark roar is copyrighted. He's even had a real dinosaur named after him—a Triassic ceratosaur called *Gojirasaurus quayi*, discovered in 1997. The previous year, he won an MTV Movie Award (only one of three fictional characters to ever receive it, the other two being Chewbacca and Jason Voorhees). And in 2004, he finally got a star on the Hollywood Walk of Fame...just as he was being "retired" by Toho for a minimum of ten years.

It was also the fiftieth anniversary of the *Gojira's* 1954 debut. To commemorate this, Toho released the uncut version of the original film with English subtitles, which was twenty minutes longer than the US *King of the Monsters* recut and yet unseen by most English-speaking audiences, who discovered the unexpurgated version to be one of the very first monster *noirs*. Unrelentingly grim and contemplative, it is one of the *darkest* monster movies ever made, and one that significantly restores the historical resonance of the tragedy of the Lucky Dragon Five—in *King of the Monsters*, the sequence is shoved deeper into the narrative and snipped down to a mere thumbnail for an American market that would not relish being held in so responsible a light. As several commentators have pointed out, though, *Gojira* is not an anti-American film so much as an anti-nuclear war film. Reviewer Dan Schneider summed up the difference between *Gojira* and *Godzilla, King of the Monsters* as "the difference between a great novel and a great comic book."

Ironically, Roland Emmerich's domestic 1999 reboot *Godzilla* is virtually a blow-for-blow remake of...*The Beast from 20,000*

Fathoms. If that lantern-jawed CGI faux-Zilla (nicknamed GINO for "Godzilla In Name Only") depresses you, then check out *Godzilla: Final Wars (Gojira: Fainaru Wozu,* 2004), which includes a scene where the real Big G kicks GINO's ass in Australia. (Earlier films take potshots at GINO, too—witness the scene in *Godzilla, Mothra & King Ghidorah: Giant Monsters All-Out Attack* [also known as *GMK, Gojira, Mosura, King Gidora: Daikaiju Sokogeki,* 2001] where cadets question recent monster devastation in New York City: "Was it Godzilla?" "They say so in America...not in Japan.")

Although Godzilla's mandated 10-year "retirement" commenced with the 2004 release of *Final Wars,* a really cool full-CGI version of him—the first ever attempted—cameos early (in what is more or less a dream sequence) during *Always Zoku Sanchome no Yuhi (Always Sunset on Third Street 2,* 2007), where the Big G wipes out the newly-completed Tokyo Tower, in 1959.

"Gojira" is also the name of one of the anti-whaling boats in the Sea Shepherd Conservation Society's fleet, out of Australia. Christened in 2010, one of its missions is to harass Japanese whalers! (Gojira is also the name of a French heavy metal band that has donated proceeds from its recordings to the Sea Shepherd Society).

It's easy to suffer or ignore the worst that Godzilla movies have to offer: cumbersome wrestling matches with increasingly absurd opponents (I'm looking at *you,* Gigan); shameless padding to feature length, or the endless second string of strident and repulsive children. But it's all compensated by one of my favorite outings, *Godzilla vs. King Ghidorah (Gojira tai Kingu Gidora,* 1991), which features one of the most deliriously insane plots of the whole series. Really, you'll bruise your head from smacking it in disbelief and wonder.

But as we await the Big G's inevitable cinematic resurgence, Duane Swierczynski has some stories he wants to tell you about our lifelong battle against giant monsters. Like Queequeg in *Moby Dick* (literature's first punk!), he tends his idols and rituals, eats a lot of rare meat, and prepares us all for the final conflict. In a mythic sense, these modern stories root all the way back to Leviathan. Witness Gustav Dore's famous illustration of *that* big beast—just add two more heads to that thing, and it's King Ghidorah!

———————

(This was written especially for my pal Duane Swierczynski's 13-issue Godzilla *comic book series from IDW, and was published in issue #2 [July 2012].)*

A HOME
IN THE DARK

Californians don't even get out of bed for less than a 5.0.

What is more annoying is that any temblor at all is classified as an "earthquake," thereby making the news, which prompts a flood of e-mails and phone calls from the East: *"Are you okay?!"*

Trust me, we're fine. We didn't even notice the calamity, and probably slept through it. If a luxury liner takes on a little water, that's not news; if the ship keels over or sinks, that's news. If a race-car driver whined to national media about a slight rear-end shimmy at 180 MPH, he'd be laughed out of the pit, whereas if he crashed and made a fireball, it would be noteworthy on the old daily feed. Most Southern California quakes are akin to one misstep while strolling. It might throw your balance off for a moment but you keep walking. Think of how your bed wiggles side-to-side when a cat jumps onto it, or your partner merely seats him or herself on the opposite end. That's what most local seismic events feel like. It's not worth mentioning until skyscrapers keel over and fissures swallow cars. But everybody has seen certain movies, and in their dark, secret hearts they want to hear that bridges have collapsed and wholesale panic reigns, because that would serve us all right for living on the Left Coast, Sodom to New York's Gomorrah.

The irony is that many of those *"are you okay?!"* messages come from zones that catch twenty tornadoes per year. Or cities so frozen that the dead cannot be counted until the spring thaw. Or New Orleans.

Most of my fellow Los Angeles sinners hear quake news the day after, usually during wakeup coffee, since for some mystical reason a lot of the minor temblors strike unerringly between 2:00 and 5:00 AM. These little ground shivers start far out in the desert and radiate the same as ripples in pond water, diminishing in force as they peter out. Or the infamous San Andreas fault will hiccup while it (and you) are fast asleep. Maybe it just had a nightmare and needs a drink of water. Maybe a dinosaur woke up. Or perhaps somebody (not you) just had themselves some terrific sex. *Did the earth move for you, too?*

By the time there is a rumble and some odd motion, by the time you can ask yourself *is it a quake*, it's over. One view holds that frequent tremors are a good thing—it's the earth adjusting itself. Take *that*, you smug mid-Westerners, living in your fool's paradise where nothing ever wiggles. One day without warning your entire town will plummet into a yawning crevice, because your topography has failed to compensate tectonically.

In Los Angeles, when the whole city shakes, it's from movies bombing at the boxoffice on opening weekend...especially those bloated CGI tentpoles with budgets in excess of the gross national product of many small countries.

The notorious Northridge quake of '94 struck at 4:30 during the wee hours. It's called the Northridge quake even though the epicenter was in Reseda, about sixteen miles from my house in the Hollywood Hills, which isn't as glitzy as it sounds. That was a 6.7 magnitude for twenty seconds, reaping a tally of 57 dead, 9000 injured, and a gross cost of around $20 billion. By the time it reached my house, it knocked some books off a shelf and assassinated a dinner plate, which left me short one matching place setting and became bothersome enough that I had to buy an entirely new set of dishes. Tragedy is relative.

The way I discern a mild quake is by glancing at a candle sconce that hangs down from my fireplace mantel. It's made of cast iron in the shape of an owl. If that thing is rocking to and fro on its own, it's either an earthquake or my house is possessed by a sardonic poltergeist. I felt a nudge and glanced at the owl. Sure enough. It was three o'clock in the morning, the "midnight of the soul," as some poets would have it—although that reference actually comes from an old hymn, "If, On a Quiet Sea."

I was up and feisty at 3:00 AM because that's when I can get the most work done. Phones and texts and Tweets and prompts all subside by ten o'clock, and anybody who comes banging on the door after that deserves to say howdy-do to a gun muzzle. The clock measures seconds more prudently. Even my online connectivity seems more forgiving at night. You can feel the hostile outside world ease its grip just a notch for downtime, relaxing into the more ancient rhythm of tides and phases of the moon. I have never understood why regular citizens still cling to the outmoded notion of keeping an invasive telephone right next to their sleeping place—"for emergencies," they'll always tell you. Right. Then again, I would never permit a TV screen in my bedroom, either. It would make me feel like an invalid. And since most of the walking world has eagerly embraced the notion of constant, unrelenting contact, it only makes sense for them to be hooked up even while they're asleep…and if that's not an Orwellian dilemma, I don't know what is.

Not that I'm a Luddite. What I was doing was writing and proofreading online manuals for Javascript—that's right, helping *strangers* navigate the chop of internet commerce, meta-indices, interoperability consortia, HTML validators, and are your eyelids getting heavy yet? I've even touched upon such exotic topics as Tesla's free energy converter (you can actually see the genius' blueprints online) and the realities of copyright law in an age where most common users get all huffy if you tell them everything they see is not for free, and stealing is still stealing.

In fact, it's the job that helps me turn off all the "devices," since being nakedly tracked on a 24/7/365 basis seems too much like additional wage work. I won't say our brave new world is bad; I'll just say some aspects seem more aimed at obliterating my privacy than they should be.

I was working from home—what once was called "telecommuting," but that never caught on—in the middle of the night, without having to dress for the job, comfortably at home in the Hollywood Hills.

Again, not as red-carpet as it sounds. My house is above the flats in Beachwood Canyon but not nestled in the shadow of the Hollywood sign, which is on a whole separate mountain (Mount Lee). My house was here before most of the others in the Canyon, built in 1926 during the first construction rush attendant to the Hollywoodland real estate development. Time passed and people built more houses, virtually anywhere they could fit, resulting in a mad mashup of architectural styles all chockablock with each other. The badly-maintained, serpentine meander of roads that feed this area is more sundered and pocked than the Ho Chi Minh Trail, and practically none of the residents ever use a garage for actual parking—the overage of vehicles parked curbside exacerbates this urban arteriosclerosis and keeps the fire department screaming about access. Each resident has visitors, and company means more cars, and non-locals rarely have any skill when it comes to parking on steep and already-narrow streets. Fat Navigators and Escalades jut into the roadway and quickly steam up your kill urge. It's a jungle up here. People don't walk. They have *their* people walk their dogs or air out their children. The only pedestrians you see up here are lost tourists, looking for the goddamned sign that's in plain sight. They think it's a restaurant or amusement park or something you can *go to* in order to enjoy an entertainment experience. You see bumper stickers that read: *Why is it called tourist season if we can't shoot them?*

The interesting distinction of my house is that, against the odds of rampant superdevelopment, there is a vacant lot to either side. It is nestled into the backside of a mountain, designed to relax against the bedrock instead of somersault downhill if there's a seismic event.

If it was earthquake-bolted, then the structure would be married by girders to the rock, which would vibrate everything loose. The '50s and '60s homes cantilevered out of the cliffside are in more danger of rattling downward than my place.

To my immediate south there is a deep valley—more a fissure—which offers a drop of about fifty feet from my rear patio. There's a huge fallen tree full of termites spanning the deepest point, where underbrush has grown unchecked. Of course it's technically a lot, but only a lunatic or a filthy-rich gambler would ever think about building something there—you'd have to blast out the entire hillside from above, then build a "stairstep house" straight down. It was easy enough to look up on the internet, and turned out to be so unbuildable that it was astonishingly cheap.

The empty parcel to my north is on the same kind of land I am (the top of a hummock). It sold to a buyer eight years ago and ever since then the fellow has been fighting the zoning commission over variances for the home he plans to build there. Lately, ominous heavy trucks have shown up to pour immense foundation caissons of concrete that required anchor holes thirty-five feet deep. Construction will take at least another eighteen months. I suppose it was inevitable. The eventual eyesore will rise to three stories, but the lot is set back and to the left of my view, which means I'll never even see it from anywhere except my kitchen.

I'll know it's there, though, crowding me.

Which is why I wanted to buy the other lot, the one with the dead tree. To keep from being surrounded. A bargain at the price, especially for land in Los Angeles.

That wasn't very likely, though. The economy was not cooperating with my dreams. This year made *last* year look like a birthday party (clowns and all), and last year had been dire. I was running out of breath in the mortgage marathon, gliding on fumes and hoping to place my few meager work bets appropriately. One gig can change everything—especially in Hollywood—but the trick is nailing that one gig in your sights with the bottomless stealth and patience of the high hide...then taking it down like a former lover and not giving up until you've feasted on its heart.

My creditors were not likely to appreciate my good intentions—another reason for avoiding voice messages that always mispronounced my name. After a suitable grace period, minions came to pound on the door to ascertain whether the property was, in fact, occupied. This happens as a matter of course. Tenants often die without telling anyone.

The entire nation was defaulting on its obligations and ducking the check faster than a hanger-on at a group dinner, but such parsimony was accepted, even encouraged so long as you were the size of a bank or a political campaign, the size of history's other Big Lies, the super-size of "too big to care." Those of us not powerful enough to raise our own debt ceiling were doomed to scandal and ill repute. Even mighty Kodak went bankrupt just prior to the 2012 Academy Awards, and kicked up a minor brouhaha about removing its imprimatur from the venue for the high-profile distribution of golden statuettes (not solid gold—never, in fact—but a gold-plated alloy that put the unit cost for making an Oscar at about five hundred bucks per, in case you were overcome with curiosity).

It had been a down year. It happens, and your tale of woe is no worse to you personally than someone else's travail is to them. Nonetheless, the harpies of finance were unwelcome as I tried to hold fast and scan the barren ocean horizon for signs of land. The stress can sneakily deplete your metabolism of vital nutrients, and before you realize it, you become lightheaded, exhausted, and angrier than usual.

I was at that precise precipice of disorder when I caught a man skulking around outside, taking pictures of the house. This was the same day as the ground's most recent predawn shudder, the last mini-quake that would rake in the messages of concern from afar: *Are you okay?*

Whole books have been written about the global allure of the Hollywood sign, and the reasons tourists make hadj to photograph it. If you drive up Beachwood any time—even in the middle of the night—there they are, trying to immortalize themselves in the vicinity of an icon they only vaguely comprehend, arms outstretched in bizarre, balletic poses, pretending to "hold up" the sign for the camera, absurdly proud that they are the first to have thought of this perspective trickery, confidently smug that "it wasn't what I thought it would be," as though they had devoted any thought to the process at all. One does not see famous people on the hoof, for this is a neighborhood where neighbors keep to themselves, except for the usual irritants such as the "homeowner's associations" made up of bored hausfraus, the unfamous or the busybodies.

Adjacent to Griffith Park and Bronson Canyon, the hillside clusters of homes are backed up to the wilderness area surrounding the Mulholland Dam. The manmade reservoir is called Lake Hollywood for the same reasons the concrete spillway that bisects the San Fernando Valley is called the LA River—to confer a false sense of nature in the midst of the urban. The real neighbors in this locale are the often-startling wildlife: deer, coyotes, bobcats, raccoons, skunks, rattlesnakes, and all their prey. The coyotes are savvy, organized, and know which day is garbage day; they compete with the Mexican scavengers who come to raid the recycling bins. They (the coyotes, not the Mexicans) will boldly snatch your housecat or small dog for a snack if it wanders into the world. The dreaded rattlers are more rumored than seen, more feared than experienced, but the phobia generates from the concept that they can fit through the same small apertures through which lizards, scorpions, spiders and impossibly tiny mice often gain access to even a secure home. Most often, if you spot a rattler, you need do nothing. They buzz as a warning, and unless cornered, will flee as fast as their snaky belly scales can transport them, which is very quickly indeed. Just how fast, you can never know if you've only seen them on TV or behind glass.

Ever-frantic and meddlesome, local citizen's groups wax dictatorial about animal encounters, advising you to lock up your offspring, call Animal Control, and live in a tightly-wound state of perpetual panic. Above all, they caution, don't feed the critters. I called bullshit on that long ago, saddened that such people would never experience the wonder of seeing a deer standing on their front lawn in the predawn. The beasts were here before us; they *lived* here, and we needed to appreciate the fact that they had allowed our cohabitation, not that they had been given a vote. A lot of my leftovers went over the side, into the valley with the broken tree, half as tribute and half as practicality—my garbage disposal had clogged up once and I never wanted *that* nightmare to happen again.

Sometimes, though, the wildlife got pushy and failed to abide by the unspoken covenant of inside versus outside. Such as the time my car began to malfunction as a result of a giant rat setting up housekeeping in the engine bay. It was the inviting warmth of the motor that attracted this invader; during a cold snap it must have seemed like a resort, parked there by the narrow curb. Rats love to gnaw things; if they don't their teeth grow out of control. This one chewed up my hoses and wiring. I opened the hood one afternoon to put in more power steering fluid (my first guess as to what was going wrong with the car) and was confronted with a wonderland of shredded plastic, a nest of repurposed insulation and Styrofoam littered with nut husks, orange peels, and little ratty footprints. Quite without warning, very much like Wack-A-Mole, a startled rat head poked up from the engine configuration and withdrew just as quickly to make his escape. He hit the street with an audible thud and I watched his enormous rat caboose beat a doubletime retreat down into the underbrush to the south. The damned thing was practically the size of a meatloaf; how the hell had it squeezed itself into the convolutions of the motor?

After getting the engine refurbished, I saturated it with a repellant—never was a substance more aptly named, since this was composed of such ingredients as dried blood (the first item on the label), seaweed, ammonia and other noxious compounds, guaranteed to drive away the hardiest of creatures. It stank up the car for a month but performed as advertised. Lesson learned and logged. It was so vile you had to wear latex gloves and a paper filter mask when applying it, because if it got onto your garments you could smooch them goodbye.

Even pushier, the goddamned tour buses were starting to snake up onto my street, invariably getting lost right in front of my house, or worse, disgorging outsiders and foreigners to snap odd angles in their ceaseless pursuit of the Hollywood sign.

The guy I caught in front of the house that afternoon was not a tourist. I spotted him through the kitchen window and immediately knew this was some minion of the bank, sent to photograph my home in preparation for more harassment.

Like the rattlesnake, I had been cornered just enough to strike.

I went outside and braced him before he could jump in his Prius and get away. I had a gun tucked into my pants when I did it.

California is a state in which you have to be extremely cautious when it comes to the deployment of firearms, even as a threat. On the topic of defending one's home and hearth against bad guys, here is how a friend with the LAPD put it to me:

You can't shoot them in the yard even if it is your property. If you do shoot them in the yard, drag them into the house and put a weapon in their hand. A butcher knife will suffice but a gun is better if you've got one that doesn't trace to you. You have to establish that you acted in fear for your own life, not like Dirty Harry. You have to establish that there was no other option. Now you know and I know that a reasoned discussion is probably not going to take place in the midst of an intrusion. But if you put them down, be ready to prove they were intent on doing you bodily harm…you might even have to injure yourself to prove it. Simply shooting someone doesn't prove what the Penal Code calls "specific intent to kill." The idea is that you acted to prevent violence, not cause further violence.

Thus, if I walked out onto a public street and stuck a gun into the face of Prius-boy, I would be committing a crime…unless the gun was unloaded, and stayed tucked as an implicit threat rather than a definitive one. If I waved the gun in his face, I would be guilty of the diminished charge of "brandishing a weapon in a threatening manner," something almost impossible to prove, even though the mere act of pulling your jacket aside to exhibit a weapon counts as "brandishing."

From the window, the guy with the Prius had the rodential look of a frustrated screenwriter remanded to menial subsistence tasks. He was antsy and did not want to be here. He was like a process server or a meter maid, slogging through a job he hated (and which no one would ever thank him for) in order to reap a wage.

I thought of squirting him with the noxious animal repellant. That would at least fuck up the rest of his day and cost him some duds, and return some of the degree of headache I had suffered at the whims of his fiscal masters.

It wasn't the day for rapier-like gestures.

Once I was on the boil I frothed over more quickly than I ever could have imagined, the black, penned-up rage (born of one humiliating month after another of mounting debt) hitting critical mass almost instantaneously. I charged up my walk, yelling at the sonofabitch to remove his ratty ass from my sight. He spotted the gun instantly; I never even had to touch it.

"I'm calling the police!" he blurted as he backpedaled. His thumbprinty tortoiseshell glasses made his eyes two blank white circles.

"I'm standing on my own property," I said.

"You're threatening me!" He dropped his keys and awkwardly dipped to retrieve them while monitoring me.

"I'm threatening that camera." I pulled the gun, a lovely nickel-finished Sig .40, and placed it atop my mailbox, still on my property. I didn't need it. Two steps more and I was between Prius-boy and his car.

He retreated rearward, toward the high curb that was the only barrier to the deep crevasse of the empty lot below. If you weren't careful while parking, your wheels might bump over it and you'd be halfway to a nasty end-over-end plummet. His eyes prayed for intervention but there were no dog walkers or joggers to bear witness. He was still formulating his next half-assed protest—something about how I had no right—when he crossed one foot behind the other and stumbled over the curb.

To either side of my frontage there is a classic old Hollywoodland streetlamp from the 1920s, an upright concrete post with a single apothecary globe and the un-nostalgic designation of "CD-803" to denote its style. The globes are high-impact weatherproof plastic now, and the bulbs upgraded to modern halogens. Every time the power goes out in the Hills—that is to say, almost every time the Santa Ana winds blow harder than a breeze—the timing on the street lights gets screwed up. I remember that when the invader with the Prius and the nosy camera fell down the hillside, the streetlamp was on even though it was mid-day.

I had been working all night. Slept until noon. He had assumed I wouldn't be home, just like a burglar.

Next to the southern streetlamp is a gnarled pepper tree. When the guy got tangled in his own legs and fell, he grabbed for the streetlamp. He grabbed for the tree. He missed both and gravity took him. He made a little *whup!* sound as he fell.

On top of the mountain bedrock there is a layer of permeable topsoil laced with frangible caliche. Rain and wind belabor it to treachery. If you try to plant a foot in it for purchase you'll sink ten inches, your center of balance will be thrown, and you'll still fall. Nine times out of ten, the branch you grab to arrest your descent will uproot or disintegrate. I learned this when I once roped down into the depression to harvest some paddle cactus for my front yard. It was growing wild all over the lot, threaded through vines and dead wood. No way I would attempt going down there without a belaying line; it was just too steep. I made it to the curb in time to see the guy's feet flail up into the air as he began a backward somersault and started a minor avalanche of loose rocks and debris. Many of the stones are shaped like dinosaur eggs and locals collect them to decorate their walkways. Weather delivers them regularly from the constantly-eroding hillsides.

The man fell all the way down, disappearing into his own self-generated dust cloud. The sliding sound was akin to a heavy bag dragged quickly over gravel. The gauntlet was brimming with pointed sticks, rusted metal, critter nests, jagged stone and decades-worth of poisonous litter. In seconds the only sound was settling rockfall. The dust cloud wafted away, hazing the air, almost the same as if there had been another minor earthquake.

I picked up the guy's camera, dropped near the curb next to the streetlamp, a place where you could regularly find the morning-after effluvia of late-night curbside sex. Balled tissues, dead 12-packs of lite beer, the biologically translucent Glo-worm of a flattened condom or two, once a single shoe, once a pair of viral-looking Jockeys (hanging from the tree). It is dark and remote enough up here to tempt wily fornicators lacking a safe house in which to fuck. Up by the scenic lookout near the reservoir, you could sometimes see parked cars with no earthly reason for being there…until you spotted the steamed-up windows and the pressed ham against tinted glass.

There was no cry for help from below. The Prius was still parked in front of my home.

Dammit.

I couldn't depend on the coyotes to eat the guy with anything approaching haste.

The day had just gotten larger. I stood guard, watching, waiting, and nothing new happened. After what I thought was a suitable period, I reluctantly went back into the house to fetch my climbing rope.

Just as I had when hunting cacti, I jerry-rigged a rudimentary harness with a six-foot piece of rope looped back on itself and secured with fisherman's knots. You twist the loops into a figure-eight and step into it. I tied off against the streetlamp and began to back down the nearly seventy-degree slope, carefully.

The air smelled of allergen-laden vegetation, dust, and creosote bushes. Ten feet down from street level, the valley was a mausoleum of haunted house trees, broken edges jutting up no differently than pungi sticks. A lot of transients had pitched a lot of garbage down here despite the residential trash receptacles up and down the street. Aluminum lawn chairs, now rusted to match the foliage. Crushed beverage cans, shattered bottles, even the butt of an old refrigerator poking up from the strata like the prow of a half-sunken ship. From my balcony vantage I could discern none of these things in detail because new growth had interlaced to form false canopies and hidden deadfalls. Somehow the spooky branches shifted position to foul the straight line of my rope, and I slipped, planting my hand into a dark jellied mass of some animal or foodstuff in mid-decay, still moist.

Further down, there were bones—small animals, eaten by bigger ones. Looped around the intact neck of a Corona beer bottle with a logo at least twenty years out of date was a pet collar for some long-lost companion named Erky. Tiny paws and hearts alternated around its sun-bleached surface. Small dog or large cat, Erky had been delivered to pet heaven a long time ago. You always saw posters and homemade flyers for MIA pets down by the Beachwood Market. They faded over time and were always replaced by new flyers, new victims.

My descent quickly became a sort of archeological tour, like that stretch of highway in Colorado that takes you through history one layer of sediment at a time. I had no idea there was this much sheer *stuff* down here. Rotten chunks of plywood. Twisted spires of forsaken rebar. Sundered foundation concrete frosted with asphalt, as though someone had torn up an old road and dumped it into the nearest available open space rather than truck out such cumbersome waste. An ancient bicycle that had somehow gotten folded double, tires long decomposed to fibrous spiderwebs. A wealth of cubbies and sinkholes in which whole tribes of creatures could set up housekeeping unobserved.

It took me twenty minutes to rope down to the bowl of the valley, which rose again to present a rock wall to the curve of the residential street below mine. This was the furthest a person could conceivably fall…and there was no person other than me. The line of rope defined the path of a spill, and there was no chance Mr. Prius had taken an abrupt turn on the way down. It was against physics.

He had fallen down the hillside and vanished as though swallowed by the earth. I know; I checked. It was unlikely that he had rallied enough to climb out to the next street; surely a tumble such as his would have snapped a bone or two. I would have heard him. I had expected to find him unconscious and bleeding. My hope was to assist him back to the world, explain my situation in the face of this larger catastrophe, and beseech some small human mercy or common understanding, which was foolish—this guy represented the *bank*.

My foot sank into a scatter of junk with the sensation of grinding crushed ice underheel. The pile was mostly dried brittle bones, the leftovers of some wild food-chain picnic. Among them I found a nearly intact skull, elongated with pronounced canines, bigger than a rabbit or raccoon skull. It was from a coyote. Something down here had eaten a coyote, or it had opted to die and decay in this hidden spot. Or other scavengers had enjoyed take-out. There were redtail hawks here, and whole murders of ravens. Even seagulls, occasionally. They swooped down and snatched prey and had been known to lose bits of their quarry in flight. Once I found a single white cat paw on my deck and had to suss out how it might have gotten there.

Some unseen thing slithered heavily through the lean-to of dead eucalyptus branches to my right. I froze the same way I did whenever there was an earthquake, waiting to see if that was all. I backstepped into more bones with a potato-chip crunch. Gravity had brought them to rest here, a bargain bin of two-for-one calcified runes.

There was a little clotted spout sticking up, which turned out to be the mouth of a small, squared-off bottle. A shred of petrified label clung to it with an insectile iridescence, but was unreadable. There was embossing near the neck of the bottle and when I wiped away the scabs of dirt I could see that it read *3-in-1*.

Jesus. 3-in-One oil had not been in stoppered glass bottles since 1910, when they went to screwtops (I looked it up). This could not have been idly loitering around the surface for a century, waiting for me to pick it up as casually as dropped change. For antique bottles, one had to dig. Unless a seismic event helped push ingrown treasures upward, as is the nature of earthquakes.

Near the bottle, already mottled with dust, I found an iPhone, still warm.

I pocketed these finds and wasted the last few moments of waning daylight in a half-hearted look-around that could not honestly be called a search. There was no Prius guy down here, and I was in trouble.

During my grubby ascent, a hypodermic pain pierced my thigh and I instantly concluded I had gotten nailed by a bougainvillea vine. It's not much of a fantasy to claim these plants, émigrés from South America, are actively malign. Used as decoration by people who don't have to tolerate close contact, its woody tendrils invade and dominate adjacent plantlife while its fat, annelid roots steal and hoard groundwater from competitors. The vines bristle with waxy black thorns that are mildly toxic. Sweep the vine aside and two or three more thorns will invariably bite you. It fits my definition of a parasite since it thrives on murdering its neighbors. The puncture in my leg, beneath my pants, began to itch madly.

Later, with the now-empty oil bottle on my desk, I noted that no pestersome phone calls had come in for the day. Of course not— they had sent a guy to photograph the house. Some hammer was about to fall.

The call list on Prius guy's iPhone confirmed that he was acting on behalf of one of my mortgage companies. His car was still parked out front—locked and alarmed. If it sat there for longer than two days I could call a special number and have it towed as an abandoned vehicle. It happens often up in the Hills, and Prius was on the hot list of desirable autos for theft, conveniently enough.

Any second I expected hostile banging on the front door by a man who would resemble a revenant from a zombie movie or *The*

Monkey's Paw writ new, demanding his camera and iPhone and at least a quart of my blood. Or worse, police cars with flashing lights and a waterfall of questions.

Note that I said the "now empty" oil bottle, above. After I took a hot shower to wash off my climb, I found a hobo spider perched on the comforter of my bed, near where I had flung my trousers. It had crawled out of my pocket, hence out of the oil bottle, to sting me for disrupting its routine as I climbed out of the valley. I should have smashed it in revenge, but instead plonked a drinking glass over it to scoop it up for closer inspection.

Hobo spiders are locally mistaken for the dreaded brown recluse, mostly because…well, they're brown and their bite can raise skin lesions. It's an aggressive little beast because it can't see very well. I found out that it is a funnel-webber, an import from Europe in line with the gag that goes nobody in LA is actually *from* LA. It raked its metallic legs along the inside of the inverted glass, impotent and imprisoned, now. Its life was up to me.

The reflex to eliminate him didn't feel right. I had invaded his territory, usurped his home and stuck it in my pocket, and if anything his response sting was more in the manner of a toll to pay. I finally walked out onto the rear deck and cast him back into the valley from which he had come. I worked over the tiny ulceration on my leg with Benadryl.

My appetite had zeroed out and sleep was a joke.

Waited. My TiVO was two-thirds full but no drama could engage me since I already had a better one of my own.

Had a drink. Didn't help. Ditto cigarettes.

A hundred times, I looked out the front door peep-hatch to see if the Prius had magically vanished. It was still sitting there, squat and inviting only as a new nightspot hang for the rat with the big butt, or his posse.

The night was cool and clear. My house is at the same elevation as the observatory in Griffith Park, two mountaintops to the east. The hardier stars shone against the barrage of city light, stubbornly declarative, almost arrogant since their light took so long to reach us that they might not exist anymore. Carl Sagan once said the Earth was a dot, a mote of dust suspended in a sunbeam. My problems meant nothing to the universe at large.

That's when the earth below my feet decided to shake again. This was more than a wiggle, it was a rumble as the ground tasted and tested a modified arrangement. A 5-point or better, the kind where they advise you to get under a lintel or dash outside. I was already outside.

Some of the stars above me blotted out. Maybe they were dead, or had all clicked off at once in an unlikely group, but that wasn't it.

There was an enormous shape, rising up from the valley, blocking the starlight the way an ancient redwood can bisect a postcard view, dominating it. It wavered almost mesmerically in a kind of cobra dance—albeit a cobra with a mouth that could swallow a limousine. I could not see a face, features, or eyes, just the absence of light where it lingered, but I knew it was looking down at me. I thought of Prius guy's camera, inside on my desk. Yeah, the flash of a strobe would solve—and probably end—everything.

There had been no earthquake.

The dark jaws distended and a steaming tube of putrescence was ejected to splatter the lawn five feet from my shoes. Amid the strings and tatters of partially-digested tissue was most of a human skeleton, topsy-turvy in order. And a pair of half-dissolved tortoise-shell glasses.

The shadow withdrew into the earth.

Gloved and masked, I gathered the bones into a trash bag which I disposed of far from home. I got rid of the glasses separately, as I did the camera and iPhone, less their destroyed chips. I never found the guy's car keys, which was normal for my credit line of luck.

Two days later the Prius was towed away by the city.

The spider bite eventually healed, leaving a tiny white scar. It took several months to subside. Among the general effects of the venom I found out that it was purported to cause "intense headaches, abnormalities of vision and feelings of malaise."

Construction on the lot to my north was halted due to unanticipated geo-thermal stress fractures in the concrete, so read the report that judged the ground beneath that one lot to be unusually unstable, moreso than the original survey had reckoned.

I still toss leftovers over the side. Coyotes and other wildlife come to eat the offerings, and sometimes, something larger eats the eaters. There are rumors of a mountain lion loose in the vicinity. Pets continue to go missing, as is normal for this neck of the woods.

You've seen dog's paws twitch while they're sleeping. If you stumble in your mind while dozing, you're not really falling down, but the galvanic jolt of your body is enough to wake you up. Nowadays when I feel the house get jostled by that stealthy tremor in the dead of predawn, I don't fear earthquakes as much. I know that it is only the guardian of this old place, dreaming.

....

The Traps of Nostalgia

(2007)

It is said that people relive their first childhood in rehearsal
for their second, which is a high-toned way of suggesting that
as each of us descends into senile decrepitude (should we last
that long), we might hold dearest those comfort-zone trifles that
floated our boats as children. Or, to put it in a slightly jollier way,
by the time we're 70, we'll have everything we wanted when we
were nine years old.

What gets overlooked in all this handy pocket psychology is
the value of obsession—its causes, nourishment, and reason.

When I was nine I thought *World Without End* was perhaps
the most perfect expression of everything I had come to love in a
sci-fi, horror or fantasy movie—that extremely unwieldy nomenclature having been more recently (and elegantly) summed up
by the Germans as the *roman phantastiche*, or if you will, stories
of the fantastic. Whether it involved a winged dragon, a haunted
house or a rocketship full of robots was immaterial; what mattered to me was: *is this a monster movie or not?* That youthful
clarity of focus has over the course of years been subjected to all
sorts of deconstructionist analysis, a kind of scrutiny that at its
worst causes wannabe experts to squander more and more time
debating inconsequential trivialities such as which guy was what
monster in which suit in how many frames of a film the world
at large has forgotten. At its best—and this is the part that gets

overlooked in the white noise of pop minutiae—what we're really talking about is a fragile window of time, how long it was open, and the effect it had on those bedazzled by its import.

World Without End (1956) predated the George Pal production of HG Wells' *The Time Machine* (1960) and is in fact an inversion of that basic plotline: In a far-flung, post-apocalyptic future, the Earth's surface is dominated by atomically-mutated cavemen while the technologically-advanced, "normal" folks cower in subterranean bunkers where they can at least enjoy air conditioning and maid service. In *The Time Machine*, our normal folks are beautiful, illiterate moron children unaware they are being bred as food stock by the subsurface Morlocks; in *World Without End*, they are impotent from living for centuries in "a hole in the ground." Both scenarios present reductionist threats to the human race as we know it, or knew it, and it remains for right-thinking white he-men from the past (our present) to kick ass and set things back on track. In both cases the unspoken mandate is that this course-correction will involve *a lot of sex*, and pronto, dammit.

What did *World Without End* offer this nine-year-old? Easy: A rocketship. Time travel. Man-mutant firefights. Genetic monsters. Weapons galore. Guys in tights and metallic skullcaps. Leggy babes in Alberto Vargas drag. In one single, glorious, Cinemascope color spectacle, you got sci-fi (rocketships and the protocol of space travel), horror (the mutants with their melted-wax, multi-eyed visages) and fantasy (accidental time-travel). Monster movie? Check. The idea of bestial throwbacks making off with hot women was straight off the cover of every pulp adventure magazine ever conceived. It really did seem for a while there that the only guy who could salvage our future was Rod Taylor (the hero of both films).

If you know the details of the above description, you are probably already doomed.

Now, what did it take to engage this mythology? Our intrepid nine-year-old had to trawl the pages of *TV Guide* with archeologist fervor, seeking the correct glyphs, in this case the hot-button designates *(science fiction)* or, even better, *(melodrama)*. He or she had to dutifully note the time this myth was unspooling on some local TV station, or risk never seeing it. To fulfill this need he or she frequently had to connive various means of that most important transgression of single-digit preadolescence, *staying up past bedtime*. Commercials be damned. I don't know about you, but I believed that if I sat closer to the television, and opened my eyes wider, I would be able to absorb more of the movie, or at least impress upon my mind the imperative of logging this information in as much detail as possible.

Stanley Kubrick once said that interest versus fear produced learning on a scale comparable to an atomic bomb versus a kitchen match. Reinforcement for the visual was provided by several venerable monster magazines you already know. That interest, obsession, addiction, physicalized in a limited number of mementoes and periodicals, suggested an imaginary community of like minds. What you had was a nation-full of isolated, individual keepers of the flame mostly unaware of each others' presence except in the abstract—there was no cohesive community, thanks mostly to the limits of our entertainment technology. Inevitably, aficionados had to hoard whatever material was to be had, and not just because there wasn't much of it. More importantly, the reactor of interest had been stoked and needed regular feeding.

Nearly all collectors, in their secret heart of hearts, view themselves as archivists, librarians, historians; each perhaps the lone repository of a special cumulate knowledge. Someone else, somewhere else, might collect exactly the same stuff you do, but without your unique perceptions or conclusions. Many Monster Kids of the Shock Theatre era and the golden age of horror hosts can be likened to monks quietly plying study in cells all across the nation. One or two or a dozen might connect, infrequently and at great effort, but generally—and I believe this true—we were all mostly alone with our monsters.

The exigencies of collecting monster movies were daunting. Even 8-millimeter condensations required special equipment and money. Far more rewarding, it was, to discover the trick of making audio tapes of same—first on a little 3-inch General Electric reel-to-reel [max recording time about 12 minutes per side] with the mike in front of the TV (if you could ever get the rest of your family to *shut the hell up*), later into cassettes (which could miraculously record a *whole movie* on a single tape) fed by leads wired directly to the TV speaker...if you were cunning enough to unscrew the cabinet.

Then came the dawn of video time—per *Video Watchdog's* Tim Lucas, about 1980. During most of the 1970s I knew people who had videocassette recorders, but it wasn't a prevalent thing and certainly out of my reach, although I once considered buying a reel-to-reel video recorder—for *three hundred bucks*—just to capture some treasures in *some* form, for later improvement. Moreover, the selection of public/official/sanctioned movie releases was elementary. It would take years, charting the rise and fall of the laserdisc, before decent libraries could be amassed and a reasonable selection of titles could be sought, or aspired to. I wasn't interested in *Gone With the Wind* or *The Sound of Music*, I wanted *Monster on the Campus*. During this period I also acquired the first prints of my 16mm collection. Terrific; even *more* costly gear.

After that, holy *crap* did things change.

Frank Dietz asked me: *Why do we do the things we do, from courting these increasingly antique phantoms to rendering art depicting same, trying to make modern sense of loves acquired in childhood?* The easy answer is there is already plenty of disillusionment in the world for those who wish to collect *that*. We can skip past the excuses of recreation, or hobby. What remains critical is not all the little things gained, but the big thing on the cusp of being lost—the era of which we are all joyously willing casualties.

Some years back, a friend of mine stood in the living room of my apartment holding a then-new videotape of (I think) the 1931

Frankenstein. "I love that I can have this," he said. "That I can now hold it in my hand and watch it whenever I want. I would not take that away from anybody. But you know what?" He wiggled the cassette in the air. "This is *too damned easy.*"

Meaning that anybody who wanted to see the film could just go buy or rent it, today. Such people might not appreciate how hard it was to see such a thing, not so long ago. Nor would they comprehend the absurd lengths to which many of us went, repeatedly, once upon a time, to see it, or perhaps discover a photograph from it, a reference to it, an essay about it. Some people would see only a black-and-white relic with a rubber-foreheaded monster, glacial pacing, outmoded drama, primitive cinema, an irrelevancy. Some other people, however, will see a culmination of a lifetime of devotion, and be fulfilled by that small, private pleasure. It depends largely on one's perspective...and whether or not one has slogged through the basic coursework, done the time in the monk's cell of childhood, and above all...

...preserved the recognition that such things, hard-won, can likewise be *lost* again with amazing ease.

And there are, um...*how* many versions of *Frankenstein* on DVD, now? Feeling smug and superior yet? DVD lasts forever, or so we are gulled until the next replacement medium becomes a corporate cash cow.

Flash forward to 2007. After much experience in DVD production, I and certain like-minded others sought to convince Warner Brothers, the current rights-holders to *World Without End*, to release a DVD version, possibly with a few added extras from experts you may know. Response on the executive level was sobering: Marketing wisdom and consumer tracking indicated that only 2000 or so copies of such a release would sell, putting it well below the radar of even cursory consideration, even if it was piggybacked with several other low-wattage movies and misrepresented to the public as a package titled *Lost Science Fiction Classics*, or somesuch.

It may not be an A-picture, a reliable revenue stream, a classic or even noteworthy to the commonweal, but what if you want to know about it, a decade from now? Chances are you will probably be able to download it from a central library hub (you don't need to be told that the golden age of DVD is already over, right?), but what if you're curious above and beyond the content of the film per se?

Most likely you will be getting your information from archived pieces like this one—if you can find them at all. Not only has the print medium been elbowed into its twilight (thus gradually eliminating those musty stacks of magazines in the garage), but the window for available oral history on your favorite movies is inexorably sliding shut, too—just ask Tom Weaver. Soon enough all you will have to consult is second- and third-hand accounts, because even the paper trail for movie production is evaporating, in an age where most of that information is on laptops and hard drives, frequently lost to file transfers and format glitches—more frequently than anyone cares to acknowledge, least of all the bean counters in charge of what used to be major movie studios.

When Brian Helgeland went back to the vaults to reconstruct his director's cut of *Payback*—a movie less than a decade old—he found all the digitized Avid files were...just...gone. Disappeared. He and his editors luckily found the original film elements, and expressed mild astonishment that they were compelled to re-cut actual film on an actual editing table, something they admitted neither of them had ever done before.

Now pause to consider the astonishing naiveté of filmhounds who blindly assume studios keep complete files on production, or know where anything can be located. During the advent of DVD supplements, some of these gaps blindsided everybody (like missing stereo mag tracks for major classic films). Then recall how often those DVD supplements, double-dips and deluxe reissues had to rely upon notoriously truant bits of "lost" footage or audio brokered via longtime fans. It rarely matters because the studios take all the credit anyway.

Think there are enough cracks through which stuff may fall, yet?

The hitherto-invisible community of monster fans has been handily networked by the internet. I am a fan of the internet. So this simple caveat should not surprise you: *All those goodies can still vanish in a hot second, and often do.* Beware.

(For two more examples out of dozens, I clicked a few links as I wrote this and found that the fabulous and monster-o-centric *Giants and Girls* website has evanesced into the ether, probably forever. Tough luck if you didn't download all those cool photos. The website of my evil twin, monster cultural historian David J. Skal, has likewise gone down to the pixel boneyard—blog included. Unlike printed matter, no matter how obscure, when websites click off no physical artifact remains in the real world; it is genuinely as though the sites never existed at all.)

Books have always fallen in and out of print; but today, in the age of what psycholinguist Dr. Murray S. Miron calls the "discretionary illiterate," maintaining relevant print resources is as old-school as watching a movie made before, say, *Payback*. Don't depend on old dependable books hanging around forever, because fewer and fewer massmind people care about perpetuating them.

All your relevant resources in whatever genre face the type of obsolescence of indifference that keeps that dream-DVD of *World Without End* out of my hands (and if that title surfaces to make me a liar, there will always be another title nobody gets to see or possess).

Students of the vintage stand in defiance of time. They "merely" maintain that their loves merit overview and consideration. Even the stuff of Frank Dietz's caricatures, for example, simultaneously exults the canon and invites new converts...but through interest, not fear or obligation. If a nine-year-old can manage it, so can you.

Think time travel is impossible? I say that if you have read this far, you've just done it.

———————

(This was written at the request of Frank Dietz for his self-published book of illustrations, 7ᵗʰ Voyage of Sketchy Things. *And David J. Skal debuted a "relaunched and improved" website, monstershow. net.)*

A GUNFIGHT

When the gunmen came, Proctor had just finished swabbing his armpits with stick deodorant. He'd had to waste extra seconds forcing up the last-gasp sliver of the deodorant cake; he did not have a backup. If you sat and waited for an assault, your enemies were always late and you paid for it in caffeine twitch. The minute you rechanneled your attention to something more mundane, that's when the shooting started. If you crouched in a decent hide and waited for them to catch up, you'd get leg cramps; you'd start to get hungry. Plus, if your adversaries were watching, you had to present a convincing mock of normalcy so they would jump. It was worse whenever they staked you out and waited for you to go to sleep—kind of a stand-off, your alertness versus their patience. It was almost funny, like the nervous shuffle of prom dates intent on getting laid amid taffeta and ritual...an eternity of flop sweat and jockeying, paid off by a furious few moments of motion.

Proctor had just transferred the deodorant stick from his right hand to his left, which is to say he switched the big pistol to his right hand. That was when the door to his latest in-transit dive started coming apart under the racket of autofire from the hallway. His visitors had not come to palaver.

He dropped on a straight vertical and rolled, his bare back picking up bits of crap from the dirty floor and its ancient caul of carpet. A cleated workboot popped the brass from the door at lock level and a pair of no-neck weightlifter types ducked back out of their own gunsmoke.

More critical was the dude on the fire escape, waiting for his cue. He was supposed to be a surprise. Proctor took him first, with two cleanly grouped shots from the Smith—soft-nosed, 230-grain wadcutters that vaporized the glass and punched into the guy's body armor like a prizefighter. He stumbled backward from the force of the low-velocity slugs, hit the rail with his butt, dropped his piece, and fell six stories.

Maybe ninety seconds from now, some scaredy-cat would phone the cops.

The killers in the corridor had enough time to re-clip, and they bobbed their heads around the frame as though playing SWAT. If two men are coming at you through an open door, the one on the hinge side will always come through second, so Proctor delivered a fast salvo of three shots through the wall above the grime-skidded lightswitch. The building was old and the wall was lath and plaster. Proctor could see from the mummified wallpaper that water damage had occurred at some point around the Korean War. People thought walls could protect them.

The bullets shorted the fire-hazard wiring behind the switch and the lights went out as one of the fellows in the hallway made a little woof of distress and bounced off the far wall. He had been hit in the face by the shrapnel of crumbling masonry. Maybe he had taken a bullet in the cheek, after the shot had tumbled and flattened and opened up the wall. Either way, he was distracted, so Proctor moved again—never stay stationary when men are shooting at you—and concentrated on Wall Boy's amigo.

The second man stepped through and commenced fire. They had come with Uzis, which meant they were probably spewing nine-mil hardball rounds, nasty little bees indeed, but junior high compared to the loads Proctor had slotted into his own semi-auto.

Proctor always kept track of his rate of fire. Five shots down, six to go (since the Smith always had one in the pipe when cocked and locked). He took advantage of the second man's exposure and tracked his fire from floor level upward, hoping to hit him in the legs or anywhere not sheathed by Kevlar. The steel toe of the guy's boot exploded. A hard asterisk of red blossomed just below his kneecap.

And then his magazine ran dry. He fell down, thrashing.

The full-auto housekeeping had certainly downgraded the charm of the room, but not a single shot had hazed Proctor. Seven slugs had drilled completely through the satchel with the money; terrific, they had just assassinated a bag of currency.

It was always about a bag of money.

The first guy from the hall was still moving, trying to hold half his face on while he groped around for his weapon. Proctor shielded his own face from point-blank back-spatter and put the interloper down.

Okay, first wave. How many more were there?

It was efficient in its own way; Proctor still had one bullet left in the Smith, and three guys down.

He grabbed his Number Two piece, a hammerless Charter Arms Bulldog with a two-and-a-half inch barrel and five gigantic .44 Special cartridges, which he kept at hand in the event of a rare jam from the Smith. He ejected the dry mag from the Smith and topped it off. Then he moved for the hole where the window used to be.

Elapsed time, maybe fifteen seconds from the whole deodorant thing.

Fire Escape Guy had wrecked considerable havoc on an illegally-parked Ford Focus, blowing out most of its windows when he had bounced off the roof. He lay in a broken sprawl in the street, his limbs at goofy snapped-chopstick angles. Nobody had dared to get near him yet. In fact, cabs were driving around him, anxious to clear the neighborhood without blood on their tires.

Proctor sneaked out his left hand to collect the shotgun on the fire escape, unfired and therefore probably fully loaded with six-to-eight. He used his left hand in case there came hazing fire from below. He could shoot left-handed but was expert with his right.

Sure enough, somebody started popping pistol rounds from the street. The distance was absurd when you considered the hope of hitting something relevant at six stories. Reinforcements would be getting closer soon enough.

He checked the shotgun. Full tube of double-aught buck with one already chambered. Fire Escape Guy would not have wanted to betray his sneakery by racking the slide.

Proctor grabbed his jacket, his extra rounds, the shotgun and the satchel and eased out into the hallway. Nobody home. If anyone else was on this floor, they'd be eating the deck in terror, waiting for somebody else to do something. It was in these little frozen capsules of time that Proctor felt most alive. He lived in the spaces left by people waiting for the authorities to straighten everything out.

Both the stairs and the antediluvian elevator were down the hall to the right. Proctor moved in the opposite direction, careful not to expose his back to a window or other unknown space.

The satchel had its own backstory, but it was nothing new. Some guys had done a crime that had paid off bigger than expected, and as usually happens when you crew with men you don't know, assorted individuals had begun to weigh the mathematics of who deserved more. Trust was never a factor. Some guys had tried to kill Proctor and Proctor had killed some guys. Turned out that the bank-rollers—the fine citizens who had paid to set up the job, but were not directly involved in the scut-work of heisting and cracking—had messy issues with some of the personnel. Currently, Proctor had the satchel and assumed he was the only member of the work crew still breathing. At this point in any similar operation, you were a lot more inclined to keep all the dough for your trouble, so the bankrollers had made a few phone calls, and Proctor's life filled up with strangers trying to erase him.

It was about the satchel, now. Who possessed it; who thereby won. It wasn't even about the money anymore. The bankrollers would spend three times the amount of now-perforated money in the satchel just to nail Proctor, just to make their petty little point about who was or was not to be messed with.

What it was about, once again, was Proctor getting out of the building with his skin still on.

Proctor did not much believe in psychology. He was a practical man who adjudged via experience. Sometimes, he did pause to wonder whether he put himself in danger just to keep his senses highwired and keen. Maybe he was a junkie enslaved to the action.

What difference did that make? Zero. If you lived in a world of perfectly-realized paranoia, your path was clear as distilled water.

A silhouette started shooting at him from the far end of the hall. Piqued, no doubt, at the sight of two of his fellows devoid of life on the floor.

Proctor moved the second he saw the man's long coat. Long coat always means a long weapon; if you are alert, you can usually spot a muzzle winking in and out of sight around the hem when the person strolls along. Proctor dropped the satchel, the coat, his boxes of ammo—no time yet to snug them into his pockets—and fell to a kneeling position as he drew the captured shotgun, which he had snugged under his left arm, butt-out.

Long Coat was "bump firing" with some sort of military carbine, holding the weapon firm against one hip and letting the recoil pull the trigger again and again. The bullets came in high as Proctor dropped and returned fire with Round One from the shotgun. The pellets chewed a suitcase-sized hunk out of the wall and balustrade, converting it to flying splinters and plaster dust. Long Coat raised his weapon for aimed fire just as Proctor corrected his own aim, let go, and blew most of Long Coat's right shoulder off.

Proctor and those like him engaged in such antics for money. Money bought you freedom, but that freedom usually turned out to be a dead wait for the next job, the next challenge to accrue more money. He pretty much expected to die by the sword sometime, but not today. He expected his own death to be unanticipated, or at least quick. Not today. Today was just a contest to see who was sharper. Outfox superior numbers and take the prize.

No, dying was not part of his plan for the day.

On each floor, the corridors connected in a big square. That meant his opponents might generate enough intelligence to think of sandbagging him from behind. Proctor had walked the floor two hours earlier, anticipating escape contingencies. Five minutes later, and the invading gunman would have drawn down on an empty room—literally, the time it took for Proctor to put on a fresh shirt and take his leave. That time did not exist any more.

Fewer than twenty-five running steps away was a doorway for the eastern stairwell, Proctor knew, and he made for it just as two more gunmen stepped out of the elevator. If he had not had to scoop up his stuff from the floor and grab the satchel, they never would have seen him. As-is, they advanced down the hallway, shooting.

A second or two of time can make all the difference in the universe.

These were men used to making a show of extravagant obliteration, and so the hallway was gradually demolished as they moved. They were a cool team, one partner always firing while the other reloaded. They kept to the walls and presented minimum profile. They checked and cleared every doorway unaccounted for in Proctor's wake. The pattern screamed Organization involvement—first send up the thugs, then send up the pros.

Proctor had killed a lot of both in his time on the planet.

No way he could make the stairs before they made the corner. Proctor had to improvise.

He body-slammed the nearest door, popping both the deadbolt and the security chain thing. Who the hell relied on those little slide-chains, anyway? They couldn't keep out a wet fart. Inside the room a naked white man was engaged in some sordid oral congress with a naked black woman. The woman saw Proctor and his guns first. Her eyes went wide but she didn't make a sound; she was a pro, too. The man spluttered and was one tic away from yelling out his indignation. Proctor brought up the shotgun.

"No fuss. Keep doing what you're doing."

Their reaction was not ordinary. Usually, people freaked and flailed and made so much noise you were forced to unplug them. Most citizens thought it was still the 19th Century, where a cry of social alarum would bring instantaneous rescue from other concerned citizens. These two just froze, as though awaiting a sculptor to immortalize them.

Of course the two gunmen instantly spotted the damage done to the door. They were too good to play it as a blaze of glory and burst in. They knew their own shadows would broadcast in the spill of light from the doorway. Slowly, one of them toed the door wider and they kept to maximum cover, eeling around in a high-low combination.

One of them rolled prone on the floor, sighting the bed. Sharp.

Proctor knew that guy would see him under the bed immediately. In the moment it took this target information to register, Proctor had already fired. The other man, the one still standing, was delayed for an instant when his eyes tracked, almost unwillingly, to the satchel, which had been positioned on a table in the middle of the room for just that purpose—to distract him in the quarter-second it took Proctor to fire again.

The hits were crippling but not fatal. Proctor had to turn each of them off with the Smith. People such as his unwitting accomplices really should not ought to have to see that kind of carnage, so Proctor left them a small wad of bills, a banded stack of cash with a neat hole through Ben Franklin's forehead. Proctor always tipped well when service was good.

He left the empty shotgun behind, smoke still wisping from its bore.

His adversaries would have control of the lobby by now and were probably working the floors from the ground up. Proctor hit the eastern stairs and made for the roof.

The whole building was caught up in an ominous beat of sheer quiet. The kind of quiet where you could hear a pin drop.

A firing pin.

Proctor grabbed the gun muzzle peeking around the corner and yanked the man behind it into a flat-handed blow that shoved his nose up into his brain. They'd already thought of the roof; this guy had heard the commotion and ventured down, thinking the show was already wrapped.

Elapsed time from the deodorant interlude: About three and a half minutes. Uniforms would be enroute by now. Proctor had to stay clear of inquisitors. Nosy officials were rarely part of his world. The presence of law enforcement did mandate a certain urgency in his trade, however, which made schedules important. To remain mindful of the clock meant that Proctor would not have to kill any policemen unless absolutely necessary.

His newest weapon, just liberated from Upstairs Guy, was a tactical M4 festooned with Picatinny rails and a suppressor the size of a roll of paper towels. There was an aluminum handgrip for stability fore of a 30-round black Teflon mag full of 556s—serious biz. The detail seemed fetishistic and overcomplicated, but it only took Proctor a glance to notice it. This was someone's personal hellraiser, not a junk gun grabbed out of a car trunk in a hurry. This thing had a special carry-case all its own, somewhere, cleaning tools and all. The dead guy on the floor didn't object, so for the next few moments this was Proctor's weapon.

Below, silent gunmen were moving up the stairs. No chatter.

Seconds could make all the difference, and now Proctor was looking to purchase a chunk of time. He decided quickly—stealth versus delay—and aimed the M4 down the open stairwell. He kept the hammer down until the magazine ran dry, then discarded the gun. The hellacious delivery and ricochets off steel and concrete would drive back the men below, force them into a defensive freeze, or perhaps even send them after an alternate route of ascent. They would not continue up the stairs, and for Proctor that was spare time bought and paid for.

The roof presented the exotic possibility of snipers, but Proctor did not think he was that important. Yet. Once the news he had just waxed seven soldiers trickled to the ground floor, his adversaries would spare no expense, and probably burn the whole building down just to nail him.

Again, it was no longer about the money. It was about the fact that Proctor had *taken* the money.

But the money in the bag represented a year of life for Proctor. A break from his identity and calling, a rest from the rigors of crime. Once quiet and inactivity began to make his skin itch, he'd work again, but the cash cushion permitted him to be more selective, and perhaps he could avoid the haste and need that had just put him on the run, today. Yeah—use the cash from this gig to avoid jobs like this. It made perfect sense if you lived in a loony bin.

The roof meant exposure, which meant more compromised time. Proctor kneeled, sacrificing a few seconds to finally squirm into his jacket and zip up. Behind him the next roof over was fifteen feet away and one story lower. No good. He'd wind up with a blown knee, crawling around while men came to kill him; he would run out of ammo and they would not.

Trained athletes could jump almost thirty feet. No good. They had special body suits and endless rehearsal, and they never had to jump with a payload. Proctor began stuffing stacks of cash from the satchel into his jacket. The satchel was his target identifier—terrific for toting currency, but a dead giveaway when it came to visual ID.

Proctor was stuffing cash down the sleeves of the jacket. Unwieldy. He wished he'd had time to put on a shirt, which could be tucked in and then filled full with less danger of money leakage. Something—a caprice of the wind, a horripilation of the nape, or plain overcaution—turned him just as a bullet ripped through his jacket sleeve, the money beneath, and the meat of his left bicep.

Sure enough, a head was poking up from the north fire escape. The pistol in front of the head was firing, where else, at the guy with the satchel.

Proctor flattened and returned fire with the Bulldog, the kick jolting his entire body and exacerbating his brand-new wound. The head whipped out of sight. Proctor heard the clatter of metal on metal. The shooter had dropped his gun to deal with the brick chips the .44 rounds had imbedded in his face. Close enough.

By now, gawkers would be crowding the one corpse already in the street.

Proctor discarded the Bulldog. The satchel had become a personal curse. He had maybe fifteen seconds to move or be trapped here for the rest of his life.

Proctor dumped out the satchel and hurled it over the side in the direction of the gunman who had just shot him. His left arm was already beginning to throb and go needly. He grabbed several stacks of cash and broke the bands with his thumbs. Then he tossed about thirty grand in loose bills over the side in the wake of the falling satchel.

Below, there would come a heartbeat of astonishment at all the money in the air. Then the grabbing chaos would commence, magnetizing more people who would, in an instant, turn from being onlookers to become opportunists. Law-abiding citizens would gladly block an incoming police cruiser for the chance to scoop legal tender off the street. Hell, maybe even a gunman with a clear mission would pause to grab several hundred bucks extra if it was floating right in front of his face.

The money-packed hole in Proctor's arm was the type of wound you wished for, if you had to get shot—what grunts had called a million-dollar-wound back in the war. But very soon it would hamper Proctor's ability to jump even the nine feet required to achieve the top of the nearest neighboring building, to the south.

He finished stuffing his jacket, his pants pockets, knowing even this weight would retard his ability to fly. He had to keep the Smith with him—had to. Without a weapon he was even more naked. It was another couple of pounds, but he had already abandoned his backup piece, and the rest of his ammo.

He gave himself the maximum distance in running steps and launched from the roof ledge, pushing off with his right foot, his stronger leg. He had a brief in-flight nightmare about being cut to ribbons by gunmen below, but if they had come around to the backside of the building by now, they were still on street level.

The toe of his shoe clipped the ledge of the next building when he hit and rolled, nearly tearing his knee out of the socket. Tiny stones, held in ambush by thick roofing tar, skewed jaggedly into his face. Momentum kept him tumbling. He threw his leg like a rodeo rider to stabilize, but it was the leg with the freshly-wrenched knee, and he nearly screamed. Then he scuttled like a sea creature to the shade of a rickety elevator housing on the roof.

Century notes wafted on the updraft in his wake. He had lost a few thousand coming over.

The Smith was gone. It, too, had fallen.

Ten minutes ago, Proctor was in the possession of one hundred nineteen thousand dollars in a black satchel. Now, as he crouched, his leg and arm mixing their poisonous pains into a toxic narcotic that could potentially black him out, he was still leaking money every time he moved.

There was an old grocery sack on the roof, flattened and wadded, paper inside plastic. The paper was furred to the consistency of velvet. Proctor began to unzip, unload, and transfer cash to the bag, which threatened to burst at every new stress. It was still too much, even with century-stacks stuffed into his waistband. He still had about half his take. He knotted the plastic at the top of the bag to hold it. It snapped the first time he tried; the plastic had been in the sun too long.

Grimed and limping, he was going to have to shuffle back into the populace clutching the bag to his chest like a bum, thinking ruefully of the money he'd been compelled to leave behind because there was simply no room in his ratty shopping bag or his pants.

Deduct the cost of under-the-table medical. Deduct the cost for refreshed armament. Deduct the usual fee structure for no questions asked and unpapered handguns. Then new clothes and a new hide.

Supplies for his basic kit, all lost now. Subtract uncompensated recuperation time.

Great; he was going to have to find a new job as soon as possible.

On the sidewalk, Proctor was the only person headed south as everybody else was moving north in rather a hurry.

"Round the corner!" shouted a florid-faced stranger as he pushed past Proctor, aggravating his shoulder wound. "There's money all over the street! It's like manna from heaven!"

The celebratory news had not yet disrupted the routine of the drugstore Proctor found about two blocks distant. He could acquire enough astringent and gauze to field-dress his bullethole. Ace bandages and a knee sleeve. A good anonymous sweatshirt. The checker eyed his disheveled state so he voluntarily checked his ratty shopping bag. Nobody here really wanted to touch it, let alone steal it.

He grabbed a little basket and filled it. Razors, foam, toothbrush, toothpaste, floss, aspirin. There was a two-for-one special on deodorant, for the budget-minded. He bought two.

(for Donald Westlake, with apologies—DJS)

....

The Mulholland Muse

(2010)

Most people know the name Mulholland Drive from the eponymous David Lynch movie. If you go deeper, you recognize the *roman à clef* elements that were interpreted into the plot of *Chinatown*—the Noah Cross character played by John Huston is heavily derived from the machinations of William Mulholland during the period known as the "California Water Wars."

An Irish immigrant who became chief engineer of the Los Angeles Water Department, it was Mulholland who conceived and oversaw the construction of the Los Angeles Aqueduct, that "stone river" that bisects most of the San Fernando Valley, scene of innumerable auto chases in cinema (you'll know it when you see it) and best remembered as the place a gang of giant, atomically-mutated ants established an LA beachhead in *Them!* Mulholland also helped build the Panama Canal, the Colorado Aqueduct, and Hoover Dam.

Mulholland's biggest folly was the construction of the St. Francis Dam near Saugus in San Francisquito Canyon. Built in 1926, the dam burst at three minutes before midnight on March 12, 1928, wiping out a 65-mile swath between Oxnard and Ventura, virtually destroying everything between it and the Pacific Ocean under 25 feet of water, with blast waves cresting at 75 feet. More than 500 people died. Mulholland, acquitted of malfeasance, later committed suicide in 1935 at the age of 79.

The sole monument to him is a fountain in the Los Feliz area of Los Angeles.

(For anyone innocent of the checkered history of Los Angeles, or who thinks the corruption started with the Water Wars, guess what? The slimy double-dealing and power-broking runs all the way back to the roots—read a terrific book called *Bread & Hyacinths* by Paul Greenstein, Nigey Lennon and Lionel Rolfe.)

And when people are thinking of noir or hardboiled storytelling, most often they are thinking of movies, not books...even the movies that sprang from books too many noir fans have never read.

If you see a car chase on a windy road in any film from the 1940s or 1950s, chances are it was shot on Mulholland Drive. Modern noir has its back-alleys and cul-de-sacs, but its main artery is Mulholland.

You know the Crossroads? As in *"I went down to the Crossroads / Tried to flag a ride...?"* The location, if one exists, of the so-called Crossroads where one may barter with supernatural forces in exchange for wealth, talent or success is widely disputed. (Some say it's where Highways 61 and 49 cross; others say it's the intersection of two railroad lines—"where the Southern crosses the [Yellow] Dog"—and still others argue that it doesn't matter; the Crossroads can be anywhere one is picked up in order to seal the deal. Mulholland Drive has a great crossroads, at Woodrow Wilson Drive. I used to live very close to it. Go down there at three in the morning and tell me it doesn't feel just a little bit spooky; "off," somehow.

So when I was writing *Internecine*—itself a very LA-o-centric novel—I made sure to set a big scene on Mulholland Drive. A few aspects of this passage were convincing enough to fool people who thought they knew every inch of that road, and I'm talking about the folks who've driven on it from the Hollywood Hills all the way to the ocean. You have to know the tricks. You have to drive on it fast. At night. Preferably in the rain. En route are a million dark rendezvouses. Yellow-eyed coyotes and bobcats spy on your missions from the brush. You might find a corpse, or deposit one. You might even find one of Charlie Sheen's hijacked Benzes. (Two, so far.)

In sum, Mulholland is a great place to get hardboiled.

———————

(This was written at the request of editor John Schoenfelder to support the launch of the [then-] brand-new Mulholland Books website. It's probably still there...)

THE FINGER

I didn't know it at the time, but my personal monster had flown all the way to Minnesota to murder a woman I had never met, didn't even know. Dead, just because she had phoned me to harass me on behalf of a bank, in dutiful pursuit of one of many outstanding loans. Her job had been working one of those soulless telephonic rat-runs as the voice of authority who "only wants to help you", which is enough to cheese off any normal human.

How I came to have a personal monster is preamble.

In Los Angeles, very few people are pedestrians by choice. But when you walk the avenues and side streets as traffic whizzes past, you notice things on the ground the speed demons will never see, and thus never even consider. Like found objects, for example.

I have a collection.

Stray, random items out in the wilds of the world have always fascinated me. Discards, junk, oddments, lost possessions. A dead-bolt, all by itself with no door. A wristwatch with no band, which has ceased to function, cast away not into a bin, but stranded in the world, on the street. Mostly small things—not trash-heaped computer monitors or old furniture, but discoveries you can hold in your hand. A broken porcelain satyr missing a leg. Half a string of fake, formerly flashy costume jewels. Pirate booty at ground level.

Once this object had been new. It rolled off an assembly line or craftsman's table and was packaged to sparkle and attract the consumer eye. *Yeah, I need one of those.* Someone desired it. It appealed to a purpose. It got unwrapped and used. Then it failed, or was replaced by something better, or became lost by accident to end its days in the wilderness, the realm outside of the comfort of a speeding automobile. Forsaken, forgotten to all except those who had learned to watch the ground with a treasure-hunter's eye.

You could make up stories about found objects. Like the enigmatic single shoe, perched on the median, or swept to the curb, or just sitting there on the sidewalk begging the question, *what happened to the other shoe?* Everybody has seen that single shoe at one time or another in their life. There are more shoes on Earth than people, right? Even the least imaginative of us concoct, in passing, a narrative for that single shoe, because it just seems so odd.

The weirdest part is that when you inevitably see two abandoned shoes together, it seems even stranger.

More often than not, the attraction was a cheat—a shard of cigarette foil crumpled just so, as to suggest a more interesting shape, or a broken bottleneck catching the light. Then, next to the useless junk, you'd find a key. Where was the lock? They key had a purpose and was ready to perform its function, but the lock was gone or irrelevant. What if the key had been lost inadvertently? Then it would still unlock something. What did it no longer protect?

A spent brass shell casing, headstamped *Federal .38 Special.* A story there, for sure.

I got the Valley Village house when Samantha left me. She took the more expensive place way out in Agoura, halfway to Santa Barbara. She took the more expensive car. Hers was the bigger bank account, so she saw her entitlements as equitable. Her deadbeat children were still living with her, as far as I knew, way out in that suburban purgatory. I like being close enough to the city to feel its rhythms and pulse. Samantha hated the traffic. I would walk a mile for groceries and she detested having to drive a block and a half just for extra milk. The lesson seemed to be not to get involved with a partner who has a previous life, but how often is that going to come your way? Friends and lovers all arrive with baggage and damage, and the challenge of human relationships is the quest to find a co-operative compromise whereby their "ins" fit your "outs".

For example, the offspring from her previous marriage did not seem like a deal-breaker at the time. They bailed early. Minors when we married, they were now adults by definition (if not in practice), supposed grown-ups who only manifested around birthdays, holidays, or any other period that provided a good excuse to ask for more money. When Samantha and I split, they had simply moved back in with her. Not my headache, not any more.

I had the cheaper car, the back-up house, and an aborted career as a software developer and website designer, which is the 21st Century nomenclature for "unemployed" the way Hollywood screenwriters who were "between projects" were accepted as jobless. They made up their stories, and I made up mine, and neither of us, it seemed, was getting paid for anything these days.

The housing crash flipped the mortgage on my modest home, but banks could not foreclose the entire country all at once, even if they preferred the neatness of such a coup. It seemed unfair that the nation could raise its debt ceiling, but I couldn't. The government wasn't paying its bills, so why should I? The tension had stretched out to three years and counting, and while know-nothings nattered about things "getting better", I saw no physical evidence of such an optimistic rally.

Walking allowed mindspace, a vent, a chance to air out my head.

I found the finger right at the corner of Ventura and Whitsett, a stone's throw from the LA River, poking up from a clump of stubborn weed. The lot had been cleared by the demolishment of yet another brick and mortar bookstore, and was engirded by the usual sagging chain-link fence and plywood construction signs heralding the imminent arrival of something better than a bookstore. The dirt had remained unturned long enough for tendrils of green kyllinga to take hold and break surface, and the finger had been lifted from horizontal by the growth until it was nearly upright, as though it was giving *me* the finger, personally, because no one else would ever notice it.

Hey. Fuck you!

It was white and desiccated. Middle finger, definitely. Both knuckles intact. Nicotine-coloured nail, chipped. Humanoid if not human. Sawn off right at the base of the metacarpal bone. Shreds of decomposed flesh, there, but long deprived of moisture. It presented no biological threat; it was dead and dry, almost mummified. Deactivated. I wrapped it up in a shred of newspaper—another common trash item we would soon forget altogether.

Twenty or thirty possible stories there, no doubt. Maybe I could frame it in a light-box for display. People might ask what the story was and would believe anything I'd care to invent.

Except as soon as I got it home, the damned thing started growing.

———————

The morning ritual went something like this: Put on sweats. Acquire coffee. Activate monitors. Delete spam, skip blather. Note how few, if any, messages relate to fresh work, then click directly to the latest news of my own imminent job doom. Reconsider smoking. Troll uselessly around the Internet for a stray hour or so in an attempt to feel better about the fact that I was becoming obsolete *while I watched*, within my own lifetime.

Dither the spec projects for another hour. Check snail mail.

Go for a walk.

In the time it took to accomplish this well-meaning yet empty industry, the severed finger I had found the day before had changed. Before, it resembled a sad little cartoon penis. Now it had a thumb-like extension of jaundice-colored flesh and looked more akin to a crab claw.

It had also gained a smell—not unpleasant, but the arid, spicy aroma of something alive.

I put it in the refrigerator, inside the hinged transparent hatch for the butter, since I didn't have any butter.

By the following morning—and I'll admit I checked it about a thousand times—the mesh of flesh between the finger and "thumb" had marshalled itself to present the stub of an index finger. A digit, I should say, since it in no way resembled an ordinary human hand. This was more like the talon from a marble statue, bloodless and alabaster, still with that yellow tinge.

Lucerno phoned, leaving a message about some bread-and-butter work helping several digitally-challenged clients zip up fresh formats for their antiquated blogs. Lucerno, who works for some big company I can never remember the name of, had always been kind that way, while my wealthier and more accomplished friends forgot about my existence (or utility) until they needed me to do something for them, like right *now*.

The finger—the thing—had mustered into an entire hand by Thursday. I took pictures of its progress until one morning, it vanished from the fridge.

I found it in the living room, soaking up sunlight like a cat near the sliding glass door to the back yard. It now had a palm, a wrist and part of a forearm. Either I had completely lost my marbles and put it there, or it had shoved its way out of the refrigerator and spider-walked to the nearest heat source. I picked it up and the new fingers, now three plus the thumb, closed gently on my own thumb with no force or threat. It was not a horror movie moment. It was just...odd.

Odd enough that I stuck it into the freezer, in the garage. It did not try to escape, and nestled contentedly among a few frozen steaks and bags of microwave mung. The freezer was large but not huge—you could not have stashed a corpse in there—left to me because it wasn't modern enough for Samantha to claim dibs on it.

I could enumerate all the ways I tried to distract myself, but let's face it: the hand kept regenerating, even while frosted with ice crystals. It grew a shoulder. I installed a padlock onto the freezer.

This was news. I had to keep taking pictures.

From the new shoulder, a wing began to bud.

This seemed to form a pattern, a new urgency that could help reorganise my day-to-day. It had become a project with up-to-the-minute developments that needed to be monitored—a reason, in fact, to get out of bed in the face of a new day that could only offer renewed disappointment on the job front as the calendar eroded in fast-forward and the bills continued to pile up. It worked just fine for me.

Until the morning when I checked the freezer and found the lock hasp broken, and the occupant, gone.

———

I had spent my entire life avoiding this kind of pain. The stress of having your child kidnapped, or seeing your yard suddenly vacant of your favorite pet. You know the million questions already, the ones you use to torture or blame yourself; the journalist's credo—How? Why? When?

I searched the house. Scoured the yard. Crawled under the foundation with a flashlight. Disturbed junk that had a year of dust layered atop it.

The hasp had not merely broken. It had been sundered in two with enough force to dent the freezer lid. The padlock was twisted, on the floor, useless now except as someone else's found object. In another life I would find such a thing and wonder what its story had been.

The crank-style garage window was broken, its metal interstices bent outward.

My internal commotion ate the day, and when the day was over, sleep was an impossibility. There was no authority to whistle up, nobody in a uniform that could be called. This was all mine.

In any house, you grow attuned to the ambient noise. How traffic outside sounds on the inside. How heat or cold makes beams and joists sound off. What sounds belong, and which don't. So at 2:00 AM, I knew instantly that something was going on in the garage. *Clunk, thud.*

I bolted up, flashlight at hand, a gun unboxed from my closet at the ready. It was a little eight-round .380 Bersa Thunder, one of the few bestowals from my late dad. It looked like a purse gun, a toy gun, but at least it was a firearm. It was totally unpapered and I had last fired it on a range over a decade ago, back when Samantha and I were still together and both of us were wondering when the social contract of marriage would reveal unto us its secret plan to make us whole.

That was when Samantha realised she had gotten married not for herself, but for her mother, for appearances, because "that's what people did". She had duly reproduced with someone unworthy, and without a mate of current record she had nothing to look forward to except eventual grandparenthood and death. Or pooching out one last foetus, to reset the whole game. We discussed it; vetoed it. Her career had enabled us to have two homes and sufficient timespace for me to rally my own work ethic. She had risen to head of publicity for a movie studio; more than once I had declined her offer of a subsistence job in the same ratbox, because you just don't want to be around even the most loved and trusted person you know 24/7. She understood that I did not want to be her employee or subordinate. Nevertheless, entropy and stasis worked their sorcery and here we were, living in two separate houses. Our split was too reasonable, almost drained of emotion, because we both knew we were already finished.

I had the .380 because I have never understood how people ever believed they could defend their home turf from one or more intruders by swinging a baseball bat around in the dark. In their underwear. Cite me a single time this technique has succeeded… or kept the home invader from shooting off bat-man's dick with a Glock. Then let's crucify the imbeciles who keep using this cliché in movies and television.

Yeah, I was all about the truth.

Truth was, Samantha was an emotional parasite. She fastened, fed, battened, and traded up. I was the suitable man-thing to do her donkey-work and heavy lifting until deposed by a *more* suitable man-thing. I occupied the "husband slot". Her idiot fifteen-year-old son Ricky once stole my car and tried to hock it. Her seventeen-year-old daughter Shannon once offered me a blow-job to keep quiet about her indiscretions. They were a nest of vipers who would eventually be forced to eat each other, and I needed to escape their toxic family values.

Gun-first, I stealthed into the garage.

Opened the freezer.

There inside, curled up like a slumbering infant, was the finger-critter. It was nearly three feet tall. It had both arms, a torso, wings, legs and a tiny fist-like head. Its rude slash of a mouth was slathered in dry blood. Tissue gobs were clotted into the ebony nails on the claws and feet. And it held a hank of curly, coppery hair in one hand.

Samantha had curly, coppery hair.

I was so shocked by this that I missed the offering that had been left for me on the workbench, also in a pool of blood. It could have been a stray knob of meat from the freezer, but as I lifted it in my hands I knew that at last, finally, I had won my ex-wife's heart.

———

I couldn't concentrate on anything that resembled work.

The creature emerged at dusk. I heard the kitchen door to the garage open and close. Nails scratching on the floor.

Shyly, it peeked around the corner until it saw me sitting at the desk. Then in a rush and a flurry of wingbeats, it was right next to me, tilting its head in curiosity just like a cocker spaniel.

Its flesh was nearly translucent now. Fine blue veins. Its eyes were pupil-less black orbs. I wanted to blast off from my chair to clutch the ceiling like a cartoon cat. It sniffed me, hesitantly. Then it yawned, stretching, its wings unfurling and shuddering slightly at the apex of extension. It worried its claws together in a peculiar watchmaker's gesture, rocking from foot to foot.

"Hi there," I said. My body wanted to die.

But it perked up at the sound of my voice, stopped rocking, and commenced an even odder up-and-down motion. I've seen lizards do it.

It *smiled*. Its mouth was full of needled teeth and it still had dry blood on its chin.

Okay, what was the procedure, here?

"So what do I call you?" I said. "What *are* you?"

It seemed to enjoy the sound of my voice.

I almost asked if it was hungry. Bad idea.

"What do you need? Do you need to go out?"

It shook its head *no*. The move was so simple, so human that it stopped me cold. Stupid question. If it wanted out, it would go out.

It kept looking around my body to see the computer screens. I clicked to change the image and captured his complete attention.

I decided to name him Bob.

When the police showed up to inform me of the murder of my ex-wife, I thanked the dark lords that they had not come bearing a search warrant, since her fresh DNA was spread all over my garage, and they might have confabulated a few idle questions about the little gargoyle sleeping in my freezer, too.

I cleaned Bob up and pitched all the incriminating evidence into the Hollywood reservoir. Bob just brought it back the next day. Then he brought me parts of Shannon and Ricky.

He also developed a preference for long-form, multi-arc television dramas—the modern soap opera dolled up with feature film production values and presented to a non-discerning viewership as something exciting and new. It kept him happily occupied when he wasn't napping in the freezer or off on one of his midnight sorties. Religion, as Marx said, is the opiate of the masses, and nostalgia is the soma of the vanquished, but television remains an ideal babysitter, even for your own little monster.

Regretfully, I was already thinking about how to kill Bob. He could not be restrained or deactivated. He seemed to slaughter according to his own interior hourglass. No matter how I disposed of his little keepsakes, he brought them back because they were, well, for me. So I had to destroy them instead, chopping up one and flushing it down the toilet, and shoving another into the maw of the garbage disposal, which clogged and began to back up the kitchen sink. I'd never be able to scotch all the invisible evidence even a lazy forensics team might find. In due course, representatives of law enforcement returned to convey the sad news about Shannon and Ricky, and this time I was scheduled for an interview and asked not to leave town.

As I returned from my interrogation some dipshit in a long-cab Ram 3500 with "truck balls" dangling from the trailer hitch almost T-boned me coming off the 101 as he tried to change lanes and text at the same time. Bob brought back a heart…and the fake balls. He snuggled up to them while sleeping in the freezer as though they were his own personal hacky-sack.

Bob slept in the freezer because I had put him there. The cold did not bother him. He never seemed to eat while I was watching. When the faceless female voice called to pester me about my payment plans, Bob decamped for nearly a day and a half. In my own (intact) heart I knew Bob had flown all the way to Minnesota to disembowel some anonymous drone whose crap job was to hector me. And while this seemed horrific, I could not deny the notion felt really good. Bob was vitally in tune with my feelings. Bob wanted to eliminate anyone and everyone who made me feel bad about myself. He never asked for anything, not that he could speak. He fed, if he ate at all, out of my sight—probably while eviscerating whomever had pissed me off that day. When he wasn't sleeping he watched TV and hung out, always vaguely interested in whatever I was doing. His presence in the house was utterly non-threatening. In a darker humor, I wished for a burglar to chance along…not that I had anything worth stealing.

And really, how many people annoy you? Do you ever run out of candidates?

The loudmouth ahead of you in line at the supermarket. The street loon who wants change, smokes and a chance to tell you his whole tragedy. The bartender who blows you off or the potential lover who adjudges you as not young, rich, or attractive enough. Jehovah's Witnesses.

Killing Bob had something to do, I was sure, with cutting off his long white fingers. Bob did not like scissors, clippers, or anything that resembled them. I'd had to calm him down once when I was power-shredding another dunning letter from a credit card company.

I could not sneak up on him and hope to mutilate him. He had never done anything bad to me.

Define love, now. What are its covenants? Strip away the fantasies, lies and bullshit, and tell me what love really is; how it is expressed. Love is acceptance, tolerance, compromise, co-ordination, and the warmth generated by the subtle dovetailing of those qualities. A comfort zone; a safe house against the brutal world at large. Love requires patience and maintenance.

Which is why I am writing this down on non-edged paper with a soft pencil, behind the locked door of a maximum-security cell. One too many visits from the police is all it takes to get you where I am now. And I wait, because you have to be willing to wait for the best things that ever happen to you. I am waiting for the soft sound of friendly claws, scratching at the window beyond the bars.

Bob will come.

He loves me.

....

Why You'll Never See
Crow Chronicle
(Even Though You'd Like To)

(2003)

As the tenth anniversary of the feature film *The Crow* crutches up upon cinemaphiles, a few observations:

Ten years after its theatrical debut, *The Crow* stands as something of a landmark, in that there remain more than sixty fan sites up and running, with current content regarding the original film and its various sequels and spinoffs. While much of this content is rumor-based or the result of wishful thinking by hardcore fans, the fact remains that *The Crow* is very much alive on the internet...and without the emotional connection many fans feel to the spirit and personality of Brandon Lee, these sites would have bitten the dust long ago. It is that sense of tragedy and longing (extrapolated from equivalent emotions, as expressed in James O'Barr's original comic book), as well as the fundamental zeitgeist experienced by many fans who were first impacted by the film as teenagers, that has perpetuated the *Crow* mythos into the 21st Century, when other mega-hits and mega-grossers of 1994 have faded into the lagan of distant movie memory. Stop and ask yourself how much of a contemporary Goth scene would exist today, without the underlying influence of *The Crow*.

The preceding decade has seen the concurrent boom of the DVD medium as a preferred choice—it is now the way most people will see most movies. The "golden age" (if we may call it that) of DVD supplements is already on the wane, the victim of increasing regulation and prohibitive costs. Interviewees now demand fees for participation in DVD supplements, because they have been at it long enough to realize that only the studios make money from enhanced or special editions; there is no trickle-down of profit to the participants who formerly offered their time or memorabilia for free. Most DVD supplements have coalesced to glorified EPK (electronic press kit) content, massaged so as to appear more "special" than it actually is, and utilizing the hyperbolic adjectives deployed during the glory days of truly incisive behind-the-scenes extras, to ballyhoo what is, in most cases, a fluffed-up version of the same boring, superficial, cotton-candy gossip and blather one can endure forever on *Entertainment Tonight,* or the depthless publicity pieces that present themselves, essentially, as breathless shills for the newer movies seen on any cable channel.

Overshadowed by its own controversy and tragedy, *The Crow*—the original film—seemed ripe for in-depth examination. By late 2000, multiple issues on laserdisc and DVD offered pallid extras, mostly the same EPK footage, endlessly recycled, often in poor taste (see *"Brandon Lee's Last Interview!"*). The prime mover of the film, director Alex Proyas, had remained determinedly mum on the whole topic, a stone wall against endeavors to delve more deeper into background. Thus, the collators of information, severely limited as to available resources, fell back on repackaging orts and leftovers—details on the comic book, or third-party reminiscences from lower-rung production functionaries more than willing to talk in exchange for a fleeting moment inside a previously-denied spotlight. Such exploitation-of-opportunity has, over the years, deeply biased what is known about *The Crow*. It's not the whole story, but it's just *one* story, if you follow.

It took Mark Rance, of Three-Legged Cat Productions, to convince Alex Proyas otherwise, and the only way to do it was through Mark's capable administration of all the supplements for the DVD of *Dark City*, Proyas' next feature after *The Crow*. A measure of trust and professionalism had been established, and that, in turn, opened up a meager window of one-time opportunity. Frustrated at the limited or prejudiced blow-by-blows that constituted the film's history up to this point, Proyas agreed to go on record for the first and sole time...with the proviso that he could wield veto power over any and all of the supplements suggested for a new and definitive presentation of *The Crow* on DVD. The timing was good, too—Miramax, the studio of record, was interested in providing a *Crow* boxed set in the wake of their second straight-to-video sequel.

The production of a self-published book by an E! Channel publicity flack (*The Crow: The Story Behind the Film*, by Bridget Baiss) only strengthened the resolve of the principal players to do it right, for once. These principal players compared notes and unilaterally declined to service the book, which was correctly seen as an opportunistic hack-job.

The double-disc for the *Crow* portion of the boxed set, as architectured by Mark Rance, was a rich cornucopia indeed. In addition to deleted and alternate footage, a stimulating new interview with *Crow* founder O'Barr in his own cellar, a reworking of the EPK footage into its originally intended (and never-seen) format, plus other extras, Mark assembled a wall-to-wall audio commentary track, consisting of contributions by Proyas, me (as screenwriter), Darius Wolski (director of photography), Alex McDowell (production designer) and Simon Murton (art director).

Then Mark, who had been vetted to me by Proyas, asked if I had "anything else."

While on set for the duration of principal photography, before, during, and after the accident that killed Brandon Lee, I had shot over 16 hours of videotape detailing aspects of the production from several weeks prior to the shoot, all the way through to the day before the accident. Mark suggested I assemble elements of this footage into a sort of visual diary of the production, and after a helluva lot of time at an editing board, the 90-minute version of *Crow Chronicle* was born.

During 102 days in Wilmington, North Carolina (for what was originally to be a 54-day shoot), I also shot about 150 black and white photographs. I shot numerous studies of Brandon Lee in various poses to provide reference for storyboard artist Peter Pound. (I also made Brandon do a standing backflip 14 times so I could adequately capture a triptych of the jump, not having a motor drive for the camera.) Peter, in turn, did able duty as my backup cameraman. All the footage was shot onto VHS masters, which imparted a "warm" look to the footage not available from the newer and more discriminating digital cameras available at the time. Mark and I reviewed the masters and found them to be in excellent shape for re-mastering onto huge 1-inch cassettes.

(More scandal, here. Some of my footage, assembled in Wilmington as a sort of "video postcard" of the ongoing production, found its way to the expected tabloid outlets after the accident, where it was misinterpreted, completely out of context, to serve the most salacious needs of yellow journalism. How did this happen? It was stolen. Who stole it? I subsequently found out who turned a cheap dime off this theft, and rest assured that retribution is staring them in the face even now. These maggots currently live and breathe among you, falsely confident that the passage of time will obscure their crimes. They're wrong.)

Unexpectedly, Alex approved *Crow Chronicle* with one or two microscopic edits. He informed me that he was as surprised as anyone to rediscover how interesting it was. Where Mark and I had steeled ourselves for a deluge of modifications, Alex had given us his unconditional blessing. *Crow Chronicle* would transport the viewer right onto the set, to witness the first shooting of the very first scene (Tin-Tin [Laurence Mason] banging on the door of the pawnshop). To be on the soundstage the first time Brandon was introduced to the crows. To be on the streets of the Carolco backlot as McDowell, Murton and I spray-painted graffiti all over the buildings. To be perched atop the building false-front across the street when we blew the pawnshop all to hell (with a blast that rocked us, 80 feet in the air, and nearly toppled us from our precarious foothold). To agonize through the eleven takes it took to keep Brandon in focus during the Funboy bedroom scene. To see Brandon joking with the camera crew ("Hey, I've been out of focus most of my life"), then performing a recitation of *The Ballad of Reading Gaol* while setting up for the Gideon scenes in the pawnshop. To wince at the thousands of rounds fired per take in what the script called the Big Moby Shootout, or Death Cleans House (so loud that it caused the videotape to "ripple;" so pollutive, in the confines of the Ideal Cement Factory [where the set was built], that we had to blow out the gunsmoke after each take in order to breathe, or, you know, light cigarettes). Viewers would be able to see Brandon's birthday (lunch break on the first shoot day) and watch him go nose-first into his own painted *Crow* cake ("I gave myself a kiss," he said). A long montage in the makeup trailer documented Michael Berryman's transformation into the Skull Cowboy, a character later deleted wholly from the scenario. In addition, my video camera doubled duty as the "playback" machine for all the second-unit shots, under producer and effects supervisor Andrew Mason (today the producer of such things as *Red Planet, Queen of the Damned, Scooby-Doo*, and—oh yes— those *Matrix* sequels).

We even had the entire liquor store robbery by 12-year-olds "Axel" and "Chopper," a scene which nobody had the balls to include on any of the DVDs.

All for nothing.

Because when Miramax backpedaled on their signed agreement with Proyas—the one giving him veto power over the supplements—and tried to supercede his wishes, Proyas withdrew comprehensively, once and for all.

Because I enjoy Alex's trust (and a lot of people don't), I had to withdraw with him. My decision, your loss.

Ed Pressman briefly toyed with the idea presented to him by Andrew Mason, of releasing *Crow Chronicle* as a stand-alone disc. We re-edited the *Chronicle* into a very punchy one-hour form, much better and more inclusive than the 90-minute version.

Again, all for nothing.

Because time had passed, and now the morass of permissions and clearances needed to authorize *Crow Chronicle* against possible litigation (from anyone who appeared in it, however briefly) had become an insurmountable obstacle to its release if it was not under the sanctioned Miramax umbrella protecting the supplements on the official DVD set. Remember the changing tides of supplements, mentioned above? They re-conformed into a stone wall.

More time passed. The DVD boxed set was released with a hurried rescue action to fill the holes left by the deleted *Crow Chronicle*. The hero version of the EPK was swiftly re-edited to exclude Proyas and myself, in a kind of nasty, last-minute knife-twist that suggests the heightened emotions involved on the corporate end. Lawsuits were threatened. Goons were dispatched to Three-Legged Cat to scoop up materials, like DEA thugs tossing an apartment for dope. The audio commentary was globally replaced by an eleventh-hour track by Jeff Most and John Shirley (the original screenwriter).

No matter, apparently, since *Crow* fans had gained enough new material, overall, to perpetuate their speculative discussions and prolong the vitality of their websites.

So, today, *Crow Chronicle* resides in an archive, not five feet from where I type this, destined to remain in shadow, glimpsed by very few people outside of the immediate production "family." Does it have value for *Crow* fans? Undoubtably. Will the weather change and provide a new opportunity down the road? Not likely. One could say that the world had its chance for Alex Proyas to speak his piece...and the world blew it. This was one juncture where the vast legions of *Crow* fans might have made a difference, might have spoken up, might have made their desires known...and they stayed quiet, for the most part, tending their shrines to the memory of Brandon Lee, not wanting to consider alternate points of view, because a decade has passed and *they* have become the myth-makers, with little interest in anything that contradicts their carefully-crafted revisionism of what I know only as historical fact.

Sure, I'm biased, too. But the difference is, I was there when it all happened. And you weren't.

Clearance problems with the work-print edit of the actual film also contributed to the demise of *Crow Chronicle*. In tandem with the longer-running and differently-edited work-print, *Crow Chronicle* might have enhanced the alternate material into the kind of experience collectors enjoy. However, today, hardcore fans of the DVD medium would probably spend more time criticizing the occasional dodgy picture quality or iffy sound (much-enhanced by the wizards at Three-Legged Cat, but still, in some cases, less than crystal-clear) than appreciating the rare opportunity to look backward in time, using the keyhole vantage of new material and interviews on a film that did not have that much "extra" material to begin with. *Crow* fans hungry for more shots of Brandon Lee would inevitably be disappointed by footage in which he did *not* appear—shots of Wrench Street as it was being built (in broad daylight), or the church and cemetery sets after they were destroyed by an untimely hurricane, or the original set of Darla's apartment, built inside a tenement in downtown Wilmington and never used (a much-cleaned-up, substitute set was built later on the Carolco soundstage, but it was very different, and a lot less grungy. That's the one you see in the film.). It's interesting stuff, but not controversial enough to fuel renewed arguments in chat rooms or on message boards.

For film scholars, movie aficionados, and people who love *The Crow* without an agenda, it's still a loss. And somehow, that just increases the air of sadness that hovers, to this day, over the whole enterprise. I got a ton of response to the whole DVD debacle, which is best reflected in the sentiments offered by a fellow named David Kann: *"I am a Prop guy and have been for eleven years. This tragedy hit my profession hard, and every time I do a show with guns I think of what happened that night and make absolutely sure it won't happen again while I'm on a show. I don't know why I'm telling you this, except that Crow fans, myself included, look at the Chronicle and commentary you talked about as perhaps some closure to a film which has changed so many lives."*

———

(Alex Proyas finally did a somewhat neutered, stand-alone solo commentary track for the 2011 Blu-Ray release of The Crow. *Of the accepted "ten commandments" of movie gun safety today, six of them are a direct result of the* Crow *tragedy. A sizzle reel of a portion of* Crow Chronicle *was repeatedly bootlegged online [with no sound], but you'll have to trust me when I say the original footage was luminous.*

You'll have to trust me because even now, over twelve years after this article was written, you probably still won't get a chance to see it.)

TWO SCOOPS

Totally Eighties Marty primped. His skin-tight parachute pants terminated in Felony Fliers of two different colors for a distinct, though subtle mime-clown effect that whispered "performance artist" to the world at large. White linen jacket (sleeves cuffed; the sun had faded them), pastel cartoon tee, big moby hair. He scratched his nose. Smooth. His butt was packed so tight it felt like it needed to sneeze. There was gym time in his future. He preferred not to remember any time when Quiet Riot did not totally rool. At age 55-and-a-half he remained confident that his band demo, his novel-in-progress, his proposal for a reality series would blast off and soar him into the revenue bracket he had always deserved, had, in fact, labored his entire life to achieve. Image was important. Losers would never dare to wear bike shorts with cowboy boots. Losers never jerked off in the shower every morning so the contour of their penis would lie as an artful bulge, just so. Losers never got laid with the frequency of Totally Eighties Marty, or so he maintained.

The band demo just needed a *teensy* bit more tweaking; the first 30 pages of the novel had been rewritten forty times over ten years and were *excellent*; and the TV show's logline, précis, synopses and beats were completed within the secure vault of Totally Eighties Marty's brain, since his last zillion-dollar idea had been plagiarized, although he never filed any sort of complaint, because it was too sensitive an issue, to this day. "Creatives" often got emotional about their intellectual property.

Totally Eighties Marty checked his Swatch as the black-on-black limousine tooled into the dead-end alleyway that was tonight's rendez. He positioned himself so the back door lights from the Chinese restaurant would silhouette him dramatically, his visage only showing in the orange glow from his Gauloise when he puffed, not completely inhaling.

The full title of the eatery was Hung Won's Rodded Ten Tigers of Canton. There was no on-site personage named Hung Won, and those who answered the phone for takeout orders invariably said "rotted tigers." If you requested snow peas, the staff would comply by making sure that you had…no peas. And so on.

Presentation, Marty knew, was everything.

The limo disgorged a pair of bull-necked shaved apes, one black, one white, otherwise identical. Between these two ballbusters, the gentleman whom Marty had come to meet made his entrance with style and flourish, which Marty appreciated, because Marty was a connoisseur.

The man stepped out on designer shoes that cost roughly as much as a Manhattan condo. When his tailored suit rustled, Marty could hear money. The man had a monocle, a Homburg, a walking stick, an eyepatch, and a generous amount of facial scar tissue. He appraised Marty with his single arctic blue orb, which caught the light like a silver coin.

"I am Hans Bierfurz," the man said in an almost comically Prussian accent. "You would be the one they call…Scoop?"

"That's me, boss." Totally Eighties Marty grinned to show off his caps, since his handshake was disdained. "But you can call me Mikey."

The real Mikey had last dozed off with the help of a bludgeon laid across the back of his skull. When he woke up, he was inside a freezer and had grown a scruffy tumbleweed of beard. It smelled really bad in the freezer, like a toilet needing bleach, like decomposing meat that might be Mikey.

Dark and spooky, in that upright casket.

He thumped and hollered. His voice was whittled away to an icy croak. Every movement felt as though drain cleaner was being pumped through his nerve network.

The rubberized gasket on the freezer door disintegrated as the door was wrenched open and Mikey fell to the floor, fetal and shivering. He was naked except for a besmirched hospital johnnie and several IV hoses yanked taut behind him. His vanilla ass was exposed. He saw a long icicle that had formed from the end of his penis. It snapped off as he tumbled. The icicle was bigger.

"Jesus H. Jupiter, this must be some kind of miracle!" boomed a voice from above him, rattling the slush in his ears.

Mikey squinted up into the Santa-from-Hell face of his chosen medical professional, Doc Auto. The fluorescents above made the Doc into just another monster shadow from the pit. The light was no less merciless than physical blades cleaving Mikey's retinas in twain.

"You smell notably ripe," said Doc Auto.

"Mnahh hummina groky splaaa," said Mikey.

"Hold on a second." The Doc produced a small, squared-off device with round corners and a blank screen. "Your voice isn't used to talking. This will help translate."

Still balled on the floor in his own barfwater, Mikey struggled to repeat his entreaty. After a moment the iPhone talked in a sterile, feminine voice: *"What dad pluck happened at me?"*

"Take it slow, boyo. Fantasia can interpret your glottals only so far." A Tootsie Pop parted company with the Doc's lips, making the moist sound of interrupted sex. "Let's get you cleaned and up to date. You've been asleep since 2006, you know."

Mikey fainted.

Mikey woke up. This crap was not like cinema's dreamy, buoyant flow back to wakefulness. Bang to black, and the next thing he knew he was still staring at Doc Auto. From the fresher stains on the Doc's smock, Mikey had passed out long enough for the medico to grab lunch.

"One of your creditors thought to mildly nudge your cooperation by bashing you on the back of the head with a chunk of iron rebar. Poor chap panicked, thought he had murdered you, and brought you by my office for disposition. I very nearly sold you to our university's cadaver program, but their offer was lame, and it turned out you still had stubborn signs of life."

Some lovely narcotic was contouring Doc Auto's voice, causing it to speed up to chipmunk prattle and mire down to whale yawn. It was very much like listening to a warped spoken-word LP on bad headphones inside the bowel of a sunken ship.

"You went comatose and unresponsive," the Doc's molasses-to-diarrhea voice continued. "I briefly considered sawing off your head and storing it in liquid nitrogen, but then, if you revived, what would I have? A talking head with no earning skills. You owe me twelve thousand dollars for the fridge, by the way. For the electricity."

Mikey winced at a mirror when he saw the gaunt, lunatic caveperson staring back at him. Doc Auto, too, looked different—he was fifty pounds more robust and his lush Olympian crown of hair and beard had gone completely snow-white.

"That fellow you engaged to find your girlfriend? Franklyn Fuck, the detective? He left this for you about six years ago."

Doc Auto unfurled a coffee-stained invoice which Mikey struggled to read:

FROM: *FUCK*
To: *YOU*
Call when you have money. Fondest regards, FF.

"I gather he did not succeed in tracking down your ladylove before he exceeded his budget," said Doc Auto. "Oh, good, you can still cry. That means your tear ducts are still in proper working order. Mind the towel."

"*Ben hiee norvup gliddy poo mnotlick?*" said Mikey.

The robotic Fantasia phone-voice interpreted: "*Then forgot me everybody hands?*"

"Oh, no. It turns out there is something in the food chain even lower than you. It turns out your shield and standard were taken up, so to speak. There is someone out there *impersonating* you."

Mikey fainted again.

Totally Eighties Marty gave Hans Bierfurz his complete attention, trying not to come across as too hungry.

"It seems you owed money or favors to nearly every independent in the city," said the sartorial Hans Bierfurz. "Until several years ago, when the complexion of your procedure seemed to undergo a…ahh, how shall we call it? A sea change."

"I got good accounting skills," said Totally Eighties Marty. He stood a bit straighter in the presence of the monied European, not so much imitating him as hopelessly aspiring to be him. "I figure, like, see, why run around fucking everything up and pissing off all the criminals?"

Hans Bierfurz stiffened. "We are not criminals."

Totally Eighties Marty spluttered. "Of *course* not! It's just like, I mean, why not see what's needed over *here* and how what's over *there* can be used, and put the two together, synergistically speaking, am I right?"

"You squeak by in the interstices," said Bierfurz wearily. "You get lost in the shuffle and between the file cabinets. You attempt to broker favors you cannot yield and influence you do not wield to address your debts, play both sides against the middle, and emerge with a nice skim because there are always little…oversights. Entrepreneurs—the people you call criminals—have no recourse but to self-govern. And you squeak by, skulking around, wheedling, burrowing, taking crumbs from the tables of your betters. You squeak like a rat, Mikey, or Scoop, or whatever your name is. *Scheisshaus ratten.*"

The towering bodyguards chuckled on cue, one black, one white. Big chess pieces.

"When the esteemed Carelton Casper Leadman was elected mayor of our fair city, he sent the entire NYPD after you in recompense for the damage you inflicted upon his little brother, Bob. Tell me, how did you manage to evade that dragnet?"

Totally Eighties Marty's cheesy expression continued to curdle. "Umm, just lucky, I guess."

"And how did you come upon the sobriquet, 'Scoop'?"

Flecks of panic mucus were starting to accumulate in the corners of Totally Eighties Marty's eyes. "Come again?"

"The nickname. How did you come by that nickname?"

"Err, no idea, really. It's just a name."

"You must have been greatly relieved when Mayor Leadman lost his office due to that unfortunate scandal," said Bierfurz.

"I heard he got beheaded for plooking some fifth grader. None of my business, or doing, chief."

"Quite. Politics hold little interest for me as well. But you are aware there are powerful people who live in the shadows who want your head on a stick. Such as Leadman's brother, Bob. The intimates and seconds of certain other underworld freelancers. And a professional wetworker known only by the name of Angelina." Bierfurz was biting off his consonants hard, now.

"Is this a setup?" Totally Eighties Marty's expression had solidified into a moist bas-relief of Limburger. He was being challenged. It was time to grow a pair...or, in Marty's terms, time to try to imagine what growing a pair would actually be like. To simulate boldness in the absence of the real thing.

"Listen, Mister-whatever," Marty said. "There's eleventy-dozen hard cases trying to kill me all the time, and say, look—I'm still here."

"Retribution does not frighten you. You advantage your debts via the art of the small-time grifter, turning your own dregs into pocket change; consuming your own waste materials. Depressing."

Totally Eighties Marty received this as a compliment. "It's all about survival skills," he boasted. "Y'know if you drink a bottle of hand sanitizer it's the same as plugging down thirty-two shots of vodka? Truth, man. I read that on TotallyFuckingTortured.com."

Bierfurz seemed to experience a mild stab of gas, or nausea, whether from astonishment that the creature before him could read printed words, or the instinctive revulsion felt for an unclean lower life form. It shall never be known.

———

Pollydolly Prudhomme Vickerswitch owned what were perhaps the largest natural breasts on planet Earth. As she straddled Mikey, his entire upper torso was subsumed in mammary tissue, which blocked his view of any of the rest of her. He was drowning in boobage. He was living the dream.

He could feel himself being clamped below by some lubricious vise, ferociously milking him. Distantly he heard sounds that might have been the throes of feminine passion, or a trunk hostage slowly suffocating.

"*Mmmf,*" Mikey said. His own saliva ran down his jaw.

When Pollydolly dismounted, she backed into the light and Mikey got a better gander at her. This vaguely Nordic blonde stood a heroic six-foot-five on gigantic wrestler feet and possessed an impossible eighteen-inch waist. The curvature of her immense ass was planetary, lending her a disturbingly true hourglass shape, as though she had been cinched hard around the waist in youth and her body mass had exploded toward her butt and breasts, having nowhere else to run.

"How's that, sweetie?" she said, still panting laboriously.

Mikey's penis lolled in moist defeat, trying to book a plane ticket to a safe house.

A fleshy *smack* announced Doc Auto's entrance as he slapped Pollydolly on her rump. She coyly pulled the Tootsie Pop (grape) out of his mouth and slid it between her lips.

"I did some reading up on suspended animation," said Doc Auto. "One theory holds that sex is a primal urge, encoded right into the DNA, and is therefore an equally primal motivator toward resuscitation. The little virus that is you *wants to live*, so it can replicate. So we give it an immediate visceral task. That's where Pollydolly comes in. She's a true sensualist."

Pollydolly winked and bit the head off the Tootsie Pop, crunching it up.

"A jump-start," said Mikey. His voice had to battle its way up and out from some icebox down between his lungs.

"Correct," said Doc Auto, his hand remaining spread on Pollydolly's sumptuous left cheek.

Deep in the cozy convolutions of Mikey's stunned cerebrum, the brain skeeters had begun to stir toward renewed life. These imaginary parasites were charged with stoking Mikey's paranoia responses in all situations, and they worked in shifts to maintain perpetual diligence. Now they were waking up, to inflict their first new stings and sup on his watery blood.

"You put me in a refrigerator," said Mikey.

"Correct again. You were in a coma. Plus, I had the spare fridge. Except for the electrical short, it works most of the time."

"Doesn't keep your beverages cold enough," complained Pollydolly, who searched up a bacon-flavored soda and bolted most of the bottle in a single vast gulp, then belched like a Viking in marauder mode.

The brain skeeters reminded Mikey that Doc Auto had said something, sometime this year, about someone else impersonating him.

"Person eating me?" asked Mikey, still trying to fit his skull around his newfound voice.

"Precisely," returned Doc Auto. "Your removal from the world of men apparently left a void, and someone else appeared to fill it. I began to twig when I heard third-party accounts of your continued activities when I knew for a fact you were here, sleeping in the fridge. To be frank—"

Pollydolly looked around for another customer named Frank. After her rodeo-ride on Mikey, which had been scarcely more satisfying than necrophilia, she was beginning to feel a little...restless.

Mikey followed her look, battling to get his own eyes to function in concert.

Doc Auto continued: "—I thought it was residual old business, you know, an echo of your passage, as you shifted from street life to urban legend. Creditors usually take a very long time to let go of their last memory of you, especially if you are in arrears."

Pollydolly perked up when she thought she heard *in our rears*. "You got any sandwiches in this dump?" she asked Doc.

"Old takeout is all, I fear," Doc Auto replied. "Lo mein and two potstickers from Hung Won's Rodded Ten Tigers of Canton—it's actually not bad. Not to worry. I'll procure more comestibles as soon as our friend here is capable of ingesting solid nourishment. In the meantime, your more pressing task is to eat *him*."

The brain skeeters flashed panic as Mikey saw Pollydolly's lip-sticky foodhole opening for him. At his last instant of cannibal fright she changed course for his groin, to mouth him hard for Round Two. He came erect almost immediately; perhaps there was a scientific basis for Doc Auto's postulation on species survival. Then again, Mikey had not been laid for the better part of a decade.

At least she had body temperature, which was more than Mikey had.

———

"Permit me to refresh you," said Hans Bierfurz in his superior, Continental manner. "In brief, Godz is not pleased."

"What gods is not pleased?" said Totally Eighties Marty, totally lost.

"Godz. *The* Godz. Master of all those whom you deride as criminals. The one to whom all underworld debts home. The biggest of big bosses, the top dog, the ultimate authority in this city."

"Never heard of him."

The hardcase bodyguards flinched visibly.

Bierfurz rolled his eye and sighed. "You Americans have never accorded Him the proper respect. He is retired from public life now, and has gone into more lucrative private enterprise. We, all of us, ultimately answer to Him. It is possible that you are so far down on the jungle food chain that you have never personally experienced His magnificence. If the universe were an arena of fairness, you would matter so little that your assorted transgressions would never merit the slightest scintilla of His attention."

"My transmission? I don't even have a car!"

Bierfurz waved off what he hoped was a maladroit bon mot. "The *point* is, Mister Mikey or Scoop or whatever your fellow dirt weasels call you, your capacity for survival against repeatedly insurmountable odds has caught the attention of the one and only Godz. He wants to know how you do it. How, with entire platoons of assassins highly motivated to terminate your sorry existence, you always manage to scoot out from under. Perhaps we should re-christen you as Scoot."

"Like a doggy on a shag carpet," offered the darker bodyguard.

"With the worm trots," said the lighter bodyguard.

"I love shag carpeting!" said Totally Eighties Marty. "It's time that it came back, right? Like a style resurgence."

Bierfurz glared singularly at all of them, his eye tearing with contempt so toxic that he was forced to dab it with fine linen. He felt a reflexive kinship with the mythical poor soul tasked to read the Bard to a catbox full of gibbons. How to get to the point in the presence of this discursive annelid? How to, as Yankees were fond of putting it, cut to the chase? This was a mental challenge of deep subtlety. How could Bierfurz do his job, maintain his dignity, and commence the more joyous pursuit of erasing this Scoop fellow from his memory as soon as possible, especially in time for dinner? His steely eye reluctantly sought the sputtering, dysfunctional neon of the sign proclaiming Hung Won's Ten Rodded Tigers of Canton to the consumer world at large. Bierfurz did not care much for Chinese.

Totally Eighties Marty was lost in a spiel about wood paneling and circular beds, his yammer working a visible bludgeoning effect on Bierfurz's bi-chromatic bodyguards. Even money on which would try to kill him first, just to shut him up.

That was it!

"Stop talking," said Bierfurz. "Pique? Dander? If this man speaks again, please shoot him rather a lot."

Totally Eighties Marty's expression went the tint of good, sweaty Stilton. He snapped his yap faster than a bear trap.

"Now. Godz has invited you to participate in an exploratory interview. You will accept this invitation, happily and promptly, or my minions will scrape your face against that brick wall until you no longer have a head. Nod if you accept. I would counsel that you nod immediately."

The speed of a paint shaker could not compete with the alacrity of Totally Eighties Marty's nod.

"Hey, Abbott," Mikey said weakly.

"Crawl up my chute," Abbott shot back. "Do you know how sick I am of that freakin' joke? A lifetime of *hey, Abbott!* It's so goddamned old that nobody knows what it means anymore."

Life can be cruel, and the cruelty inflicted upon Abbott N. Costello was not as bad in theory as, say, being lumbered with the name Butts or Bungwipe or Pustule. Its torments were more subtle and infinite. Abbott was pleased that his parents had died horribly. Strangers expected him to manifest as a weirdo throwback in pinstripe and wingtips, dispensing impenetrable period slang about skirts and heaters and everything being "jake," willfully overlooking the fact that living in the middle of a World War before the introduction of sulfa drugs or pure penicillin was a berth to which only a nitwit would aspire.

Worse, strangers would assume somebody named Abbott N. Costello might be from the mystical other-realm of Noir, where the dames were all femmes fatales and every 'bo was on the chisel. It was a legendary place where the sun didn't shine—literally. An alimentary fantasyland.

Abbott N. Costello strove to be a realist. "You're looking trim," he told Mikey. "You've lost some weight." Empty compliments always encouraged your subject to lead the conversation.

"I'm a scarecrow," said Mikey, his throat sore, his body microwaved, his organs seemingly rearranged by a blind autistic. "I've been on ice for…a long time. Out of the loop. I need to know what's what."

Once Doc Auto had limbered up his shipwrecked corpus and pumped him full of a cocktail of painkillers and vitamins—all carefully enumerated on Mikey's yard-long bill—the burly medico had deemed him fit to rejoin society on his quest to learn more about the specter who had assumed his identity. Plus, as the Doc said, he really needed the fridge back. By chance, the only name that had swum forth from the rapidly smoothing convolutions in Mikey's besieged brain had been a mnemonic special—Abbott N. Costello. Once comfortable in the subterrane of bagmen and bookies, Costello had been downsized out of work by ex-mayor Leadman's obsession with a paperless economy (less paper, less evidence, or so Leadman mistakenly thought, to his peril). Costello was thirty-eight and looked sixty, stooped of posture, sagging as the world bulldogged his shoulders. He was infamous for his eczema. A lifetime of drugstore spectacles had pinched his cranium in the middle, corseting his mad preacher hairdo. He had liverish lips and spoke wetly. Mikey envied him the saliva.

"What's what is the economy forced me to diversify," said Costello. "The internet was a godsend for credit fraudsters. Type a couple of numbers and the bills are paid. A monkey could do it. A dickless monkey. A retarded dickless monkey with spasms. But it's such a slick scam, and it's so huge that it's undeniable. Wave of the future and all that. It buys your time back for, y'know, contemplation and introspection and shit."

Mikey longed to release a contemplative shit. A truly liberating power dump to cleanse his lost calendar. But his creaking, haunted house metabolism was not ready...yet. A major toilet event might still cause his heart to explode.

"Eight *years*," he croaked. "More, even. What happened?"

"Don't you find it odd that the economy fell apart at about the same time as you took your nappy trip into coma-land?" said Costello.

Their rendezvous was the most anonymous diner in what used to be called Hell's Kitchen (the attempts to re-name the area Clinton or Mid-Town were just one way the municipal gentrification effort had failed miserably), the kind of Greek joint where the dyspeptic waiter brought your coffee with his thumb inside the cup. Costello chowed away on a mound of biology camouflaged by what the specials board called "gravy;" Mikey could barely stand to gaze at the half-glass of cloudy water in front of him. He thirsted bottomlessly, but choking down fluid was still an epic challenge.

"I don't follow," he said.

Costello plucked what seemed to be an excessively curly pubic hair from the amoebic abomination on his plate. "See, I got this theory. It's based on that whole idea that Nature abhors a vacuum. So here you are—*were*—tootling along, causing trouble, getting every crime boss and killer in the city after your hide, one-upping them, like slapjack. But then you disappear, and after a coupla years, these dicks stop looking for you; they assume one of the other guys got you, they write you off, whatever. So, nobody is trying to kill you today, because everybody has moved on. The upside is you don't owe any money."

"Except to Doc Auto. So far, I'm liking this scenario."

"Yeah, *except...*" Costello polished his bent fork on a paper napkin but still could not dislodge a bit of crud that had been vulcanized to its surface during the last dishwasher run-through. "...there's inertia. Entropy. Your being the lowest animal on the totem pole gave a lot of people motivation. Kept many gainfully employed. The argument could be made that we have to get you back *into* hot water so the whole cosmic balance of the universe ain't disruptified."

"Except that some other idiot took my place."

"Exactly! Nature abhors a vacuum! Are you hearing me yet? You're that single grain of sand on the beach, the one poets used to talk about when people could still read. Move the single grain, you set up a different pattern, and everything in the world is changed. I heard that on some TV show, I think. Anyway, the point is, if you did not exist it would be necessary to create you."

Mikey stared at Costello dumbly. "The galaxy depends upon it."

"*Now* you're getting the bigger picture!"

"So…I'm so necessary, that if I drop out of sight, a Mikey-shaped hole is filled by another, bogus version of me by the secret masters of the universe?"

Costello nodded, re-attacking his excuse for food.

Mikey nodded along with him. "That is, hands-down, the stupidest goddamned thing I have ever heard in my entire life, and that *includes* a UFO abduction I'm not sure really happened, either."

Costello shrugged broadly. "Life is stupid; whaddaya want from me?" He leaned forward to invite confidentiality. "You were abducted by aliens, too?"

"Long story." Mikey tentatively sipped his water, which tasted soapy.

"You're like Rip Van Winkle Lite."

"You've been in circulation, A.C., I haven't. So—how would I be most likely to get a look at this poseur who thinks he's me?"

The brain skeeters reminded Mikey that for the first time, he had been presented with the concept of something even lower than himself on that cursed totem pole. Somebody whose head would be just below Mikey's ass, and shit always plops downhill.

While Costello ruminated on possible answers, Mikey made the social error of trying to fill the silence with more conversation, a flaw of people who never had anything to say, yet never stopped talking in a doomed quest to buttress lousy self-esteem. "So, Abbott N.

Costello. I guess you've been asked this a million times, but what's the 'N' stand for?"

Costello's brow furrowed, then darkened into an oncoming thunderhead. "Norma," he said. "Long story."

────────────

The Deuce had died decades ago, just as Hell's Kitchen had. The 42nd Street murderer's row of grindhouses and sex emporia had caved in to the nagging demands of civic disdain, core renewal, overpriced development, and most importantly of all, the need to fleece Big Apple visitors of discretionary income. No longer could one enjoy the sights of used needles in the gutter, whores on the stalk, hustlers on lupine lookout for victims, or the "supermarket of sex" offered by such defunct adults-only wonderlands as Porn Again or XXX-Mecca. A Laugh Factory now stood in the space formerly occupied by the mighty Show World—five floors of hootchie-koo, peep booths and amenities for that contingent of the populace too early to succumb to the bounty of the internet, for reasons best left to future anthropologists. The bums sleeping in refrigerator boxes had all relocated to the garment district (better picking in the bins there, during winter). Now it was as though Walt Disney had retrofitted a concentration camp into a kid-friendly tourist attraction, and Totally Eighties Marty paused in a moment of silent eulogy for a lost and, to him, superior era.

He stood mid-block between 6th and 8th Avenues, where a single lone sentry from more stimulating times held fast. Across the street waited the marquee of the old Eros Nightingale, unlit and waned to the cancerous yellow of rotting teeth. It did not beckon. The security gate was kicked in and half-closed (the only remaining position permitted by its dysfunction), which acted as a sort of dam for accumulated litter and the occasional dead body.

On the marquee: *Blood Enema Butcher, Homos Walk Among Us*, and *Blacktopus* (*"Eight New Ways to Die, Yo!"*).

Encoffined within the cataracted ticket kiosk was a skeletal figure of indeterminate sex who might have been an animatronic puppet, its moves herky-jerky and unimpeded by grace or nutrition. Closer scrutiny coded this guardian as female, done up in baby-doll flapper drag—a fright wig with a jaunty bow, malignant beauty spot, and about twenty layers of foundation troweled on like spackle to provide a rough canvas for the purely illustrated illusion of red Betty Boop lips and wholly absent genuine eyebrows. From Totally Eighties Marty's view of her in the booth, it was very possible that she did not exist from the waist down.

"Ya want, fuckface?" the apparition wheezed.

"I want to buy a ticket, lady," said Totally Eighties Marty, just stiffly enough to advertise what he mistook for dignity.

"Who the fuck are you?" It was like watching a mummy from the Thirties suddenly come to zombie life.

"Name's Scoop, but you can call me Mikey," he winked.

"The fuck does that mean to me, asshole?"

"Ticket," said Totally Eighties Marty. "I'm here to see the Big G."

"Oh," said the haggard woman-thing, with an expression that suggested a fart had just blown up the wrong internal pathway. "In that case, that'll be five hundred fuckin dollars." She swigged from a transparent flask of turbid brown liquid that was either rotgut or formaldehyde, probably both.

Totally Eighties Marty took a backward step in shock. "Five hundred bucks?"

The beef-jerky-and-Brillo enchantress on the other side of the milky bulletproof glass expelled a death rattle of tangible foulness and seemed to focus on him for the very first time. "The church-like aspect once enjoyed by those who grew up during the heyday of the motion picture experience has been replaced by corporate blockbusters, by franchises that serve only the need of the revenue stream," she said. "As the quality of home entertainment equipment exceeded and indeed, surpassed the desire to seek movies outside of one's own portico, the societal value of 'a night at the cinema' was diminished and impaired. It is a valid argument that moviegoers today are paying an unfair and biased premium for the privilege of watching what is essentially the same Blu-Ray disc they could watch at home, for less risk and expenditure. This compelled the formerly burgeoning cinema industry to re-conceive both its aims and its appeal during a period when, frankly, it was staring Death right in the face and ignoring its portents. That multiplex boom you witnessed when those pants of yours were new? That imploded. Whole cinema shrines got turned into gyms and wine bars. In the current economic climate, the more stubborn adherents found themselves faced with the oldest challenge in the world: adapt or die. They needed to offer an experience that could not be enjoyed from one's sofa, and so pure cinema—as opposed to "branded entertainment events"—got relegated to the status of opera or ballet, dependent on a diminished core group of patrons. Inevitably this cost more money, a lot more, and the present conflict is this: How much more income can be derived from a dwindling pool of aficionados—the last movie generation of the 20th Century—before they die themselves and eliminate the market entirely? This is the question that vexes all of us. So…that will be five hundred dollars, fuckhead. Pay up or move along."

Totally Eighties Marty saw the light: this was a cunning formality designed to repel the casual cineaste in favor of a more exclusive clientele, those not interested in all at watching a big screen. Six hours later, after calling in four markers (pending debts to Scoop) and visiting eight cash machines (using spurious bank cards attributed to Scoop), he ponied up.

After all, it was the notorious Scoop, not Totally Eighties Marty, who was taking this meeting.

Abbott N. Costello had put his ear to the street and advised Mikey of a rendezvous between this so-called, faux-Scoop and a gangster who went by the handle of "Godz." This intel had cost $250, neat, to be disbursed by Doc Auto from Mikey's rapidly ballooning past-due bill. Also on the check in addition to Costello's lunch was a cash advance—everything had increased in price during the time Mikey had been "away"—and the cost of the pistol weighting Mikey's overcoat pocket. The overcoat had been an "extra" from Doc Auto, provided that Mikey returned it with reasonable wear and tear. Ditto the sidearm, an abused old Police Positive whose cylinder clunked to the floor the first time Mikey checked it. It was loaded with vintage cartridges that might or might not fire, depending on the humidity. It worked best as a receptor for hopeful karma.

Ice-cold air was swapping directions along the natural wind tunnel of 42nd Street between the East River and the Hudson, flag-snapping the overcoat, which hung two sizes too large on Mikey's emaciated frame, smelled like cat pee, and coyly revealed several faulty seams through which the frigid breeze sought to chill his bones, to *re*-refrigerate him.

When the rebar had kissed the back of Mikey's skull some eight years, seven months and three and a half days ago, iPhones were just beginning their population explosion and "tablets" meant dope or the Ten Commandments. Two Presidents ago. Carelton Casper Leadman had come and gone, as mayor. There was no such thing as Snapchat. The season finale of *The Sopranos* was yet unbroadcast. His last chance at desperate love, one Jacqui Quisneros, had evaporated into the same timeline that had written off his debt puzzle and consigned him to Earth's roundfile. Time defeated everything. Time won, in the end.

He noticed a preponderance of citizens on the hoof, seasoned New York pedestrians, apparently talking to themselves like garden-variety street loons...then deduced: *those people are on the phone*. In the same way vices became habits, formerly lunatic behavior had metastasized to the New Normal. It was now possible for anyone to leave their entire brain behind at a coffee shop or bus stop by accident. A stranger could find your brain and wipe it clean and sell it for a profit, while simultaneously assuming your credit identity long enough to earn you felony time. People watched TV while driving, now. Screens were everywhere—big advertising ones, tiny hand-held ones—and everyone experienced the world right in front of them via an electronic window that blocked the view of the living and real with pixelized simulacra. There were even more surveillance cameras on the streets than screens, and everyone Mikey saw seemed obsessed with *recording* every single thing that transpired, everywhere.

Not a very rich loam, for an outmoded grifter. Or—flip the bad news to good—an unprecedented opportunity.

From what Mikey witnessed during his stroll to the Eros Nightingale Theatre, it could be argued that iPhones and other "mobile devices" (as he heard them called) were actually an invading alien race who possessed and enslaved human beings for their own perpetuation. They landed on your hand, they took over your entire life; they demanded your obedience, punished noncompliance, and pushed out anything that would distract constant notice from their soul-swallowing little screens, the windows to *their* world. And Earthlings seemed overjoyed at the subjugation. Eager, in fact, to help the invaders multiply.

This lent Mikey an unlovely flashback to the UFO abduction he had mentioned to Costello. *Don't go there*, the brain skeeters warned.

While Mikey understood the concept of paying good cash money to be dominated, this was different.

Suckers and marks galore no longer saw a problem in *spraying* all their personal information hither and yon, like thumb-tacking your tax return and sex profile to a phone pole in Times Square, where *just anyone* could page through them, laughing.

Not that Mikey had ever filed, of course.

But during his absence, even *stealing* had become okay if not strictly legal—certain kinds of stealing, such as the purloinment without pay of movies or books or music or artwork or photographs in the thieves' paradise once fancily called the World Wide Web. Virtually everyone with an internet connection was, by definition, a common crook, and Mikey disliked the idea of simpleminded, do-it-yourself competition.

Not that Mikey had ever illegally downloaded anything, ever.

But if *anybody* could shoplift anything, that ability ceased to fit the definition of a skill, or worse, a talent. Not just any mook on the street could have survived Mikey's history of death-scrapes and close calls, and in this regard he wanted to feel special and unique, if only to himself and the brain skeeters. It was the sole shred of ego he permitted himself. The only thing that was *his*, truly.

Unless it was hijacked by some dog-fucking pedophile shit-eating turd-jerkoff scab-sucking mother-humping Satan-fellater.

Which it had been, most certainly, except for the scab part.

Godz, *il capo de tutti capi* of East Coast crime, the A#1 head honcho and chief *frommage* of all activities sublegal, the personality Totally Eighties Marty had referred to as the "Big G," turned out not to be so big after all. He was an imposing (though underwhelming) six foot one, not that He ever stood up from His Rascal scooter anymore. But if He did, the super-sized Vibram Finger Heels on His massive feet would have added another half-inch. Everything, from His "personal mobility vehicle" to His designer shades, was oversized and custom-cut. This was necessary due to the kingpin's eccentric dimensions, not to mention His fat, scaly-green tail.

"You're Godzilla," said Totally Eighties Marty.

"*Gojira* Godzilla, in point of fact," said the fire-breathing Japanese city-stomper in a hiss of atonic steam. "First name, last name, *birth* name, for another fact. You're here to tell me things I *don't* know, pinwheel. And don't ask for my autograph unless you want to die very painfully over an extended period of time, say, a decade. I ask the questions in this crib."

It was difficult to parse all the input received by Totally Eighties Marty's eyes. Tessellated armor-plated flesh, check. Glowing dorsal spines, check. Huge luminous eyes and stalactite dentition, check. Fat trident hands, check. That was why the Vibrams had struck Marty as odd—they only had three toes each.

"But you're supposed to be, like, *four hundred feet tall...*"

Godzilla sighed and rolled His eyes, which put His minions on high alert. There were at least fifteen of them, like a clenched fistful of Secret Service rejects in mirrored sunglasses, expressionless bone-breakers all, fidgeting with state of the art firepower in many assorted configurations. Several were women at least by broad taxonomic definition, but there was not a single Asian in the room. They were fanned in a defensive deploy, some close at hand, some near windows on the far end of the vast but low-ceilinged space, which had been repurposed from storage to a lush and utterly hidden office.

"Movies and reality are two different things," Godzilla said by way of weary rote. "Do I need to drag a blackboard and pointer in here? No? Good. That goddamned Bierfurz warned me, and I'm beginning to see that it would be better for all of us if you discontinued the flapping of your lips. But unfortunately, I need you to say certain things and please don't make us wait while you guess what they are."

Totally Eighties Marty now realized Who had schooled and rehearsed the boxoffice ladything in the serpentine pocket history of motion pictures as commerce. After all, it was called show business, not show friends—the one aspect of the form that had actually *defied* the passage of time and remained as relevant as any enduring truth. Totally Eighties Marty appreciated this acknowledgement of the past with an eye toward the future. Still, though, he could not prevent himself from blurting out: "But, isn't—?"

A stern reptile finger was waved in warning. "What did I just say about asking questions? You were about to ask a question anyway, weren't you? A *stupid* question. I can smell it radiating off you. Okay, here's my deal: you ask a question, and Booger and his mates there will shoot you rather a lot. Are we crystal?"

Totally Eighties Marty nodded fast, which was good, because it kept him from swallowing his tongue.

"To save time, permit me to recap," said the Big G. "Llewellyn, if you please."

A previously unseen helper, unarmed, appeared out of the ambient dimness to wire special reading glasses around the huge batrachian head. He held a data screen in his left hand. Totally Eighties Marty looked closer. The device was actually wired *into* Llewellyn's hand; several cables and metabolic interfaces snaked up his arm to worm beneath his shirt-sleeve, and the guy's middle was divided by a belt that was all power-paks and wireless hook-ups. Llewellyn himself was a lifeform that thrived under digital light. His nourishment was measured in ones and zeros. His sad, spotty flesh was merely a life support system for the screen fused to his hand, a true palmtop. He was what came next on the iPhone's evolutionary timeline. The radiance of the little screen was never absent from his face except when he was attending directly to his superior; Marty sensed that Llewellyn was one of the few human beings in history allowed to touch his reptilian master without tasting instant death.

The King of the Monsters executed a deft, space-saving half-turn in His Rascal, which was adorned with racing stripes and the backswept logo *Chariot of the Godz*. He buzzed His way on fireproof wheels to an equally gigantic desk with cutouts that accommodated both Him and His scooter for close work. Stacked neatly thereupon were duly accumulated files and dossiers; Godzilla paged through the topmost of these while another helper bloomed forth from the bad peripheral light: a geisha with large blue eyes and skin the color of fresh snowfall. She lit a cigarette, screwed it into an ebony holder about a foot long, and parked it in the right-side jaw-corner of Godzilla's dinosauric mouth.

"Okay, circa..." The big lizard squinted through a double-take. "Jesus. This goes all the way back to late 1980s, about the time I was making that movie where I kicked Biollante's *cachetes*. He was some mega-stupid DNA monster dreamed up by a *dentist*, if you can believe that. And Wentworth—god, what a freeze-dried twat *she* was. You helped precipitate her demise, along with several of her wingmen, which caused your debts to leap-frog to the Cherub..."

Godzilla scanned the files at a fast, efficient rate, His gaze back-tracking whenever they skidded across some factoid almost too weird to be believed. His eyes pounded the data until it succumbed to His logic, then they proceeded until speed-bumped again by yet another fantastical Scoop story.

"You did the Cherub and his imbeciles about the same time I had to tackle King Ghidorah again. I did an atomic heel turn and was a bad guy and good guy, both. Let's see...you were in to the Cherub for about $25K...everybody died except you, *again*...and that brought you under the scrutiny of Boss Rigg, at about the same time a hired gun named Angelina came calling for your sorry rump, because of what you'd done to old frosty-cooze Wentworth. I gather they were indulging some sordid and too-trendy same-sex relationship; yawn-a-rama. This dates to around the turn of the century; same time Megaguirus and those swarms of pesky Meganula all ganged up to be one giant rectal nuisance for me. Then I had to slap down King Ghidorah yet again; that three-headed dingbat never learns...plus Mothra—*again*...while you were, hmm..."

More page flipping. Totally Eighties Marty stayed totally silent, reveling in victories he had not earned.

"...Pymsdyke, Garibaldi...Mister Bart and Cleo; I remember those tough guys...the guy the Cherub called Cobbler; old Lightbulb Head...Mechagodzilla; Mothra *again* (it seemed to make Godz madder every time he had to say the name)...I had to take a break after *Final Wars* but it looks like you kept chugging right along...oh, holy shit, here comes Casper Carelton Leadman right before he was mayor. And his little brother, Bob. You were attempting to impregnate Bob's girlfriend?"

"No!" said Totally Eighties Marty, trying to look offended. "That was a total misunderstanding." In point of fact, he had no idea what Godzilla was talking about. He lacked access to the information the best money or the best hacks could acquire. As an imposter, he was tissue-thin, but that had never mattered until now.

"Yeah, you were porking her," Godzilla muttered to Himself as He moved on to the next page. "It appears you are quite the mad-dog killer, Mister Scoop. A death machine. Pardon me if I say you don't look like a Terminator or the Grim Reaper, yet the road behind you seems paved with dead bodies, most of them people who had an interest in killing *you* at one time or another."

"Well, see, I—"

The iconic monster atomically-spawned in 1954 stretched, joint-crackingly, and let loose a roar known unforgettably across time and space: *Aheeeh-raaahhhhhh-urrrrungh!* His staff and body-guards all covered their ears as politely as possible. The whole cadaver of the Eros Nightingale Theatre trembled to the foundation. Totally Eighties Marty felt his colon try to jump out of his throat. He saw demon steam jet from the flared canine nostrils. He forgot whatever excuse he had been fabricating.

Godzilla wheeled about in His Rascal to nail Totally Eighties Marty with His laserbeam gaze. "From the record, Scoop, you destroy everyone who gets in your way. I apologize for my earlier disrespect because it seems that you are a lot like me."

"Yeah, well, see, you cut right to the steak, Mister G. You're like, I dunno…inspirational. Is there a higher benchmark than you? No! You're famous all over the planet! *Off* the planet, even!"

"Please spare me unnecessary groveling," said the undisputed Tokyo Terror. "I can still barbeque you with a sneeze." He held another page before His crenellated face. It reflected whitely in His bifocals. "Ah, here's a very precise summation of your debt structure composed, I believe, by ex-Mayor Leadman himself…*very* detailed. It appears you agreed to assassinate ten designates of Mr. Leadman at $7500 per head, then you reneged."

"The circumstances were not optimum," Totally Eighties Marty said, still lying his ass off because he had no idea what the Big G was talking about.

"Hmm. Your response was to attempt to defenestrate the younger Leadman to his death. Along the way…at least five more casualties, including Roach and Ratso, along with Mssrs. Beveringswithe, Muzykansky, and the elaborately-named Mr. LeBlanco-Pinche-Dolorosa, whom I believe you also knew as Poker, Peeker, and Porker, am I correct?"

"Sure thing," said Totally Eighties Marty, having never heard of any of these guys, either.

"Do you have $75,000 to balance the scales for what you owe the Leadmans?" said Godzilla, who snickered. "*Scales.* Pardon the pun. Also pardon the rhetorical question—it's clear from your wardrobe that you do not have two dimes to rub together. Seriously, dude, the Eighties sucked enough the first time around. We need to bury them. Even I had to bring my oeuvre current with a reboot. Royalties, merchandising…you know."

"I don't have seventy-five large," said Totally Eighties Marty.

"*Psssht.* It is but pocket change; a non-issue. What I would like to propose is that you receive a stipend in return for my on-call use. Since the evidence suggests you can survive anything, and obliterate anyone, I'd like you on my team."

"That would be rad," said Totally Eighties Marty. "Like, I *knew* seeing you would be a good idea. You say it, Boss, and I'll do it."

"Excellent, Scoop—if I may call you Scoop."

"Totally."

"Fine. I would like you to kill *this* woman."

Llewellyn displayed his radiant hand to present Totally Eighties Marty with the only photograph of "Angelina" known to exist in the free world. It was an old surveillance camera side-view in the dark of an elegant, cat-suited blonde who resembled one of those supermodels you can never recall by name. Except for her eyes, which caught glints of light like polished scythe blades.

"Stone fox," said Totally Eighties Marty, who had never met Angelina, nor fought her, nor escaped her killing embrace the way the real Mikey, and the real Scoop, had. For most mortals, meeting Angelina led to fighting her, and there was no third part. Mikey—Scoop—had been the sole exception in the universe, to date.

"From what I can glean, Angelina is equally interested in a rematch with you, Scoop," said Godzilla. "Her excision would clear my playing field, so to speak. I have her secret contact number if you'd like to proceed directly."

"No, uh, why don't you just give it to me—"

Another earsplitting roar pushed all the air out of the room. Several of the gun-toting operatives were forced into a backward step. Llewellyn was compelled to dab at a fresh, thin nosebleed. Even the geisha winced. Godzilla's eyes had gone slightly scarlet.

"Wrong answer, Scoop. If we are to become co-workers, you must execute commands instantly, yes? Otherwise I'll just feed *you* to *her*, to get the results I want."

Totally Eighties Marty had his palms up, defensively. "I get you. Totally tubular. Wicked clear. I'm your man."

This was three minutes before the real Scoop—the real Mikey— entered the room.

———————

Not while Mikey was standing on the freezing street, did the feeling come. Not while crossing the same street, with the usual reflexive sensation that crosshairs had settled on the back of his neck. Nor had the odd feeling proclaimed itself while he was dealing with the desiccated hag occupying the boxoffice of the trashed husk of the Eros Nightingale Theatre. She was an obstacle, and Mikey was accustomed to slinking past obstacles. Never approach an objective directly. Never use the same path for retreat. The brain skeeters insisted.

Once inside, Mikey hugged the peeling walls and allowed his spotty vision to acclimate. He saw sentries, bodyguards, tough guys—no matter what the era, they always littered the territory, and years of stealthy cowardice had schooled Mikey in avoiding these sub-conflicts, also mere obstacles. Speed bumps enroute to an objective, so judged and dismissed by the brain skeeters.

From Boxoffice Hag, he had learned that "Scoop"—whomever *that* was—had been inside the building for about twenty minutes.

His mind tinkered together the too-familiar picture: there would come a room in which a meeting had been called. The room would be full of people with weapons, kowtowing to some big-shot master criminal, or several, as "Scoop" did his damnedest to squirm out from under this week's big cartoon safe, falling toward his head. The brain skeeters always giggled at the imagery.

As had occurred many times previously during his pre-freezer existence, it would be "Scoop" versus the bad guys, or worse guys.

And that was when Mikey experienced the singular feeling of déjà vu. Not the flashback sensation of walking into another death-trap with no secret weapon, as usual. This was more a nagging itch of over-familiarity, as though he was watching the doomed drama of his cursed life play out the way it always played out…except from a new vantage point that brought a weird twinge of, what? Security? Comfort? Upper-handedness? As if he were not participating, but *watching* the whole train wreck, from the safe side of a one-way mirror.

The fated conflict always happened the same way: Mikey's foes would outnumber him, out-gun him, and make fun of the "Scoop" nickname while their leader—some extravagant grotesque—would detail the ways in which Scoop was about to die. Scoop—that is, Mikey—would brace for impact, indulge the despair of hope, and prepare to marry up with oblivion. Then—always—the doors would burst open and some unanticipated third party would intrude to butt-fuck the whole fiesta, hot lead would sizzle through the fetid air in all directions, ironic injuries would be suffered, and Scoop—the real one—would miraculously skin free to piss off another foe another day.

Except that now, today, it was Mikey himself who was the unbidden guest, the third party intruder, because some Scoop-*manque* was already inside, assuming his position on the chopping block. It was Mikey himself who was about to bust through the door with a gun in his hand.

If only he could locate the correct door. He had ascended to what he rightly assumed was the second-floor mezzanine, which once led to a balcony for the moviehouse; shoot-up and jerkoff central for the raincoat crowd from the bygone glory days. The entire balcony was gone, or perhaps it had escaped. The dark void of the former auditorium promised a harsh fall and a protracted expiration. The dank air that pulsed from this gloomy pit reeked of toilet malfunction, bum sweat and age-old stale popcorn. Across the carpeted floor was a series of double doors...but which one housed the conclave? Mikey realized he was not walking on carpeting, but a burly down of olive-drab mold that had overtaken the floor. There were recent footprints still perceivable. He followed them.

Mikey *really* wanted to get a look at the person whose life was such a gutter-ball that becoming a fake, substitute Scoop was more attractive than less encumbered options such as plastic surgery, the witness protection program, or suicide. So when he found the correct set of doors, he paused, for the tiniest moment, to put his ear to the seam and try to eavesdrop the temperature of what was going on inside.

That was when a meaty hand the size of a catcher's mitt clapped the back of his neck, and began to squeeze.

Nobody was more taken aback than Totally Eighties Marty when the porcelain-skinned geisha glided up and stuck her hand in his pants. Like Llewellyn, she too had digital interfaces and transmitters coiling up her arm. Her grasp gathered his penis (even through the too-tight parachute pants) and closed upon it.

"Amaterasu is a sensitive," said Godzilla. "Much better than optical recognition." His minions exchanged gruff glances and chuckled.

She smelled of night-blooming jasmine and never made eye contact. For the only time in his life, Totally Eighties Marty tried to will away his incipient erection, but he was outclassed as soon as his Joe Namath knitted slingshot brief was breached.

Amaterasu gave Marty's prick a tug. Then she smiled to herself, eyes still lowered. These two things occurring in the same 24-hour period nearly caused Marty to embarrass himself in front of a bunch of dudes via inadvertent over-ejaculation.

Then Amaterasu turned her hooded gaze to Godzilla and said, "This *kusottare* is lying. Kill him."

Totally Eighties Marty's hard-on deflated within two heartbeats as the geisha withdrew her hand, sniffed it, and spat on the ground through extended fingertips. Llewellyn was snickering, no doubt at transmitted data. Godzilla was smiling in the way only a rattlesnake can smile. His minions went weapons-hot like a Nazi chorus line.

"What a bother," grumbled the Big G. "You can deceive others. You *cannot* deceive me. To so attempt is disrespectful."

This was when an exterior patrol lookout named Christian opened the double doors, using Mikey's face.

"I spied with my little eye something beginning with *fucking trespasser*," said Christian, his mirrorshades capturing a great wide-angle view of Godzilla as he spun about in his Rascal.

Godz released a slightly radioactive burp, no more harmful than sushi marinated in wastewater from Fukushima Daiichi. "If Bierfurz didn't send him, then I'm bored already, and please massacre these two, will you?"

"*Wait a goddamned minute!*" shouted the new interloper, heaving and failing against Christian's vise grip. "I'm here to see Scoop! Who in this room is Scoop?!"

"That would be me," said Totally Eighties Marty, still fretting about his dingus.

The stranger—Mikey—struggled around to face the King of the Monsters, nearly completely overlooking the fact that he was talking to, well, Godzilla.

"And you're the boss here? You're in charge?" Mikey's face was bright red now, due to his circulation being shut off in other areas by Christian's devastatingly effective standby hold.

"You shouldn't ask him direct interrogatives," said Llewellyn mumbled to Mikey's image on his palm screen.

Godzilla snorted—more steam—and exchanged his cigarette holder for an ebony toothpick preferred by Amaterasu, once she finished with the hand sanitizer. His glare of dissatisfaction considered potential victims, in different order, until it settled on Mikey.

"What. Are you?"

"The real Scoop. This fellow is pretending to be me." Mikey lunged against Christian's restraint but remained immobile except for his most vital tool: his big, flapping mouth.

"Impossible," said Godzilla, his breath pre-heating, his scooter locked for the recoil of a fireblast. "Who would want to be *you*? You look as though you lost your shopping cart back at the madhouse. Explain."

"This man is an imposter," said Mikey.

Quickly twigging to the challenge, Totally Eighties Marty shot back: "No way. *I'm* Scoop. This butt-stain is a fake."

"He lies," said Amaterasu.

"Which one?" said Godzilla.

Both men yelled and pointed at each other as far as they were able, since Totally Eighties Marty was now being pinioned by a minion. *"Him!"*

"Don't listen to him!" Mikey beseeched. "That name, that fucking *name*, Scoop; all my life I've been tormented by it. It was laid on me by a crook I hated, years ago; it stuck to me like snot to an eyelash; every scumbag and reject and clot of human shit in the city learned it, and every time I tried to get ahead, do a deal, elevate myself up out of the sewer or get some respect or just buy a tiny bit of fucking peace, there was that *name* again, blowing me down, kicking out my plug, and by the way, I really did have to elevate myself out of a sewer once. A literal sewer, where I was duct-taped to the Cherub's headless corpse! Boss Rigg and Angelina weren't in that sewer, but they shit all over me anyway! You want names and dates, I can give you chapter and verse, but if life is a big bowl of excrement, I've eaten two bowls too many with two spoons, all because of that humiliating name, Scoop! 'Scoopy this; Scoopy that;' every lowlife in the whole fucking city, constantly, never-ending! And nearly all of them *underestimated* me because of that name, and I'm still here, and they're not!"

A rope of free drool rappelled down from Mikey's clenched teeth. He was husking desperate air in and out like a distance runner.

"You want Scoop, motherfucker, you've got him! I'm him! Scoop, that's me! Scoop! *Scoop!* Are you deaf?! *There's only one Scoop, and it's me!*"

Godzilla had both big paws over His ear-holes. "Gawd!" He said, "*Enough,* by the twats of the *Shobijin!* You're making my sinuses hurt. Stop babbling!"

There came a single beat of eerie quiet as no one in the room made a sound.

Then the lizard-in-charge adjudged thusly: "There's only one way to resolve this cluster-fuck," He growled. "*My* way." He drew in a vast, limitless breath. Gallons of air whooshed into Him.

"Oh, shit!" squeaked Christian in the voice of a comic book mouse. He released Mikey and high-tailed it out the door.

This sentiment was echoed by most of the minions—the smarter ones, anyway—who dived or fled for the nearest incombustible cover. The team leader, the one called Booger, had speedily assumed the classic duck-and-cover in the footwell of an abandoned military desk.

Amaterasu backed gracefully away, into darkness, while Llewellyn had already been distractedly pulling on a fireproof coverall in anticipation of his master's habit while watching all this hooting and yelling transpire to a timecode on his screen. He had enough time left to flop the garment's foiled hoodie over his head.

Leaving Mikey and Totally Eighties Marty naked, essentially, to the oncoming holocaust.

Lava-colored liquid fire napalmed forth from Godzilla's open maw in a radiant spray as His spines iridesced with self-generated power and the entire room lit up as though hit by a blue searchlight. Everything flammable sprouted flames. One of the minions was caught in mid-air as he leapt for a sheet of corrugated steel—useless demo turned lifesaver—and landed with both his shoes on fire.

Godzilla buzzed His Rascal in a ninety-degree arc, vomiting acetylene-hot sterilization in a drooping flamethrower stream. The abrupt upsurge in temperature did not faze Him. He rose majestically from His mobile chair and struck a power-lifter pose as the searing firefall continued to erupt from His face.

Most of the blistering assault flew over Totally Eighties Marty, who had fallen to the floor after colliding with Mikey. Mikey rolled and came up behind Llewellyn just in time to feel the fire-spray divide around them in a forked path with Llewellyn as nexus. Unaimed gunfire hammered away as the magazines in an entire arsenal of dropped weapons overheated instantaneously and the cartridges exploded. Godzilla's minions knew better than to hang onto their hardware when the boss had one of his "fits;" they had been burned before.

And as Mikey knew from rough experience, even the best minions frequently cut and ran. Another constant that had changed little during the ensuing years was that reliable help was *still* hard to find, for a reason.

Mikey spotted Amaterasu's dropped dispenser of hand sanitizer on the floor at his feet. He scooped it up in case he needed to salve burns…or something.

Godzilla roared afresh and unleashed another buffeting oral poot of incendiary plasma. Totally Eighties Marty scrambled to standing, then slammed into shock at the sight of his smoldering left arm, which stuck to the floor and did not come up with him. It had been flash-fried to carbon.

Godzilla grabbed Totally Eighties Marty with both reptilian paws, bit off his head, and swallowed it. Steaming blood blew ceilingward in a broad fan that partially doused the back of Mikey's borrowed overcoat, which was also burning merrily. Then the King of the Monsters began to lurch about, stomping on small things and crushing them.

Llewellyn flipped up his smoke visor and spoke over his shoulder to Mikey: "He gets this way, sometimes. We always have to find a new building, afterward."

The rest of Totally Eighties Marty disappeared down the gullet of the super-lizard, to the accompanying crack of sundered bones.

"That really is Godzilla," said Mikey wonderingly, stepping out for a better look. "*The* Godzilla."

"Oh, yes," said Llewellyn, checking Fahrenheit stats on his board. "Don't let his demeanor fool you. He is a capable administrator and has a really good dental plan. He'll be upset for awhile and then Amaterasu will calm Him down the way she always does. He..."

Without preamble, the legendary monster had turned to make Mikey taste the fire directly. Mikey was a step and a half too far away from Llewellyn to regain him as a shield. He saw the fireball generating inside Godzilla's throat, cremating the dregs of Totally Eighties Marty as fuel. The cheap pistol in his pocket was too hot to grab and would probably explode like a grenade. Mikey did the only thing he could think of.

He hurled the hand sanitizer into Godzilla's fulminating gullet... where it detonated on contact with the hot plasma, exploding with the force of thirty-two shots of vodka, just as the late Totally Eighties Marty had surmised. The effect was like blowing out a runaway oil well fire with dynamite. Stealing its breath.

Godzilla's eyes rolled skyward and He plonked thunderously to the floor, temporarily sidelined by oxygen deprivation.

"Well," said Llewellyn, watching the whole sequence on his screen. "I've never seen *that* happen before."

"He's not gonna be mad, is He?" asked Mikey.

"Normally, yes. In your case, not so likely. You see, with Amaterasu's help He had already learned which of you was the bona fide. This gave me time to review your digitized history, such as it is. My sense is that upon recovery, He will feel a latent kinship with you—after all, you both seem to survive no matter what time and fashion hurl at you. That's enough for now. Were I you, I would concern myself with evacuating before this rat-trap cooks down to cinders and ash. Expect to be contacted at a later date. But tell me something: with all the downside aspects of being Scoop, why would you now claim the name so fervently?"

Mikey replied, "Because it's the only thing I've got that's all mine."

The Eros Nightingale Theatre burned for most of the following night, to the delight of news cameras and the joy of realtors who had been seeking some way to quietly torch the last eyesore on the Deuce. No one saw or recorded the exit of a small, shabby figure in a big, smoldering overcoat.

On the way down the back fire escape, the overheated junk pistol in the coat pocket discharged a single round that had finally sizzled to a boil. It blew off the toe of Mikey's left shoe but missed his foot. In a rare moment of what Abbott N. Costello would have called introspection, Mikey thought, *now there was a piece of actual, genuine good luck.*

A grumbling Chevy Impala blocked his path. It had nosed out of the alley before him like a huge Moray eel. Classic '65 ragtop doused in beetle green, a hydraulic hopper with 20-inch chrome wheels. It disgorged a quartet of surly bangers who all pointed guns at him.

"Hey *puto*, we hear you're the dude they call Scoop."

"That's me," said Mikey. "But I don't know what *your* problem is, Pablo."

All hammers clicked to full cock.

The balance of the universe, it seemed, had been restored.

....

Two More Scoops...
of Celluloid

(1)

It Don't Mean a Thing if It Ain't Got That *Thing*...

(2009)

That hollowed-out ice-coffin from which the 1982 Thing thawed? I sat inside of it.

That is my complete and sole hands-on connection to the movie.

Having spent a significant portion of my existence dabbling in the tiny but potent subgenre of "arctic horror," my initial reaction to *John Carpenter's The Thing* was point-specifically over-critical, based on my knowledge of how DEWLine bases were run in the 1970s and 1980s. To wit: No arsenal—maybe a single pistol, locked in the station chief's desk (the Antarctic Treaty banned firearms, not to mention flamethrowers, and they only used dynamite to blow up septic pits full of calcified human waste). No fully-equipped operating theatre—not for a mere twelve guys, not when stations of 25 men had a single first-aid competent member if they were lucky. No lumber lying around—every single stick of supply had to be specially flown in. No exterior door locks—what for? It's not as if a stranger is going to stroll up and knock, on an icecap in the middle of hundreds of miles of nowhere.

But without a little dramatic license, you don't have drama.

While present-day received wisdom has *The Thing* as an enduring classic, most people seem to have forgotten (or never knew) how reviled it was upon release. It was, in a word, a flop. What Universal Studios envisioned as its "own" version of *Alien* was roundly trounced in the marketplace by *E.T.: The Extraterrestrial* (from the same studio). It seems staggering now, but *The Thing* failed to earn back its $15 million pricetag, which *included* prints and publicity.

But *The Thing* and home video were new at the same time, and that's where the movie found its audience. Presently it is a tantalizing memoir of a vital, proactive form of moviemaking, a time-capsule from a pre-CGI world that has aged like fine wine instead of decomposing into camp nostalgia. It passed the test of time and walked into the canon of classics on its own two pseudopods.

Every scene, every effect and every line of dialogue have been immortalized by constant scrutiny and study...which I doubt could be said for the likes of *E.T.* (*"Phone home"* doesn't have nearly the resonance of *"you've gotta be fucking kidding,"* if you follow me).

I first met John Carpenter at Forrest J Ackerman's house during a press conference for *The Fog*. Since I was in cahoots with Universal Licensing, I was frequently on the lot at the same time Mick Garris worked there as a genre publicist during the extremely fertile days of *Conan, Cat People, Ghost Story, Videodrome* and *An American Werewolf in London*. We met up at least once a week and one day Mick asked if I wanted to see "Carpenter's set." This was August or September 1981. We walked through a powered-down version of the iced-in Norwegian outpost (no filming that day); I recall it being blazingly hot outside, which means that Mick probably headed north to shoot his 16mm footage for the "making-of" that December (which essential short still has not been included as a supplement to any disc release.)

Apart from featuring *The Thing* in the first-and-only issue of the *Universal Studios Science Fiction, Fantasy & Horror Newsletter,*

Mick also made sure to provide a little collectible handout of the original John W. Campbell story, "Who Goes There?"—what today would be called a chapbook. Part of the "legend" of the 1982 *Thing* resides in the idea that the movie hews more closely to Campbell's story than the 1951 film, when *anybody who has actually read the damned story* can tell you it's more like an even-money split. The 1951 *Thing from Another World* basically ends a third of the way into the source tale, when the invader is fried in an electric flytrap. For the rest of the short story, the characters stand around talking about what the invader *might* have been. The 1982 film basically extrapolates that talk into a linear plot (the blood-test scenario is quoted directly, even to the line "crawl away from a hot needle, say") and uses most of the character names from Campbell ("McReady" became "MacReady"). One important point missed in all this comparison is that the 1951 film is about a functional unit of men (talky Hawksians) versus an outsider; the 1982 version presents a loose commune of misfits and exiles (taciturn Carpenterites)—outsiders themselves who must collaborate against a more menacing outsider. For this reason, the Carpenter film is not as "nihilistic" as frequently claimed: By the end, the outcasts are bona fide heroes by virtue of their self-sacrifice.

The 1982 film is one of those rare revisions (not "remakes") that could admirably stand alongside its earlier version on a double bill, like the 1978 *Invasion of the Body Snatchers* or the 1986 *The Fly*. Tim Lucas more correctly summed it up as Carpenter's "graduation" from the shadow of his idol, Howard Hawks. And Carpenter memorably achieved his often-stated covenant of doing a monster movie where the featured creature was not obviously a man-in-a-suit—a shortcoming to which even the powerhouse *Alien* had succumbed.

Its longevity has proven out. I still watch it at least once a year, to this day.

Scrutiny reveals that the Thing covertly nails a third of the Outpost 31 crew—Bennings, Norris, Blair and Palmer. The "dirty drawers" discovered by Nauls belong to Norris, who was Thinged by the wandering dog (the alien replicates Norris so perfectly that it even copies his heart condition, and suffers an unanticipated coronary). It's interesting that Palmer and Norris provide arguments for keeping the suspect MacReady outside, since at this point in the story they are *both* Thinged. I will leave you with three questions to test your own *Thing* chops:

What happened to Fuchs? Did Blair burn him?

Who got to the blood if Garry and Doc Copper are both human?

And finally, when did the Thing get Blair?

(Special bonus question for die-hards: Who is Jans Bolen?)

(2)

Back to Andromeda

(2010)

Hall: "Where's the library?"
Dutton: "No need for books—everything's in the computer."

One of the few regrets of my adult life is that I never got to meet Michael Crichton, who died too young, November 2008. Eminently emulatable, he had conquered publishing, film and television and remains a personal hero. I was hooked from the moment my father returned from his Arctic DEWLine duties bearing a paperback first printing of *The Andromeda Strain*, which I plowed through while in high school. Then immediately re-read, and re-read again.

I still have that paperback.

Subsequently I devoured everything Crichton wrote—the "John Lange" potboilers written to pay his way through medical school; the landmark *A Case of Need* (written as "Jeffrey Hudson;" a stingingly strong pro-choice novel done prior to the Roe v. Wade decision); even the dope fantasia *Dealing*, written with his brother as "Michael Douglas." Even his book on the artwork of Jasper Johns. Even the one Crichton book not likely to ever be reprinted—his prescient rumination on home computers, *Electronic Life*, written in 1980.

And the attraction was always: This guy really knows what he's talking about. He convinced me.

About halfway through the novel *Timeline*—not one of Crichton's best—there is an explanation of quantum physics that even I, science mook, could clearly comprehend. Crichton came to represent for me that bridge between incomprehensible technology and common understanding.

But, it has been argued, his characters all suck.

But, it is further argued, he uses the same plot over and over. A motley team of high-tech wiseguys are collected into an exotic location where they become outfoxed by their own security systems.

Both essentially true.

Both criticisms were brought heavily to bear when Crichton was profiled in *Time* magazine. So I wrote *Time* a letter saying I never read Crichton for characters; I read him because he allowed me to cross that bridge. At least I got to defend him in print, not that he needed it.

The Andromeda Strain novel is loaded with citations, some of them from scholarly works authored by the characters in the story, a revelation that just blew me away. Crichton *made up* those references credibly enough to veneer his characters with academic respectability; they, too, knew what they were talking about.

Therefore, Crichton lied brilliantly, to escort readers to places they might never venture willingly.

That, to me, sums up the charter of a really good writer.

(Which is why the fast-and-loose pseudoscience of *Jurassic Park* doesn't bug me. The reader has been cunningly pre-biased toward being convinced because he or she, more than any other consideration, *wants* to get to those dinosaurs.)

In 1970, I decided there was just no way that a movie of *The Andromeda Strain* could be as engrossing as the novel.

In 1971, I was proven about as wrong as I could be.

The plot recounts "the four-day history of a major American scientific crisis," in this case the microbiological Armageddon posed by a "brand-new form of life" brought to Earth by one of our own space capsules, which touches down in a small town and immediately wipes out most of the population. In a state-of-the-art lab complex buried in the Nevada desert, our assembled team of specialists races against time to determine the nature of the enemy.

With nearly forty years of hindsight, *The Andromeda Strain* remains one of the most flat-out suspenseful movies ever made from a science fictional premise. Watch the early scene in which console men gradually stop what they're doing to listen to a horrific encounter solely via radio speaker; it's a textbook of tension-building at the hands of director Robert Wise, who wisely stuck to Crichton's compressed timeframe (96 hours) to make every plot turn seem imminent and threatening.

It is one of the last science fiction films to be wholly populated by adults. No celebrities, prettyboys or youth-demographic compromises.

It is one of the few not overwhelmingly beholden to the spectacle of special effects.

It is one of the *very* few in which scientists *act like scientists*, and one of the even fewer which depict the numbing tedium of procedural research—albeit efficiently (the pacing never lags).

It is rife with aching ironies: The entire earth is threatened by an organism the size of a pencil point. The Wildfire lab's deep technology is subjugated by a sliver of paper. When Andromeda mutates to a noninfectious form, it is at its most dangerous. If the fifth member of the team had not been waylaid by appendicitis, then Dr. Leavitt would not have suffered an epileptic blackout while doing the other doc's job.

In the novel, the team is all male. Screenwriter Nelson Gidding suggested making one of the scientists a woman. The result: Kate Reid's Dr. Ruth Leavitt is the single best piece of casting in any science fiction movie, ever. Middle-aged, paunchy, outspoken, wise-cracking and rebellious, she smokes, has shitty eyesight and allergies, and keeps her epilepsy a closely guarded secret. She's about as far away from Ripley or Raquel Welch as you can imagine, in an award-worthy performance never considered for any trophy.

You don't get more rock-solid or utterly believable than her colleagues, either—Arthur Hill, David Wayne, James Olson (in his single best performance in a feature film, period) and Paula Kelly. (You'd never know it from this movie, but Kelly, an accomplished singer and dancer who enjoys the weird distinction of being *Playboy's* first full-frontal non-Playmate nude [in 1969], stepped away from acting after two Emmy nominations to pursue her musical career. She still gigs!)

No characters die off in reverse order of their credits.

Gidding and Wise concocted a form they called the "cine-script," which incorporated all the printouts and schema seen in the book, as well as the multi-screen effects seen in Wise's subdivided Cinemascope frame—a very visual approach, at the time, to mirror Crichton's inclusion of graphs and charts (laboriously handcrafted on an IBM Selectric). Wise's masterful command of composition for the 'scope frame is seen in numerous split diopter shots.

The film also features Gil Mellé's groundbreaking electronic score, the most arresting aural furniture since the "tonalities" of *Forbidden Planet*. The first issue of the soundtrack album was a hexagonal disc inside a silver sleeve that "flowered" open, to compliment the Andromeda organism's stop-sign shape. Watch closely and you'll see this "hex" theme reiterated all over the film.

If trivia is your heroin, try spotting the following actors in bit parts: Michael Pataki (Count Dracula in *Dracula's Dog*) as the Mic T., Bart La Rue (Irwin Allen and *Star Trek* regular) as a medic, Lance Fuller (of *This Island Earth, Voodoo Woman* and *The She Creature*) as a bystander, or Glen Langan (the Amazing Colossal Man himself!) as a cabinet secretary. For a long time, Crichton's own silent cameo (during James Olson's first operating theatre scene) was obliterated by the pan-and-scan nature of VHS. Wise himself donned surgical greens as a stand-in for the same shot, though he's unrecognizable. And visual effects maestro Douglas Trumbull named his daughter Andromeda after working on this film.

Years later, Crichton noted that his very first visit to a movie studio was to Universal during production of *The Andromeda Strain*. He was shepherded around the lot by a young hotshot named Spielberg, then on the brink of directing his first *Night Gallery* episode. For years following the release of the movie, those glorious stainless-steel Wildfire sets were part of the studio tour (they pop up regularly in other productions, too, like the "Spanish Moss Murders" episode of *Kolchak: The Night Stalker*). A lot of viewers don't realize that the top of the Central Core set is actually an Albert Whitlock matte painting.

This is also one of the first movies to regularly use a scrolling readout for time, date, and location to place action—a now much-overused device by filmmakers who feel the need to tell the audience with a insert title that an establishing shot of the Golden Gate Bridge means, in fact, that we are in San Francisco.

Forget the egregious 2008 TV-remake. Amid all its persiflage about buckyballs, wormholes and time travel, it didn't even get the plot point about acidosis and rapid breathing right.

Forty years later, *The Andromeda Strain* has not only earned its slot as a modern classic, but also remains as one of the handful of films that wears its respect on its sleeve, honoring the book on which it was based.

It convinced me.

THREE MISSING
FOOTNOTES FROM
THE BAD TIME

1

The monsters came for Claudia at night, just after the stroke of eleven. They functioned better at night. This forced human beings to adopt a nocturnal cycle for sake of simple alertness. It threw daytime people off; made their responses sluggish. Inconvenience was the first and least problem for a world of the pampered and lazy. Every subsequent aspect of this newest enemy seemed to translate as a hard, law-of-the-jungle advantage. Perhaps this really was the twilight of the old gods.

If one waits long enough, any hoary old prophecy will come true.

The Black Widowers were essentially impervious to most simple bullets. Their skin was too thick, crocodilian. They made armor out of the fleshings of their own dead for assault. It was cultural with them, an honorific remembrance, to strap on the remains of your comrades to add their power to your own, like successive layers of dense, plated leather. It made them even bigger.

They breached the front door of Claudia's hide with all the subtlety of a Sherman tank through a plate glass storefront. They met defense, but with conventional firepower it took many more slugs to slow them down. The battle math had been skewed; you could waste fifty cartridges just to stop one of them.

Also inconvenient.

Claudia Ballantine had been raped by a Black Widower during the early days. Trapped by four of them, actually, and violated on top of a rancid pile of restaurant garbage in a steam-clogged alley. One had held its catcher's mitt-sized hand over her face the entire time, muffling her screams. Two had held her legs. And one had penetrated her. It had felt worse than a champagne bottle kicked into her vulva, fat end first.

The impregnational member of a Black Widower—what would be called a penis on a human male—was frighteningly martial. Large enough to hurt; weaponized enough to damage. It was tessellated with anchoring barbs similar to the spines of a candirú fish. Once seated in a human female vagina, it was difficult to remove even with surgery. The spines did not withdraw. After copulation the organ could be ripped free by force, but they tended to detach from the owner. The Black Widowers grew new ones. The first wave of them were all males. Their adaptive biology mandated that all their brood stock be sourced in other metabolically harmonious species.

Claudia's blood gushed. The grotesque phallus snapped off inside her, and when she awoke, it was still inside her. Nearly dead from hemorrhage, she managed to stagger to a hospital, back when such things were still readily available.

Even more inconveniently, the semen of a Black Widower was dark and acidic. Its composition included an enzyme that sterilized the womb once impregnation was achieved. It was still one egg, one sperm—one of the reasons they were able to procreate with human beings—but the result was parasitical and cannibalistic. This was a fetus that demanded and took everything from the host-mother, including her ability to become pregnant again, if she lived.

That was one extra cruelty of the Black Widowers—you almost died, but not quite. Not until you disgorged a new Black Widower. The earliest victims frequently tried to kill themselves. The first of record was a woman named Martha Steckler, famous because she had shot herself in the temple with a .45 and technically died, but the demonic little zygote waxed and was born anyway. Black Widowers gestated quickly. The mother did not need a functional brain. The brood female became a meatbag of nutrients, and rarely survived.

Claudia had been one of the rare ones. Surgeons had managed to extract the nascent monster from her body. The excision had been inelegant and hurried, complicated by the inexperience of doctors with monsters.

Where they came from, whether from outer space or the molten core of the Earth, mattered very little. They seemed to be the collective spawn of bad dreams, visited as a punishment of godlike severity. They changed the face of civilization, first pushing a lot of people out of jobs simply because they ate refuse and worked like bulldozers, quickly inciting every so-called minority to avail itself of at least one major urban riot—thus was the razing of downtown Los Angeles chronicled as THUMP, or more onomatopoetically speaking, the Total Hispanic Urban Metro Panic. A supreme irony was that Spanish utterly confounded the Black Widowers, and later became a potent tool for coded human communications during their reign.

But it was human hysteria, not incursion by outsiders, that destabilized most of the cities. This blame was later overlooked, per the hard and fast rule that history is written by the victors.

The new enemies had skin the texture of indifferently-mixed concrete, their complexion an oxidized copper green, like the Neil Simon gag about very new cheese or very old meat. They were at first denigrated as humpbacks, mutants, mandroids, tylopods, and many more pejorative things due to their unfortunate visual association with camels and hence, Iran and Arabia. They were a new minority. They didn't care. Prejudice outside their own kind was for them a non-issue, which demonstrates how little they regarded human beings as a threat. One gander at us and they knew they had more stamina.

They were not animals, nor subhuman. They were highly motivated to survive and make more. More motivated, some argued, than a world full of human beings grown so complacent that they procrastinated when race annihilation landed on their doorstep. Soon enough, the new masters would not need human beings at all. They already controlled half the country and most of the highways.

And killing them was as difficult as bludgeoning a camel to death with a chopstick. It could be done; better to pack a bazooka.

Human social order collapsed pretty quickly.

Claudia survived, mostly confined to a wheelchair, her body an Expressionist work of scar tissue from ribcage to knees. She became one of the ten most wanted enemies of the Black Widowers. Her tracts against them were famous; history-making. She was the voice of the underground, speaking at first from the online cloud—back in the good old days before what came to be known as the Digital Pearl Harbor.

The arrival of the Black Widowers was the first punch of a one-two combo. The second hit was an electromagnetic hiccup that plunged the United States back to analog and hard wiring. It was akin to bucking along at 90 per and slamming your transmission into reverse; the last thing you see in your rearview is parts spewing all over the highway before you accept the fact you are now stranded. The cloud evaporated. Cellular communication, gone. The Internet went bye-bye. This massive fail was forever linked in memory to the coming of the Black Widowers regardless of whether they engineered it. They shouldered the blame, and why not?

Linotype machines were pulled out of mothballs. Newsprint returned. And Claudia Ballantine continued to work on a manual typewriter, placed on a board across the arms of her wheelchair. She became a rallying voice for the human cause, the victim/survivor who had prevailed to become stronger. The Black Widowers did not care about martyrdom (or symbolism); now they wanted her dead and silent more than ever.

When the Black Widowers came through her door, Claudia had been writing about the horror of the breeding camps.

Until the first generation of human hybrids, no one had ever seen a female Black Widower. The new hybrid females had their own special biology, which rejected human male sperm in favor of consuming it for the protein. Adventurous humans on both sides of the sexual divide took copulation with a Black Widower (or a hybrid Black Widower female) as a kind of ultimate dare. They generally wound up regretful, crippled, or dead. Hybrid brood females were highly prized within the Black Widower hierarchy, in part because they could produce creatures of three-quarter purity, but mostly because they were hardy enough to survive more than one birthing cycle.

Aware of the human disinclination to surrogate-host their new generations, the Black Widowers themselves began to strategize countermeasures, which meant abduction and imprisonment. Farming. Claudia had photos acquired at great personal cost and smuggled to her by a rebel named Styles. At least the point of a death camp was to kill you. This was worse, so Claudia wrote in unflinching prose about a nightmarish topic, ever vigilant against a threat that was anti-human and therefore, evil.

Reporters regained their value. Before, news had been marginalized by entertainment and distraction. Now it was once again a risk to speak the truth. Not a political risk, but actual jeopardy of life.

Claudia sprawled from her wheelchair and crawled for her tunnel hole-up, a contingency planned from the beginnings of her exile. She was unable to take her own life because the automatic pistol with which she had been supplied did not already have a cartridge in the chamber. No time for her to remember to work the action to chamber the round. Those few extra seconds were sufficient for the Black Widowers to find her, and take her again.

2

The girl in Claudia's cell was hugely pregnant. Black Widowers gestated in about three months—the same as snakes—and the young were independent at birth. The same as snakes.

"You're not pregnant," the girl said when Claudia opened her eyes.

Claudia had been deposited in this dank place, her dead legs skewed before her in the manner of a child at play, one tucked beneath the other in a figure-four. Her back was against a moist wall and the only available light ebbed through a rectangular slot that had been crudely carved from the center of a thick industrial hatch, like a freezer door. Apart from the lingering odor of stale feces and urine, there was another familiar smell, atonic, metallic.

Claudia had passed out at least once. Time had become vague. The Black Widowers had been educating themselves in the use of intravenous drugs to pacify prisoners and obtain touchy information. Claudia's head thudded with migraine, a blowoff from whatever they'd stuck her with.

Her cellmate was visible in the nicotined light. Claudia had to acknowledge her fellow human, so she fought to agree.

"No," she said. "Not." The utterance sparked lightning across her frontal lobes.

"You're lucky," said the girl, shifting her legs to accommodate her swollen belly. "I'm Cecilia. CeCe, they call me."

"*They* call you?"

"Well, no—I mean, like my Mom and my friends. My boyfriend."

The idea of a family, friends, a partner, seemed so alien to Claudia that she almost swooned. The girl could have been talking out a fever dream. From what she could perceive in the infected light, Cecilia could not have been much past age fifteen.

"Boyfriend?" Claudia heard her own voice as a dry, glottal croak. It echoed flatly. The acoustics and the lingering icebox aroma made her realize their prison was probably a decommissioned refrigerator truck. The dimensions were right. The other smell, the not-unpleasant one, was the smell of an aluminum ice tray after the ice had thawed.

"That was Brent," said CeCe. "He's dead. They killed him to get me."

Too aware of her own story, Claudia was reluctant to passively take on the crushing burden of this stranger's tragedy, so she forced herself to speak again, cutting off the oncoming tale of woe. "How long have you been here?"

"I dunno," said CeCe. "I dunno what day it is. I think I missed my birthday." Her voice battled with an oncoming floodtide of tears. "When I was twelve, I remember my Mom got me a cake. Candles. People gave me presents. Not fancy stuff but gifts, you know. That all seems like a million years ago, now."

Age twelve to age fifteen, ballpark. The world had fallen apart in three years. Put that way, baldly, the truth made Claudia want to start weeping, too.

"How come you're not pregnant?"

"Can't," said Claudia. "Not possible."

CeCe shuffled around, unable to find a comfortable position but leaning forward, too happy for the company. She was gaunt with greenstick limbs, stylishly bald. Tattoos. Jewelry, too, Claudia thought, until she recognized the glint of metal at CeCe's left ear as a stapled tag, the kind used on livestock.

"Then what do they want you for?" said the girl.

It was almost a challenge—the healthy young colt calling out the desiccated elder. *I can make babies and you can't.* It had been the fundament of this young girl's life and still had elemental power. Her future had once been limited to bad marriage and indiscriminate reproduction. Now at least she was fulfilling some obscure goal as a woman. Put two people in a cage and one will try to assert dominance over the other. That was what CeCe was attempting in her childish way. Claudia was in too much pain to argue...then she thought, *well, then, why talk at all? Why do anything?* If two human prisoners could not connect with each other on the most basic level, then they were ceding defeat without a struggle, and that was not what Claudia's post-rape life had been about. Claudia *never* went for the easy win.

"You see the undergrounds? The papers?"

"Yeah, I've seen 'em." Meaning: CeCe did not read them. "I miss Tweeting."

"I'm 'Nightingale.' I've been writing about the Black Widowers ever since they—"

A flush of artificial excitement from CeCe, as she overrode: "Wow, you mean like you're *famous*?"

"Infamous," Claudia said, hoping not to have to explain the difference. "They want to shut me up."

"That's *gotta* suck."

"Yeah, it does, actually. But not as much as letting one of those things rip its way out of you."

"It hurts," said CeCe, cradling her belly. "Hurts to even touch."

"It's still not fully formed," said Claudia. "You can kill it. I can show you how. It's not easy, but..."

"No! No way! I can't!"

Oh, god, Claudia thought. *This kid still has some delusion that the parasite inside her is hers somehow, a child, not a monster.* The pull of genetics could be that strong; the species taboos against aborting offspring were forever ingrained on a cellular level.

"You can. You can beat them."

"No, you don't understand."

Adults never understood anything.

"I *have* to have it," said CeCe with histrionic emphasis. "I *want* to have it. It's the only way I have of fighting back, see."

CeCe half-crawled, half-rolled to get closer to Claudia, agitating the sour air. Desperation was surging out of her skin in waves. Her flesh was bad, patchy and mottled.

"You're right," said Claudia. "I don't understand."

"I have to be careful," CeCe whispered, practically into Claudia's ear. "Sometimes they listen. Sometimes. What's wrong with your legs?"

Claudia adopted the same confidential tone. "Dead issue. They got me once, tried to impregnate me. I was able to get it out, but from the waist down, I'm history."

"See?" said CeCe, trying to make her voice even quieter. "You said, 'you can beat them.' And you beat them."

"Not really. I thought we could get a movement going. An uprising. An underground railroad, a resistance, a grassroots rebellion." Her big words were ricocheting off CeCe's skull with none of the intended effect of chewy prose. "Never mind. I tried, though. I tried to do what I could, and some people listened, but never enough. Too scattered, too battered; no organization."

This youngster could not even be bothered to read the bulletins and calls to arms. Claudia's revolutionary fervor was a generational conceit with a definite spoilage date. Past due.

"No," whispered CeCe. "What I'm saying is I can beat them, too." She indicated her belly. "This has to be born."

"Why?"

"My birthday, when I was twelve?" said CeCe. "There was this guy, Mom called him Uncle Lucky, and he kept constantly trying to get into my pants. He was older than me, and he kept *pressing*, right? Well, Uncle Lucky got lucky. He got my cherry. And I started losing weight and Mom took me to the doctor. *Wham*, HIV positive, just like that. I got the swollen, what do you call them?" She massaged her jawline.

"Lymph nodes," said Claudia, with growing dismay.

"They said sometimes it takes ten years but this was *fast*. Good days, bad days. I thought I had the flu. Then we got some drugs, and my hair fell out. So, see, this thing comes out, it's gonna have AIDS. I'll die, but I was gonna die anyway. And this thing will infect 'em after I'm gone."

The oxygen felt vacuumed from Claudia's lungs. This child whom she had dismissed as hopeless was making a bigger stand than Claudia could ever hope to achieve.

Claudia extended an arm and CeCe snuggled into her, with a tiny grimace of pain.

"It's moving," CeCe said. "Like claws, inside. The big one, its thing is still inside me too, but it doesn't hurt as much. Like it got smaller."

"It's being assimilated by the baby," said Claudia. "Eaten."

"Don't call it a baby," CeCe said. "It's not a baby."

She managed to fall asleep, briefly, in Claudia's arms. Right now, for this fleeting moment, she was Claudia's child, and Claudia wept, knowing it was very likely that no one in the world would ever know CeCe's name.

Claudia and CeCe both died in captivity. In the decade that followed, the scourge of the Black Widowers diminished them to zoo specimens and carefully-selected culls for scientific research. AIDS clipped the berserkers like a scythe to wheat. Future historians would liken the invasion to a world war somewhere between a pandemic and a natural disaster, the sort of slate-wiping change that the whole planet undergoes every so often. People were overcautious about crediting the Black Plague of the 20th Century for saving such a world, and consoled themselves with memorial walls and calendar holidays. While Claudia Ballantine's legacy was appropriately footnoted, her prediction about CeCe came true—no one ever knew who she had been.

3

Jag 39 had lived his entire life, very nearly, as a prisoner despised by his jailers and hated by most of his own people. Half his existence had been lost in endless tubes of narcotics and he frequently could not distinguish any palpable barrier separating his dream life from his "waking" life. Much of his sedated narrative consisted of a perpetually-enhanced and augmented retelling of his long-ago freetime, since his now-time was a plunging repetition of cells, bars, restraints and sterile rooms.

Most often he replayed the story about the only time he had taken one of the grub women, the pale ones designated as brood stock. At least he had completed his rite of passage ritual, part of which involved hammering a sharpened stick of consecrated wood through the crown of his *puquel*, to open the passage through which future generations would flow. Prior to this had come the fasting, the trial by flame, the dream isolation and the spiritually cleansing compounds that had been poured into his eyes, ears, mouth, nostrils using a carved tube (also of wood) which was then rammed past the defensive flap of his anus. Before the seed-hole was opened, all other bodily orifices had to be purified with a thick herbal muck that always burned, and inscribed scars.

Judged fit to reproduce, it remained for him to accomplish his first prowl with the three elders who had prepared him. Always three. The grub-women had become more difficult to harvest; rumor had it that they were being hidden or killed by their own kind. But there was always one to be hunted up, and they were all pale and shrill and fragile. Care was taken because they came apart easily. One elder muffled the shrieking face because grub-women made a lot of high-pitched noise that was annoying. The other two held the wormy legs apart. It was important for them to bear witness. The production of progeny was key to the survival of all. Jag 39 mounted this rather disgusting brood mare in a shower of its own blood. There was no pleasure in it. Well seated, he felt the decompression in his groin as his payload was delivered. His *puquel* broke off inside her and one of the elders chuckled. It would grow back. And the sharp stick would penetrate it once again. It was humiliating and painful, but repeated often enough, one could get used to anything. Honor accrued in the number of brood mares seeded.

Of course, he had not been called Jag 39 when all this happened. It was sad that he could not remember his real name. Once, during a period of lucidity, he had asked one of his keepers for the meaning of his new name. He had suffered to honor his forgotten name; surely some kind of status applied to its replacement.

Because you're a jagoff, the porcine grub-man had replied. *Now git to the far end of the room or I'll taze you again.*

When Jag 39 next awoke, he found his *puquel* had been docked again. The keepers kept doing this to see how fast it would grow back.

Fluids were ducted from his body by the pint in a near-constant draining. He was called *typhoid mary* more than once—perhaps this was another real name, with weight and value. The imprimatur had something to do with his human mother, long dead. Jag 120 once protested that Jag 39 was not the only one to be brought low by mating with humans. Something had polluted their bloodlines, some quality that had begun their subjugation. Many died quickly. More had gone mad, resigned to their dark future as lab rats and oddities, silently hoping for fortune turn again, fruitlessly trusting in some unknown messiah. The balance of power was tidal; it always shifted eventually…though probably not in their lifetimes.

Once, Jag 39 woke up while the keepers were removing his *puquel* again. Either that, or the practice had become so common that they had neglected to anesthetize him. They merely put it in a clamp and pulled it off. It went into a jar like all the others, its head unpierced, its potential denied.

Pull off my skull instead, Jag 39 thought. The pain would be as intense, but at least it would stop. His overseers were unsympathetic.

This time, however, Jag 39's sex organ did not regenerate as rapidly. What was forming inside the armored cubby between his legs was different. Perhaps he was mutating, or evolving in a protective response to repeated trauma. The other drugs made it hard to maintain a chain of thought.

Like many prisoners of many races past, Jag 39 thought about ways to hasten his own death, to deny his imprisoners the pleasures of this bottomless torment. Like many before him, even humans, he thought that the most honorable way to die would be to take at least one of the enemy with him. Some of these synapses of thought took days to travel inside his head, thanks to the medications, which were really no better than the caustics applied for his ritual passage to adulthood. It was all part of *becoming*…something else.

And something new was definitely happening, even perceived through a blurry haze of chemical hallucination and back-dreaming. For one thing, the keepers stopped shocking him. For another, they changed his nutrient diet. He began to feel fuller, stronger, more whole. They lost interest in tearing off his *puquel* at every opportunity, probably because it had finally refused to grow back.

But Jag 39 alone knew that it *was* growing back, in a form he had never seen. He needed an elder to explain it to him, but fraternization was almost nonexistent.

Turns out you're good for something after all, the fat jailer taunted him. *Finally we got an antibody we can use.*

Jag 39 was not sure what this meant. His regular jailer was pink and bristly, offensive to the senses. He always smelled like carrion. If there was one human to kill to purchase the honor of his own demise, this was the prime candidate.

The member evolving between Jag 39's legs had a lot of the properties of his lost *puquel,* but it seemed folded back on itself, almost defensively. It made sense. Contemplation of it, between sessions to suck the blood and antigens out of his body, used up a lot of time.

Things got more confusing when the fire broke out. Smoke occluded the thick, shatterproof panels of pre-stressed laminate. Strobes etched lightning in the smoke as klaxons bleated ear-piercingly. The sequestration cubicles occupied by Jag 39 and his kind self-bolted in automatic lockdown. Black Widowers could be suffocated; it had been proven in tests. Better they suffocate in their holes than be saved for later use. Replacements could be easily acquired, or, as it also had been discovered, bred to order.

Inside Jag 39's cell the heat reached one hundred sixty degrees by the time he placed his spread palm on the transparent surface and felt that it had begun to soften. It would not break, but it would melt. Outside the cell it got even hotter. The flames roared with a waterfall sound, feeding on the multitude of incendiary liquids and materials in the lab. Heat that could fry a human being from the lungs out was no problem for Jag 39, who had in this very room learned patience, above all. If one waited long enough...

His depleted muscles throbbed with the hunger for incipient action. There was plenty of commotion outside, the sound still

muted by the plastic panels, as functionaries scurried to save samples, prevent pressurized tanks from exploding, or salvage hard
drives—anything, in fact, before the thought of freeing the live sub-
jects of their scientific inquiry. Black Widowers were too dangerous
to liberate, even during a catastrophe.

A frightening-looking creature paused before Jag 39's cell. It was
the tubby pink sentry, clad in an insectile mask of goggles and hoses.
It was pointing at Jag 39 repeatedly. Then it displayed its middle
finger, to what purpose, Jag 39 could not understand.

Jag 39 reached through the softened glass and clutched his tor-
mentor by the throat. The liquefying plastic sizzled on his exposed
skin. He yanked the guard's head off his body. Gushing red blood
doused the licks of fire that scared up on Jag 39's arm.

Six escaped the lab during the chaos that ensued.

They banded into the nearby mountains for sanctuary, compar-
ing wounds, damage, memories and mutations. They hoped others
of their kind had survived other experiments in other places, but had
no way to know, being newly unleashed and completely ignorant of
the world. They bonded by what they could recall of the old rituals,
or estimate. They gave each other real names. Jag 39's new name was
Skedshya, which meant "first one."

That was because he was the first to discover that he had self-
impregnated, having become parthenogenetic. The time had come
to begin again.

········.

¡Qué la Cancion!
or:
The Dream of a Masked Man

(2001)

When you see the furniture, you pretty much know where you're headed: The rainswept neon night, the fallen-angel city, the trenchcoats and fedoras, big buglike vintage autos, femmes fatale, the cigarette smoke unreeling toward the ceiling, the half-empty bourbon bottle, the half-closed office of private investigation, the betrayals and the mournful darkside music—all of it iconography we have chosen, for better or worse, to shortform as hardboiled, or *noir,* or both. And that's it.

If you know in advance you're reading a hardboiled novel, the game holds few surprises for you. If you know you're watching a classic film *noir,* not only are the house odds against the anti-hero, but it's foregone that the Main Girl will die in the end, or dump him. And he'll have a conscience that's battered but clear. And most of his friends and allies will be dead. And on top of that, it'll be pissing down rain.

Same with superheroes. As soon as the social misfit with the oddball powers or goofy Spandex costume shows up, it all becomes as predictable as a Godzilla sequel—a lot of stuff gets destroyed, whole crowds die en masse, the threat is allayed until the next sequel, and nothing ever really changes.

Sonambulo doesn't live in these worlds; he challenges them.

"Down these mean streets a man must go who is not himself mean, who is neither tarnished nor afraid," wrote Raymond Chandler, in "The Simple Art of Murder," speaking of detectives more than half a century ago. Chandler did not know he was writing the playbook for all the present-day pretenders to his throne, from the overrated best-selling xeroxes to the worthy descendants and inheritors, like Crumley, like Goodis, like Willeford. "He must be a complete man and a common man and yet an unusual man." That's Sonambulo, which brings us to the topic of *enmascarados*.

The essence of the wrestling mask in the *cultura de lucha libre* is that the man beneath it could be anyone from a migrant worker to deposed royalty. (In fact, the distinctive oval shape of the eyeholes in El Santo's mask design was inspired by Dumas' *The Man in the Iron Mask*, and the legend that the interior of the mask had been rusted out by decades of the tears from its captive king.) The masked man could, in short, be any member of the audience in walking street-life, which is why luchadors—heroes and villains both—have a social status that transcends the mere playing of parts. As Chandler notes of his ideal detective, "He must be, to use a rather weathered phrase, a man of honor—by instinct, by inevitability, without thought of it, and certainly without saying it. He must be the best man in his world and a good enough man for any world."

Outside of *lucha libre,* most of the time, references to guys in wrestling masks are played strictly for laughs, summoning this potent cultural image only to mock it. Not so, in Sonambulo's world. Attackers frequently deride him as "fat" or "old man," usually before getting their heads shoved up their asses. That's the price you pay for no respect. Per Chandler, "He will take no man's money dishonestly and no man's insolence without a due and dispassionate revenge."

Ah, but what about sex? Chandler had that covered, too: "He is neither a eunuch nor a satyr; I think he might seduce a duchess and am quite sure he would not spoil a virgin; if he is a man of honor in one thing, he is that in all things." The women do not call Sonambulo "fat" or "old man." They look at him the way that siren on the splash page of "Mala Noche" regards him.

We know that, like Santo, Sonambulo had a glorious past, from hardcore Greco-Roman grappling to film shoots staffed with a bevy of bodacious bloodsucking beauties straight out of *Las Vampiras*. As enmascarado, he's central to the narrative, and solitary—that is, he doesn't have any masked buddies or allies that we know of. He walks the mean streets (or drives in one of a variety of luxurious rides) alone, and is accorded the automatic respect of bad guys and good guys alike, and nobody ever mentions that mask, just as they wouldn't if they were dealing with enforcers like Santo or Blue Demon or Mil Mascaras, whose vintage Sonambulo shares.

It's worth pointing out here that the Sonambulo saga plays out in modern-day real time, despite the post-World-War trappings. You have to look closely, but you'll see that seductive aspects of past decades have interleaved—Forties suits, Fifties car culture and science fiction, Seventies cult looniness; all side-by-side with drive-thru taco stands and ponytailed malefactors. Sonambulo's world is itself dreamlike, a fantasy potpourri in which dial phones and 500-channel cable can comfortably coexist.

Sonambulo takes a bullet. It's the first thing we see happen to him, before we even get our first glorious, full-page look at his countenance. He packs an automatic (in a world otherwise armed with revolvers) but never shoots anybody. In combat, to Sonambulo, "old reliable" is a folding chair, the weapon of choice in the bloodiest ring battles. We do glimpse a brief flashback to a lucha match past, but Sonambulo, who has the arcane power to read the dreams of others, cannot dream himself, because...well, that's getting ahead of the story, into the spoiler zone.

Maybe someday we'll get an idea of the circumstances that drove him away from the squared circle.

In a nice nod to Mike Hammer, creator Rafael Navarro has blessed Sonambulo with the ever-tolerant and always-available Xochti. She is his Velda, and if you don't know what that means, you really should be reading something else—about more guys in Spandex, maybe.

Okay, one Navarro story: It's the middle of the night and Raf is painting a velvet banner in a corner of my living room. He mentions a longterm jones for Linda Darnell (born Manetta Eloisa Darnell), especially her performance in a movie titled *Fallen Angel* (1945). I said, "I've got that right here; you want a copy?" And his whole face lit up.

And if yours just did, too, you're ready for what *Sonambulo* has to offer in its pages.

———

(Rafael Navarro's first three issues of Sonambulo *have been assembled into a glorious trade paperback titled* Sonambulo: Sleep of the Just (The Collected Case), *now available from 9th Circle Studios. Visit the* Sonambulo *website at: http://www.sonambulo.com.)*

THE GHOSTING

Ever see one of those paranormal investigation shows? The kind where a nightvision camera spooks around an abandoned house purported to contain haunts? Shaky-cam jitters and whispered conjecture? *"What was that?! Did you hear a sound?!"* And later the intrepid ghost busters sit around and compare notes with some hysterical local, and the payoff is always the same:

"Right there, on the tape—is that something?"

"Definitely something."

A bunch of emotionally excitable idiots concur that "something" happened, every week. They want it to be something preternatural; they *need* it to be something "other"—or there's no episode next week.

They make "something" out of nothing, literally. And you do, too. Of course, making up things is the essence of entertainment. You make a tacit pact to endorse the patently unreal for the purposes of your own amusement or enlightenment. But those people on those ghosty shows have never come within rumor distance of an actual disembodied spirit.

Believe me, I've learned a lot about this since I died.

The first thing you need to know is that ghosts are a fancy of the human mind, not the ghost mind. A willing suspension of disbelief by living beings hungry to embrace a romantic concept of post-mortem existence. A wish-fulfillment in terms convenient to drama.

Here are the bullet points:

(1.) Ghosts cannot see you. They have no idea where you are. They can hear you, sometimes, but it's all vaporous white noise. It's like trying to follow a sketchy radio broadcast of a rapidfire speech in Mandarin.

(2.) Ghosts cannot interact with the living world. They cannot move objects. They wish they could. Poltergeists? Please.

(3.) Ghosts cannot manifest to living people. They have no control, conscious or otherwise, nor can they communicate backward, past the slammed door of death. Death is a disempowerment.

There is a single conditional, highly specialized exception to (1), (2), and (3), which I'll get to in due time.

(4.) Ghosts can see other ghosts, which is a pain in the ass because every ghost of every person who ever died is *still hanging around*, and this afterlife (if you want to call it that) is really overcrowded, which doesn't matter in the sense of pure physics, because ghosts weigh nothing and don't absorb any space. If this is Purgatory, there is no maximum capacity.

(4a.) "Pain in the ass," above, is necessarily subjective.

(5.) If you're enchanted by the notion of a spirit-lamp salon with the likes of Einstein, Sophocles or Oscar Wilde, forget it. Most retain only vague memories of their walking lives. They are ghosts of their former selves.

(6.) Nor are they the perfect versions of their ex-selves. They remain as they were when they died, tumor-ridden, decrepit, insane from dementia. The scenario where you reunite with your beloved as freshly-minted youngsters? Not bloody likely. The only things missing are the oxygen tanks, poop bags and IVs. And most often your own people won't remember you, anyway. Not after the post-mortem time disorientation.

I wish ghosts could be as the living imagine them. That would solve a lot of problems. Hell, it would even be fun. Revenge from beyond the grave? Sign me up! A jingling bell to indicate to your survivors that you approve or disapprove? If only. That stuff about a loving reunion with your most beloved pets? Forget it—no animals here, although some of the dear departed are pretty beastly.

About the actual circumstances of my death I have conflicting and unreliable memories. The heart pumping, blood flowing period all seems like a half-remembered nightmare, inaccurate and with huge holes of jump-time unaccounted for. I *think* my name was Ernest but that might have been a convenient name I popped in to make the narrative flow, to bridge the void of identity common to sleeping thought. The "I-guy." The point of view character. Ernest Protagonist.

Ernest did not have a ghost mentor. He learned all the rules via bitter experience. He remembered that thousands of people attribute odd feelings, inspirations and insight to the presence of supernatural entities, the guiding whisper of the spirits of the deceased. It doesn't work that way. A living person passes through, or intersects, several hundred ghosts every day (because of the overpopulation Ernest mentioned; the sheer crowding). The ghosts are aware of the collision—sometimes—but the people never are.

The dominant human need that endures is the desire to invent explanations that address the *why* of it all. Only then, as a ghost, can you learn true despair, because the rules work randomly and no one hands out a guide or manual for coping with the afterlife.

Or this damnably frustrating between-life…if, indeed, there is another existence to suffer after one has been a ghost. But Ernest has seen people from the dawn of time still hanging around. There's no census. Surely *someone* has moved on to…something. If so, there's no intel; no reports from back from the new frontier. Ghostly day-to-day is like the world's worst holding area, out where the buses no longer run.

A world of nothing, where Ernest longs for "something" to happen. Anything. There's no rhyme to the scheme, and if there's a God, he or she or it or they are certainly not here, either, nor are any of religion's most suspect entities.

A riverbank has no awareness of the flowing water that shapes it. There is a relationship there, but each side is powerless to influence the other intentionally. Stuff just happens. During rare instances of lucid contact with fellow ghosts, Ernest has seen and felt the crushing desire to flip a playing card, to nudge just one Ouija planchette. But ghosts cannot interact with the world from which they have been evicted.

Ghosts are *lost*. Trying to grope backward, to meddle in the affairs of living beings, seems defeatist and regressive. They want to retreat instead of advance. As it turns out, everybody living or dead wants something they cannot have.

A ghost can sit on a park bench, but only because that ghost's imagination says *you are now seated on a park bench*. He occupies no space and there is no physical contact. The fact of being seated is a figment of that ghost's desire to perform a mundane human activity. Ghosts don't need to sit, and from what Ernest has witnessed, they mostly just mill around in denial. They don't need to eat—that's a given—and they don't need to sleep. Rest versus exertion and the need to refuel are human conceits.

Ghosts are awake and aware all the time, which is why so many of them are incomprehensible or delirious.

Which is how Ernest got the first inkling that he was different, because he managed (or thought he managed) to fall asleep, and have a dream.

———————

The dream was about a woman named Camilla.

She was dark, almost Ethiopian-black, with big, expressive eyes in a streamlined, pantherish face and a tiny, fetching gap between her two front teeth. Small in build, compact, capable. Elegant hands. A smile that could light up even the world of the dead.

Now, wait, Ernest thought. *Is this a legitimate dream or am I porting old leftovers of sense memory?*

Camilla folded her arms and shook her head, waiting for Ernest to figure it out.

Is this how it starts—the destabilization, the craziness? Am I thinking backward or looking forward?

And you know what happens in a dream when you start to perceive it as a dream.

You wake up.

———————

The dead don't dream, Ernest was told by a soldier named Kimani.

Kimani had died in furious combat in some war. He was still wearing his battle fatigues, bloodstained because half his head was gone, but his uniform still obligingly conveyed his name to the universe of ghosts. The military strip of canvas over his left breast pocket said who he was (or who he had been) in faded black stenciled letters.

Is imagining a dream the same as dreaming? Ernest asked.

You miss it, Kimani said, therefore you want it. Doesn't make it real. You want to think you can still dream.

Everything wanted by everybody is essentially a dream, said Ernest.

Kimani replied, that kind of thinking is for the living. Not us. You were not sleeping. You wanted to sleep, so you convinced yourself you were asleep. Not the same at all. You sleep in battle. You try to convince yourself that the battle is a nightmare. But the battle is what is real—and the world where there is no constant battle is the dream.

Do you remember how you died? said Ernest.

Kimani shrugged; almost chuckled. I feel asleep, he said.

———————

You already know the croaky old saying about what happens if you die in a dream...

...but what if the dreamer is already dead?

In a flash of stupidity I realized I had become one of *them*— the psychic philanderers, the quixotic wanna-believers, concocting unlikely weird tales to trap the unknowable in a box, no better than

a caveman inventing fear-based moon myths and fire gods to blame
for his burdens of tragedy.

However, the dream of a ghost cannot be elevated by calling it
an experiment, because no proofs apply.

Which is why it took me more than a year to get back to Camilla,
the first time. That "year" is figurative, of course; an approxima-
tion. Imagine sitting on a folding chair in an empty room and doing
nothing for a year. Time is slippery for a ghost and cannot be reliably
measured. (Ghosts cannot truly sit, either, as I concluded earlier, but
you get my point.)

Sometimes the only privacy you can enjoy is inside your own
eyelids. Harder for ghosts, because you are noncorporeal and can see
through your eyelids, anyway. You can put your nonexistent head
down on your folded nonexistent arms, but that's like using X-Ray
Specs to spy on the next floor down. More ghosts, is what you see.

Difficult, it is, to perpetuate even the illusion of a mock of sleep.

The few ghosts that seem rational are usually irrationally needy.
Thus, you don't find a lot of sympathy in Ghostland. Everyone here
is more tragic than you think you are now.

I thought I had the melancholy bit down, until I met the
departed spirit of a person formerly known (she thinks) as Beatrice.
Becoming a ghost was her goal. It was better, for her, than the tread-
mill of paying bills and growing old alone, all the black jokes the
cosmos sees fit to dump on your head when you are most vulnerable.
All Beatrice ever wanted to do was *nothing*. If Ghostland had cable
TV, she'd be in paradise.

Another myth laid to rest is that ghosts are naked. Kimani's
uniform put the lie to that. In Beatrice's case, her death apparel was
a small blessing. No ghost is nude unless they died nude, and they're
rarer than you'd think. Jean-Paul Marat is probably wandering
around here somewhere, clutching an inadequate bath towel. Oh,
and that photo snapped at Père Lachaise supposedly depicting the
shade of Jim Morrison lurking near his own gravesite? Total fabrica-
tion; a bamboozle. He's not wearing the right shirt.

Here's the good news: *Death is not the end.*
Now guess the bad news. Right: *Death is not the end.*

It took a lifetime of reflection before Ernest realized that his "dream" of Camilla was not his dream, but *hers.*

Camilla was alive, dreaming of Ernest (whom she had never met), and Ernest's ghost was somehow hooked into the circuit. Hence, the exception to the "ghost rules" I mentioned at the beginning.

This opened up all kinds of speculation. Was Ernest a figment instead of an actual dead guy? Was there a special dispensation category for ghosts permitted to walk the dreams of the living, so that in time they might perhaps qualify for other, more traditional ghostly benefits? Was there a pathway back to waking life embedded somewhere in this code?

Sufficient, for me, that a stranger's dream-state might somehow provide a foothold on the world I'd left behind, if only by proxy. In due course, Camilla would naturally believe that *she* dreamed *me* up, when in fact I had been there—wherever—all along. Perhaps ghostly cross-talk was possible.

Ernest knew this because he had done exactly the same thing once, while he was an alive person.

Ernest's dream lover had been a woman named Miranda.

That brought the pain and frustration of trying to remember life, with all the roadblocks I have already described. Life as me. As Ernest, or whatever my name had been.

There was an old newspaper cartoon once featuring a wandering ghost who complains, "I spent this year as a ghost and I'm not sure where home is anymore." Imagine feeling like that *all the time.*

And yes, I'm aware I keep saying "you"—second person present tense—and then shifting gears without warning. I confected "you" as an imaginary audience, third person passive, overlapping with my first person present indicative. That should give you an idea of how things slip and slide where I am; I'm playing to a crowd while I'm actually talking to myself.

I told you it was confusing.

———————————

Greg Stiler used to be one such person who thought he knew the difference between dreams and reality, not to slam a nail in the idea too blatantly or anything. He knew an entire bogus lifetime could be sped through in the drowsy minutes that separate two hits of the SNOOZE button.

When he was a kid his worst nightmare was of waking up and preparing for school, then resignedly tromping to whatever his first period class had been...only to then wake up for real and begin the process all over again. But—and this is important—he dreaded the *idea* of the school-dream, not the dream itself. He did not experience what ordinary people called nightmares because he knew they were dreams, and never thought them nightmarish. Odd fantasias of his mind, yes, but not pragmatic waking reality. Snakes, phobias, even dying were rendered subpotent by his clinical fascination with their subject matter and nonlinear flow. In a way he was like the Senoi, the ancient Malaysian hunter-gatherers who were said to experience group-dreaming. The Senoi way was to go for the full sensation, good or bad, because they saw the dreams themselves as instructive rather than hazardous.

Deep-dreaming was also a terrific way to avoid conflict with his wife, Nora, especially since Greg was in the midst of a long-term affair with another woman. Some of his waking hours were wasted—privately—in a bottomless depression, because he had only managed to see his ladylove, Miranda, twice in the past year. He thus dreamed-awake of seeing her more, confabulating some future or alternate life that would permit him to speak directly to Miranda's eyes and deepen their tenuous relationship so that interlopers might not breeze it away by accident or whim. Especially his own wife. But access was not up to him.

Miranda sometimes behaved as though she was resentful in response to Greg's covetousness; a whiff of subordination that did not parse with her character. Time was squandered in catch-up, since their meetings had become so rare. There was no villain to fault and no blame to place. She once compared their relationship to two dust motes with no control over how they collide in a strong wind.

"Relationship" was really the wrong word for what they had, or shared. It seemed to fit Greg's marriage to Nora perfectly, though: At first there was practicality without romance (one could say sex without love), which freighted in its own skill-set of problems. Their mutual itch-scratching slowly unfolded into a passionless comfort zone. Exposure seeded familiarity, which then yielded something *akin* to romance—a convincing simulation of an actual, yet-uncaptured emotion. Familiarity surrendered to ultimatums. You know—the usual jet rollercoaster of two people blithely hoping they'll come into sync by accident. The downside was perpetuity without love. The dangers were clearly marked, hazard cones on the superhighway of human interaction.

With Miranda, there had been longing, infatuation, painful emotion, delirious consummation, and now this…void.

Greg Stiler wrote down exactly those words, trying to encompass on paper what had thorned his heart. It seemed dry and academic; too sensible. New trajectories needed to be sought. More contact with Miranda might come as an inadvertent upside, a fringe benefit of a blind gamble.

Try this, he thought: Replay old tapes.

He recalled the shape of her face from their last encounter. Gamin, banged, eyes sparkling with promise.

I need to see you more, he told her.

You know that's not up to me, she told him.

He held her face in his hands and saw her boldly naked beneath the diaphanous white nothing she wore. They plundered each other with a kind of sad desperation, as though one of them had to return soon to solitary confinement. It was easy to lose his senses in the thickness of her hair. The fantasy was sex, as an opportunity for contact. The reality was mad coupling that lost them crucial time, every time.

It became as stressful as two married folks having a capsule fling, forming a fragile time-bubble inside which they existed for one another free of outside influence, including atavistic guilt, responsible to nothing except the ticking clock. A complete secret, hermetically sealed.

With sudden clarity he saw it from Miranda's side. She was probably enduring just as much internal strife, perhaps more, solely to keep seeing him.

Greg's work suffered as a result, but no one noticed. His home life suffered too, and Nora noticed.

Greg pulled down a nice wage and health package by working as an in-studio camera operator for the news at four, five, six, eleven. Nora wore the ring on her finger, lived with Greg and tortured herself over what might be wrong with their relationship.

There was that word again—*relationship*. Wholly inadequate, begging obsolescence; cripes, what we need are some new clichés. As far as Greg could see, relationships were social role-playing structures intended to reinforce the incumbency of the status quo. He had read that somewhere. Structures—the blind zombie-walk of how one was presupposed to behave in a majority-vote, mutually-agreed-upon universe of normalcy—were death to him. He had tried to counterprogram and avoid the snares of the mundane. His job was structured. His marriage with Nora was structured. Dead ends require shunts to inhibit explosive decompression. Hence, Miranda.

Greg shared Miranda with no one. Not drinking buddies, co-workers, relatives nor strangers. He tried to keep her locked up inside his head, but occasional leakage was just the sort of thing that would set off Nora's alarms.

What is wrong with you? Nora would ask, leaning forward and furrowing her brow in concern. What's up with you?

Nothing, he lied, knowing his lie was actually pretty close to the truth.

Nothing. Day after day of non-news could erode your sanity if you actually bothered to pay attention. Local crimes, high-speed police pursuits endlessly documented, celebrity gossip, "human interest" stories of interest to no species, some war half a world away, some epidemic that did not involve upscale urban white people, some panhandling charity, the no-win charade of weather (*storms a-coming; button up; oops, maybe not*), suspects are presently sought, if you have seen this child, the eel-like morph of rules—what were laws yesterday became notions today, from vices to habits and back again—the assaultive cacophony of buy this, go here now, do that right away, keep up, go for it, just do it and try not to snap so *shots rang out* before *he turned the weapon on himself,* the end, see you next newscast.

Nora accepted the idea of stress at his job, but that was not the same as capitulation. People in *relationships,* you see, are supposed to dig. They feel a responsibility to delve all up into your biz. Perpetual cross-examination provides flaws, even if none exist at first. Ceaseless scrutiny, too many rats in a box, the result is generally the same.

There's something you're not telling me, Nora said.

It's nothing, he said. No *thing.*

He had not expected to see Miranda that night, late, and here she came in that wispy gown. Perhaps that was part of the sorcery: You had to *not* think about her for her to manifest. Unfair, but what was fair?

Nora was the reality—pragmatic, mundane and responsible. Miranda was the fantasy—exotic, dangerous and unpredictable. Greg was the man on the tightrope between them: *Careful. Tread cautiously. Watch the next step but don't think about it or you'll plummet. Is there a net? I forget.* Forgetting was a problem with Miranda. Greg lost so many pieces of her after each encounter that he feared he was editing her, leaving out something bad or blithely overlooking a flaw that might depreciate her status in his memory. Nora was much more present, therefore much more accountable. She had nothing better to do. Miranda flew in, flew out of Greg's life so randomly that there was no time for her to become boring, normal, or everyday.

It was at self-contemplative junctures such as this that Greg wondered how other people, his co-workers for example, managed to live at all with their catalogues of predetermined behavior, the rote ritual of their existence. On that alien planet, "partners" or "couples" were supposed to engage in a never-ending subsurface war that somehow demonstrated their compatibility or at least reassured their collision as not random. Shari was supposed to belabor Max about his inadequacies in front of his friends. Max, in return, was supposed to publicly poke gentle fun at Shari's slight weight gain. Barbara felt compelled to endlessly declaim on how she could have done better had she not stuck with Tyler until their union became a tar pit, sucking her down and trapping her bones for future study. Tyler felt he needed to point out Barbara's catastrophic untidiness as a measure of what he had sacrificed for her—yet another flaw in a thick and meticulously-annotated catalogue of tiny, annoying sins that proved Barbara was in fact some kind of mythological Nemesis. All this in public, at heightened volume, so eavesdropping strangers could nod their heads and quietly agree that your life was a living hell, and boyoboy did the world fuck you over. Laurie played he-said she-said to prove the uncaring universe was actually in her corner. Stefan occasionally fantasized about murdering Laurie just to silence her natter, but nothing serious, of course. Then came the complications of offspring and previous generations of judgmental relatives, all of whom got an ephemeral vote in one's nonexistent democracy of life. Shirley's parents disapproved of Mort. Mort stayed with Shirley for the kids. Mort and Shirley's satellites busied themselves forever digging a pit of opinion that became bottomless and inescapable. Their lives were so crowded with external noise pollution that they had ceased living long ago, no better than their DNA—they consumed, mated, excreted and would eventually die.

Miranda was, therefore, Greg's safe house.

Great, Greg thought. I'm in love with a ghost. A phantom. A woman unlike any I have ever known.

Of these, there were three general categories.

The categories included another, earlier ex-wife and at least five long-term live-in partners. It seemed slightly more respectful than subdividing his past loves by body shape, hair color or worse, sexual hit lists. Each category was named for the woman or girlfriend who engendered the type. The Beckys (never *Rebecca*; that was another subphylum entirely) were vivacious, flaky and ultimately impractical. The Katherines (including the *Kates* and *Katys*) were appealing but always booby-trapped with some infirmity (physical or mental, real or imagined). Greg began to fall out of love with his wife Nora (diminuation of *Eleanor*) the moment he realized she was another Victoria, the type for which he suffered the most pronounced weakness—strong-willed and determined yet clueless, educated but not smart, contrary and argumentative but not brave. Like a magnet that can attract or repel; rejection that flipped into temptation. The Victorias, the Noras always had multiple facets, suggesting a depth that never quite surfaced but traditionally drew Greg, moth-like.

Miranda did not fit into any category except her own.

You really dislike women, deep down, Miranda once told him.

No, he protested, knowing the knee-jerk immediacy of his denial might expose him as a fraud. I want to figure them out. They entrance me. They are the closest thing to an alien species I'll ever meet in this lifetime, and I want to know them.

Until you sleep with them, Miranda grinned. What made her so wise?

Greg would admit some truth in this, to the extent it did not do irreparable damage to his ego. Yes, he did tend to relish the pursuit more than the capture. He sought the moment of capitulation, that knowing look or phrase that signaled yes, I'm yours. But, he argued. But you have to start a relationship somewhere. One supposed that another one might admire some artist type from afar, and draw conclusions based on perceived simpatico. But. But for most humans, it had to begin with the elemental attraction, pheromones, physical attributes, and the synapse-fast bottom-line that first sparked to mind regardless of whether people would admit it or not: *I want to fuck you; do you want to fuck me?* Yes. No. Perhaps.

Amoebas managed to eat, reproduce, excrete, die without so much cultural fuss.

You see? said Miranda. You speak in terms of romance, but your meaning is in terms of conquest—pursuit, capture, capitulation, biological imperative. You just used that word you hate so much—*relationship*.

She was being willfully obtuse. If most things in our Western civilization were, as the saying goes, "done to pay a mortgage," then even the broad umbrella of that maxim withered before the even more dominant imperative: The base reason for anybody doing anything was to get laid. It was coded in the genes, buried under false fronts and protocol, a sleeper-bomb guaranteed to detonate with each and every encounter, no matter who wound up waking up with whom. All media, all culture, *everything* was vectored back toward the grim basic wiring of simple reproduction…which was not and never had been a danger, when it came to Miranda.

If you had me more, if you had me whenever you wanted me, our time would not be so special, she told him. She did not use the dreaded hot-button word, *relationship*. Damn, she was sharp.

That was pretty much how their last meeting had gone. They had made love anyway, with a strange inevitability, as though their numbered days were heralded, and now somebody was counting down. The less he saw her, the more he thought about her. It was crushing, toxic, to chase Miranda this way in his mind. Patience was required.

But if Miranda turned out to be a predator, Greg would be exposed as the world's biggest mark. Another warning flag.

The more he thought about what Miranda had said, the kinder he was to Nora, which of course raised her suspicions. At night, he awaited her.

Pretty soon, a year had passed and he had only seen Miranda twice. He wondered what else she might be up to. Prying was not in the ground rules of their time together; it was one of those mutual, unspoken agreements. It was impossible not to believe that she might be staying away on purpose.

I love you, Miranda had said without hesitation.

Nora told Greg *I love you* as well, but the message his brain received was oddly different. Disproportionate, deformed somehow.

A typical conversation:

Her: That's really annoying. Stop it.

Him: What?

Her: The way you keep staring at the tits of every woman on the street. It's crass.

Him: I am not staring. I am acknowledging them and moving on.

Her: You were staring like you were thinking about fucking each and every one of them.

Him: For a microsecond. It's just male coding. The breast is a natural bullseye. A circle within a circle within a circle.

Her: Uh-huh. You certainly looked hypnotized.

Him: It was a glance, not a look.

Her: It was not a glance. You were going back for seconds.

Him: I *look* at people. I can't help it. The planet is full of them. On your world I'm sure it's different—equitable, fair, non-sexist androids who are never offended by people noticing them.

Her: Unfair. You're trying to put it all on me, like I'm nuts or something.

Him: *This* is totally unfair. Women check out men's asses all the time, and we can't throw your little tantrum because our backs are turned.

Her: Mm-hm. So someone is checking out your ass? Who?

Obviously Nora had graduated to the phase where Greg became property—slightly more intelligent than a cat, slightly less needy than an infant, slightly guilty no matter what, requiring constant monitoring in her fervent hope that eventually he would slip up and justify all her suspicions. Nora therefore became Greg's concession to a world in which he did not wish to live, but found himself trapped.

He wanted to tell Nora I love you as best as I can, but please don't expect me to do it in terms of what you call a relationship. They had only been married several years; in Greg's mind, there was still plenty of time to try and force his thoughts into cogent speech.

You were talking in your sleep, Nora told him. And by the way...who's *Miranda?*

———

It is rare but not unheard of to experience a dream with "conscious point-of-view cognizance," otherwise known as lucid dreaming. Presumably this sort of awareness—knowing you are inside of a dream—permits manipulation of the dream elements. After all, it's *your* brain.

Trapped in some kind of hotel...the rush-rush schedule always an issue, an imperative...snakes by the thousands...Freud's ghost is on the verge of shitting himself with ectoplasm...this is all such a knee-slapper...

...unlike the time-wasting dream psychedelia in books and movies, made-up stories, where some character always goes *huhh!* and sits up into the camera for a cheapo shock effect.

Greg recognized the setting—the hotel. The "lucid" part came with his perception of the dream *as* a dream while *within* the dream. As for the snakes, that was a too-simple oneirological checklist of fear versus hidden threats, or subconscious callousness, sexual temptation, or transformation (depending on how you felt about serpents in general). Greg's special new point of view made the dream like a chapter play or serial, where the narrative progressed and a little bit more was learned with each installment. Usually the thrill of finding out what happened next was the saboteur that rushed him awake, too soon. Conventional dreams generally terminate around a crisis point, what would be called a climax in sex, or fiction. The danger in this more sophisticated form of dreaming was built-in; the moment you become aware you are inside a dream, you run the risk of waking up at that moment before you can build anything. But then Greg discovered that he could fall back asleep and *resume the story* right where he'd left off.

You are hereby dared to convince a single soul that this would not be more tempting than the formiciform day-to-day of the waking world.

It took forever for Greg to find Miranda again, and when he did, he tried to force her to be a perfect version of herself, which was impossible despite the bent physics of dreamtime. It became more important than ever for Greg to deny the waking world entirely, to hold it at bay indefinitely, during the dreams which were the only opportunity he had to see Miranda again.

But he was so excited to find her after such a long break that he blew it, and woke up back in the world where he would have to arrange half-truths in such a way that Nora didn't think he was cheating on her.

Wasn't it the same as their entire argument about ogling women on the street? Come on, viewing audience: more guilt, or less? Vote now.

Miranda looked Greg eye-to-eye and told him: The only way for our love to endure, the only way to preserve the intensity of what we have now, is for me to never become more real for you than I am right now. As if you had found the perfect love of your life and she died. No one can ever compete with that kind of bond.

Greg's denial of this was stronger than Miranda's love. Wasn't *he* in control, here?

Miranda tried to tell Greg that she was a fantasy. He did not buy it.

Miranda tried to tell Greg she was dead. Ditto.

And finally, Miranda stacked the deck, telling him volatile things that would cause him to acknowledge the dream state, and thus awaken.

Greg perceived this as a rejection. Miranda had rejected him, and pretty soon Nora left him, and the nights became full of hours during which Greg could not sleep at all anymore.

The decay arc was long and lonely. And when Greg Stiler finally managed to fall asleep—still hoping to find Miranda one more time—he was behind the wheel of his car. He died.

———————

Now, I don't know offhand who Greg Stiler was, but I vaguely suspect he might have been me. Which explains a lot about my meet-ups with Camilla.

I cannot tell Camilla that our entire intersection is doomed, because she is my only surcease from this daunting forever of ghostness. By not telling her, I doom her as well, possibly to the same fate suffered by somebody named Greg Stiler. Only the loss of everything makes you this selfish, about a single thing.

It's no secret that many people prefer dreams to waking experiential reality. For one thing, dreams—as we have seen—lack the boring bits of the narrative. Even the routine is tinged with incipient excitement, a-crackle like ozone in the air. Other people believe the dream state to be just as experientially valid as waking life. Or that waking life and the dream-realm can flip-flop within one consciousness, sometimes at will. Just ask any opium addict. No wonder Muslims believe dreams to be the only way they can receive revelations from God.

Happy endings are for children's storybooks, Kimani tells me (with half a face). The closest we come to living is when we ask questions. For the answers to be obvious, or provided at all, would negate the whole purpose.

But Camilla is in such an agitated emotional state that she has become the way Greg Stiler used to be: she prefers sleep, encourages its opportunity, does it too much because she's a hopeful explorer. Ernest Protagonist must wait around for Camilla to (1) figure out the system in order to usefully deploy it at will; (2) flavor her dream lover according to her needs and wants, her tastes and her prejudices, her desires and fantasies; yet (3) somehow recognize that her preferable dream mate came with baggage of his or her own, that he or she needs a new name because it is the current fanciful incarnation of me. I. Ernest Protagonist, and possibly Greg Stiler, too, and who knows how many others.

Because Camilla needed to be warned about what had happened to Greg Stiler and Miranda. If you are the dream lover and the dreamer *dies*...well. I already know what happens, ghost hunters. An eternity of the endless non-society of other ghosts, as I have described. Endlessly. For the dreams of Camilla seem to be rare fortune indeed, unlikely to happen more than once to such a poor spirit as myself. Did it happen more than once to Miranda? I wonder.

Which leaves me, Ernest Protagonist, ghost, waiting eternally for Camilla (who does not know me, remember) to fall asleep again...and perhaps dream me.

From what I said earlier, you should have surmised that this is not the sort of story that has either climax or resolution. *That* is exactly why you never want to be in my position—no closure, ever. That is why becoming a ghost, with only a slim chance of living in the dreams of the living, is the final big joke of the cosmos.

Which leaves me, Ernest Protagonist, telling stories to you (himself) in the afterdeath. Making things up, if you like. It passes the time.

....

An Introduction to
Catacombs,
by John Farris

(2008)

In the lagan of contemporary horror fiction, few writers balance mainstream accessibility with stylish literacy as does John
Farris, whose work slips the snares of genre to plumb, as he
has said, "strange states of life." His principal platform most
frequently encompasses advanced states of perception (psycho-
kinesis, psychic twinning, doppelgangers, dream projection),
human mutation (advanced telepaths, regressive animal hybrids)
and the obscure playbook of African sorcery. His standard practice is to employ a suspense/thriller structure, re-imagining
mythologies or inventing whole new ones, and recombining
them with aspects of the puzzle-box crime novel, the eccentric
casts of glitterati fiction, and outright Grand Guignol. He is also
a mordant sociopolitical critic who writes with a refreshingly
adult sexuality—in all, strongly counter-programming against
the tired tropes of horror. As Stephen Gallagher noted, "Farris
isn't one for finding a comfortable spot and then sticking in it.
Many authors would stop dead at such a point of success and
get into the cloning business. (In his work) I can't identify any
pattern other than a restless wandering around a recurring set
of themes."

In the interests of full disclosure: I have been a Farris reader since I discovered a used paperback copy of *When Michael Calls* about five years after it was first published. Before my first novel came out in 1987, my publisher sent a manuscript copy to John Farris for a blurb, or something. A year after the book had come and gone, an editor in the New York publishing offices handed me an envelope that had been sitting around in my file; it was a letter from John Farris.

"I don't read much fiction these days," he wrote, "mostly because I am particular about what I put into my head." There followed a page and a half of the most extravagant praise I could ever have wished for, tempered by the knowledge that this man sat down and flipped a stack of unbound manuscript pages (which had to have produced an unwieldy mess) and based his thoughts on actually reading my novel, not defaulting to a logline synopsis.

Some years after that, I got to meet the man himself. Since then we have shared numerous drinks and dinners and hours upon hours of talk; I subsequently dragged him onto the internet in 2001 with his own "official" website, *Furies & Fiends*, mostly because it was a crime that there existed no workable online bibliography of his output. Then I dragged him into the backwaters of the small press by editing a collection of his short fiction (*Elvisland*, Babbage Press 2004), and further dragged him into the deranged snakepit of television by adapting one of his short stories into the *Masters of Horror* episode titled "We All Scream for Ice Cream" during the 2006-2007 series season.

I recently brokered some of his early output—Gold Medal-style hardboiled paperback originals written as "Steve Brackeen"—toward the good offices of Hard Case Crime, which plans to republish them with (I hope) suitably lurid covers.

So I can no longer pretend any sort of objectivity.

But it is all in pursuit of getting word out, grabbing people by the scruff and telling them to pay attention. John Farris has seen the luxuriant coverage enjoyed by many writers with far less talent, principally because he is a very private man who likes to let his work do the talking and is not wont to parade himself publicly.

He had already achieved best-selling celebrity at age 23, with *Harrison High* (Rhinehart & Co., 1959), a grittier riposte to the then-popular *Blackboard Jungle* subgenre, which spawned five sequels and a movie adaptation (by James Gunn), *Because They're Young* (1960).

Following a trio of mainstream novels (*The Long Light of Dawn* [Putnam, 1962], another "Brackeen," *The Guardians* [Holt, Rinehart & Winston, 1962], and *King Windom* [Trident, 1967]), Farris took what he termed "baby steps" toward a style that would later come to be known as "psychological horror" with his next three novels: *When Michael Calls* (Trident, 1967), *The Captors* (Trident, 1969), and *Sharp Practice* (Simon & Schuster, 1974)—straightforward suspensers about an apparent haunting, a kidnapping, and a serial killer, respectively; correctly summarized (by Gallagher, again) as "popular mainstream (whose) common angle of approach was a kind of heightened, erotically-charged contemporary realism." This led Farris to categorize his watershed novel, *The Fury*, as "a thriller with occult overtones," although it is as much about black ops, assassins and bureaucratic dirty tricks as psychic twins, telekinesis and new mutations of human evolution.

In 1973, Farris wrote and directed *Dear Dead Delilah*, at about the same time Tobe Hooper was changing the complexion of horror cinema by ruminating on chainsaw massacres down Texas way. *Delilah* is almost a "lost" film in the pantheon of 1970s horror movies and the new wave they engendered, in much the same way that everyone knows *Halloween* (1978), but far fewer know *Black Christmas* (1974). (The movie version of *When Michael Calls* also featured an eerily prescient murder in a Hallowe'en spookhouse, as a body smashes through a display of lighted jack o'lanterns.) *Delilah* was screen dame Agnes Moorehead's final picture.

As fortune would have it, *The Fury* (Playboy Press, 1975) was a calculated strike by Farris just as horror fiction experienced a rejuvenation during the late 1970s—the success of this book (best-sellerdom and a film adaptation by Brian De Palma [1978], from a Farris screenplay) cemented his alliance with the genre for most of his subsequent output. This adventurous tale, of adolescent psychics beleaguered by sadistic government operatives who wish to exploit their nascent magical abilities, explicated another major Farris theme: the costs exacted when people fail to acknowledge the power of preternatural beings who have been among us all along.

All Heads Turn When the Hunt Goes By (Playboy Press, 1978) is Farris' take on the "family curse" novel, a grim, downbeat story of the failure of redemption against the indomitable will of an African snake goddess. Informed by a keen eye for the idiosyncracies of aristocracy in the American South, it is also a story of generational karma debt—and who must pick up the bill, no matter how innocent they seem.

Similarly, *Shatter* (W.H. Allen, 1980) is about the sins of the fathers visited upon the sons, but without the supernatural element. It reads more like an abandoned screenplay idea, or a re-take on *All Heads Turn* with the snake goddess rinsed out, and courts another recurrent Farris theme, blurred identity.

And sure enough, assorted encyclopediae and reference texts started coming to me, as though I had some kind of lowdown on this John Farris: *Write an entry on* The Fury *for us. Summarize Farris' career. Tell us why you like* All Heads Turn *so much... because we can't figure it out...*

John very kindly wrote an introduction to a collection of mine (*Black Leather Required*, Ziesing 1994). Now it's payback time.

A painter, John Farris sometimes organizes his narratives around specific color palettes—decayed greens and golds for *All Heads Turn*, and blood-red for *Catacombs* (Delacorte, 1981), his epic twist on *King Solomon's Mines*, concerning the crimson diamonds discovered deep in a Mt. Everest tomb built by the feline race of Zan, who, though long dead, still exert influence over the locale and the stones. As the author reminds me, the book "is maybe the best example of what I mean when I say nowadays, 'I don't write books; I paint them.'"

H. Rider Haggard was enjoying a hell of a resurgence-by-proxy in the early 1980s: 1980 had just hosted Michael Crichton's *Congo* (same theme) and 1981 saw the premiere of *Raiders of the Lost Ark* (same theme, with its brains kicked out). Where Crichton deployed his usual savvy for flavor-of-the-month technological hardware, Farris brought on a legion of dirty tricksters, a whiff of the supernatural, and not one but two powerful, credible female leads.

Longtime readers of Farris will be compelled to notice his predilection for strong female characters, some of the best-written in all contemporary fiction. In *Catacombs*, Erika Weller and Raun Hardie are fully-fleshed, flawed, brave and resourceful women, not mere girl-skins mouthing "male" dialogue. They *have* to stand out, considering that the first section of the book literally teems with characters—so many, in fact, that the set-up is a dizzying opera that mandates close attention from the reader (one cunning trick is that the book's so-called Part One is ninety per cent of the novel, a la Trevanian's *Shibumi*). It is equal parts adventure, political thriller, travelogue, and supernatural suspense, by turns poetical, then hardboiled. In other words, *not* a beach read.

But all that makes it sound stuffy, and it is not.

Consider, for example, Erika's rape. (And for those allergic to "spoilers," please grow up.)

No nick-of-time cliffhanger "save," here. The assault, courtesy of a pair of British poachers who banter like lost vaudevillians, is given to us from Erika's point of view, serious as a nuclear meltdown. Normally tough and resilient, Erika, wounded and ill, has given herself over to despair: *"The jolting, humiliating attack couldn't concern her"*—and she defangs it in her mind as a "rompering," which allows her to keep her wits dispassionately enough to witness, with dream-like amazement, the almost immediate dispatch of her abusers in a machine-gun passage that exemplifies Farris at his most potently descriptive. Not one to gratuitously abuse his heroine, Farris sides with her by rendering her attackers derisively, even finishing one off with a wince-inducing pun.

Come to think of it, the title of the novel is a pun, too. The sense of humor with which Farris leavens his thrills and terrors is always arch and incisive, cynically comical, and too often overlooked in the reader's mad dash toward genre tropes—another way in which Farris and Trevanian are bitingly similar.

There are the normal and expected passions for a Farris adventure novel: the clandestine mission, the race against time, the intrusion of the paranormal into everyday governmental black ops, and the choking frustration of stifled communication among hyper-competent and self-realized characters. Make that *smart* characters—there are very few stupid people in John Farris books, apart from political mooks and government bully-boys, when used as spear carriers or local color. You have to have a sense of humor to write this sort of thing consistently, but even dogs are supposed to have a sense of humor, which means what we are really talking about here is wit. You, presumably, have read witless books and know the difference; if not, then *Catacombs* can demonstrate it for your edification.

This novel also represents Farris' recurrent love affair with the African continent, echoed in other works but here given the full-immersion treatment (the author cites seminal reference works in a rare Afterword). To quote bush pilot Philip Goliath, *"the beauty of this land is like a narcotic."* The characters of Matthew Jade and Lem Mestizo permit Farris to alloy his attraction to various forms of American Indian shamanism with the forces at work in the Catacombs, resulting in a peculiarly inclusive echo effect—the observation of one kind of mysticism through the lens of another, if you will. Unlike most treasure-hunt tales, the objective here is not a dead place, a long-forsaken tomb or mine, but a still-living locus of incalculable power, a place where the laws of physics bend. The race to the prize is exacerbated by this unfathomed power—the legacy of the cheetah-people of Zan—itself combining with the geothermic threat of Kilamanjaro about to blow its top, and the forces in collision are an unstable marriage indeed, one which Farris controls as adroitly as one of those guys who can juggle a chainsaw, a cream pie, and a baby. Then he uses the chainsaw to cut a piece of pie to feed to the baby, all in mid-air.

Another fascination, for the life and work of Nikola Tesla, creeps past late in the book to help explain how the ancient bloodstones might form a kind of forcefield to block nuclear attack (Tesla got a broader role in *Wildwood* [Tor, 1986], where he appears as a character). If you look very closely, there is also a tip-of-the-hat to the writer who essentially put paid to the entire spy-thriller genre, Rod Whitaker (a.k.a. Trevanian), late in the story.

In an age where far too many grownups are congratulating themselves for reading young adult fantasy novels (making them what psycholinguist Dr. Murray S. Miron has termed "discretionary illiterates"), *Catacombs* awaits as the type of novel that hits all the best-seller marks, yet traditionally eludes the readers of best-sellers. Neither impenetrable nor over-intellectual, it is merely complex, multi-spoked, and therefore more rewarding for the attentive reader. Per Farris, it is "both a premier circus act and painting of a unique landscape." Like King Solomon's diamonds, like the bloodstones themselves, it is a treasure awaiting an overdue rediscovery. By you, right now.

THE CHILI HUNTERS

At issue was the loss of Sonny's virginity. To stop thinking and talking constantly about getting laid and at last, take action.

Sonny's primary focus was Penny, from his seventh grade science class. She'd been around before, but this year Sonny saw her with new eyes. While the easygoing fifth-period teacher, Mr. Janowitz, dutifully presented the workings of the carbon atom, Sonny concentrated on the back of Penny's neck. The lackluster plaid dress her mother had probably bought for her, which Penny forced to look better by virtue of her own budding shape. Her beautifully smooth teenage calves, not a zit or mole or scratch to be seen. Penny liked Sonny. Sonny knew this because she had actually spoken to him.

Then there was Skip, Sonny's partner in (imagined) crime and constant passive nag. Talk to Skip, and within seconds the conversation was about jerking off, specifically Skip's talent for this young adult pastime. If masturbation was an Olympic event, Skip would have qualified for Team USA. Skip would whip out his dick and start stroking just to demonstrate (for anyone who did not flee immediately) how far he could ejaculate (several feet). But his experience of physical intimacy with the opposite sex was hobbled at the fifth grade level of "you put your thing in her pee hole." A seminal fluid spill into a girl's navel could get her pregnant. That sort of intel.

Penny's sudden and surprising availability had come to pass because of a talk she had with Sonny, originally about Skip. Her girlfriends feared Skip.

Sonny gallantly shouldered Penny's backpack to walk her home.
That was, hell, at least half a hour where they could talk about *any-thing they wanted*, unchaperoned and as free as you can get when
you're fourteen and trapped in suburbia.

"Yeah, Skip is really…*special*," she said, clenching her teeth and
giving an eye roll.

"He whacks off *all the time*," Sonny blurted, desperately hoping
this would not sound too forward. He was painfully aware of the
interruption in the topography of the back of Penny's dress. She was
wearing a bra now. Not so, one slight year ago.

"I hate the sex stuff," she said, staring dead ahead. "Like, Miriam
and Candace, they're always *talking* about it, and dropping little
hints like they *know* something, and they don't know shit."

Their stylish running shoes crunched gravel. They were technically on the outskirts of an Arizona burg that had sprawled to
fill an entire valley. Their current alma mater, Florence B. Hogan
Junior High ("Go, Vipers!") was newly-constructed to handle the
growth of the town-turned-small-city. Last year, the old junior high
on Sixth Street had gone to double shifts when the new one fell
behind on completion. The student body was split in half—first
group, six AM to noon, no lunch; second group, noon to six PM, no
lunch. Penny had been in the former, Sonny, the latter, so it was as
if she had vanished for a year and come back transformed. Sonny
loved the late shift. It allowed him to sleep until eleven o'clock in the
morning and come home when it was getting dark. He could stay
up late. He could do stuff he wanted to do as his household retired
around him. For Penny to arrive at school by six AM, she had to rise
at, what? Five, at least. Sunup. That must have taken some stamina.
When Sonny overdid his late-night personal time, their schedules
had *almost* touched at the ends. But now FBHJH was open for business, the kids in the tract housing had their own new school, and a
lot of them simply walked to and from in the vast amount of flat,
open desert parcels that had yet to be civilized. Less than a mile
away was the city line, past which people could still legally burn

their own trash. Skip's family had a mobile home out there; Skip had demonstrated to Sonny how an aerosol can could explode like a grenade when you lobbed it into the fire of the trash barrel, which was a charred oil drum. It made Skip want to rub out another spasm, of course.

But now Sonny and Penny were talking about sex—or at least, talking about talking about it—and she had said she *hated* it. Sonny had to tread very carefully. His insides already felt like a highspeed pileup on a slick freeway; was this what hormones were all about? Why didn't Mr. Jankowitz talk about *that* shit? That was scientific, right? Give a guy some warning about his own biology, for christ's sake. It was terrible. It was wonderful. That back-and-forth could rip a teenager apart.

"Oh, like Miriam and Candace would know anything," Sonny ventured. It was cautious. It was chivalrous—let Penny carry the topic if she wanted to.

"That's just it," she said. "They drop all these little hints about who did what with so-and-so, and it's all just *rumor*, it's—"

"Hearsay."

"Yeah, that's the *perfect* word."

Score one for Sonny, having come up with the perfect word to describe her distress. He had read the word in some horror paperback. Score one for books.

These kids could have been any color. Any race. They were Americans trapped in the fast-forward world of the 1970s. Their suspicion was that Mr. Jankowitz had once been a hippie. He still wore a home-made peace symbol belt buckle, which seemed to be an astonishing lapse on the part of ever-morphing dress code. His hair was shaggy but not long—technically—but he had cropped it on behalf of the teaching gig. Within a year, Mr. Jankowitz would be fired by the school board for taking a sick day in order to testify as a character witness for a friend that had been arrested for marijuana possession. Pink Floyd's *Dark Side of the Moon* album was still brand new. Sonny, Penny and Skip all owned it, and there was some chatter about proposing "Time" as that year's class song (as cruelly honest and depressing as it was), although the jocks would vote it down in favor of "Rocky Mountain High."

"Dottie bragged about going out with that guy Mario in his car," Penny said. "He was all over her, to hear *her* tell it, but I don't think they actually did anything except make out. But boy, Dottie talks like she went *all the way*, you know, hot and steamy, and it's just to make everybody else *jealous*, and it just sounds, I dunno…"

"Cheap?"

"Yeah, *perfect*." Her eyes went into laser focus as she tasted the word for herself. "*Cheap*."

Penny always spoke with a lot of *emphasis*, in aural italics, to get a point across. This was mesmerizing because while doing so she would frequently touch Sonny's arm to make sure she had his undivided attention.

Several points:

First, being in Arizona, every school had a large compliment of Mexicans in the student body. People were just beginning to call them Hispanics or Latinos (when they weren't calling them spics or taco-benders). Very often, they came into the local school system late, or failed certain disciplines and got held back a year or two. This meant that a few of them were actually old enough to *drive their own cars to junior high school*, a point not missed by the rest of the boys not yet old enough for a learner's permit. Female attention naturally skewed toward candidates with independent transportation, making the passed-over male contingent feeling as if they had a war on their hands since they were incapable of competing with wheels. The hottest, the sexiest, the most desired girls *always* went for the guys with the cars. Against that, it looked lame if you rode a bike to school or took the bus, which is why Sonny preferred walking.

Second, Dottie's braggadocio had already labeled her as *potential slut*, which required no truth at all to grow into *town pump*. If she kissed somebody in public on Monday, by Wednesday all the doper kids would be lining up to ply her with weed and cop a feel.

Adolescent females in the Arizona school system had to remain up-to-date on their perceived status rankings, which had the additional perk of keeping all the males in a state of high hysteria. Thus, Penny was expressing the view that she was not like Dottie, not at all, keeping Sonny bottomlessly grateful for the simple joy of speaking to her without an audience of their peers.

"Still, I hate all that," Penny said. "The *not knowing*. You ever feel like that?"

Sonny could feel his face flushing red. "Too much," he admitted.

"So you're a virgin, is that what you're telling me?"

Red became scarlet became crimson. Sonny felt sucker-punched and it was abruptly difficult to breathe. He had to hide his alarm inside his skin and not let her see it. How he responded to her frankness was at once the most important thing in the universe. The world ceased to exist around him—no desert, no home or school, no family or food at the end of his trek. There was only *right goddamned now.*

"Sure," he said, thanking his voice for not cracking. "Like… you?"

She sighed as if confirming an inner fear. "I hate *that*, too."

"It could be worse," he babbled. "I mean, we're not sick or crippled or retarded, our homes are okay…I mean, like, so many guys I know are all: My dad's a drunk, my mom's a whore, my brother's in jail, my sister's a junkie, my *other* brother is a Mormon…"

She snickered brightly, sharing the tension-release with him (instead of using it against him). "Yeah, boo-hoo-hoo, I *stayed in this goddamned town* and now I'm a loser!" She stopped Sonny with another touch on the arm. "But, listen. I have an idea."

Third point: For lack of any better recreational activity or secret clubhouse, many tract kids developed the ritual of the midnight sneak-out. There was no destination apart from the 24-hour convenience market a mile or so distant, near the highway. To reach that goal, you crossed a lot of undeveloped desert land threaded with half-assed bike trails, with the dirt stomped flat so you could see it by moonlight alone. The trick was to find a way to escape your own home once everybody else in the house had gone lights-out. The finish was to re-enter unobserved so that as far as family history was concerned, the walkout had never occurred.

It was the sort of crap you invented when you were fourteen and bored.

Some kids snuck out to get high. Or copulate, mostly by surmise. Largely it was hanging out. For a good part of the year, the desert was absolutely freezing at night, yet nothing tasted better than a cold drink from the convenience mart at those times. It was special, private, and personal. Best of all, it was *getting away with something*, which temptation was never lost on Skip, with whom Sonny usually hooked up on such missions.

Penny destroyed that whole pattern when she proposed just such a rendezvous with Sonny, for the purpose of terminating their mutual virginity.

"But not inside," she said. "Not in a house. Outside, where the stars are. So if anything goes wrong, I can remember the stars and not some cheesy bedroom in my house, or your house. Some stupid picture on the wall."

"Yeah," Sonny nodded, mouth dry, head spinning. "Your parents' bed or living room or something. Den decorations." Or my bed, he thought, wincing at how gross his own twin bed could become. It was a single. It was not designed for two. But he knew what Penny was actually saying, in the spaces between her carefully-ventured words.

The whole "slut" thing was uber-important, and hovered like a malignant ghost. It was as frightening as the pejorative "fag" for guys. It would be years before anyone would write about gender policing as a bullying ritual, but for those who had choked their way through *The Scarlet Letter* in English class the cultural warning was clear. Penny was a non-slut frustrated by her own inexperience. The social options of "slut" versus "nice girl" versus "ugly" did not provide a large enough menu. What she was saying—and it took courage to say it—was that for certain people, there was another option. They had to meet on mutual ground, as adults almost, and agree not to fall in love or anything stupid unless that, of course, followed naturally. They would not have the excuse of being stoned or drunk, the thing that would entrap so many of their classmates. They would be responsible and just get it over with.

They would be *getting away with something*, bigtime.

"Tomorrow night," she said, and gave him an unforgettable kiss to seal their secret pact. The kiss boded well.

"Yeah, if the Chili Hunters don't get us," Sonny said.

She smiled at that, and waved goodbye as they split up for their separate homes. It was a tiny, inconspicuous wave meant only for him.

How the hell was he going to sleep *tonight?*

———

Sonny had heard stories about the Chili Hunters ever since his family had moved to Arizona, back when he was starting third grade. Nobody had ever reliably seen one, and that lent the boogeyman myth enormous potency.

To hear other kids tell it, Chili Hunters were sort of a cross between the *chupacabra* and a clan of mutant cannibal mountain people, resentful at being elbowed out of their desert lairs by rampant development. Their breath stank of garlic, moonshine and onions. Their farts were stomach acid, brimstone and sulphur. Their teeth were file-sharpened and their finger and toenails resembled corn chips. They had yellow eyes. When they *got you*—because you had been misbehaving—they made chili out of you, and ate you, which was why no rumored victims had ever survived to describe them for real.

They shat out your bones.

The Chili Hunters only *got you* at night.

Sometimes they mated with human beings, but were not human themselves.

They might have been part animal. They possibly appeared as black-hole shadows, reflecting no light. They conceivably spent their daytime hours living in Hell, which was accessed by hidden rock tunnels. After that, the stories got a little ridiculous.

"There's something wrong with the tip of my dick," said Skip.

Sonny was busy flipping *Sticky Fingers* to side two. "Oh, god, *don't*," he said.

Too late. Skip already had his penis out. "It's got some kinda, I dunno, crusty shit on it."

It was a timing game for Sonny. See how long Skip could go without mentioning his dick. The record was usually about fifteen seconds.

"Maybe you're wearing it out," said Sonny, fighting not to look.

Skip's member was uncircumcised, the first one like that Sonny had ever witnessed. It resembled a kosher frank with a florette of skin at the business end, similar to the twist of plastic that tied off a bread bag. It was thin, but long in comparison to Sonny's own, not that they had ever matched up outright.

"Do you think, like, when you come, it's like bullets in a gun?" said Skip. "You've only got so much ammo for your whole life, then you run out?"

"If that was true, your ugly alter-ego would have dropped off years ago." He was finding it difficult to spiel the usual chatter toward Skip. His order of mental priorities were first, Penny; second, sundown; third, what was to come after.

"I heard Beth Mossman sucked off Ramon Velasquez, in his car." Skip's eyes were gleaming. "Sucked it, swallowed it, *everything*. Went back for seconds of his hot sauce. Man, what a *slut*."

There was not a shred of evidence to support this conjecture.

"I wonder if she'd, you know…"

"Wash that thing first," said Sonny. "Look up *smegma* in the dictionary, fool."

Skip's dick was at parade attention now. He was idly stroking it like a pet lizard while some endlessly recycled triple-X movie played in his brain. "Oh, thanks, doc—like you know so fucking much about anatomy!"

That's all about to change, Sonny thought. His other thoughts were as scary as skydiving.

"Put that away before it goes off and hurts somebody."

"Do you *ever* get a boner?" Skip asked as he stowed his equipment.

"Sure." This line of inquiry was vaguely irritating to Sonny, as though he was dealing with a child.

"Wet dreams? You ever come all over yourself?"

"Do you *ever* think of anything else?" Sonny mocked his pal's tone.

"I'm an adolescent street soldier fucked over by the world," Skip said. "No rules, no limits, no future! These are the best years of our lives and I want to get out there and start…coming!"

Sonny harbored severe doubts as to whether the living hell of junior high, or even high school, could ever represent a best possible world. Skip's unceasing sex talk grated on his ears now because Sonny's horizon had already changed; the picture of Penny in his mind was not that of a school slut or spunk-bucket, someone to be used and discarded like a diaper.

Is that how it happens, growing up? he wondered. *Shit changes while you're not looking and all of a sudden you have to learn a whole new set of rules?*

"Let's go get a slushie," said Skip. "See if those Cathedral High assholes will buy us some beer."

"No, I don't feel too hot, Skip." Sonny touched his forehead in the universal gesture, to sell the lie. "Think I'm getting a fever. I just want to lie down."

"The fever is your need for pussy, like immediately. It's a sickness, boy, I've seen it before. You need to lie down on top of Holly Whittier and spooge on her tits."

It struck Sonny that perhaps porn films were Skip's only working reference model. A lot of up-down and inside-out rutting, but with the finish always visible—*now pull out and come on her face and hooters.* Maybe this was elementary birth control for those who did not know any better. Or natural selection in action.

Cold fear stabbed his lungs. Was this what Penny expected of him? What were her models? They really should have discussed more, yesterday, when their futures were completely imaginary.

Holly Whittier was a fixture on the student council and a big sports booster. Her reputation quivered in the twilight zone between "nice girl" and "slut," pending a transformative event that could yield adequate gossip.

Sonny had heard Penny say that Holly's father whupped Holly's ass if she did not bring home straight A's. That he kept his daughter barricaded at home like a princess in a tower, when she was not trackably doing time as a cheerleader, a student officer, or yearbook coordinator. She was always pleasant but her smile seemed frozen in place, like the smiles of politicians Sonny had seen on television. Like Nixon, when he went live and lied to the whole country. For the first time, Sonny pondered Holly Whittier not as a teasing object, but as someone who might be suffering an indescribable inner torment. Holly's rumors were not that different from the tale spun by Sonny's own mom in regard to the way she had escaped *her* youth. Flash-forward to Holly twenty years from now, chain-smoking in front of a TV, not knowing her child was about to sneak out in the dead of night to have sex. Flash back to the unlovely mental image of your own parents doing the deed that created *you*, of your mother screaming and bleeding and pushing you out into the world, to wax into a viral miscreant who could only think about getting laid.

The pattern had to be broken, otherwise the morbid example of Mike Dohler and Vicki Fortnam became the waiting fate that waved at you from the end of the street, taunting you with your own doom.

Mike and Vicki, seniors, impregnator and impregnatee, had a plan to get out, blow town, build a life. Mike's Barracuda was found abandoned on the highway not all that far from a very popular convenience mart. But no bodies, fugitive, dead, or otherwise.

"Chili Hunters got 'em," Sonny's little brother Barrett concluded immediately. You even heard it from adults as a throwaway, a gag followed by a knowing wink.

This sort of thinking could drive you bananas, even without the sex angle. ·

While not feverish, Sonny's cranium did feel swollen because it had too much to contain. Was *that* what sex was—a release of all this pressure?

"Yeah, you do look kinda dizzy," said Skip. "Don't cough on me, man, that's all I need is to get sick. Cuts into my ditching time."

"You mean your whacking time."

"Yessir, and fuck you too. I'm gonna bounce. I'll catch you on the flip...unless the Chili Hunters gobble my ass, right?"

Sonny grinned. Skip was not always as bad as he *could* be. But the stuff in Sonny's head right now was not for buddies. He was about to leave the kid stuff, and the Chili Hunters, far behind.

———————

Sonny had graduated. At age ten, the Chili Hunters would have been sufficient threat to keep him from nightwalking. At fourteen, childhood seemed decades gone, and lurking midnight boogeymen were not enough to belay the temptation of the bedroom window, which offered clandestine escape and endless promise.

Still, what if the myth had a basis in reality? What if the Chili Hunters were just real-world, fucked-up people like outlaw biker meth-heads or dope fiend rapists or homeless derelicts gone malignant? It lent a tangy risk to each extracurricular excursion. The more times you went truant on your homewatch, the less threat there was to what Sonny could now recognize as a social lie designed to enforce obedience. Santa Claus was a crock, too. Religion was not far behind. But the mold of a man stems from the mind of a child, and superstitions have a habit of lingering (which handily explained Catholicism).

Sonny's little brother Barrett claimed to have seen a Chili Hunter outside of his bedroom window, a couple of houses ago, when Sonny and Barrett had still shared one room. It was a bit silly because the room was on the second floor with no purchase, but never mind. Now Sonny had his own room, and his own window, which opened onto a slope to the front porch roof—important because there were no sleepers to be alerted directly below. From there it was a silent ninja drop to the lawn. Reentry was achieved by climbing the support for the far corner of the porch. You stood on the rail and did a fast pullup in order to get a foot (just in time) chocked into the Y-shaped crossbeam, being careful not to grab the rain gutter, which would come loose with a shriek of nails and bending aluminum. Sonny knew his placements as surely as a rock climber, and had done the exercise so many times it could be accomplished with his eyes shut. How many catlike paces across the sloping shingles. Where the squeaks lived. When to stop and when to drop.

The night was chilly, but not dead cold. The sheer *freedom* of being out in such a night, breathing its air, completely on his own recognizance, was simply one of the things that made Sonny feel a bit giddy.

Not the main thing, however.

Courting rituals were another imposition. Inside the pockets of his cargo jacket (his knapsack would have been too cumbersome for maximum stealth) were two small bottled waters, a flashlight, some candy and granola bars (which he knew Penny would like), and several different brands of condoms obtained long ago from Skip (who had hundreds, like an unused collection, some so old that the foil had begun to abrade from the packet). To secure prophylactics from Skip directly would have raised undue alarm and inquiry; these hardy samples were two or three years old. They had been at hand, no fuss, now amplified in importance beyond being mere guilty curios.

Sonny snapped loose a wilting red rose from the front bushes. It was cheap, lame, corny and better than nothing (he hoped) as a gesture. A thorn pierced his palm and he sucked a fat, welling blood-drop.

To walk the precisely-gridded avenues at night, even under the infrequent streetlamps, would be foolishly cocky. Sonny had a favorite route that involved transecting a few backyards and moving along the dirt-road alleyway provided for trash collection. It was a challenge to get past without setting off a few local dogs, penned in but vocal. There was always the chance that somebody's growly beast would be running rogue on Sonny's map; he had been chased once or twice. Next came the feeder road, a dark ribbon of hot-top that bordered the tract. It was called Access Street—no lie—and was entirely bereft of lamps. Beyond it was the first acreage of yet-undeveloped desert scrub.

This time of year was too cold to fret about rattlers, but the area was still lively with coyotes, rabbits, skunks, possums, raccoons and the occasional, mostly-rumored bobcat or puma. Smaller rodents aplenty. Hundreds of different lizards. They all made their own raids, one time or another, on human garbage cans. You could still glimpse deer crossing the road or sometimes loitering in your front yard.

Seen from above, the threadwork of trails through the raw land parcel coalesced semi-regularly into wider circular meeting spots where earlier kids had originally set small campfires, quickly finding that the light gave them away at night, and the smoke did likewise during the day. Sonny knew most of the twists and turns by heart and lunar glow. It was a maze of mesquite shrubs, alien-looking ocotillo plants and still-green tumbleweeds, what Mr. Janowitz had described as *xeophytes*. Typically, most vegetation here had spines or thorns; their defenses were always up.

Adults never came in here unless they came to clear and build. At the far east end of the square mile or so waited the much-beloved convenience mart, waiting for the highway to get bigger so it could reap more trade.

This part of the world belonged to the teenagers. Even the trails were invisible from the road. You stepped around a big fist of paddle cactus and vanished. As he let the landscape envelop him, Sonny knew there was nothing to fear. Nothing except discovery, attack, betrayal, disillusionment, heartbreak. Nothing to fear here.

———————————

Once or twice, Sonny thought he could hear the sound of rubber soles, running fast across hardpan, the source of the noise difficult to fix. Not big carnivores or Chili Hunters, but most likely Skip, on the prowl to shadow his good buddy and find out what was *really* going on, and whyfor the feigned illness, and—even more likely—seeking an opportunity to fuck up everything at precisely the wrong moment. When everyone was bored to death, it was that much harder to exclude your friends from anything potentially diverting.

This was not one of those times, dammit.

Sonny's respiration hitched as he was forced to acknowledge that—even worse—it was all a trap, a trick engineered by Skip to humiliate him.

Not out of the realm of possibility, certainly, no.

Worst of all was the thought that Skip might be out here during their nightwalk hours as a spy, furiously pounding his meat from the vantage of a secure hide.

"Sonny." Penny's voice, a whisper. "Over here."

They embraced without even thinking about it, a clean, honest moment. She smelled like life itself. She seemed touched by the flower he'd brought.

"I guess this makes this a *date*," she said.

"You don't have to—"

She blocked his protest. "Shh, no. I know what you're going to say, and it isn't like that. You think *you're* nervous? Me, too."

"My mouth is dry," he said, worrying about his breath. He chugged half of one bottled water and offered her the other, which she also seemed to appreciate on a level that bespoke considerations taken.

"I want you to kiss me," she said. "Kiss me like you mean it."

Sonny did his best. It would be wonderful to just linger here, wrapped up in each other, doing this. They didn't have to—

"Shh." She put her hand on his crotch and gave a gentle exploratory squeeze. Her throat vibrated against his mouth. *"Hmm. I want to see it, okay? I want to hold it, first."*

To one side of this little clearing there was an inexplicably large boulder jutting up from the ground. Penny backed him into it and sat him down after she had unbuckled his belt, leaving the rest for him to do. It turned out the boulder was not the only thing large, or jutting.

"It's so *smooth*," she said with vague wonder.

"Wait! What was that!" Sonny might have heard movement in the brush, or imagined it. Reality and dreams were merging. Before she could tell him to *relax, slow down, take it easy, don't worry*, he had to explain.

"Sorry—I sorta got the idea that Skip was out here, screwing around, y'know? It figures that he might."

"But you didn't *tell* him," she said. "That would be bad. This is for us." She encircled his erect, exposed penis with her impossibly soft hand.

"No, no way. Never..."

She moved her hand up once, down once, base to tip. She said *wow* under her breath...

...and Sonny ejaculated all over her hand, emitting a miniscule grunt of alarm.

"Oh *my*," she said, smiling at him.

"Oh, god," he said, shifting around, thoroughly repelled by himself. He shifted uncomfortably on the rock. "Jesus...I'm sorry... it's not..." He petered out. So to speak.

But Penny was not mad or disgusted. She looked at the glistening stuff in her hand with an almost scholarly expression. "I've always heard that people having sex always yell out *god, jesus, christamighty*. I guess it really *is* a religious experience. But hey...I told you not to worry, okay? Don't worry about small talk and excuses. Here."

She stepped out of her jeans, yanking them over her Doc Martens, then hooked a finger into her sensible cotton panties to liberate them in what appeared to Sonny to be an incredibly graceful move. Then she took his hand like a lover and guided it to her groin.

"Here," she said again.

He felt a velvety architecture different from his own, taboo, forbidden, and moist. Wet was supposed to signal excitement, for girls.

She moved closer to re-collect him, and already his dick was standing up again. He was fighting to disallow the intrusion of mental images of Skip.

"See?" she said. Hard was supposed to signal excitement, for boys. This was the simplest possible exchange, unencumbered by acrobatics or hardcore filigree. "Now, let me see if I can do this right…"

As though by magic she produced a condom. Miraculously, she had brought her own and Sonny needed to assume she had acquired it more or less the same way he'd gotten his, if he wanted to protect himself from more brutal conjecture. She used her teeth to initiate a tear in the packet since she was one-handed, still discarding her clothing. She unrolled it while making a face that said it was difficult to tell one end from the other. Its principle was pretty simple, though. "Safety first, and all that," she added, as though the thought needed voicing.

His penis was actually pulsing toward her as she applied the rubber. No, she did not seem to be an adept at this, which made Sonny's fear decompress. Quickly enough, by trial and error, she figured out how to make the latex cooperate. She grew closer and closer, until there was no space between them.

She aimed the blunt head at her labia, then all at once came forward and sat in his lap, facing him. He could feel himself slide up into her. After a first tentative contact, she put her hands on his shoulders and engulfed him to the root in a single motion. Without thinking at all, he thrust up to meet her. To join her.

"Ow. *Ow*," she said in a sharp inhalation going rigid for just an instant.

"Oh god, did I hurt you?!" It came out as one casseroled compound word: *ohgoddidihurtyou?!*

"No, it's okay," she said, pushing up, then slowly easing back down. "Stings a little. I figured there would be blood, right? I brought some maxi-pads and stuff. No it's—*ahhhh*—okay. Keep doing *that*."

Whatever it was, Sonny was committed to keep doing it. The sounds Penny made were mysterious, possible pain or pleasure equally, expressed via knife-sharp intakes of air through clenched teeth as she rode him.

Soon enough Sonny could feel his own imminent boiling point. Now he understood why boring writers (in English class reading assignments) had called orgasm "the little death," *La petite mort*. It was like death and rebirth all in one accelerated moment.

Penny seemed to clench up with a gasp. Then she hugged herself tightly, wafting down and expending breath as if blowing out candles, until meter gradually returned to her breathing. *Oh.* The last breath in a long plume.

Sonny felt he could stay this way forever, holding her tight to him, doing no more than listening to her breathe...until over her shoulder he spotted his friend Skip's face in the bushes.

He bolted upright, pants in disarray, holding Penny by the arms so she would not be catapulted backward to fall.

"*Skip!* You motherfucker! Goddammit, I *knew* it!" He got his jeans to half mast and tried to take charge, somehow. "Stay right here," he cautioned Penny. It was time for Skip and Sonny to have their first genuine fight. Sex and violence, all in the same hour. Sonny was no longer a child.

"It's all right," Penny said meekly. There was a smear of blood on her right thigh, visible in the moonlight.

"It's not all right!" Sonny yelled, blushing with rage. His hand closed on his flashlight, raised, spraying its beam into the air as Sonny prepared to clout Skip with it.

Skip did not answer, or move. His face, partially concealed by the scrub, wore only the calcified expression it had when Skip had died. The rest of his body was on the ground ten feet away, with the crotch wholly bitten out in a wet semi-circle. It would not remain there for long.

Sonny turned back to Penny, utterly derailed. "What *is* this?"

The air around them roiled thickly with the stench of garlic and onions, hydrochloric acid and brimstone. Mildew, fertilizer and cemetery rot.

Penny, still happy, nodded over Sonny's shoulder, speaking to the gigantic dark shape that loomed up behind him.

"He's ready," she said. "And so am I."

Faux-God of the Mouse Haus

A story of mass death and mouse caretaking
Or rather, the lack thereof.

(1999)

Bob the Snake Man is a very good friend of long standing, who lives to this day in the Southwestern desert area of the United States, still one of my favorite environments. Bob is a self-taught herpetologist who wound up running the reptile department of the Phoenix Zoo before returning to private enterprise, and he has always had snakes in his house, ever since the first time I stayed there way too many years ago, when the count was a mere three corn snakes (one of which escaped and holed up in the wall heater at the foot of the couch where I was sleeping).

Under Bob's tutelage I learned how to handle venomous and non-venomous serpents, as well as frogs, geckos, and assorted other amphibians and reptiles. Whenever I laid over at Bob's place enroute to somewhere or other, there was always an exciting new variety of critter awaiting, usually in the room where I was supposed to sleep. The first time it was a timber rattlesnake.

Bob accumulated a whole gang of reptiles. Several visits later, the snake count was 35 and a whole room of the house had been converted into a "snake room." This is where we chased around a beautiful mangrove snake which managed to squirm out of its tank and bite Bob right on the web of the hand before recapture. The mangrove is mildly venomous, a rear-fanged exotic. "What do we do"?" I said. Bob said, "We wait and see if anything happens to me." Like I said, it was a panic bite, and ultimately juiceless.

We marveled at the sheer strength of an eight-foot python named Pedro, who punched Bob right in the cheek with its snout and laid him out. Pedro was mostly blind that day, due to an imminent skin shedding, and got startled. Never forget that snakes are essentially one big, long muscle.

Bob's reliability in handling the lower orders became well known locally, primarily because people who find snakes in or around their homes usually (oddly enough) call the fire department. Bob arranged for the fire department to relay-call him whenever this happened, on the condition he got to keep whatever snakes he collected. I tagged along on a couple of these "snake calls," which invariably came at about two in the morning. Generally some panicked person would SOS all fluttery about finding a rattler under a sofa or porch or in a crib or something. Nine times out of ten it was a gopher snake—great fakers, big, long, aggressive, and capable of making the most horrendous hissing noise, but not venomous. The *tenth* time, however, it was usually the biggest goddamned rattlesnake we'd ever seen.

We got shat upon, pissed on, whiplashed and bitten in the process of sexing snakes, something you really don't want to taste for yourself. Trust me on this one.

But it came to pass that Bob asked me to snake-sit once, while he was out of town. It was a basically easy regimen of poop-scooping, lightbulb-replacing, watering...and feeding. Easy if you remember not to reach into the sidewinder cage with your naked hand, the kind of mistake you only make once.

The "feeding" part involved the Mouse Condo. This was a terraced rack of multiple cages out in the garage, containing about a thousand mice and pinkies (baby mice) arranged according to size—that is, "serving" size. Many snakes will only eat live food. Constrictors have got to pounce and suffocate, and poisonous snakes live for the killing strike. Therefore you don't want to drop in a live rodent large enough to do damage to the snake when the rodent realizes it is not supposed to leave the tank alive. Pedro, for example, would consume big rats or small rabbits in excess of several pounds; these had to be stunned so they were still warm when consigned to their last role, as dinner. The smaller snakes could handle smaller, frisky live food just fine.

So every trip to the Mouse Condo usually reaped a shoebox full of agitated victims-to-be. Once, my then-girlfriend Paula leaned her head against the jamb and gave me a Look, as I was pulling drawers and boxing up a body count.

"Kinda makes you feel like God, doesn't it?"

"Yep. I'm not only picking them out, I'm going to watch most of them die within the hour. But all of these guys are marked for the big D, anyway."

Sooner than I thought. The Condo was air conditioned against Arizona's brutal 115-degree summer heat by two huge units, which, because of a malfunctioning hose, had to be refilled with water manually. I misjudged just how fast a reservoir of water could evaporate in an afternoon, and when I visited the Condo again, I was stopped dead by That Smell—the aroma which brings the news that a whole bunch of little furry critters have just bitten the big one.

We began rushing survivors into the house, where it was cooler, and scooping out casualties. Soon enough we were stuck with between 17 and 30 deceased meeces that even the snakes wouldn't eat.

"You really know how to charm a girl," Paula said as she helped me body-bag ex-mice. "I can't remember when I've ever had this much...eh, something."

I was not asked to snake-sit for Bob's next out-of-town trip. The incident did set me to thinking about Christians, though, and what might befall them if their "god" simply fucked up by forgetting to refill a cooler!

———

(This never-published, hopelessly unmarketable biographic curiosity is included here on a very sad note: Bob died in 2014, aged 57, by suicide. Treasure your friends while you have them, and if you love them, tell them so while they're alive.)

WARBIRDS

"Warbirds was real," said the old man sitting across the table from me. "I seen 'em. More real than gremlins, say; less real than the weight of a pistol in your hand."

I had traveled several hundred miles to listen to this man reminisce about my late father, and he was spinning me a tale of flying monsters, his spidery white eyebrows gauging how much hogwash I might buy. We'd never met before and all the trust assumed implicit between us was mere courtesy, standing at ease until something more fundamental could replace it.

I should have paid more attention to that part about the pistol.

"Good man, your Dad," said Jorgensen, top turret gunner. That would be the Martin turret on the B-24D. Blame my homework. I knew each crew member by their position; I'd based a lot of my anticipation on a photo I found from 1943—one of the few times the entire core team held together long enough for a snapshot. I appended last names to each man, my roster denying them their full names or nicknames, and back then *everybody* had a nickname, usually a diminution of their given name: Bobby, Willy, Frankie, no different from kids in a neighborhood mob. And kids these guys were. As I sat there drinking coffee served by Jorgensen's sister Katie, that defocused black and white photo was sixty-five years old and most of the fresh faces were barely out of their teens. At least two of the crew had lied about their age in order to join up. Jorgensen, today, was not pushing eighty, he was pulling it.

One more burden. He suffered arthritis that had closed his hands to cramped claws. He wouldn't admit that he was a bit deaf, even though his hearing aid was plain to see (one of the older, bigger ones, a behind-the-ear rig with a so-called "flesh-colored" braided wire that snaked to a box stationed in his shirt pocket. His eyes were blue, paled by a patina of yellowed sclera. Polished spectacles. He was bowed but unbent by time and expected me to believe what he told me, because, after all, he was my elder, and what do kids really know, anyway?

Brett Jorgensen, like most men in bomber crews during World War II, had come out of training and landed in Europe as a sergeant. He joked that before the Normandy invasion, German prison camps were overcrowded with thousands of shot-down sergeants. He leaked items like this to suss me out; was I for real and did I know what I'm talking about, or was I just another ground-pounder who had seen fit to drop the last Great War from history and memory?

"Sergeants and lieutenants," I said, dumping powdered chemicals into my lukewarm coffee. Jorgensen drank his straight, black. Naturally. If you repeat what a person tells you, usually they illuminate.

He pushed back from our table, then moved forward. He had a tough time finding biz to do with his hands, since they had degenerated to basic grasping tools. I felt a sympathetic twinge; not for the first time.

"Your Dad was a sergeant, too, outta Chicago. He tried to train on AT-6s but wasn't a very good pilot. He pulled back'a the bus, twin Fifties." He snorted out a chuckle and searched for a napkin. "This one time, he got his butt cooked by a piece of flak that came through the fuselage and tore through his flight suit and wound up sizzling against his ass."

"Yeah, he told me about that one. Bernberg airport, part of Berlin's outer ring of protective bases, mission number three, March of '44."

"You *have* been paying attention," Jorgensen said. "Well, then, maybe you won't find this story so weird. You've seen war movies. Ever seen combat?"

"No, sir." I was in high school when the draft lottery was instigated. I drew a fairly high number on first cull.

"Well, it ain't like that, and aerial combat is a whole different gorilla. Mostly what it is, is a lot of noise and panic and somehow, if you live through it, you try to figure out later why you're not dead. In the moment it's all adrenaline and the kind of fear that makes you shit yourself. Plane coming apart around you, bomb loads dropping, ten big Fifties all snackering away, enemy fighters throwing twenty-millimeter cannon shells at your snoot, and around you, *all* around you, you see other planes going down—guys you knew, trailing smoke, blowing up in midair, and you want to look for chutes but there's no time. You ever listen to that heavy metal music?"

He painted such a vivid thumbnail that I was momentarily lost in it, groundless. "What? Oh, yeah, some. You know."

"I never liked it," said Jorgensen. Pause for me to construct a mental image of Jorgensen sitting down all cozy with a Black Sabbath greatest hits disc. A taste of Mudhoney thrash. Perhaps a jot of some Norwegian speed-metal band's idea of meltdown.

"Know why? It sounds like combat, that's why."

The B-24 Liberator called *The Turk*, according to its nose paint, chomped into the ground and belched flaming parts all over the runway shoulder while what was left of her crew scattered. Two crewmen still in thermal suits were flattened by the explosion. One did not get up to slap himself out. Fire crews hustled from one half-extinguished conflagration to this new one as other crippled heavies tried to dodge the debris and land. Liberators—nineteen tons each, empty—were packed and stacked on approach and literally dropping out of the sky. A tower spotter was busy counting returning planes and racking up a death toll.

The weather, typical for England, was an oppressive haze of fog and overcast. Blazing planes seared painfully bright peepholes in the mist, hot spots that corkscrewed black contrails of smoke toward the sky.

Wheatrow, a just-arrived belly gunner from Oklahoma City, as blond and corn-fed as his name, rushed up to Harry Mars, a lieutenant who was the *Shady Lady*'s co-pilot. Mars stood with his hands thrust into his back pockets, an attitude he affected when he had no idea of what to fix first.

"Jesus H. Christ!" said Wheatrow. "What hit her?"

"Came in with her nose wheel cocked and didn't watch the crash film, I guess," said Mars. "Welcome to Shipdham, laddie buck."

Shipdham was a parish in Norfolk, a jut of the Isles northeast of London, now home to the 44th Bomb Group and one of the Allies' coastal rally points for European missions. This British postcard of pubs and cottages had been despoiled by Nissen huts and landing strips, engirded by anti-aircraft batteries, then overrun by brash American flyers demanding to know what was really going on. Usually loudly and with a pointed absence of tact—cultural shock, writ large.

Watching a gut-shot B-24 slide home was almost operatic in its extravagant horror. Liberators were big-bellied birds that ceased to look ungainly only in flight. On water ditches they tended to "squash," making survival ten times less likely than if you splashed a Flying Fort. The *Turk*'s skipper took the lousy hand he had been dealt and played it by the manual, feathering his two working engines, stomping flaps and keeping his snout off the tarmac as long as possible. His locked-down starboard wheel had snapped on impact, guttering him into the mud and shearing off the right wing between the huge Pratt-Whitney engines. Then something had caught fire. No bomb load, little ammo, and littler fuel, but something aboard had touched off and blew the beast apart at the waist like a firecracker in a beer bottle.

Practically everything aboard these planes was flammable, anyway, and the fire would not be extinguished by the United Kingdom's omnipresent cold, gray mud and moisture-laden air.

Everybody got more bad news from Madsen in the mess hall, which doubled as the briefing shack. Wheatrow checked the mission board for *Shady Lady.* Their space was still blank. Madsen was a stiff piece of Sam Browne-belted British business, with a swagger stick he employed as a pointer and map-whacking tool, addressing a full complement of fidgeting officers and noncoms in the too-small corrugated hut.

"...a total of one hundred nine-point-two tons of five-hundred and 1000-pound bombs, fused at a one-tenth of a second nose and one-quarter-second tail, were successfully dropped from eighteen thousand to twenty thousand feet. Apart from the Messerschmidt plant at Regensburg—"

Madsen's swagger stick whacked the map and a general cheer went up at this.

"Yes, yes." Madsen waited it out. "Two other targets in the vicinity were hit, successfully severing air, water, and electrical lines. A screw factory and a rubber plant. Of course some machine parts were left salvageable, but not without major testing and repair."

Nearly nine hundred lit cigarettes formed an inversion layer of smoke in the dome of the hut. Wheatrow recognized a few faces fresh from his training in Casper, Wyoming; guys he'd shipped over with, guys with unmemorable names. But now he was socked in with his new crew, the fresh meat on their plate. He sat next to Sgt. Jorgensen, who was rocking in his folding chair.

"All this Limey ever talks about," said Jorgensen. "Screwing and rubbers."

Alvin Tewks, a cowboy from California, leaned in from Jorgensen's far side to jerk a thumb toward the *Shady Lady's* navigator. "Ole Lieutenant Max, he *married* a Limey almost as soon as he hit the beach. Ba-boom!"

Tewks immediately cringed under the scrutiny of Lt. Keith Stackpole, bombardier and nose gunner. He was, after all, talking about an officer. "Shit," he said. "Sorry, sir."

Stackpole, one of the grownups among them at age 22, held out a flat hand. *Keep that blather stowed.* Just as they were raiding the Axis, a similarly militant contingent of British ladies were raiding homesick Yanks, in a potent atmosphere of material privation and imminent death. Max Gentry, their green-eyed navigator, had claimed different. He had fallen in love. Of course he had. He had also bought himself a double truckload of ribbing and bullshit, which Stackpole admired him for bearing with a calm deference that suggested he was acclimating to the whole indigenous stiff-upper-lip posture. As long as Gentry did not start wearing a flight scarf or speaking with a nasal accent, Stackpole would be A-OK with the *Lady*'s map-man.

Stackpole passed a cigarette to Sgt. Jones, the radioman, who broke it in half and passed it on to Sgt. Smith, his best buddy, engineer and right waist gunner. Smith and Jones. Sometimes you had to laugh to keep from crying.

"To hell with all the scores," Jones groused. "How *many*?"

"Forty, fifty, something like that," said Smith. Both men lit up off the same match.

Wheatrow's expression curdled. "Out of how many?"

"Two hundred, something like that." Jimmy Beck had appeared behind them, since there were no more seats. The tail gunner wore military-issue glasses and transferred his smoke from one hand to the other to permit Lt. Mars and their pilot, Lt. Coggins, to squeeze in. Every fact and statistic, no matter how clear, was *something like that.*

Wheatrow lost his breath. "Two *hundred*...?!"

"Out of a total of one hundred seventy-seven B-24s," Madsen boomed from the paltry little stage upfront, "at least one hundred twenty-seven and possibly as many as one hundred thirty-three reached and bombed the target. Forty-two aircraft were shot down or crashed enroute—"

"N-root?" said Tewks, still with a newcomer's fascination at the British penchant for not speaking English.

"—of which fifteen, we estimate, were lost over the target."

"We're not on the mission board, again," Coggins said to Stackpole.

"In addition," said Madsen, "eight planes landed in neutral Turkey and were interned. One hundred and four returned to base, and twenty-three to other friendly bases, for a total loss of fifty. The casualty tallies at present are four hundred forty men killed or missing in action. We are informed the Axis holds twenty of the missing crews."

Wheatrow felt his stomach drop away. One mission, nearly four hundred fifty guys lost. The crews of forty-five lost planes. *Something like that.*

"Goddamned Krauts," Jorgensen muttered.

Madsen delivered the cold comfort part of the briefing: "A total of fifty-one enemy fighters were downed."

"Great," said Tewks. "Almost one fighter for every bomber fulla guys."

Some of the men applauded anyway.

Lt. Mars was already past it, ribbing Beck. "Hey Jimmy—know what the life expectancy is for a tail gunner in combat?"

It was an ancient joke for these youngsters. At least three of them chimed, "Nine seconds!"

"Thanks, fellows," said Beck, exhaling smoke. "I feel a whole lot better. Warm inside."

Coggins silently scoped reaction among his crew. Good. Big death numbers would make them all hate the Fuehrer a little more tomorrow, and maybe that hate could help him bring them all back alive, not barbecued in bomber wreckage like those poor sonsabitches aboard the *Turk*, whose skipper was currently logging bunk time in the hospital with his left arm deep-fried medium rare and his leg busted in four places.

This was war. This was important. In 1941, six months before Pearl Harbor, The US Army Air Corps had been renamed US Army Air Forces under General Hap Arnold, and this hut-full of belligerent Americans had a lot to stand up for. Tons to prove. Now, their pride was pricked every day. The warriors of the clouds were *almost*

as legitimate and autonomous as the Navy or the tank jockeys. After
the States entered the fray, the War Department reorganized the
Army Ground Forces and Army Air Forces into co-equal commands, but the shuffle would not result in something called the
United States Air Force until after the war. Many of the veteran
fliers still wore their Air Corps insignia with understandable self-
esteem even though they were all now part of the AAF.

The pride did not count for much when you were rousted out
of your rack at one o'clock in the morning. Half the guys in the hut
were aware of the intruder even before he clicked on his flashlight.
That would be Carlisle, the C.O., so that would be Carlisle's beam
bouncing off Coggins' bald cueball skull in the chilly darkness.

"Coggins," Carlisle whispered. "J.J. Wakey-wakey."

"I'm awake," Coggins husked, rolling over.

Carlisle seated himself on the edge of the cot. "Listen, I hate to
do this to you, but—"

"What time is it?" Everybody except Tewks was awake now.

"One-fifteen. Look…the mission. Can you make it?"

"Sure," said Coggins, as if he was sure of everything.

"We're leading the Eighth this morning, and we need the whole
group to muster maximum effort."

"What's he saying?" said Wheatrow, rubbing his face to
consciousness.

"Shh," said Beck. "It's a surprise."

"It's a big deal," said Carlisle, louder now, for the general benefit.
"Heavy flak, then fighters. An oil refinery. I know your crew isn't
quite combat-ready, but we can't co-pilot you out with a more experienced guy because—"

"My crew *is* combat-ready, sir," Coggins returned, and nobody
contradicted him.

There it was, then. The thing Coggins would later describe as a
"massacre."

Coggins had gotten *"Shady Lady"* painted on his ship during
his North African leg. This green crew was sleeping inside a hut

that several days before had been occupied by a completely different crew, now MIA. Tomorrow, who knew? Technically, they had flown four of their 25-mission stint, but had always been recalled or otherwise aborted. They had yet to make it all the way across the Channel. Their much-vaunted first mission had decayed into a complete embarrassment when they lost a supercharger at 12,000 feet and had to turn back and dump their bombs in the North Atlantic. Their right waist gunner, a Texan named MacCardle, had been seconded out to an active combat crew on their twelfth run, *Hometown Gal*, leaving a slot that had just been filled by Wheatrow.

A belly gunner from a ship called the *Double Diamond* had related the mission to Coggins: "I saw the *Ratpacker* take an 88 shell right in the cockpit. It heeled over with a full load of bombs and cut *Hometown Gal* right in half. I didn't see any chutes." Was MacCardle alive or dead? Nobody knew, and past a certain minimal concern, it was a bad idea to care too much.

So here they were: Scalding hot coffee, joints cracking in the accursed British damp, struggling into their gear, sleep dirt blurring their vision, becoming roly-poly flyboys. Electrical suits, flak vests, backpack chutes for the pilots, chest chutes for the rest, Mae Wests, helmets, goggles, oxygen masks. They all smelled like wet sheepskin and leather.

"Goddamned fog," said Tewks on the truck to the field. "Too thin to eat and too thick to drink."

Visibility was zilch. "We're going to have to follow a Jeep just to find the runway," said Stackpole. "Where are we in the formation?"

"Coffin corner," said Coggins, trying to make it sound normal.

"Oh, outstanding," grumbled Beck, the Guy in Back.

"What?" said Wheatrow, damp blond hair plastered to his head inside his flight cap.

Lt. Mars recited the verdict: "Outside edge of the box, rear element."

"So the flak can kill us easier," noted Beck.

Jorgensen boffed Wheatrow on one thickly-padded arm. "Newcomer position. For virgins."

"We're supposed to tag along until there's an abort," said Coggins. "So we can fill in." At least they had graduated from the aborts. Coggins had pulled the wire from the brim of his garrison cap with pliers, to permit the proper "mission crush" when he donned his headphones.

Stackpole was whistling "The Way You Look Tonight."

And *Shady Lady* abruptly loomed up before them, filling their world. Dull green, bitch mother, sky lover, their womb, their fate.

The 44th Bomb Group was known as the Flying Eight-Balls, the first Liberator unit in the AAF, though not the first to Europe, which distinction went to the Ninth Air Force's Pyramiders. The Eight-Balls flew their first sortie in support of Flying Forts in November of '42, and as the other groups converted to night missions, the Eight-Balls were left in the unenviable position of being the sole Liberator group assigned to daylight bombing raids. There was a lot of talk about one Lib, *Boomerang* by name, part of the 93rd Bomb Group's October 9th raid on Lille. She came back wearing thousands of holes, destined for scrap, but her pilot and crew chief fought for her, patched up her bullet punctures with aluminum, and she became the first B-24 in the Eighth to complete her fifty missions. Her men defended her honor and she repaid them with their lives. Not to put too fine a point on it, snickers aside, the Lille mission was also the breaking point for command, which was compelled to incontrovertibly report that the B-24 was a better bombardment craft, hands down, than the much sexier "glamour girl" B-17—the Libs were faster, longer-range, capable of ferrying heavier bomb loads with superior armament. In essence the history of the Eight-Balls was the saga of the Liberator in wartime; aerial conflict had birthed her, and she would be practically obsolete by VJ Day. Many of the 24s at Shipdham had arrived with the newer armor, self-sealing tanks, turbo-superchargers, and the retractable Sperry ball turret.

Which is where Wheatrow was headed this morning.

"Big pot-bellied bitch," said Mars, echoing the words of a skipper named Keith Schuyler.

"I like big women," said Tewks. "More to grab on to."

"She moves fast for a big'un," said Coggins. He might have been talking about his wife back in the States, or his aircraft, thought Jorgensen. Like the difference mattered. Maybe his old lady's wingspan was longer than her fuselage.

The flight crew had completed hoisting 500-pounders into the *Lady's* bomb bay, and the ten Fifties aboard were glutted with eleven thousand rounds of ammo in disintegrating link belts. Coggins' men began levering themselves into the underside of the plane. There they'd spend the next twelve hours in almost unbearable cramp, pissing through relief tubes, sucking artificial air, fighting not to die. God help you if you were struck with the trots in mid-mission.

Mars clambered into the co-pilot bucket to Coggins' right, noting that the skipper, as usual, had locked his seat full-forward. You'd think shorter men would be ideal for bombers, but the jokers back in San Diego or Fort Worth always liked to rack the pedals just out of reach for an average human being.

"Could be a milk run," Mars said, snugging in.

"Could be a nightmare, if fighters pick our group to plaster," said Coggins, not looking at him. He mashed down his (now-wireless) cap to accommodate his headphones.

They ran through the preflight check with the flight engineer. Mars stowed the control latch overhead (so it would not slap him in the face later) and popped out the hatch to check movement on the ailerons, elevators and rudder. They were starting up from a battery cart so he killed the ignition switches. The engineer pulled the props through by hand, six turns or "blades" each, starting with #3, inboard to outboard. The process was dull, administrative, and by rote, but even a misstep at this stage could cause an explosion, from a closed intercooler or an overlooked supercharger switch. The flight engineer placed the wheel chocks and stood by with a portable extinguisher for the actual engine startup, #3 first, to drive the hydraulics. At 1000 rpm the dials read properly:

45-50 pounds for the oil pressure, 4 1/2 inches for the vacuum pumps, about 975 pounds pressure in the accumulators, for braking power. Coggins throttled to one-third power while Mars amplified the fuel mix to auto-lean. After taxiing out, Mars would rev all four powerhouses to "exercise" the props.

Coggins went on the air: "Checking interphone."

"Christ, I can't even see past the nose of the plane," Mars returned as the crew began to check in from their positions. As usual, the fog would lift only when they broke above it.

Stackpole's voice: "Bombardier, roger." He was down by their feet, near Jones, at the radio station, who said, "Radioman, check."

Behind Smith always came Jones: "Roger, left waist."

"Rodger-dodger, you old codger." That was Tewks, across from Smith at the right waist gun.

"Top turret, Jorgensen here." If Mars or Coggins turned around, they'd see Jorgensen's boots on the turret footbar.

"Wheatrow. Ball turret is okay." The poor lad had to be dogged in and lowered away, without a chute. No room for a chute. To use one, he'd have to clamber out—with help—and strap one on, theoretically while the aircraft was plummeting earthward in a fireball. Easy peasy.

Lt. Gentry jack-in-the-boxed out from his station to give a thumbs up. Per procedure, he had to be heard, so he was.

"Heads up, Jimmy," said Coggins.

"The tail is ready, Skipper," said Beck from what Jorgensen had called the "back of the bus."

In that moment, Coggins seemed to compress from the weight he imagined on his yoke. Mars' eyebrows went up. Coggins finally cracked a half-smile and said, "This goddamned seat's too short."

Despite their bulky gear, armament, and sleepless disposition, when the *Lady* lofted skyward it felt like riding in a limousine. They finally got to see some daylight and blue sky. Every little taste of reward was deeply important.

At 3000 feet they all lit up cigarettes, because at 10,000 feet they'd have to go on ship oxygen. Then sheer ball-sweat would have to carry them until they turned around, empty, showed the Continent their tail.

"We got swamped by Focke-Wulfs," said Jorgensen. "One-nineties everywhere. After flak always comes fighters. And the next thing I know, Mars is screaming into his intercom that *Vargas Doll* was on fire, just off our left wing. I couldn't *not* see it from my turret. Flak hit an oxygen bottle near ole Jonesy's head and blew his radio apart. Wheatrow's electrical suit shorted out and burned him. Everybody's yelling, the guns are all blazing; Focke-Wulfs zipping pass close enough to spit on. Tewks snapped his gun tether and accidentally shot up our right stabilizer trying to nail one of the sonsabitches and we started to shake like a drunk old whore. And that's when I saw it, first time."

"The Warbird," I said. Katie had dutifully refreshed our coffee. Jorgensen's older sister was also in her eighties. The last Mrs. Jorgensen had died a decade ago.

"At first I thought it was one of them Stukas," said Jorgensen. "When they dived, they made this weird whine. Then I saw its wings flap and I thought, *this ain't no airplane.* It was nearly as *big* as a fighter. Wings like a bat, snout like one of them needle-bills. Eyes like onyx and pewter." He cleared his throat. "About now you're thinking to yourself, gee, this old coot has lost his marbles, right?" His feathery brows arched, to indict me.

"Actually, no sir. I could never get my father to talk about the war, but some of the *Shady Lady*'s other crew had a few tales to tell, over the years it took me to find them. I've heard weirder."

He seemed to arrive at some momentous inner decision. "Well, okay, then, as long as Katie's in the kitchen or watching soaps or whatever it is she does with her free time." No protest came from the back of the house, so Jorgensen was satisfied we were in confidence, here.

"I thought the same thing you just probably thought," he went on. "That it was a hallucination. I don't think so. I just saw this big, impossible thing coming straight for me, claws out. Next thing I know, all my plexi is gone and I'm laid out on the deck with my head tore open. Still got the scar." He smoothed his hair back to favor a white line that zigged from his left eyebrow up into his scalp. It resembled a knife wound. "Damned near lost my eye. By the time we were back to base, I was in shock from loss of blood. I barely remember the haul back home. They told me later that the belly turret was gone when we landed, and so was Wheatrow, the new guy."

"The whole turret was just gone from the plane?"

"Yeah—pretty tough to do with just cannon fire or machine guns. And all of us would have felt a direct flak hit. Jerry was using 128-millimeter guns for flak, so if Wheatrow had been blown out of the ball by a burst, we would have known about it because half the plane would have been on fire. We had seven thousand pounds of incendiaries and our wings were full of high-test gasoline."

"You think that—"

He overrode me. "I don't think. I suspect. Some things I know. Now, I suspect what happened to poor ole Wheatrow, but I'll tell you what I think: I think that a war that big doesn't just go away because you shake hands and sign some paper."

"Or nuke a couple of cities into Japanese-flavored vapor." I didn't mean it to sound that flip, but Jorgensen stayed on track, either ignoring it or being polite.

"Think of it: the whole world at war. Years of war. Every birthday, every Christmas, the war is still there. Then we suddenly get all civilized and agree to pretend there ain't no war. Sometimes I think… sometimes…" He petered out. Why bother? He barely knew me, and I was just the callow spawn of one of his old crewmates, Jimmy Beck, who'd died five years ago and never sent a holiday card, ever.

"It ain't about heroics or glory," he said, starting up a different avenue of attack. "Where you're up there in the air, shooting all around, guys bleeding and guys hollering, explosions, it's about keeping your skin on. Sheer survival. If you believe in God, you pray constantly to yourself, silently: God, please don't let me die on this mission. If you believe in good luck charms, you tote 'em. Stackpole had a little Kilroy sock doll his wife made for him, and you better believe we all treated Kilroy like one of our crew; made sure he was accounted for on every mission. Gentry had a St. Christopher's medal. Wheatrow came with his rabbit's foot, even though that wasn't very lucky for him *or* the rabbit. And your Daddy had this ritual. Before he checked his guns he'd pull the first slug out of the chain belt, and write the date on it, and put it in his pocket next to his heart."

A fifty-caliber round was nearly six inches long and weighed more than a roll of quarters. My father had flown at least eight successful missions over enemy territory. I wondered what had become of the bullet collection.

"Everybody does stuff like that," I said, although my father's quirk was news to me. "You don't need combat to believe in little rituals, patterns. Who does it harm?"

"You're missing the point." He waved his hand dismissively.

I seemed to be part of a larger picture, one that was right behind me, part of a vista that Jorgensen could perceive, but I could not. He was seeing it right now.

"That feeling, that battle feeling, it's come back," he said. "Every day. Just little bits at first. More every time. Not flashbacks, not jitters. I'm not senile, goddammit. It's as real as the part in your hair. Now I'm gonna tell you what I believe, and I'll call you a liar if you tell anyone else, but I'm saying this out of respect for your Dad."

He was passing something on to me, a weight more massive than I expected, and it was everything I could manage to not interrupt him with all my wise modernity.

"I think we woke something up back then, with all that conflict. All that hate. All those lives, feeding the war. Something that big doesn't just stop, there one day and gone the next. I think maybe it got gorged and fat, and it went to sleep for awhile. We had other wars, here and there, but they weren't the same. This war had a child.

It birthed up something bad. Something that awoke from its nap, and realized, why, it was hungry again, and it hadn't yanked *all* of us out of the air, where it feeds."

"The Warbird. But why you? Why now, after all this time?"

"You want logic from me? I don't have it. All I have is the thought that maybe some of us were supposed to die back then, and didn't. And it knows who we are, and it's got a little checklist, like a menu. And we're easy pickings, because it waited, and now we aren't full of sperm and vinegar anymore. We can't run away and we can't shoot back. The Warbird is on the wing again, eating leftovers, and none of this matters, because who in hell is going to believe a crusty old fart like me?"

"Mr. Jorgensen, my father died of a heart attack. A thrombosis. He technically died four times before he died for real and stayed that way. He had a quadruple bypass. An angioplasty. He had two pacemakers in his chest when he finally went down. Nobody was more stubborn than him when it came to dying. And he did not die in fear, or pain. He accepted it. He didn't act like he was…" I hated that I had to grope for an appropriate word "…haunted."

"Yeah," Jorgensen said. There was a hint of *gotcha* in his eyes, past the tears he was manfully damming back. Men of his generation were not supposed to cry, ever. "But you just said he never talked to you about the war, did he?"

"Yet you talked to me about the Warbird." He was not funnin' me in the way of a wacky grampaw. He was dead serious, and the admission had cost him in emotional viscera, reeled out and inelegantly splayed for inspection. Whether I was trustworthy or not, I had fallen into that bizarre gap that permits people to confide to strangers intimacies they would never reveal to their closest loved ones. I had gotten an explanation. It seemed unfair to retroactively impose preconditions now.

"I did, didn't I?" he said, coming back into himself. "That was stupid of me. I'm sorry, young man. I'm sorry for your Dad, and I'm sorry for dumping this on you. You seem like a stand-up fella. I'd a been proud to serve with you. But please don't let this foolishness hector you none. I'm past it. I'm at the end of my rope and I'm hearing things every once in a while, and the joke is, I don't even hear so good. Senescence can be liberating. Bet you didn't think I knew a word like *senescence*, now didja? I looked it up."

Sometime later that evening, Brett Jorgensen put the muzzle of a vintage Luger beneath his chin and blew the back of his head apart with a nine-millimeter hollow point.

I had left him alone to do that. Made my excuses, said my goodbyes, and sincerely promised to keep in touch. I had, I realized, abandoned him.

From what I could piece together later, he'd had the pistol for over half a century.

Brett Jorgensen, the man I had just spoken with, had been the son of immigrant parents from Oslo, Norway. His middle name was Eric. After the war he had graduated with a degree in political science from the University of Missouri, courtesy of the GI Bill. Two marriages, three children. His obituary would be cursory. He had done time at a brokerage firm and retired with a decent nut. His down-home manner of speech was mostly a put-on. Nobody much cared that he had once risked his life daily to drop fire on the Axis war machine. Since 1939 he had smoked two packs of Luckies a day and never caught a smidge of cancer.

Apparently he had made several attempts at a suicide note and burned them all in a punchbowl-sized ashtray as self-pitying drivel. Near the ashtray and butted smokes was a pewter frame with a photograph of Teresa, his first wife, his big wartime love, his girl back home. He had buried her in 1981 after pathologists dug out a tumor the size of a deflated volleyball from her insides. Against popular odds, he had fallen in love again and ultimately buried his second wife, Milicent, in the same cemetery in New Jersey.

The Luger had not come from enemy spoils. Jorgensen had fought Germany in the abstract but never glimpsed a Nazi, except maybe for one time when he swore he could make out a face, grimacing behind goggles and a leather flight helmet, firing salvos of twenty-mil cannonfire right at his noggin, ten thousand feet up, lost in foreign clouds. That had been mission number six, railyards at Bremen. Or perhaps that cruise had been Hamburg, a munitions factory. Or another kind of factory, something like that.

He never thought he would live to grow old. Yet it was all they ever talked about, stranded in Shipdham, flying missions: Marry that girl back home. Raise that family. Carve out that piece of the red, white and blue pie. Survive to accomplish it all.

He hadn't trusted a politician since Kennedy. He remembered the outrage of the world focusing on that single assassination, and recalled where he was and what he was doing when he heard the news. Today, all people knew was that Kennedy had been some kind of randy, dirty joke. Sordid exposes; muck-raking. John F. Kennedy had been a war hero, dammit all to hell. If the revisionism was true, then what had Jorgensen been fighting to preserve, way back when? He had seen that cartoon, the one captioned *We Have Met the Enemy and He Is Us*, and thought, *I wish I could tell when that meeting took place, because I missed it.* His country's flag was still the same, but he had seen too many men and women, hypocrites all, standing before that flag and lying. Even his political science degree seemed a cruel trick, permitting him to perceive too much, and he stopped entertaining notions about fighting for a country in which he no longer seemed to have any rightful place.

He had loaded the pistol at half-past three AM, alone in his den, fifteen feet away from where we had shared coffee. He knew the sounds of fighter planes in the air, ours and theirs. What he was hearing then was not a police helicopter, or semis crawling up the interstate. To make sure, he pulled out his hearing aid and all that remained was a screeching noise that came from no kind of aircraft, not even a Stuka bomber.

This is guesswork, I know, but now I can see it, clear as expensive stemware: An old man rips out his hearing aid and the world falls silent. The mantel clock stops ticking, the outside world goes away, the creaks and settling lumber of his home cease their punctuation of the night, and he is left alone with the sound of the Warbird. He finishes his bourbon, snubs his Lucky, and pulls the trigger with closed and tearless eyes, hoping his sister will understand and forgive him. There is a loud noise and the war comes pouring out of his head.

Just another old fart, self-destructing.

Except that now I can hear the sounds, too. Sounds that cannot be mistaken for anything else. Now I see strange black shapes in the night sky. Hungry, still unsatiated, coming back for more.

Bloodstock Film List

35mm prints

The Abominable Dr. Phibes

The Adventures of Robin Hood

The Andromeda Strain

A Boy and His Dog

The Cabinet of Dr. Caligari (silent)

A Clockwork Orange

The Creature from the Black Lagoon

The Curse of the Cat People

The Day the Earth Stood Still

Demetrius and the Gladiators

Demons of the Mind

Doc Savage

Earth Vs. the Flying Saucers

Fantastic Planet

Fantastic Voyage

Forbidden Planet

The Hunchback of Notre Dame (silent 1923)

It Came from Outer Space

Ivanhoe (1952)

The Lady Vanishes

Mark of the Vampire

Metropolis

Mutations

The Phantom of the Opera (silent 1925)

Planet of the Apes

Play Misty for Me

Psycho

Saboteur

The 7 Faces of Dr. Lao

Slaughterhouse Five

Schlock

The Sea Hawk

Shadow of a Doubt

Sherlock Jr. (silent)

Silent Running

Sinbad & the Eye of the Tiger

Son of Kong

Tales from the Crypt

Tarzan, the Ape Man

Theatre of Blood

Them

Thief of Bagdad (1940)

The Thin Man

The Thing From Another World

THX 1138

2001: A Space Odyssey

The Valley of Gwangi

Waxworks (silent)

When Dinosaurs Ruled the Earth

The Wizard of Oz

16mm

After the Thin Man

Angry Red Planet

Arsenic and Old Lace (1944)

Between Time & Timbuktu

The Birds

The Blob

Blood & Roses

The Body Snatchers

The Bride of Frankenstein

The Corpse Grinders

Curse of the Werewolf

Dark Star

The Day of the Triffids

The Devil Doll (1936)

Dr. Strangelove

Evolution (1923 silent)

Five Million Years to Earth

Flash Gordon (1936)

I Was a Teenage Werewolf

The Incredible Shrinking Man

Invasion of the Body Snatchers

The Invisible Man

Island of Lost Souls

Jack the Giant Killer

Jason and the Argonauts

Journey to the 7th Planet

Journey to the Center of the Earth

Just Imagine

Little Shoppe of Horrors

Lost Horizon

Lost Weekend

M

Monster on the Campus

Mysterious Island

Mystery of the Wax Museum

Night of the Living Dead

North by Northwest

One Million Years BC

Plan 9 from Outer Space

Prince Valiant (1954)

Queen of Outer Space

The Rocking Horse Winner

San Francisco

7th Voyage of Sinbad

Son of Frankenstein

Tarzan and His Mate

The Time Machine

This Island Earth

The Unholy Three (talkie)

The Uninvited

War of the Worlds

....

Afterwordia

Because Brontosaurus

These things take time.

In the case of collections of my own short stories, loyally rendered by Subterranean Press since 1997, the book you are holding took nearly a decade to coalesce. The wholesale public slaughter of traditional story markets is one reason. The so-called "death of publishing" (see below) is another. Then there were novels to write—five of them since 2008, an additional reason for the slowdown.

Another process which absorbs hella time is the contemplative maze of self-searching done in quest of a *theme* for the book. That's right: actual cognition is invested in seeking some umbrella quality by which the stories presented might become unified in purpose; some overarching manifesto...which usually declares itself obvious long after the collection is completed. You know—something to make nominal sense out of a seemingly puked-together morass of otherwise-unrelated text. This trend was pointed out by several reviewers and critics in regard to past collections, and by now the ritual holds fast, and who am I to correct such folks by telling them they're just making this shit up post facto?

During the assembly of this book, paleontologists decided that the designation *Brontosaurus* was once again okay, after having lumbered us for several decades with a more "proper," more unwieldy term—*Apatosaurus*, which just *feels* wrong in the mouth. Gluten intolerance panic became a vast joke on foodies. Pluto was a planet, then it wasn't, then it was again, and the jury's *still* out. Chocolate, red wine and caffeine? Good, then not-so-good, then the experts are all forced to admit they *just don't know one way or the other.*

That's kind of how the title of this book came about. I changed it at the very last minute (as you'll find quoted in another piece herein, more like "11:59:45 and counting"). Then changed it back again.

Because Brontosaurus.

Not until I attacked the flap copy did I abruptly recognize this book is completely overrun with monsters, actual *monsters.* Which is a good thing.

Even better: Zero vampires, per se. Ditto zombies—at least technically, meaning "zombies" as the average dumbass would define them in these zombie-glutted times. *(Pause for sigh of relief—whew!)*

Actual *impossible* monsters, to lift the observation from Francisco Goya.

(In 1799 Goya published *Los Caprichos*, a series of 80 editorially inflammatory prints calling out every injustice he could see, and one of the most popular was #43, *"El sueno de la razon produce monstruos,"* or "The sleep of reason produces monsters." The fuller quotation is: *"Imagination abandoned by reason produces impossible monsters; united with her, she is the mother of the arts and the source of their wonders."* Do check out the entire set, which is wonderful. At my suggestion Kasey Lansdale also repurposed *impossible monsters* as the title of an anthology—another fine Sub Press book, I might add—which makes me feel like I still have a modicum of savvy when it comes to slapping titles on things.)

Monster stories are a seeming anachronism in a world of instant trend-mongering and 140-character attention spans. They reek of antiquated notions of horror, a genre currently hamstrung between forensic shaky-cam torture shows (the "new") and the sun-bleached antiquity of haunted houses and possessed children (the "classic"). Monster stories don't fit in. Are quaint. How retro. Insert derisive smirking and callow, superior disdain anywhere along this sequence: *Oh, look, a monster—how terribly old-skool; let's kill it, problem solved, the end, next.*

Both the world of horror and the world in general need more monster tales, ghettoization be damned. Originally coined to describe deformed humans, the teratological definition of a "monster" is anything abnormal or hideous. The classical definition is the mirror of fiction (or art in general) held up to reflect our downside characteristics as parable. A great many horror stories hinge on the concept that bringing folks back from the dead is not a particularly good idea; that covers everything from *Frankenstein* to this week's zombie apocalypse. Or the monster is the *bete noir*, the black beast beyond our control—you know, like politicians.

We all watched "horror" as a genre fall victim to the lunkheaded and perpetually-unfair conflation of horror *fiction* with *scary movies*, as a slew of slashers (both maniacs and resurrected dead) elbowed "classic" monsters aside with evolutionary inevitability.

Once the *Psycho* wheel turned, we became *surrounded* by monsters that look just like your friends and neighbors. Who indulge shooting sprees in public venues. Who wear suits and populate wood-paneled rooms while sucking your lifeblood and voting themselves raises. Who would murder you for being in "their" lane, in traffic. Who are so numerous they no longer qualify as aberrational. Or who spend years destroying you, slowly and patiently, in the name of love. These monsters became the "new normal," and they still fit the distorted-mirror analogy described above. So it's almost a chilly relief to deal with monsters who unabashedly fit the label as it used to be.

No wonder old monsters seem cuddly. Each one comes with a handy shopping list of ways to destroy them. Wolfsbane, curses, salt water, religious tchotchkes, ancient tomes. Catch up on Dracula's cinematic history sometime: by the time the first Hammer Films cycle was done, there were so many ways to wipe out Dracula that's it's a miracle he ever set foot outside his castle, the big fraidy-cat.

Watch how old gangster movies similarly kowtow to the dumb concept of "the criminal mind"—silly, basically, because most old-time criminals really were as dumb as a clinker brick. The *smart* ones never got caught, you see...or documented. But the concept of the essentially "perverted" criminal brain was used over and over to illuminate the difference between normal folks and bad folks.

Norman Bates was an imaginary creation and Charles Manson was for-real. They and all their satellites contributed to the rise of what Alan Harrington termed "psychopathic man." It doesn't matter that other contestants throughout history have been proven crazier or have higher body counts because all of a sudden, social miscreancy has become pop culture. *Famous* and *infamous* have blended together—what matters is your ability to get on TV news or become a flashfire internet sensation, not the warp and woof of your cranial convolutions.

Always remember that normalcy is the majority's form of lunacy.

In fiction—movies, books, TV, storytelling—the turning point summarized by the watershed character that was Norman Bates inevitably sprouted several divergent branches on the Crazy Tree. Some psychos now had to be extravagantly overstated, if for no other reason than to keep pace on the style curve. Hence, splatterpunk, torture porn, human deconstruction in all its moist, crimson detail; all that stuff you claim not to see, but peek at anyway. But the fact they were fictional ceased to be relevant, as *reality* and *unreality* blended together in public cognizance the same way *famous* and *infamous* did, just above.

Cruelty is not synonymous with *horror*, but they frequently share the same iron maiden.

Not that most people could tell the difference between what was real and what was pretend, since you'll find them criticizing movies for not seeming "real" enough and whining about reality for not being as fantastical as, say, advertising. The overarching need for most non-players is to ensure that *everything can be complained about, constantly*...and nothing is ever *good enough*. This is the yield of a society that has transitioned from the experiential to the observational, whose members won't risk anything themselves, but will endlessly berate others for attempting anything.

To stay safe (an illusion), they watch instead of do.

It is the mindset of the hopeless, the lost, the doomed, the defeated, the hammered-down, the ones who decided early on that life fucked them over, what's the use, the game's all rigged. They appear to be living, but they're only marking time until the roof caves in. They're just waiting around to die.

Where did the actual people go? They disappeared into their own hands, their minds enslaved to their new portable brains. They *literally* "talk to the hand." Are shallow. Get you steaming mad. Cause wrecks. Have as much intellectual fiber as a Cheeto. (See "Two Scoops" for a further bit of timely rumination on this topic.)

Simultaneously, and slowly but inexorably—like the way the Mummy moves—"ordinary" monsters gave way to more daunting threats like the Mortgage Monster, the Cancer Creature, the Demons of Despair and the Time Terror, all levies exacted in exchange for becoming a grownup (legally, if not practically). Fear of a potentially stalking werewolf dwindled to nothing next to the horror of dealing with banks, taxes and tumors. As we matured and were urged to put away childish things (according to the first letter of the apostle Paul to the Corinthians, a biblical passage often read—ironically, one hopes—at weddings), our monsters became like soft toys next to adult responsibilities, yet all the more comfortable and comforting as we gradually realized all those Others and Outsiders were our *own* reflections in that eternal mirror. Staking a vampire became child's play when compared to the fear factor of waiting for your number to come up in that most grown-up of games, Ambulance Roulette, and only when you become the star of *that* show do you acknowledge that a 911 call is a full-on dress rehearsal for your own death.

At some point when I wasn't looking, movies got replaced with "branded entertainment events" and the concept of the cinema-as-church went swirling down the ole fuckhole. For some, the upside is that now we have what used to be called "a major motion picture" for every fairytale, comic book and video game ever conceived. Two hundred million dollar children's stories.

At another point, book publishing got replaced with...well, air. The Cloud.

Magazines—once of critical importance in the foundation of a writing career—also evanesced to foggy memories in that miasma. Their fate was already written by the precedent of music downloads, where money is exchanged for...more air.

TV shows became drawn-out, soap-operatic, 75-hour "movies" while movies became very much akin to TV series, with each sequel, reboot and remake being an "episode." Streaming downloads snatch this program material right out of the (you guessed it) air.

One of the dire predictions of classic domed-city science fiction has come true in a way no one ever expected: They are now *selling us air*—literally!

(Remember the scene in the original *Rollerball* where there comes an electronic hiccup, and Jonathan E. asks what was lost and the Librarian responds: "The whole of the 13th Century"? Who would have pegged *Rollerball* as a predictive film? This catastrophic data loss is going to occur in your lifetime; get your fiddles ready to saw when Rome burns...again.)

(And you don't even want to know how much it irks me to have to write "the **original** *Rollerball*," there.)

Access has superseded *possession*. Possession means artifacts; physical baggage. Access means...well, everything to

Generation Z (roughly, those born after 1995), who are "digital natives" instead of "digital immigrants," who live in a post-linear, post-logical, post-literate world where images mean more than words; who are, as another clunky coinage had it, "screenagers."

Everything has flipped upside down or evaporated, and lots of people spend oodles of time bitching about it. The inheritors of the planet have flopped from left-brain to right-brain behavioral matrices, and challenge those who would judge them by 20th Century standards.

Another ten years from now, the things you and I write or say will be even *more* incomprehensible to the rank and file of ordinary citizenry.

You all know the intricacies of progress, and the current popular iterations that drive you mildly insane every day. What I want to know is: Just when and how the heck did we *deactivate* natural selection? Real-world stupidities lapped the movie *Idiocracy* into understatement. We're living on the Planet of the Shaved Apes—right now!—with neither the encumbrance nor charm of time travel.

Several of my media-centric observations can be found in more detail or from enhanced perspectives in a different lobe of this book.

Such changes are mere steps in the dance we rehearse with Death. One day we'll be called upon to show what we've learned, do the dance for real, and—as Robert Bloch famously said—learn at last the joke that makes skulls smile.

And what resides in the skull? About three pounds of brain, so we're told. Except in this left brain (supposedly the analytical, logical, objective half) you'll find the fiction, while in the right brain (supposedly the intuitive, thoughtful, subjective half) you'll find the non-fiction.

Yes—nonfiction. Criticisms, essays, editorials, interviews.

Up until this present volume, I never thought to include nonfiction pieces in story collections even though the half-life of articles and suchlike ephemera is much shorter than the window of vitality for a short story, which can at least get re-bought and reprinted. Often begged for free or otherwise wheedled via reciprocal blackmail, returned favors, or bogus charity, nonfiction writing absorbs as much time and burns as many calories as fiction, but is most often only as potent as it is timely, which is to say nonfiction usually gets a single shot one shot before it dies forever.

Like my past collections, this book contains thirteen stories. What I dumped in *at no extra cost to you* is thirteen additional pieces—nonfiction columns and intros and spasms I thought (a) might be worth your attention and (b) parallel enormously with the "monster theme" I imposed on this book as an organizational principle. If you look closely, you might see how the nonfiction observations "bleed" into the fiction from time to time.

About twenty years ago I wrote a series of 41 columns for *Fangoria* Magazine, mastheaded *Raving & Drooling*. Postmortem, these were corralled into a stand-alone book titled *Wild Hairs*, which did me proud. Inevitably there were leftover or subsequent raves and drools that came along later...such as whenever Fango would near another milestone, like their 250th issue, or 300th, or their 30th anniversary.

(After that last one, they stopped asking. They probably assumed I was dead by that point.)

Traditionally, I also have been loathe to include publication data on the legal page for a book, based on (a) the idea that people who really need to be thanked or acknowledged will be covered right here, in an Afterword, and (b) the transcription of such data is zombiatically repeated by others, book unto book, with neither reason nor common sense applied; people just do it because they think it makes their book look more "official"—the same way hack novelists feel a wholly by-rote, copycat need to quote the work of someone *a lot better than them* at the beginning of a novel to evoke a completely spurious simpatico...another stupid writerly habit that needs to die, die, *die*, already. Then comes

(3): the utterly wrong-headed notion left by an "original publication" hit list that the first publisher and/or licensors *own my work*. For these nonfiction snacks, though, appropriate annotation has been provided, along with an update or two (I did the same thing in *Wild Hairs* but it was a lot more daunting).

Got that? A, B, and 3. Pay attention.

Now, as for the short stories herein...

There was once a time when fiction had to pass muster as writing. This was before the Titanic of publishing struck the iceberg of the Internet.

Today you can read an un-vetted holocaust of would-be writing that looks and sounds genuine because its enthusiastic creators learned the magic tricks of presentation and marketing, arguably before they learned anything about actual writing. You can process mega-tons of crapola until your eyes bleed, on the off-chance that some of it inevitably will have a knack or twist or surprise, or a micron of inspiration or talent, but it's usually too digitally exhausting to investigate to any depth of critical thinking.

It might be called "illiterature," except that term is already taken (to mean the republication of written work in non-written form, such as an audio book or a film based on a book). Ditto "subliterature"—a negative term for popular work whose appeal is toward a general audience that does not necessarily have to be literate to enjoy it.

But bad writing has always been around. Bad writing did not cause the downfall of the traditional publishing industry.

When people cite the "death of publishing," they're actually talking about assisted suicide. For decades, 'twas ever thus: publishers found ways to spatter ink across the cheapest pulp paper they could find and vend the resultant package at an obscene markup. How do you think they came to afford all those fancy Manhattan offices? And you've seen the results of "traditional publishing" trying to hang on, trying to milk the old system for *just one more year* like a geriatric hooker. I do not mourn their eviction.

Their fate was writ large by the whole Napster brouhaha more than a decade and a half ago—to which they paid no attention. It was a huge, blinking neon sign: *this is what's going to happen to publishing, this phenomenon that killed the "album" concept of music*...and for the most part, everybody ignored the portents.

Because bad news is, y'know, *soooo* depressing.

Almost as horrific as "Facebook depression," which you can look up if you don't know what it is.

Combine the concept of writing—or typing, at least—with the concept of online social media if you *really* want to get depressed, as in genuinely, clinically suicidal.

But the idea of actual editors (that is, people with editorial talent) did not die alongside the outmoded publishing models. Such editors are rarer these days, and more difficult to find, like the two-toned Australian lobster, but they are not completely extinct. Hard Case Crime founder Charles Ardai is one such glowing example, and Charles is in *absolutely no danger* of being courted by the kind of self-styled wannabes who brag about their "darkest book ever" (because it took them *all weekend* to write) and make sure you know their daily word count beneath Facebook banners where the word "author" is part of their screen name.

Because amateurs. Because analphabetism.

Real, live, bona fide professional short story writers are a strange sub-species to begin with, considering their heyday flat-lined decades ago. Long gone are the days a new story by Ray Bradbury hit the *Saturday Evening Post* and everyone was talking about it the next day, or asking if you, too, had seen that recent Charles Beaumont story in *Playboy*. You'd think that shorter fiction would be a perfect fit for a more attention-deficient age with myriad newer, faster, flashier distractions, but no. When people want to brag about reading—or pretend they champion it in order to appear literate—they want to point to a *novel* and say, "I finished *that.*"

But—and pay attention, doomcryers—the statistics on readers have *always* been dire. We're talking single-digit percentages.

Always, like, since forever. Go check out the latest Pew Research Center numbers. They sound pretty rosy until you consider that they're based on how many people read "one or more than one" book per year. Now consider all the people milling around you, and how many of them are congratulating themselves for reading books intended for children or teens.

Now subtract all the diet and self-help books. Subtract those flash-in-the-pan, ghostwritten celebrity masturbations. Subtract anything from Oprah's Book Club. Et cetera. Pew does not distinguish between "books" and "fiction;" plus, they include audiobooks as "reading."

No wonder it is becoming more and more of a chore to explain this whole "reading for pleasure" thing to people.

Working off the principle that the best dealers are addicts, too, how does one embark on such a goal as becoming part of an endangered species on purpose? For many writers of my generation, I suspect a large portion of the credit or blame must go to Scholastic Press, a.k.a. Scholastic Corporation, still in business today after over 90 years (did you know Scholastic holds the exclusive United States publishing rights to the *Harry Potter* and *Hunger Games* books series?). Through their catalogues, grade-schoolers could order paperback books, and the best part of the catalogue (especially for pre-teens besotted by monster magazines) featured horror anthologies like *Stories of Suspense* (1963, ed. Mary E. MacEwen) and *11 Great Horror Stories* (1969, ed. Betty Owen). Between the covers of those two books alone waited Poe, Lovecraft, Finney, Bloch, Stoker, Kersh, Collier, du Maurier, Dahl, Daniel Keyes and Shirley Jackson. The latter book was in fact my first exposure to the work of Gerald Kersh, and the gateway drug to such exhilarating follow-ups as *Tales for a Rainy Night* (1961, ed. David Alexander); *A Treasury of Great Ghost Stories* (1965, ed. Ira Peck); *Horror Times Ten* (1967, ed. Alden H. Norton); *Speak of the Devil* (1967, ed. Ned E. Hoopes) and whole shelves more. My personal all-time favorite—due in no small part to the berserko, Richard Powers-styled cover painting—was *Monster Mix: Thirteen Chilling Tales* (1968, ed. Robert Arthur). Nor should we overlook that cornerstone volume for the starter-set library of many a young monster fan, *The Ghouls* (1971, ed. Peter Haining). Presently there are more than 200 such volumes not ten feet from where I sit typing this, in the "anthology corner" of my office, and that's just counting the books actually on the shelves.

The last truly nationwide magazine market for short stories was the cumbersomely-titled *Rod Serling's The Twilight Zone Magazine* and its digest-sized spinoff, *Night Cry*. TZ premiered in 1981 and was published by Montcalm, which had given the world *Gallery*, *Fox*, and *Lollypops*, among many other fine adult publications. A horror periodical with the distribution of a national men's magazine? Sign me up! I virtually swarmed TZ with submissions, and wound up being published in it and *Night Cry* so many times (until the demise of both, in 1989) that I had to concoct pseudonyms because, in the words of editor T.E.D. Klein, "the magazine doesn't appear to depend on a small coterie of writers too openly."

Twilight Zone's arc described the ascendancy of horror fiction from Stephen King's breakout to Clive Barker's breakout, then it withered and died in 1989. For the genre of short horror stories, there was still one last, glorious orgasm in store, courtesy of Larry Flynt—who sponsored *Rage* Magazine for about two years-worth of monthly issues in the mid-90s. *Rage* had *Hustler's* distribution apparatus, full-color interiors, great story art, and was deeply receptive to horror for its very brief lifespan. (The *Rage* title was subsequently appropriated by on online LGBT monthly).

Then horror fiction scuttled back to the ghetto from whence it had issued in the 1970s—the small press, micro-presses, and assorted themed anthologies. Many of these latter have numbers after the titles and a real, live editor-with-portfolio to sift out the chaff (they also usually feature stories by the two most prolific authors in horror, Manny Moore and Anne D'Others—you'll find their names on nearly *every* cover!).

Should you care to perform your own winnowing, a bottomless pit of internet horrors awaits you. Some ambitious sites attempted to replicate the magazine model in digital form; few lasted. E-books remain interesting—nearly all of my older books have transmogrified to this form by now—and surprisingly, the demand for concurrent audiobooks is growing modestly but steadily.

The preceding Kentucky windage is to set the stage for my dedication for *DJSturbia*, the biggest ever, to be found on its own page immediately following this desultory rigamarole. Some of those cited are obvious and fundamental; some are obscure and unread today. Some are primarily novelists, who dabbled; some wrote very few stories, but important ones. I read them all. It is an assembly of people who had an impact on my written work, large or small, via *their* work. Many latter-day writers and peers do wonderful work, but cannot be said to be influential because we were all forming up at the same time. By no means is this list comprehensive. It is more of a browse, not a be-all, end-all catalogue to spur debate over inclusions versus exclusions. This is personal, timely for no longer than the span it would take to read it, and subject to perpetual amendment; a sampler of styles and their capacity for effect, recommended so that *you* might make a pleasant discovery or two in the process of wading through all this back-matter.

But the stage-bows do not stop there, and some of them actually repeat in the thanks I owe them for enabling these chunks of text in the first place.

For Nonfiction: Jim & Marian Clatterburgh, Frank Dietz, Michael Doyle, John Farris, Tony Timpone & Michael Gingold, Tim & Donna Lucas, Drew McWeeny, Mark Morris, Rafael Navarro, John Schoenfelder, Duane Swierczynski, Jerad Walter, Tom Weaver, and the entire cast and crew of *The Crow*, forever.

For Fiction: John Joseph Adams, Mike Heffernan, Stephen Jones, S.T. Joshi, Joe R. Lansdale, Kasey Lansdale, Bill Schafer, Darrell Schweitzer, and original Splat Packer John Skipp.

For Subterranean Press, long my standard-bearer: Bill Schafer (for 20 years!), Gail Cross, Geralyn Lance, and Yanni Kuznia. I am also proud to bring my brother Tim Bradstreet into the fold as this book's resident jacket artist. The signature sheet and endpapers are the work of my long-gone but ever-present other-brother, Grant Christian (1959-1981).

Accomplices include: Keith Rainville, for hiking the long, hard *Outer Limits* road with me; S.T. Joshi & Jerad Walters of Centipede Press for resurrecting the dead; Wrath James White and the staff of Killercon 5; Tom Monteleone (for the fastest book proposal and sale, ever); John Scoleri for buffering me from both eBay and Facebook; all the Farris clan—John Lee, Mary Ann, Pete & Heather; the entire cast and crew of *Mob City,* to which I'll add LA's Queen of Noir, Joan Renner; the stalwart responders of LAFD Station #82; Ashley Largey (for helping babysit me in the emergency ward); Underworld denizen Ken Mitchroney (for pie); John Schow and all the little Schows (including the newest, James Schow, Jr., born 2014)...

...and my ladylove, the stupendous Kerry Fitzmaurice, who is also a pretty good proofreader.

And the rest of my family? Those collections mentioned earlier, and those other books you can see listed in the front of this one? They're not zombies either but they keep *coming back from the dead.*

It's up to you to determine whether they'll stick around for a while.

—DJS
May Day, 2015

Dedication

To All the Short Story Writers Who Matter,
My Gratitude and Admiration

Including but not limited to: Robert Aickman, Louisa May Alcott, Brian Aldiss, Dante Aligheri, Kingsley Amis, Poul Anderson, Mark Alan Arnold, Robert Arthur, Isaac Asimov, Robert Asprin, A.A. Attanasio, Paul Auster, J.G. Ballard, Honore de Balzac, Sabine Baring-Gould, Clive Barker, Laird Barron, Charles Beaumont, Stephen Vincent Benet, Alfred Bester, Ambrose Bierce, Earl & Otto (Eando) Binder, Algernon Blackwood, James Blish, Robert Bloch, Michael Blumlein, Boileau & Narcejac (Pierre & Thomas), Jorge Luis Borges, Anthony Boucher, Ray Bradbury, Max Brand, Alan Brennert, Poppy Z. Brite, Charles Brockden Brown, Fredric Brown, Larry Brown, Edward Bryant, Charles Bukowski, William Burroughs, Lord Byron, John W. Campbell, Ramsey Campbell, Orson Scott Card, John Dickson Carr, Robert W. Chambers, Raymond Chandler, Suzy McKee Charnas, Paddy Chayefsky, G.K. Chesterton, R. Chetwynd-Hayes, Arthur C. Clarke, Samuel Taylor Coleridge, John Collier, Wilkie Collins, Joseph Conrad, Harry Crews, Aleister Crowley, James Crumley, Roald Dahl, Lester Dent, August Derleth, Philip K. Dick, Thomas Disch, Arthur Conan Doyle, David Drake, Guy de Maupassant, Daphne du Maurier, Lord Dunsany, Amelia Edwards, T.S. Eliot, Stanley Ellin, Harlan Ellison, Helen Eustis, Philip Jose Farmer, John Farris, Howard Fast, William Faulkner, Charles G. Finney, Jack Finney, F. Scott Fitzgerald, Gustav Flaubert, John Ford, Christopher Fowler, William Gay, Johann Wolfgang von Goethe, Nikolai Gogol, David Goodis, Charles L. Grant, Davis Grubb, Melissa Mia Hall, Allison V. Harding, L.P. Hartley, Nathaniel Hawthorne, George Gissing, Lafcadio Hearn, Ernest Hemingway, Chester Himes, Michel Houellebecq, Robert E. Howard, Rachel Ingalls, Washington Irving, Shirley Jackson, Henry James, M.R. James, George Clayton Johnson, Franz Kafka, Gerald Kersh, Daniel Keyes, Caitlin R. Kiernan, Stephen King, Rudyard Kipling, T.E.D. Klein, Nigel Kneale, Harry Adam Knight (John Brosnan), Kathe Koja, C.M. Kornbluth, Joe R. Lansdale, Nancy Lambert, D.H. Lawrence, Stephen Laws, J.S. Le Fanu, Fritz Leiber, Elmore Leonard, Thomas Ligotti, Jack London, Frank Belknap Long, John D. MacDonald, Carson McCullers, Larry McMurtry, William March, Gabriel Garcia Marquez, George R.R. Martin, Richard Matheson, Richard Christian Matheson, Ardath Mayhar, Cormac McCarthy, Michael McDowell, Patrick McGrath, Jay McInerney, A.A. Merritt, Michael Moorcock, Vladimir Nabokov, O. Henry, Fitz-James O'Brien, Tim O'Brien, Stuart O'Nan, Arch Oboler, Chuck Palahniuk, Dorothy Parker, Mr. Poe, Fredrik Pohl, Joe Pulver, William Relling Jr., Jane Rice, Theodore Roszak, Ray Russell, Saki (H.H. Munro), Budd Schulberg, Rod Serling, Michael Shea, Lucius Shepard, Lewis Shiner, John Shirley, Robert Silverberg, Clifford Simak, Dan Simmons, Curt Siodmak, Henry Slesar, Clark Ashton Smith, Michael Marshall Smith, William Browning Spencer, Norman Spinrad, Robert Louis Stevenson, Peter Straub, Theodore Sturgeon, Lucy Taylor, Thomas Tessier, Hunter S. Thompson, Trevanian, Mark Twain, A.E. Van Vogt, Jules Verne, Gore Vidal, Kurt Vonnegut, Karl Edward Wagner, Ian Watson, Andrew Weiner, Manly Wade Wellman, H.G. Wells, Eudora Welty, Donald Westlake, Dennis Wheatley, Oscar Wilde, Kate Wilhelm, Charles Willeford, Jack Williamson, F. Paul Wilson, Mehitobel Wilson, Gahan Wilson, Douglas E. Winter, Cornell Woolrich, Philip Wylie, John Wyndham, Chelsea Quinn Yarbro and Roger Zelazny.

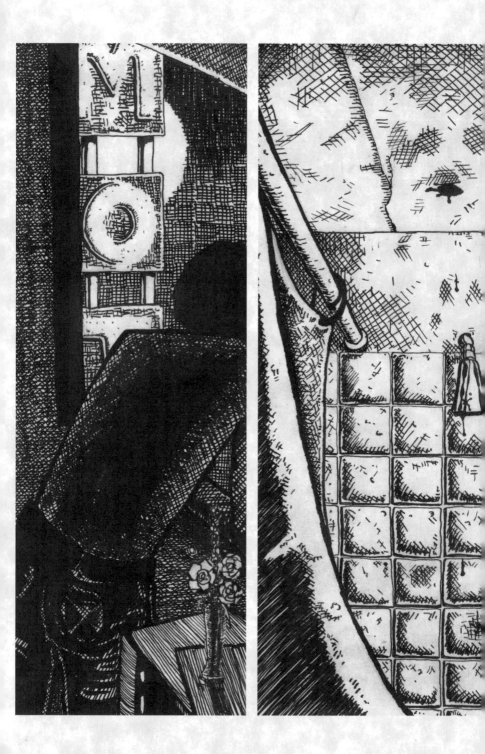